SCOOP
of the
CENTURY

The Fateful Odyssey of
Reporter Stella Weiss

Scoop of the Century

Published by Mindstir Media, LLC
45 Lafayette Rd | Suite 181| North Hampton, NH 03862 | USA
1.800.767.0531 | www.mindstirmedia.com

Printed in the United States of America
ISBN-13: 978-1-7347069-8-7

SCOOP
of the
CENTURY

The Fateful Odyssey of
Reporter Stella Weiss

MICHAEL BRIAN SCHIFFER

PROLOGUE

PRESIDENT FREDERICK JOHN WAHL AND HIS WIFE, Svetlana, were preparing to fly on Marine One from the White House to Joint Base Andrews. There they planned to board Air Force One, which would ferry them a short distance to their favorite North Carolina resort. Svetlana emerged first from the White House and walked alone to the helicopter. After she climbed aboard, the president made his grand entrance, strolling across the lawn and waving to onlookers with exaggerated gestures.

Marine One lifted off on schedule and headed east down Pennsylvania Avenue. Suddenly, something went terribly wrong. In flames the craft plummeted to the street, killing everyone on board.

NTSB, FBI, and CIA task forces investigated the incident. The FBI and CIA immediately suspected terrorism, and NTSB soon reported that the crash had been no accident. But then the investigation stalled, even though the country's most experienced agents were on the case. They had made no headway in identifying the assassin and released no further information on the status of the investigation. Frustration simmered in every corner of the country.

President Wahl's narrow Republican base was furious that the government had not identified the left-wing terrorists whom they believed had killed their leader. Wahl-lovers insisted that left-leaning "deep state" operatives in the federal government had orchestrated a cover-up.

Democrats urged Americans to be patient, to let the investigations run their course. There should be no rush to judgment.

Despite a nationwide clamor for information, the agencies remained silent. Members of the press longed to write the story of what so far seemed to be the perfect crime. Instead, as the three-month anniversary of the assassination approached, newspapers rehashed earlier stories and chided the federal agencies for withholding important details.

PART 1

CHAPTER 1

IN YEARS PAST, Stella Weiss would have barely heard her landline's ring above the chatter and clicking keyboards in the busy newsroom. Today, the ring was loud and clear because more than half the desks stood vacant after two rounds of severe budget cuts. On the staff of the Los Angeles Times, Stella was one of the fortunate reporters still working at the venerable newspaper. She soldiered on, hoping that the next pink slip would not carry her name.

Glancing at "caller unknown" on the phone's display, Stella hesitated briefly before answering her direct line on the fourth ring. The caller was a male computer voice. "I can offer you the scoop of the century about the crime of the century." The call ended abruptly. Another joker, she thought to herself. Just for a moment, though, she entertained the wild thought that this joker might not be joking. After all, he must have gone to some trouble to obtain the number of her direct line.

Until last year, most Americans would have identified the 9/11 attacks on the World Trade Center and Pentagon as the crime of the century. Now, Stella knew, that crime had a rival: the assassination of Frederick "Fred" John Wahl, late President of the United States. The life of the least popular president in recent American history had ended on November 16, three months earlier. In addition to Wahl and his 23-year-old wife, Svetlana, the crash of Marine One had killed two aides, two pilots, three secret service agents, and a motorist.

Because the federal investigations had failed to find the perpetrator, any new and verifiable information about the assassination would be a stunning development. In a further flight of fancy, Stella imagined that this scoop might lead to a Pulitzer Prize-winning story. Maybe the Joker would make contact again. Just in case, she forwarded the direct line to her iPhone so she would miss no call in real time.

CHAPTER 2

IN HER LATE THIRTIES AND OF MEDIUM HEIGHT, Stella's black hair was coiffed in an Afro kept fashionably short. Her complexion was light brown and unblemished. In addition to African and European ancestors, her almond-shaped eyes and high cheekbones hinted at an East Asian forebearer.

Stella's beat was city government, where corruption was rife. She latched onto a story like an angry pit bull and didn't let go until the wrongdoers were bloodied and her story was in print. The Times building was located near the Los Angeles City Hall, where her frequent walks down the corridors of power had worn out many pairs of sneakers. Stella's exposés of corruption and incompetence had won local recognition but not yet a Pulitzer Prize.

In getting a story, Stella sometimes made risky and unconventional moves. A former deputy mayor, Albert Roussel, had been accused by whistleblowers of pressuring city agencies to award no-bid city contracts to his relatives and business partners. A high-octane team of San Francisco attorneys convinced the assistant D.A. not to file charges; the attorneys also helped to hush up the affair. This much Stella's sleuthing had revealed. Incredulous at the chicanery, she waited patiently for an opportunity to nail down the truth of Roussel's corruption.

The opportunity arrived when a drunk Roussel missed a curve on Mulholland Drive and drove his Maserati into a ravine. Found alive, he was hospitalized in serious condition. At a costume shop on Melrose Avenue, Stella rented a complete nun's habit. Wearing that outfit with her face barely showing, she talked her way past the security guard outside Roussel's private room at Cedars-Sinai Medical Center on Beverly Boulevard. A devout Catholic, Roussel panicked when he saw Stella, certain that she was an omen of his imminent demise. She convinced him that even a nun could improve his fraught situation with the creator if he confessed his crimes to her. And he did.

Stella didn't know it at the time, but her secretly recorded interview with Roussel turned out to be a deathbed confession. His condition worsened after their encounter, and three days later he died of a massive stroke.

CHAPTER 3

NEARLY FOUR DECADES EARLIER, Stella Weiss had been adopted by a prosperous Jewish married couple who had suffered three miscarriages. The Weisses had raised the eyebrows of their relatives and Beverly Hills neighbors by welcoming a Black baby into their family through a private adoption. Her father, Daniel, was an endodontist who owned a boutique practice in Brentwood. Her mother, Rachel, was a patent attorney who did consulting gigs with cosmetics firms and worked from her home office.

A precocious child who learned to read before starting kindergarten, Stella had many advantages denied to others in less affluent families. Public schools in Beverly Hills were excellent as well as safe. Other parts of Los Angeles County suffered endemic violence and strife. When Stella was in middle school, four L.A. cops brutally beat Rodney King, an unarmed Black man. After a jury acquitted the officers 13 months later, violent protests broke out in south-central Los Angeles. These events were so fully covered in print and electronic media that even children were exposed to the stories. Instead of instilling fear in young Stella, the news prompted her to admire journalists; it seemed like a glamorous career.

An inspiring English teacher at Beverly Hills High School fanned Stella's ember of interest in journalism into a steady flame. Her teacher taught that journalism was seldom glamorous. It was hard, sometimes frustrating or dangerous work, but done well, the teacher emphasized, journalism could have positive effects on peoples' lives.

She graduated from high school near the top of her class, and went on to earn a journalism degree at the pricey and prestigious University of Southern California. There she became editor in chief of the Daily Trojan. In an irony Stella fully appreciated, she had been the beneficiary of what many people called "white privilege." Owing to a combination of nature and nurture, Stella had grown up to be a confident and self-assured Black Jewish woman.

During her junior year at USC, Stella held an internship at the L.A. Times. She so impressed her supervising reporter, Malcolm Klein, that he extended the internship into her senior year. After Stella's graduation, the Times hired her as a cub reporter on the city desk.

Stella wasn't the only workaholic among Times reporters, but her ability to capture key interviews and get answers to the most penetrating questions yielded impressive—and newsworthy—results. Politicians and bureaucrats had come to fear a call from Stella Weiss. They knew she possessed a high-fidelity crap detector that was always turned on. As one city councilman learned the hard way, refusing Stella's interview request could itself become a story.

Although intensely dedicated to her work, Stella was not averse to dating and the possibility of finding love. She had tried the more popular dating websites, but had not found her soul mate. What she missed, even more than a meaningful relationship with a man, was the killer story that would propel her into the pantheon of immortal reporters. She was intent on becoming the next Bob Woodward or, she would chuckle to herself, the next Carl Bernstein.

CHAPTER 4

THE JOKER'S SECOND COMMUNICATION came by email with the subject line "scoop." The sender was "knowsitall," and his terse message was shocking: "I am the president's assassin. Weapon was a Steyr AUG A3. More to come." Stella googled the weapon and was astonished to learn that it could fire a full magazine of 42 rounds in about six seconds. This assault rifle had an effective range of nearly 1,000 feet, but it could reach almost a mile. A low-flying helicopter, she presumed, would have been an easy target. At this realization, she felt flu-like chills go through her entire body.

Accepting the Joker's claim at face value was out of the question. Stella had to verify his tip. Beth Perkins, an acquaintance from college, was currently a criminalist at the FBI lab in Quantico, Virginia. The reporter seldom requested sensitive information from Beth, but now she believed it was necessary.

Stella knew that calling Beth posed a risk to her friend. She could be fired for leaking information from an ongoing investigation. Stella had earned Beth's trust over the years, never publishing the off-the-record factoids she furnished. She picked up her iPhone, brought up her contacts, and tapped in Beth's personal number.

"Beth, thanks for answering. I have a lead on the weapon used in the president's assassination. Could it have been a Steyr AUG A3?"

"I'm not working the case, but I'll snoop around and see what I can find out. Where did you get this information?"

"You know I can't tell you that."

"Of course. It's always a one-way street with reporters. We give and you take."

"At least that way I avoid publishing inaccurate information. I can tell you this much: I learned about the weapon from an anonymous source, and I have no idea who it is."

"I'll get back to you if I find out anything."

"Thanks, Beth. I'd really appreciate your help on this one."

Beth called an hour later.

"Our people claim they have no firm fix on the weapon, but the scuttlebutt is that the Steyr AUG A3 is the strongest contender. Marine One was supposed to have ballistic armor, but it apparently protects only against handgun fire."

"Thanks," said an excited Stella, and ended the call.

Stella next looked up what the FBI had said in the days immediately following the crash: virtually nothing. In the information vacuum, seemingly well-informed reporters speculated that it had been an assassination, not an accident. They further conjectured that the weapon had probably been a rocket-propelled grenade. Perkins' admission that it was an assault rifle enhanced the Joker's credibility. Even so, Stella wasn't ready to believe the assassin himself had sent the messages. What she knew so far was tantalizing, but anyone could have made an educated guess that a powerful assault rifle had brought down Marine One. She needed more information before she would believe that her Joker was the killer.

CHAPTER 5

STELLA DROVE HOME to her modest apartment in Park La Brea Towers. This unique housing development, built by MetLife in the late 1940s and showing its age, included more than a dozen 13-story towers containing over 4,000 units. Its central location and proximity to museums, Fairfax Avenue, Farmer's Market, and the upscale Grove shopping center ensured its continuing popularity.

Stella paid $2350 plus monthly pet and parking fees for a 710 square-foot, one-bedroom apartment. The rent was a sizable slice of her paycheck. She took advantage of the complex's amenities, including swimming pools and a gym. Her body was a taut as her mind.

The groaning elevator took the reporter to the fifth floor, where she walked down the dingy hallway to her door. The flickering fluorescent bulbs furnished enough light for Stella to slip her key into the lock. She walked in and placed her black Michael Kors purse on the glass-and-chrome coffee table, pulled out her phone, and plopped down on the beige microfiber couch. Tabitha, the overweight orange cat she had rescued from a shelter, joined her. She scratched Tabby behind the ears, and the feline began purring contentedly. Stella's gaze landed briefly on her Picasso prints, Three Musicians and Girl Before a Mirror, which graced the wall opposite the front door. Living so close to the L.A. County Museum of Art, she had indulged her interest in modernism, buying prints and visiting exhibits when she allowed herself "me time."

She checked her phone, but the Joker had sent no messages or emails. Stella did find an email from her editor, Malcolm Klein, who furnished feedback on the draft article she had turned in just before leaving for home.

Her story was about the diversion of library funds to the city's motor pool. She identified two mid-level managers who had conspired to make the transfers so they could purchase high-end Mercedes for their exclusive use. They had cleverly obscured their misdeeds, but Stella had scoured the city's financial records and unraveled the imperfect cover-up. She named the wrongdoers and expected a minor scandal to erupt after the Times published her story.

In her characteristic style, Stella animated the story with the views of people affected by the wrongdoers. Her conversations with librarians and library patrons supplied pithy quotes that enlivened the financial details. Libraries in south-central Los Angeles had once hosted special Saturday afternoon programs that welcomed neighborhood children and their parents. Famous authors would, for a fee, read from their own books to a semi-circle of enchanted children. Because of the budget shortfall, this popular program—among others—had been axed. Stella hoped her story would hasten its return.

Malcolm had made a few minor wording changes to the draft but left the story's content intact. A preoccupied Stella paid scant attention to Malcolm's tweaks and thanked him. She was nursing a high level of anxiety, hoping the Joker would call or email soon.

Meanwhile Stella was famished. She opened the fridge and removed a bowl of leftover pasta primavera. After heating it in the microwave, she sprinkled crumbled feta cheese on the veggies and pasta. Into a flute she poured a few ounces of pinot noir from an open bottle, and sat down at her vintage red Formica-and-chrome kitchen table, a gift from her parents. Stella ate slowly while reading the New York Times on her laptop.

Because the three-month anniversary of the assassination had just taken place, the New York Times and other papers were speculating anew as to who brought down Marine One and how they might have done it. Stella steeped herself in these stories, gathering background

18

information on the assassination and its aftermath that had appeared in print during the intervening three months.

Assassination stories had driven news of the February primary elections from the front pages of the major dailies. Editors had discovered that dramatic retellings of the event accompanied by horrific images of the wreckage attracted reader eyeballs and sponsor dollars.

Marine One had just taken off from the White House grounds, heading to Joint Base Andrews. On the tarmac, its engines already warming, Air Force One was ready to fly President Wahl and Svetlana to their favorite resort in North Carolina. But Marine One fell short of its destination.

The crash site was in the 1200 block of Pennsylvania Avenue. Since 9/11, first responders in Washington arrived in droves after the initial 9-1-1 calls, including D.C. Metropolitan Police Department, D.C. Fire and Emergency Medical Services, U.S. Marshals Service, Secret Service, National Park Service Police, and the FBI. One reporter who arrived 10 minutes after the crash described the scene as "total chaos." Firefighters battled the blaze for almost an hour before gaining the upper hand.

The D.C. police cordoned off Pennsylvania Avenue for several blocks in all directions, far beyond the scattered wreckage. Officers ordered gawkers to clear out and step beyond the barriers. People in buildings that fronted Pennsylvania Avenue were ordered to stay inside or leave by another exit.

Stella learned that the FBI had assumed the worst—a terrorist attack—and treated the four-block zone as a crime scene. One article quoted an FBI agent's lament: "the opportunity to interview witnesses was lost when the D.C. police sent away people who might have seen something."

Descriptions of the crash site, which included three cars on the street, went into gruesome detail. These accounts bothered Stella, for there was no need to describe the charred body parts scattered amidst the wreckage. The FBI sent in a team of senior criminalists who were joined by NTSB field investigators. After the field recording had been completed, the human remains were removed. NTSB hauled off the wreckage to a hangar at Joint Base Andrews where the craft was painstakingly reassembled and studied.

Stella read that, despite weeks of relentless pestering of the NTSB and FBI, reporters had learned nothing about the cause of the crash. The government's silence was ironclad. However, six weeks after the event, the NTSB publicly ruled out mechanical failure and pilot error. Apparently, that left only sabotage or a terrorist act. Secrecy merely amped up speculation and fueled countless conspiracy theories, many of them propounded on fringe websites. Had the president's antics finally led someone in the government to commit a desperate act? Perhaps, one foreign correspondent opined, France or the U.K. had become exasperated by the president's cavalier treatment of long-standing alliances and had sent a hit squad. Wahl had destabilized the post-WWII world order that had been built and presided over so effectively by previous presidents of both parties. Right-wing commentators were confident that unnamed left-wing extremists or Muslim terrorists had done it, condoned by deep-state operatives. Talking heads on Fox News insisted that a leftist took matters into his own hands, disappointed that calls for the president's impeachment had gained no traction in the House of Representatives. Stella took notes on the various theories of the crash, wondering where the Joker might fit.

CHAPTER 6

AS A REPORTER AND CITIZEN, Stella paid attention to national politics, but it was not an obsession. The city beat had narrow boundaries and she usually stayed within them. But the assassination story was different. If only...

Her phone sounded off. As she looked down, her heart skipped a beat because the Joker had just sent an email. "Food truck involved. Await instructions." She pondered the two sentences, gripped by apprehension. Stella couldn't recall reading anything about a food truck in any of the crash-related articles. Probably, she reasoned, a food truck's connection to the assassination would be known only to people in the NTSB and FBI—if anyone.

She pondered her next move. If she tried to verify this factoid by calling Beth at Quantico, she might be putting her friend—or herself—in jeopardy. She ruled out that move. Stella knew she would have to sit on the Joker's information. But, in her mind, the mere specificity of his food-truck claim increased its credibility. Tabby rejoined Stella on the couch and was soon purring contentedly.

"Await instructions" might mean the Joker wanted to set up a meeting. She wondered if his next communication would allow her to respond. The Joker sent no further missives that night or during the next two days. Stella was puzzled by his silence, fearing he had ended his tease, or maybe it had been a clever hoax all along.

But the Joker did not disappoint. When his next email came at last,

Stella was sitting at her desk in the newsroom. As the Joker had promised, he supplied instructions: "book round trip to Honolulu; depart 25 February, return 6 March; reserve 10 days at Queen Kapiolani Hotel."

After reading the email several times, she looked up airline ticket prices and the hotel's daily rate. Not counting food, cabs, and incidentals, this trip would cost far north of $2,000—and might easily reach $3,000. She knew it was now time to discuss this expensive project with her editor.

CHAPTER 7

MALCOLM KLEIN WAS IN HIS LATE FIFTIES, a survivor of the L.A. Times's golden age. Short and stocky, he had a gray goatee but only a fringe of white hair on his otherwise barren dome. His patrician features and penetrating blue eyes gave him an intimidating demeanor, but to his reporters Malcolm was friendly and approachable. He and Stella had a warm professional relationship that went all the way back to her undergraduate years as a Times intern.

Born and raised in Los Angeles by middle-class parents, Malcolm attended UCLA where he majored in English and political science. He spent two years in the Peace Corps, building irrigation systems in Kenya. Back in the states he enrolled at Columbia University where he earned a masters degree in journalism. After serving more than 15 years as a reporter on the L.A. Times, he had been promoted to managing editor.

Malcolm had almost always supported Stella's projects. Sometimes he went out on a limb to furnish money for in-state travel and for assistants, as she unearthed wrongdoing that could extend all the way to Sacramento. Stella wondered, what would be the most effective way to approach him for this outlandish request? Maybe the personal touch would be most effective.

She walked through the sea of desks, several empty ones still hosting dusty old PCs, to reach Malcolm's corner cubicle. Glass covered the top half of his two office walls facing the newsroom. The interior walls hosted framed clippings of significant stories he had shepherded from proposal to print. Many of them were Stella's.

"Hi, Stella. Sit down, make yourself comfortable. What are you working on this morning?"

"I've had some intriguing messages from a man who says he knows exactly how Marine One was downed."

"Oh my god, are you serious?"

"Damn straight!"

"How did he come by this information? Is he leaking it from the FBI or NTSB?"

"No, it's nothing like that." She paused briefly for dramatic effect. "This man—I call him the Joker—claims to be the assassin."

"Holy shit!"

"He reached me once by phone and several times by email. He gave me two tantalizing factoids about the crash. Then, assuming I had swallowed the bait, he sent me instructions in his last email on how to meet him."

"I assume you've tried to verify the factoids?"

"Yes and no."

"What do you mean?"

"He said the weapon had been a Steyr AUG A3 assault rifle. I checked with my FBI contact at Quantico. Beth said that the Steyr was most likely the weapon. By admitting that much, she verified that Marine One was not downed by a grenade launcher or a bomb."

"Wow! That's new and important information. What else did your Joker give you?"

"He told me that a food truck was involved, but left me hanging as to how."

"And did Beth verify this information?"

"No," Stella replied. "I didn't ask her to look into it."

"Why not?"

"I don't think it's smart to let anyone in the government know I have this information, assuming it's accurate. Beth's a friend, but she's still FBI. The assault rifle could have been a lucky guess on my part and probably wouldn't raise any red flags. If she tried to verify something as unusual as a food truck, her questions might raise suspicions. I don't want Beth to lose her job or be forced to disclose my involvement."

"I agree. Under the circumstances I think you made the right decision, though it leaves doubts about the Joker's veracity. Do you believe he's the real deal, the actual assassin?"

"Obviously, I want to believe it. In his phone call he promised to give me the scoop of the century. But I could end up being the dupe of the century, suckered into a wild goose chase—or worse. Malcolm, I just don't know. But my gut is telling me that the Joker killed the president."

He stroked his beard, deep in thought, gazing at a few of Stella's long-shot stories that had panned out brilliantly.

"Where is your meeting supposed to take place?"

"That's what I wanted to talk to you about. His latest communication told me to fly to Honolulu on February 25th and register for 10 days at the Queen Kapiolani Hotel."

"So, he fled to Hawai'i? That seems like an odd place to hide out."

"I have no idea if he's there. I can't even be sure this is a meeting with him. His communications are cryptic."

"I assume you're here to request my approval and funds for the trip?"

"Oh, wise man, you are so smart."

"I would call you a 'smart ass' in return, but someone might construe that as sexual harassment."

They both chuckled.

"How much would this trip cost?"

"At least two grand—maybe three. It's not a cheap hotel."

Malcolm grimaced. "Geez. Can't you stay somewhere less expensive?"

"I probably could, but he must have some reason for specifying the Queen Kapiolani."

"This project is going to be a tough sell, especially after you include meals and incidentals. Even if I approve it, I can't authorize a budget that large by myself. I'd have to pitch it to Alice. As you well know, ever since Alice McGuire became the Executive Editor, she has been a budget hard-ass."

"I know that. But will you try, anyway?"

"Let me think about it for a while."

"Malcolm, I agree it's a long-shot. But if he's the assassin and if he gives me the story, we'll have an incredible exclusive. If Alice refuses to approve it, I'll pay for the trip out of my own pocket. I think it's that important!"

"I see where you're coming from, but the many 'ifs' bother me. There are so many unknowns. Are you sure you really want to do this? Wouldn't it make more sense for you to turn over the tip to someone on the Washington desk?"

Leaning forward and raising her voice, Stella said, "Malcolm, you can't be serious! This could be the story of a lifetime, and I can't possibly give it to anybody else. Besides, the Joker must have his reasons for approaching me to do it. He might not want to work with anyone else."

"So, are you really willing to take the risk of going to Hawai'i and meeting up with a mass murderer?"

"Malcolm, I have to do it. I can't pass up this opportunity. I understand the risks but I'm willing to take them."

"You've always taken chances for a good story, but this? I just don't know."

Malcolm sat quietly for a few moments. While she waited, her belly fluttering with anxiety, Stella surveyed the family pictures: his sons and their families at Thanksgiving, at the Santa Monica pier, and at Disneyland. She felt no envy because children had never been on her agenda.

Finally, Malcolm said, "your gut has been right more often than not, so here's what we'll do. Go back to your desk and write up a budget proposal. After you send it to me, I'll mull it over for a while and decide whether to pass it on to Alice with my recommendation."

"That seems fair."

"But you do know that if Alice approves the trip and it turns out to be an expensive bust, we'll both be on a short leash for a while."

Stella considered Malcolm's warning but it did not affect her resolve. She returned to her desk and did some online research. An hour later, she emailed Malcolm the detailed budget; it was a gasp-worthy $3,156. A few minutes later, she returned to his office, where he was still mulling over the numbers.

He finally turned away from his computer and faced her. "Stella, I'll give your project a shot. You shouldn't have to pay for this yourself."

She breathed a sigh of relief. "I appreciate your support, Malcolm. Opportunities like this one don't come along very often, so I have to take it. Please don't tell Alice or anyone else what this is really about. I probably sound paranoid, but the fewer people who know what I'm up to, the better."

"Yes, we should keep this project under tight wraps. But I won't lie to Alice. I'll just tell her it involves meeting with a fugitive who's willing to give you deep background on a notorious crime. She can assume it's one of the long-unsolved art mega-heists."

"Thanks, Malcolm."

CHAPTER 8

IN THE LATE AFTERNOON, Alice dropped by Malcolm's office. She had read his memo requesting the travel funds, and she had questions.

Alice was a tall woman in her late forties. She had salt-and-pepper hair, dark brown eyes, petite nose, and a prominent chin below full lips. Her daily outfit, a black blouse and black pantsuit, proclaimed her considerable sway at the Times. Without asking, Alice made herself comfortable in a chair facing Malcolm and wasted no time getting to the point.

"Malcolm, I'm not satisfied with your justification for this project. This is a big ask. Is it really a huge story?"

"Believe me, Alice, it could be one of our biggest in decades."

She rubbed her chin, apparently deep in thought, then asked, "are you confident Stella can pull it off?"

"As confident as I can be at this stage."

"That's not exactly a ringing endorsement."

"Look, Alice, this project involves many uncertainties, but I strongly believe we should take a chance."

"And you won't tell me what this story is really about?"

"I promise you, it is about meeting with a fugitive, but I can't tell you any more. We can't risk having the exact purpose of this trip leaked."

Pursing her lips and raising her voice, she exclaimed, "Malcolm, do you honestly believe I would leak it?"

"Of course not, but accidents happen: overheard conversations, hacked or misfiled emails. We can't chance having anyone else knowing about it."

Shaking her head, she said, "well, Malcolm, you two have an impressive track record and have earned the paper's trust, so I'll approve the request. But we'll all have egg on our face if this story turns out to be a nothing burger."

"Believe me, I get it."

Malcolm immediately conveyed McGuire's approval to Stella, and she made the flight and hotel reservations.

****

At home in the evening, Stella dragged a compact roller bag out of the bedroom closet. She expected that her time in Honolulu would be spent indoors, but optimistically packed shorts, swimsuit, and sandals. Maybe she would find some time for exercise outdoors.

In the meantime, Stella called her parents to let them know about her upcoming trip but did not mention the destination. They agreed to drop by and pick up Tabitha before she left town. Taking care of the low-maintenance cat was a chore her parents happily undertook whenever Stella traveled.

After dinner Stella received an unexpected email from the Joker. "Good flight. Bon voyage."

She just sat there, momentarily mystified. How could he have learned about her reservation? The obvious answer came to her immediately. The Joker was some sort of IT whiz: maybe a professional, maybe a hacker—maybe both. Curious to know how far he had reached into her personal life, she scanned her inbox for his previous emails. They were gone, and she couldn't find them in the trash. She marveled at his ease in hacking commercial websites. This reinforced her hunch that he had murdered President Wahl. Stella was almost certain now that this scoop would punch her express ticket to the Pulitzer Prize awards ceremony.

CHAPTER 9

THE FOLLOWING DAY AT HER DESK in the Times building, Stella began researching more articles on the assassination published in the weeks and months following the November 16 crash. Many people had seen Marine One take off from the south lawn of the White House. Apparently, however, no one had seen Marine One just before it began the fatal plunge to the street, three long blocks to the east, though many saw and heard the impact.

Reporters had tracked down dozens of people who were in the area when Marine One went down at 11:03 a.m. Interpreting the highly varied sounds heard just before the crash proved difficult. Some people heard an explosion, some heard a burst of gunfire, some heard nothing. Echoes from surrounding buildings, ambient noise from cars and buses, and the helicopter's ear-splitting whirring and beating sounds made a coherent interpretation of the witness reports virtually impossible. Reporters found no apparent correlation between where witnesses stood and what they claim to have heard.

Stella's thorough search turned up no reports of surveillance videos of the crash or of the surrounding area before the crash. She was incredulous that security cameras in the large cordoned-off zone had recorded nothing of interest. What had happened, she believed, was that the NTSB and FBI were sitting on the videos, still trying—three months later—to piece together the incident and identify persons of interest. Meanwhile, the public remained in the dark.

An intriguing Washington Post article, dated November 29, came up in Stella's search. At the time, Republicans were still mourning the late president. Democrats initially rejoiced at Wahl's death because Vice President Joseph Shilling was, according to West Wing insiders, as dumb as a stump. Maybe, hoped Democrats, Shilling would become the Calvin Coolidge of the twenty-first century, a do-nothing dullard.

The article went on to reveal some details about the former vice president and his elevation to the highest office in the land. When the Secret Service learned that Marine One had gone down, agents quickly corralled the VP. They escorted him to the White House Situation Room where Chief Justice of the United States, the honorable Max Panovsky, fresh from a sauna, administered the oath of office.

Joseph Shilling, 44 years old, did not fit the physical mold of a U.S. president. Almost every previous president stood more than six feet tall. Even wearing his two-inch lift shoes, Shilling reached only five-nine. With short black hair, closely set brown eyes, and a small nose above a bushy mustache, Shilling's face was hardly distinctive. The new president could walk down almost any street in America entirely unnoticed.

A former Kansas governor of negligible accomplishments, Shilling had joined what some reporters called "the cult of Wahl" at the earliest opportunity. As vice president, he had no discernible duties except to stand near—but always behind—Wahl at photo opportunities. Shilling's worshipful demeanor toward the president was a source of mirth to the White House press corps. One young reporter remarked that Shilling, despite his virulent homophobia, had a crush on the president.

Wahl's murder had deprived Shilling of his role model, his idol. He was deeply disturbed by the loss; he also feared he might be the next target. A one-on-one with a Washington Post reporter revealed his reasons for worry: he believed that the assassin was most likely a radical leftist who was determined to end Republican rule. Probably, he speculated, they had employed foreign terrorists to do the job. Accordingly, Shilling made the extraordinary move of issuing an executive order mandating that the CIA and FBI collaborate on the case.

According to the Post, Shilling's fear of assassination went beyond self-interest to the interests of the Republican Party. If he were killed, then Democrat Elaine Naismith, Speaker of the House, would become the next president. He expected to guard against that unhappy outcome by appointing a new vice president, and already had a man in mind: the former attorney general of Kansas. However, an anonymous White House source told the Post reporter that, when Shilling learned that both houses of Congress had to confirm the appointee by majority vote, the new president became livid. He had come face to face with an incontrovertible truth: the Democrat-controlled House of Representatives would never confirm his man. Shilling, the Post article concluded, was unwilling to suffer the humiliating defeat.

Shilling had no hard evidence to support his fears that he was in the assassin's crosshairs. But his anxiety was stoked by an addiction to Fox News. At the very beginning of his presidency, the network's talking heads warned Shilling not to fly on Marine One, lest he suffer the same fate as Wahl. He followed the advice and traveled in a large motorcade of black SUVs to Joint Base Andrews whenever he left town. He ignored mounting criticism that the journey caused gridlock along the entire route.

In public statements Shilling affirmed that the federal government was sparing no expense in tracking down what he termed "the Democrat-inspired criminals." In private, he railed about the investigation's snail's pace.

According to a well-sourced report in the Wall Street Journal from mid-December, Shilling had once summoned the heads of the FBI, NTSB, and CIA for a meeting in the Oval Office. In a fashion reminiscent of Wahl, he berated them for not closing the case, and insisted they work harder. The president doled out verbal abuse for nearly 15 minutes, but got no response except for the platitude: "complicated investigations take time." Shilling was incensed. Almost two months after the incident, the agency heads had nothing new to report.

CHAPTER 10

STELLA FOUND A MORE RECENT Washington Post article featuring President Shilling. The reporters described an unprecedented meeting, in the White House, of Shilling and the entire membership of the FBI, NTSB, and CIA assassination task forces. The meeting took place on January 14. In telling the reporter about the meeting, an unnamed attendee paraphrased Shilling's remarks to the gathering of seasoned investigators: "I am in mortal danger because you've made no progress in identifying President Wahl's killer. The Secret Service receives a dozen or more death threats against me every week; why has no one been arrested yet? And don't forget that the Department of State says that three dozen terrorist groups are active in the world today, many of them hostile to the United States. Have they been thoroughly investigated?"

"We're working on it," said someone from the CIA.

"Well," replied Shilling, "get your asses in gear and work faster."

The meeting ended with the investigators shaking their heads. Shilling was completely ignorant of the methodical way that investigators work. An FBI agent was heard to remark, "what a dumbass. He expects a miracle."

Stories about Shilling repeatedly emphasized that he was riding the agencies hard because he feared for his own life, and he also earnestly wanted to capture the assassin.

CHAPTER 11

ALMOST AS AN AFTERTHOUGHT, Stella inserted into the Post's search engine the term "D.C. food truck." Washington, she knew, was awash in these highly regulated mobile kitchens, many of them serving gourmet-quality meals to tourists and office workers. The search captured dozens and dozens of stories; most concerned controversies over permits as well as truck owners' complaints about police harassment.

Wading through the highly redundant stories, Stella's heart quickened when she found a one-paragraph note published on November 18, two days after the crash. On the previous day, a Washington Post reporter, Landry Fairbanks, Jr., received a call from a woman. The woman claimed that a man had burst into her home on the morning of the crash and held her and her three children at gunpoint. After the man received a call on his phone just before noon, he holstered his gun and left. The woman claimed that the man's calm and officious demeanor proved he was a government agent. Her husband, the note continued, owned a food truck. The report identified neither the woman nor her husband. Stella searched for follow-up stories but there were none.

Stella had never met or talked to Landry Fairbanks, Jr., so she googled him and found an email address for the journeyman reporter. Fairbanks cranked out brief pieces daily in the Metro section, most of them about car crashes and shooting victims in the District and adjacent areas of Maryland and Virginia. She sent him an email asking for any other information he could provide about his obscure piece on the home-hostage situation that allegedly occurred on November 16.

Fairbanks replied, "I included everything I learned from the woman. She didn't file a police report, and I couldn't see any other way to track her down because she had used a burner phone. She had a heavy Spanish accent, which led me to suspect that she was an undocumented immigrant. If so, that's why she didn't call the police. But she was so rattled by the experience that, at her cousin's insistence, she decided to vent to me. I'm afraid I have no further information about the woman, but you've jogged my memory about a related event. The evening after my note appeared in the Post, two FBI agents came to my home. Like you, they wanted more information about the woman and the alleged home invasion. For almost two hours I had to endure their repetitive and patronizing questions. I insisted I knew nothing more. What I didn't tell them, but I've told you, is that she had a Spanish accent. The men in black suits with bad attitudes left unsatisfied. I never heard from them again or found out what was going on, but I assumed it had something to do with the assassination. The timing and FBI interest couldn't have been a coincidence. It was a very unpleasant experience, to say the least, and I was pissed."

Stella emailed back and thanked Fairbanks for his reply. Thinking about what he had written, she regretted that it was a dead-end for her because the reporter's story had held back no details, except for the woman's accent. Stella assumed that the Joker was referring to her husband's food truck. No way to know yet what role it might have played in the assassination.

CHAPTER 12

AFTER THE EMAIL EXCHANGE with the Post's reporter, Stella visited Malcolm's office.

"Malcolm, are you busy right now?"

"No, come in. Are you all packed and ready for your Hawaiian vacation?"

"Ha, ha. I just got some new information; it strengthens the case that the Joker—I still call him that—is the assassin."

Stella told Malcolm about her research on food trucks that led to Fairbanks's note in the Post. She gave Malcolm a printout of the note, and he immediately read it.

"Holy shit!" Waving the printout, he added, "this really does raise your Joker's credibility. I assume you contacted Fairbanks?"

"Of course. But he couldn't fill in the blanks, such as the woman's name. However, he told me something sobering. The day his piece was published, two FBI agents visited him at home and interrogated him at length about it."

"Did he feel intimidated?"

"I'm not sure about that, but he was pissed. The FBI was evidently interested in the hostage situation, and they tipped their hand by asking him to provide more details about the woman."

"Stella, I know you're on your guard, but be doubly careful, especially in Honolulu. For all we know, the FBI might be on to the Joker now, and you could get caught up in their operation, maybe even arrested."

"Don't worry, Malcolm, I'll be careful."

"Have you made travel arrangements?"

"Yes, I booked the flight and hotel. It's really creepy, though. The Joker knew my flight plans and emailed me his approval. Then, get this: when I double-checked his earlier emails, they were gone—and not in the trash."

"Oh shit. Your Joker is clearly a first-rate hacker."

"Yeah, don't I know it."

"I almost wish I were going with you."

With a twinkle in her eye, she said, "Malcolm, people would talk."

He smiled.

CHAPTER 13

IN STELLA'S PERPETUAL QUEST for a meaningful romantic relationship, she had recently been using JDate, the Jewish Internet dating site. This evening she got ready for a coffee date with Robert Levinson. He was a successful entrepreneur who had built a small but growing company based on his proprietary medical software. She had exchanged texts with him and was optimistic they might be compatible.

Stella had agreed to meet Robert at a trendy cafe in Westwood Village, near his corporate headquarters, not far from the Ronald Reagan UCLA Medical Center. As an alumna of USC, she wasn't thrilled about being in the heartland of the UCLA Bruins. USC and UCLA were fierce crosstown rivals whose students enjoyed pranking each other during football season. Even as adults, many alumni retained animosity toward the other school—and Stella was no exception.

Looking at herself in the full-length mirror on her bedroom door, Stella smiled with satisfaction. Her outfit of white blouse, pearl sweater, and black slacks was just right for a first date on a mild February evening. Eye shadow was her only makeup, as she didn't want to obscure what Robert had said was her "exotic beauty." She had studied his image, concluding that the olive-skin man with blue eyes and shaggy brown hair was not hard to look at.

After closing her apartment door, Stella took the elevator to street level, and strode to her white Volvo in the parking lot. She got in, started it up, and drove south to Wilshire Boulevard where she turned right and headed west. Every intersection on mile after mile of short blocks had streetlights. It was a slow ride, but Stella was thankful that the worst of rush-hour traffic was over. Once she passed the Beverly Hilton Hotel, she knew that the tall buildings of Westwood would soon be in sight.

She turned right on Westwood Boulevard and began the great hunt for a parking space, all of them metered with a two-hour limit. She was lucky to find a car pulling out of a tight space, but she had to wait patiently while the Cadillac Escalade went back and forth several times before it could escape. After deftly easing her Volvo into the space, Stella paid for parking at the curbside machine and began walking to the cafe, only two blocks away.

Stella was about 10 minutes late for her date. She hoped the man who promised to wear a Dodgers baseball cap was still waiting. He was there, seated in a booth, his cap slightly askew. Seeing her approach, he immediately stood up and greeted her with an outstretched hand, which she shook. But he didn't remove his cap.

"Hi Stella, I'm so pleased that we were able to get together."

"Me, too."

"Make yourself comfortable, and we can order some coffee and snacks. By the way, you are even more beautiful in person than your JDate picture."

She smiled and sat down. "Thank you, Robert," she said, but didn't return the compliment, suspecting that he had photoshopped his JDate picture.

He remarked, "this is always so awkward, breaking the ice with someone you've never met before."

"Yeah, dating these days has its strange rituals."

"Tell me about it!"

A waitress stepped to their booth and took orders for two coffees and apple pie for him, blueberry pie for her.

"Robert, your JDate profile had plenty of details about your family, but not much about your business. Maybe you could tell me how you built your company."

"That sounds like Stella Weiss, L.A. Times reporter. Is this date just a pretext so you can do a story about a budding billionaire?"

Raising her eyebrows, taken aback by his accusation, she replied, "of course not, Robert. This is a date, and I'm just interested in getting to know you."

"Fine. I'll give you the benefit of the doubt."

Stella was thinking, this guy's a dick! But she merely gave him a puzzled look and restarted the conversation, just as their coffees and pies arrived. "I know you got computer science training at Pepperdine University, so then what did you do?"

"While I was in college I started writing medical software. I came up with a dynamite program that I was sure every hospital would have to buy. With support from my parents, I hired a patent attorney, and we submitted an application."

"My mom's a patent attorney, so I understand that getting a patent can be a grueling process."

"Especially for software patents. The federal government does everything it can to put obstacles in the way of creative people."

"Isn't that an exaggeration? It's my understanding that the patent system protects the intellectual property rights of inventors."

"Then why are most software patent applications rejected?"

"Maybe they were poorly prepared or the software wasn't novel enough."

Robert was surprised by her comment, and blustered, "I'm afraid, Stella, you don't know what you're talking about."

Appalled by his rude remark, she almost stood up to leave. Instead, she said, "it's true I don't know anything about software patents, but the patent office usually has good grounds for rejecting an application."

"That's a load of crap. The patent examiners are a bunch of narrow-minded bureaucrats who enjoy stifling innovation."

"You don't really believe that, do you?"

"Yeah, I do. And don't get me started on regulations."

"Okay, I promise I won't."

But he got started anyway. "The trouble with regulations is that they drastically increase the cost of doing business. A friend of mine was trying to open a pizzeria and had to jump through dozens of hoops. Can you believe that spaghetti sauce has to be stored below a certain temperature?"

"Don't you think that food regulations like that protect the health and safety of the public?"

He shook his head and said, "that's a load of bull."

"I believe regulation is needed because businesses attempt to maximize profit, and they'll cut corners wherever they can. The government has to write regulations to protect ordinary people."

"I've never seen a regulation that we couldn't live without."

She was about to call him out on his fatuous remark, but allowed it to pass in silence. Finally, she asked, "did you eventually get your patent?"

"No, Stella. I got tired of fighting the buttheads in the patent office and went the commercial route without a patent. It's been working for my company, so far, because no other company has a product as good as mine."

"I'm happy it worked out for you."

Stella had heard more than enough to know that she and Robert were not a good match. She could not tolerate a man who was contemptuous of her opinions. This date would be her last with Robert. She was mystified as to why so many men did not respect smart women, especially women who deigned to disagree with them. Robert was just the latest in a long string of Stella's dates that had ended badly.

She took the last bite of pie and finished her coffee.

"Robert, thank you for spending some time with me. I hope you can find a woman who will dote on your every word and not question your jaundiced views. I am not that woman."

Stella stood up, put a twenty-dollar bill on the table and walked away, leaving Robert incredulous, wondering what he had done wrong.

CHAPTER 14

CONTINUING HER ONLINE RESEARCH the next morning, Stella learned that Shilling wasn't the only person impatient with the investigation's slow pace. White supremacists, neo-Nazis, and other right-wing extremists had been infuriated by the lack of arrests. They were certain their man in the Oval Office had died at the hands of a conspiracy of leftist groups and the deep state.

Those on the far right, one reporter wrote, discounted NTSB and FBI claims that the ongoing investigations might take many more months. Surely, members of these fringe groups asserted, the government already knew who had done it because federal employees were involved. Officials in these deep-state agencies were protecting the killer's identity because they had, in fact, ordered the hit. Eventually, the feds would identify some hapless loser in the mold of Lee Harvey Oswald and frame him for the murder. It was just a matter of time.

In the meantime, a few of the more militant, explosive-savvy groups had found another way to display their unhappiness with the investigations and the loss of their leader. In the middle of the night on the fourth of December, the D.C. headquarters of the Democratic National Committee was fire-bombed. Fortunately, no one was injured, and no group claimed responsibility.

The FBI swarmed into the DNC office and did a thorough forensic investigation. The criminalists were able to reconstruct the bomb, whose military-grade explosive displayed uncommon sophistication. However, there was insufficient evidence to implicate the bomber.

Two days later, a second bomb badly damaged the Washington office of the American Civil Liberties Union. Three people were injured, one critically. The FBI concluded that this bomb had been cobbled together with sticks of dynamite and detonated by a cellphone—the kind of improvised explosive device that almost anyone can make by following instructions on the Internet. This bomber also eluded capture.

In follow-up articles, reporters described a rash of right-wing violence and explosions, none of which had resulted in fatalities. The FBI concluded that these incidents were unrelated to each other, all provoked by a backdrop of social media posts blaming militant leftists for Wahl's assassination. Several bombers were caught on surveillance videos and arrested.

In further reading Stella learned that the murder of the president had taken national security agencies by surprise. Seemingly, the assassination had come out of nowhere without a specific warning or generalized Internet chatter. The immediate aftermath was filled with whispered recriminations among federal agencies for their collective failure to derail the plot. Senate committees swung into action and held closed-door hearings to pinpoint the cause of the security failure. The aged lawmakers, ignorant of modern IT, had to rely on questions furnished by their young, tech-savvy staffers. Even so, the hearings did not identify the reasons for why there had been no advance warning.

A New York Times story reminded readers that ISIL, al-Qa'ida, al-Shabaab, Boko Haram, and many lesser-known terrorist and Islamist groups had taken credit for killing the most powerful man in the world. Ordinarily, a claim by any one of these groups, if corroborated, would have provoked a devastating U.S. military response. In view of the uncertainty over which group—if any—was responsible, the government had no choice but to defer retaliation until the investigation fingered the responsible party. The national security agencies spoke with one voice, cautioning Shilling that a premature strike would feed into the narrative that the West was waging war on Islam. So many claimants, so little evidence. It was all very puzzling—to the public and to the agencies.

CHAPTER 15

THE NTSB AND FBI INVESTIGATIONS of Marine One's crash had been moving ahead, independently, during the previous three months. The lack of information sharing between the agencies was becoming especially irksome to Senior Special Agent Joanna Bartolo, who directed the FBI's task force.

In her early fifties, Bartolo had shoulder-length graying black hair, brown eyes, and a plain face that emitted earnest vibes to people in her presence. One of the FBI's most respected agents, Bartolo had managed many important investigations. She had made her mark early on by her contributions to the 9/11 team.

Joanna was married to John Bartolo, an archivist at the Library of Congress. They had two grown children and three grandchildren. The Bartolos commuted to their workplaces from the family home in the upscale suburb of Ashburn, Virginia.

Bartolo had a large team of experienced agents at her disposal and a virtually unlimited call on agency resources. However, the assassination team was working under a handicap. The NTSB was unwilling to issue a definitive report, even a preliminary report, on the cause of the crash and other pertinent conclusions. Bartolo understood the NTSB's reluctance because she was aware of the plethora of conspiracy theories that had taken root in the aftermath of the assassination of President John F. Kennedy. The inconsistencies and errors in the Warren Commission Report fed a long-lived cottage industry of second-guessers and kooks. She knew that the FBI and NTSB had to make an airtight case against any individual or group believed to have done the deed. Every inference, every conclusion, had to be backed by unassailable evidence and published in a well-edited, lavishly illustrated report. That was the plan.

Several times during the previous months Bartolo had implored her counterpart at the NTSB, Herman Kettering, to share his investigation's preliminary findings, but he respectfully declined: "we can release no report until the investigation is completed." Worse still, he had allowed FBI criminalists very limited access to Marine One's remains. Bartolo was miffed because the assassination investigation was supposed to be collaborative. In theory, it would show the public that federal agencies could work together on important cases. Despite Bartolo's repeated entreaties, Kettering wouldn't budge.

****

Herman Kettering was a small, roundish man in his early fifties with blue eyes and long blond hair trending white. He always wore a coat and tie, even when sweating over charred aircraft fragments. He was a hard-boiled, career investigator who had earned a Ph.D. in aeronautical engineering at MIT. His keen powers of observation were admired throughout the agency.

Poring over the pieces of Marine One, reassembled on the hangar floor, Kettering's crew had learned much about the crash's cause. The flight recorders indicated normal operation—no unusual turns, improper altitude changes, or speed shifts—until the crash itself. It didn't take them long to rule out pilot error and mechanical failure. Although the aircraft burned, there was no evidence of an explosion, which ruled out a bomb aboard or a rocket-propelled grenade.

What Kettering and his team found instead were five battered slugs that had entered the craft's interior as well as traces of other rounds that had damaged external parts. There was no doubt: the barrage of bullets had done fatal damage. The locations of the holes and their patterns of micro-flaring were input to a computer simulation along with the locations where bullets had made initial contact inside the helicopter. The trajectory calculations were complicated by the forward motion of the craft, which constantly changed its vertical and horizontal positions relative to the shooter or shooters. Fortunately, the flight recorders monitored the craft's orientation and speed, which were entered into the simulation. Fed these parameters, a supercomputer cranked out the most likely bullet trajectories.

The simulation yielded several significant findings. First, in all likelihood there had been only one shooter because the inferred origin points of the shots were somewhat clustered. Second, the shooter had been on the south side of Pennsylvania Avenue, firing from a height of between two and eight meters above street level. This meant that the shooter could have been on the sidewalk, in a vehicle, or in a building's first or second floor. If he had been on the sidewalk, someone would have seen him in late morning, but there were no reports of an active shooter. Two adjacent buildings from which the shots could have come yielded no indicative evidence. Satellite imagery for the time of the crash proved useless owing to dense cloud cover.

The NTSB had received the autopsy reports of the casualties, including a commuter crushed in her Bentley convertible by the falling wreckage. There were no surprises, as all had succumbed to trauma or severe burns.

****

Bartolo's FBI team, in the dark about the NTSB's findings, had been working their own angles on the crash. Their first move was to canvass Marine One's entire route, extending to three blocks east and west of the crash site, seeking videos, witnesses, and material evidence. Several businesses had surveillance videos that captured the grisly crash. In addition, Bartolo made a public plea for videos recorded on cameras and phones that were made before, during, and immediately after Marine One went down. It was her hope that someone had captured images of the assassin. That search proved fruitless: no one and no thing raised suspicions.

In repeatedly canvassing businesses along Pennsylvania Avenue, the agents had at last found one surveillance video that inadvertently recorded the vehicles parked along the south side of the street. Unfortunately, the camera had been located three blocks east of the crash site.

Zooming in on the video, Bartolo's agents noticed something curious. At 10:57, a food truck pulled into a parking space, but did not open for business. By 11:06 the truck—which was badly out of focus—was gone. That finding, along with the Post's brief article about the family held hostage, led Bartolo's team to suspect that the shooter might have taken cover in a food truck.

FBI criminalists using archaeological survey techniques searched the street and sidewalks on Pennsylvania Avenue from the crash site to the western margin of the cordoned-off zone. Seeking slugs and shell casings, agents even pawed under trees and bushes and sifted dirt in dozens of super-size planters. They found no shell casings but were rewarded by the discovery of 11 deformed slugs, some of which had ricocheted off buildings on the north side of the street and removed chips from concrete and granite walls. These were apparently some of the shooter's misses. By analyzing where the slugs had landed and the fresh chips on buildings, the FBI team was also able to identify the shooter's most probable location: the south side of Pennsylvania Avenue. Ballistics analysis at Quantico narrowed down the shooter's assault rifle to one of several models, including the Steyr AUG 3A. Joanna Bartolo was pleased with her team's progress.

****

With no real hope of success, Bartolo decided to take another stab at squeezing information out of Kettering. This time, however, she had some tentative conclusions to offer in trade. Maybe that would make the difference.

"Herman, this is Joanna Bartolo. I think we should meet for coffee and discuss the case."

"I'm in the mood for coffee, any excuse to break from processing the wreckage where so many patriotic Americans died. Discuss the case? We'll see."

"Good. I have information to trade. Let's meet tomorrow at the Hoover Building at 2:00. I'll email you details on how to find me."

"That works."

CHAPTER 16

THE MEETING BETWEEN BARTOLO AND KETTERING took place at FBI head-quarters in downtown D.C. The Hoover Building was a Brutalist fortress dedicated by President Gerald Ford in 1975. Despite the appearance of invincibility, the building was deteriorating badly, concrete flaking off here and there. It was almost universally condemned as the ugliest structure in downtown D.C.

Kettering arrived early enough to pass through the enhanced security gauntlet and still make it to the meeting on time. He took an elevator to the fifth floor and then walked down the hall to the designated room number. There he found Bartolo standing inside a small conference room. They shook hands and sat down at the oval table. Kettering's eyes were fixed on the view from the window, a grand panorama to the south where he could see the Smithsonian Castle, domes of two national museums, and the Washington Monument.

"Joanna, the beauty of this city never grows old."

"I agree."

Pointing to the spread of coffee and pastries on the table, Bartolo said, "Herman, help yourself."

"Thanks. Is this a bribe?"

"I'm desperate, so I'll try anything! Seriously, I always have munchies available during interviews. I'm trying to undermine the TV stereotype of FBI agents as uncaring, jack-booted thugs."

A smiling Kettering said, "I'll gladly accept the bribe."

Kettering poured himself coffee, added cream and sugar, and grabbed a bear claw and napkin. Bartolo took her coffee with cream but without added carbs.

Neither fed wanted to make the first move to talk about the investigation, so instead they discussed whether the Washington Redskins would make the playoffs in the upcoming football season. They agreed that the prospects were dismal.

Finally, Kettering said, "Joanna, you called this meeting, so what's on your mind?"

"We have some preliminary conclusions we'd like to share with you, provided you're in a trading mood. Nothing said at this table will go beyond my team. But we believe that sharing information could speed up both investigations."

Kettering went silent. Deep in thought, he nibbled at the bear claw, and then smiled enigmatically. "What have you got?"

Bartolo's face brightened, "does that mean you're willing to share?"

"Up to a point. I do see value in collaborating, I just can't risk the possibility of provisional conclusions reaching the press and feeding endless speculation and conspiracy theories."

"I assure you, there will be no leaks from the FBI."

"The best intentions aren't always sufficient."

"Herman, I know that. But look, we're in the same boat. We both have information. We both want to prevent leaks. We both want to nail the assassin. And we both have President Shilling breathing down our necks. Let's see if our pieces of the puzzle fit together and make a more complete picture. To show good faith, I'll go first and tell you what we've got."

Bartolo briefly summarized the FBI's investigation and preliminary conclusions. Kettering, impressed, then did the same for the NTSB. Both were pleased that, despite employing different kinds of evidence, the investigations had converged on several key conclusions. There had been a lone shooter who employed an assault rifle, probably a Steyr AUG A3. For cover, the assassin stood inside a food truck parked briefly on the south side of Pennsylvania Avenue. The rifle shots had immediately disabled the helicopter, causing the crash.

Kettering asked, "do you have a lead on the food truck?"

"There's only one video of the truck, which we didn't find until late December. Unfortunately, none of our IT people could extract a license number or other identification from the badly pixilated image. All we had was the truck's color and basic shape. You know, Herman, there are hundreds of food trucks in the greater D.C. area. We mistakenly assumed that the truck was registered in D.C., but it wasn't. Even after we expanded the search area, it still took us more than three weeks to track down the right truck and its owner. None of the local jurisdictions were in a hurry to answer our requests for information about licensed food trucks. Finally, we got what we needed. The truck owner is an undocumented Guatemalan who sets up shop only in Alexandria, Virginia. His truck is in compliance with city regulations, and he doesn't have a criminal record."

"Do you think he's the assassin?"

"I don't think so. I'm dubious because of the woman who was being held hostage on the day of the crash."

"What do you mean?"

"Didn't you see Fairbanks' note in the Post's Metro section published two days after the incident?"

"No, I didn't. Who wants to read about all the mayhem in Metro section? I see more than enough at work. So, what was it about?"

"A woman called the reporter, Landry Fairbanks, Jr., on a burner phone. She claimed that she and her children had been held at gunpoint in her home during the morning of the crash. The man left without harming anyone after he received a phone call."

"Joanna, did you track down this woman?"

"She didn't give the reporter her name, address, or any other information in her call, but she did mention that her husband owned a food truck."

"Hmm," said Kettering, finishing the bear claw and contemplating a second one, "did you interview the reporter?"

"Yeah, I sent two agents to his home. He insisted, credibly they said, to have published everything the woman told him."

"Are you thinking the assassin had an accomplice who held the truck owner's family hostage while he used the truck as cover for the shoot?"

"That's our thinking right now," she said while sipping her coffee.

Just then Bartolo received a call. "I'm sorry Herman, I have to take this."

She listened for a minute, then said, "thanks, Marty. Good work."

Bartolo turned back toward Kettering. "Herman, I just received word that we got the warrant for a person of interest in this case. He's been involved in radical causes and was also arrested for vandalism at the protests on the day of Wahl's inauguration. Unfortunately, the case against him was dismissed because the D.C. police couldn't tie him to a specific criminal act. Now, with the warrant, we'll tap his phone, search his phone records, and identify his social media contacts. Oh, and we'll do a deep dive on his financials. I can't say any more about him at this moment, but he's been on our watch-list for years."

"Do you think he did it?"

"At this point, he's our most viable person of interest, but he's wily, always comes a hair's breadth short of getting in a jam. Honestly, right now there's not a shred of evidence linking him to the crime, but I'll interview him and see what happens."

"And where does the investigation of the food truck stand?"

"We have to be very careful. These people—Francisco and Isabella Sanchez—are undocumented. And, of course, they're obviously afraid of any contact with law enforcement. I'm going to send two Spanish-speaking female agents in nurses' uniforms to interview them at home. We hope the Sanchezes can describe the man and his accomplice. Once we gain their confidence that we're not going to report them to ICE, we'll swab the food truck and house for any residual DNA and dust for prints, but at this late date we're not optimistic we'll find useful evidence."

"Yeah."

"So, what's the NTSB's next move?"

"All our findings so far are preliminary. We will continue working with the evidence until we're confident there's nothing more to learn. We're in the process of refining all the measurements and tweaking our simulation, trying to make the conclusions more robust. After we're done with the investigation—and that could take six more months, maybe a year—we'll write a report that justifies our conclusions and makes them immune to second-guessers."

"We'll face the same problem when the time comes to report our findings."

"Let's keep in touch."

"Of course."

They shook hands. Bartolo walked down the hall to her nearby office, and Kettering left the fortress and grabbed a cab to NTSB headquarters at L'Enfant Plaza.

CHAPTER 17

THE INTERVIEWS WITH THE GUATEMALANS were fruitless. The nurses' uniforms did not fool Francisco and Isabella. Despite the agents' repeated declaration that they were health workers and not from ICE, the couple refused to cooperate and answered no questions. And Isabella even denied she had called Fairbanks at the Post. Francisco and Isabella were silent for reasons beyond their fear of deportation. In the house and in the food truck, the intruders had threatened to kill their children if they ever spoke to anyone from the government. The agents left disappointed that they had nothing to bring to Bartolo.

Bartolo was unhappy but not surprised when she debriefed the agents. She knew that Francisco and Isabella had made a good life in the United States, fleeing unspeakable horrors in violence-wracked Guatemala. Their children had been born in the United States and were being raised as Americans. The Sanchezes were simply protecting their family in the only way they knew how. But Bartolo also had a responsibility to gather evidence from the couple's home and food truck.

On an early Saturday morning several days later, two teams of FBI criminalists brought search warrants to the Sanchez residence, a small row house they rented in Woodbridge, Virginia. When the FBI vans pulled up, neighbors viewed the frightening scene from their upstairs windows, fearing that the Sanchez family was about to be arrested and deported.

The criminalist teams knocked on the door several times. Francisco finally decided that they had no choice but to open up. At the request of the criminalists, he also surrendered the keys to the food truck, which was parked on the street. The couple sat on the couch in their living room, comforting their young children. The two-year-old was wailing uncontrollably despite being in his mother's arms.

The criminalists methodically collected samples in the house. Isabella obviously kept the place very clean, even as her children generated constant clutter and confusion. The furniture was old, not antiques but thrift-store quality. This was a family that, they judged, had limited disposable income.

After completing their sweep of the house and taking DNA samples from the couple and fingerprinting them, the criminalists returned to Quantico where they processed the evidence. Their efforts had been for naught: the samples from the house yielded nothing to implicate the assassin.

The second criminalist team, Helen McCarthy and Andrew Lechtman, tackled the truck, which carried the Virginia vanity plate TACOMAN. It was obvious from the moment the pair stepped inside the mobile kitchen that Francisco took pride in keeping the gleaming stainless-steel surfaces immaculate.

McCarthy asked, "do you think we should bother sampling the food prep areas?"

"He has to sterilize these surfaces every day. I don't think it's worth our time. After all, it's been many months since the incident. Let's look for surfaces the shooter might have touched that Francisco doesn't routinely clean."

"That sounds right to me."

McCarthy thought to herself that this truck was as spotless as a hospital operating room. She let out a sigh of exasperation. Then she looked up and spotted an unusual ceiling vent next to the chimney-like ventilation fan seen on other trucks. The odd vent had, she estimated, a surface area of about two or three square feet. The unpainted aluminum vent was hinged on one side so that it could be pushed open, allowing smoke and aromas to leave the truck. Perhaps, she thought, it was the original vent; the truck, after all, was very old.

"Andy, look up at the ceiling vent."

He did and asked, "what are you seeing there?"

"The metal on the vent shows signs of unusual bending."

"Yeah, I see. Someone pushed it out of shape and then tried to bend it back."

"Helen, what do you think it means?"

"The vent was designed to open up to about 30 degrees. If the assassin used it as a gun port, he might have pushed it open farther to get a better view. After he left, Francisco would have tried to bend it back, but it retains traces of the shooter's actions."

"Right. So the assassin probably stood on the stool, bent the vent, and fired from there."

"Well, given that scenario, we need to take extra care to swab the vent for DNA. Maybe the assassin screwed up and gave us a gift."

When they had completed their work, the truck team thanked Francisco and Isabella for their cooperation, assuring them that they were not in any kind of trouble from the government. The criminalists returned to the Quantico lab and during the next few days processed their meager finds. The truck vent did yield DNA, and it was not Francisco's. That was the good news. But there was also bad news. Whoever left the DNA was not in CODIS, the FBI's combined law-enforcement DNA data base, or in any public ancestry-DNA data base.

****

Bartolo was in her D.C. office when, a week later, she received the criminalists' reports online. "Shit, shit, shit," she said after reading the conclusions about the fingerprints and DNA. But Bartolo was pleased that the truck team had found another piece of the puzzle. The damaged vent with the unknown DNA strongly indicated the assassin had used the Sanchez food truck as his shooting platform. If only there had been a DNA match or brass on the floor.

As a courtesy to her NTSB counterpart, Bartolo called Kettering and filled him in on the searches of the food truck and the Sanchez home.

"Overall, that's disappointing. But with your image of the food truck in place, we can use the vent as a data point to help refine our next-generation simulation."

"Good, I'll have a lab tech send it to you."

"Thanks, Joanna."

"Anything new on your end, Herman?"

"Nah. It's like we're slogging through molasses, but our preliminary findings are still holding up."

"That's good to hear."

"Any movement on your person of interest?"

Joanna replied, "our data feeds are ongoing but we're not moving on him yet."

"Let me know if anything happens on that front."

"I will."

CHAPTER 18

AS A PERSISTENT WAHL HATER, Bryan Feldman was among hundreds of radicals and would-be terrorists whose social media posts caught the FBI's attention. None of Feldman's public posts had passed the high threshold of being regarded as an actual threat to the president.

From Feldman's confidential posts, the FBI learned that he had been in contact with many far-left groups that detested and defamed the president. The FBI also knew he had participated in many anti-Wahl demonstrations. One post from late July put Feldman squarely at the top of Bartolo's suspect list: "the only solution to Wahl's reign of terror is assassination."

Bryan Feldman had been disenchanted with Frederick Wahl long before the Electoral College had elevated him to the presidency. Feldman's father, Jay, owned a construction company in Philadelphia. When Wahl choose Philadelphia for his new corporate headquarters, he hired Feldman's firm for the drywall job on the 22-story building downtown. Not only did Feldman satisfy the onerous contract specifications, but he also completed the project two weeks ahead of schedule and on budget.

Despite receiving monthly reminder invoices, Wahl stalled on making the final payment—25 percent of the total project cost. Fraudulently claiming that the drywall installation was substandard, Wahl never paid the bill. It was a near-fatal blow to the family-owned company. Jay never forgot how shabbily Wahl had treated him. And he passed along his hatred of the man to his oldest son, Bryan, who was 14 years old at the time of the job.

As a youth, Bryan had been a prodigy in math and science. After graduating from high school at age 16, he won a full scholarship to Johns Hopkins University where he studied computer science and earned a Ph.D. Even before finishing his dissertation, the 21-year-old grad student was courted by MIT's Lincoln Laboratory to join one of their teams in Cyber Security and Information Sciences. They offered Feldman a post-doc, which he happily accepted.

When Feldman's post-doc ended, he signed on with a large aerospace company in Bethesda, Maryland. The government denied him top-secret clearance on the basis of his political activities and social media posts. The company still wanted Feldman, and so they hired him in their commercial division.

Feldman never forgot his inherited hatred of Wahl. As soon as the man declared for the presidency, Feldman began making inflammatory posts on social media. Every new presidential outrage led to a new spate of snarky witticisms. And he especially relished photoshopping Svetlana's head onto pornographic images and posting them on social media.

Apprised of Feldman's activities, Bartolo's team monitored his outbursts closely, but the young man never crossed the line. Even so, Bartolo decided it was time to interview him. And she wanted to do it herself.

****

Feldman lived in a two-bedroom condo in Wheaton, Maryland, a northern suburb of D.C. Other than state-of-the-art computers and a host of peripherals, he had furnished his condo sparsely from IKEA's offerings. His home was a bachelor pad where he occasionally hosted like-minded women he met at political meetings and demonstrations.

At 7:00 a.m. on a brisk, late January morning, Feldman got out of bed slowly so as not to awaken Janice, his companion *du soir*. Hearing a car pull into a parking space in front of his first-floor condo, he padded to his bedroom window, pulled the heavy curtain aside, and peered outside. He recoiled in horror at the sight of an unmarked black SUV bearing government plates. Two large men in dark suits exited the vehicle and headed for his hallway; he feared they were coming his way. Confirmation came a few seconds later when he heard a loud and insistent knocking on his door.

He hollered, "give me a minute to get dressed." The FBI agents were in no hurry and stood silently in the hallway. Feldman hastily put on jeans and an old MIT sweatshirt and opened the door part way.

"Who are you, and what do you want?"

Feldman's appearance met the agents' stereotype of a radical left-ist; probably a Jew, they judged by his surname, black curly hair, olive skin, dark eyes, and beaky nose.

The agents ignored his question and asked, "are you Bryan Feldman?"

"Yes, I am. Let me ask again: what do you want?"

"You'll find out soon enough. Put on a coat and shoes because you're coming with us."

"Let me see your IDs."

Feldman shuddered at the sight of the IDs but they appeared authentic. He was scared shitless and had no idea what they wanted. True, he had been arrested on the day of Wahl's inauguration. In fact, he used a brick to smash the windows of a Lincoln limousine. Because no videos showed his face, the judge in a bench trial dismissed the case against him. Regardless, he thought, that incident had been a matter for the D.C. police to pursue, not the FBI.

Mystified, Feldman decided that resistance was futile and could only make matters worse. "Okay, I'll come with you, but can you tell me anything? Am I under arrest?"

One of the agents said, "you're not under arrest as of now. We'll be taking you to the Hoover Building where Special Agent Bartolo will interview you. That's all we know."

Just then Janice from behind the half-closed bedroom door said, "what's going on Bryan? I hear voices."

"I have to go downtown. Will I see you tonight?"

"I doubt it," she replied coolly.

The three men left the building and stepped into the SUV. Silence prevailed on the 50-minute trip downtown during rush hour.

CHAPTER 19

AT THE HOOVER BUILDING, the agents escorted Feldman to the small conference room on the fifth floor. He marveled at the impressive view through the window but was in no a mood to enjoy it. Bartolo entered the room and lowered the window shades, ending the distraction.

"I am Senior Special Agent Joanna Bartolo. I know who you are."

Bartolo offered her hand and Feldman hesitated briefly before shaking it. Pointing to the offerings on the table, she said, "help yourself, and take a seat."

Glancing at the table, Feldman appeared surprised to see coffee and an array of pastries. He took a mug of coffee with cream and a cheese Danish.

There was a third man in the room, also an agent. He remained seated and said nothing, but took notes on a tablet. Feldman pointed to the silent man and asked about him.

"He's agent Lawrence Chesley. He's here to take notes and prevent me from beating the crap out of you."

"Oh," he said, not realizing it was a joke.

On the drive downtown Feldman had begun to think of other reasons why Bartolo had summoned him to FBI headquarters. Maybe it had something do with his anti-Wahl posts on social media. He knew they had been provocative, but he was confident that none of them went so far as to threaten the president. Surely, he thought, the FBI didn't care about a little artistic photoshopping of Svetlana Wahl.

"Mr. Feldman, we know that you have radical leanings and have taken part in violent demonstrations."

"I assume you're referring to the vandalism that occurred on the day of Wahl's inauguration. But surely you know that the charges against me were dismissed."

"That doesn't mean you were innocent."

Feldman and Bartolo both knew that the D.C. Metropolitan Police Department was hopelessly inept. That's why most of the cases against several hundred people had been dismissed. There simply wasn't enough evidence to link specific people to specific acts. Feldman realized that Bartolo couldn't arrest him for that crime, unless he'd unknowingly trashed a federal vehicle. Most likely, he surmised, this visit downtown was about something else.

"Mr. Feldman, you have come to our attention as a person of interest in the investigation of President Wahl's assassination."

Feldman was stupefied, speechless, his mouth agape and eyes open wide. He finally asked, "are you going to read me my rights?"

"I can, but I prefer to have an informal conversation with you. You'll notice that I'm not recording it." In fact, the room contained several hidden microphones and video cameras that fed recorders in an adjacent room. Although Bartolo had lied to Feldman, recording the interview was legal in D.C. because one party—Bartolo—had consented to it.

Bartolo continued, "you've posted a large number of anti-Wahl hate messages over the years. And in the months before the assassination they increased in frequency and virulence."

His composure returning, Feldman blurted out, "that's because Wahl was doing more and more outrageous things. Fox News brainwashed millions of people in this country. But people who can still think for themselves were appalled by Wahl's behavior. He was a vindictive son of bitch with no morals, no interest in the lives of working people. The scum of the earth, a despot. So, yeah, in my social media posts, I simply expressed my utter contempt for the man. In my hatred, I was just more open and more forceful than other people."

Surprised by Feldman's bluntness, Bartolo hesitated briefly before moving on.

"After the media began carrying reports of Marine One's crash and the presumption that the president had been killed, you posted…wait a second." Bartolo scrolled through her tablet. "Ah, here it is. You wrote, 'ding dong the witch is dead, the wicked witch is dead.' Were you referring to the president?"

"Of course. This country is much better off without him. He was a despicable human being, totally unfit to hold public office. And that was a widespread judgment according to polls taken in his last months in office."

"Mr. Feldman, do you own any firearms?"

"No. I have nothing to do with guns. Never owned one, never will."

Bartolo realized that this conversation was going nowhere. She needed to focus Feldman's attention.

"Okay, Mr. Feldman, let's go back in time. What were you doing on the morning of the assassination?"

"Let's see, that was…"

"Friday, November 16."

"Ah yes, I know exactly where I was when I heard the good news about Wahl. I was at work. Someone in another cubicle yelled, 'turn on the news. The president's been killed.' So, I immediately clicked on the live feed from CNN and watched their reports."

Bartolo showed her disappointment with a frown. It was a credible alibi, easy enough to verify.

"Can anyone corroborate your story?"

Feldman gave her an incredulous look and said, "of course. My co-workers and I went down to the conference room because it has a 60-inch TV. We sat there mesmerized during the rest of the morning, and even stayed through lunch. I'm sure my co-workers will remember my joyful outbursts."

Bartolo's frown deepened. She could no longer stand being in the same room as the man who had such deep hatred for the late president. Wahl's many faults aside, Bartolo believed that Feldman had disrespected the office of the presidency, and thus the United States itself.

"Mr. Feldman, assuming you weren't involved in the crash of Marine One, do you have any ideas about who might have done it?"

"If I did—and I'm not saying I do—I wouldn't tell you. Even if you waterboarded me."

"Waterboarding was the CIA's game, not the FBI's." She took a deep breath and said, "we're done here. I'll have someone escort you down to 9th Street. I assume you can find your way home from there."

"Actually, I have to go to work—I'm late as it is." With more than a hint of sarcasm, he added, "thanks for breakfast."

On 9th Street, Feldman walked north, jogged over to 7th, and continued north until he reached the Gallery Place Metro station in Chinatown. After waiting seven minutes, he boarded a Red Line train in the direction of Shady Grove.

Later that morning, an FBI criminalist packed up Feldman's coffee mug and drove it to Quantico where it was processed for DNA. When Bartolo was informed that the DNA did not match the unknown from the food truck, she was not surprised. She also sent two agents to interview people at Feldman's workplace. As she had anticipated, Feldman's alibi was strongly confirmed. "Damn!" she muttered.

****

Feldman had been the number one person of interest, but many more anti-Wahl protesters had raised suspicions. A lifelong Republican, Bartolo didn't look forward to interviewing other leftwing radicals. Her team in D.C. and in many field offices around the country had been picking up hundreds of Wahl haters. They were also prioritizing interviews with people who had shown sympathies with Isis and other terrorist groups.

Bartolo was aware that the United States was currently dropping bombs on nine sovereign nations, in many cases without the targeted country's permission. Any one of these countries might have provoked a person already holding a strong grudge against America to have committed the crime.

At times Bartolo seemed overwhelmed with the scope of America's enemies. We've messed up in lots of places, she reluctantly admitted to herself. She was especially worried about the Palestinians. After all, Wahl had publicly ruled out a two-state solution as a diplomatic goal. Immediately after his pronouncement, rioting in the West Bank and Gaza resulted in dozens of deaths. She wondered if America's bungled foreign policy in the Middle East was behind the assassination. If so, the FBI would again be cleaning up another politician's mess.

CHAPTER 20

INSIDE THE HOOVER BUILDING, working independently of Bartolo's group, was a second FBI task force also investigating the assassination. Its charge was to explore unusual scenarios, perhaps involving foreign actors. Special Agent Richard Coppersmith headed this top-secret team, which collaborated with the CIA.

After graduating from Harvard with an M.A. in Russian literature, Richard—"never call me Dick"—Coppersmith had few job prospects. With his degree in hand, he went looking for unconventional job opportunities. The FBI was hiring, and had even sent a recruiter to Harvard's alumni placement office. One position seemed very appealing: document analyst. He applied and was hired. After training at Quantico, the FBI assigned Coppersmith to the Hoover Building. He served on many important teams and achieved the rank of Senior Special Agent.

Zeroing in on President Wahl's ties to Russia, particularly Vladimir Putin, the FBI-CIA collaboration was developing an extraordinary theory of the crime.

Coppersmith, tall and fair-skinned, was in his early fifties and showing his age. Almost bald, his plain face as wrinkled as a dried apricot, he had cultivated a sizable middle-age spread. Over several decades, Coppersmith and Bartolo had occasionally worked together on cases significant and trivial. Now both agents were on parallel paths, trying to pin responsibility on the president's killer or killers. They enjoyed a cordial working relationship but did not socialize outside of work.

In a meeting that took place in the conference room near Bartolo's office, Coppersmith outlined his team's theory of the assassination.

Helping himself to coffee and a chocolate donut, he surprised Joanna with news: "Joanna, we've developed a counterintuitive theory."

"Tell me about it."

"Well, as you know, a majority of agents inside the bureau and in the CIA believe that Wahl was Vladimir Putin's puppet."

"Yeah, no news there."

"The common wisdom is that Putin wanted to keep Wahl in power as long as possible so that he'd continue to promote the Kremlin's agenda in foreign policy. Let's face it, even before his inauguration Wahl was spouting Moscow's propaganda points."

"I'm following so far."

"Well, Putin's calculus changed during the months preceding the assassination. The American press was doing near-constant exposés of ties between Russians and Wahl's campaign staffers and aides— and even his cabinet secretaries. We believe this relentless airing of Russian influence was making Putin uneasy. Communication intercepts suggest that Putin was profoundly unhappy over the flood of bad press about Russian interference in American elections on behalf of Wahl, Wahl's business dealings with several oligarchs, and the secret calls between the two leaders. Reluctantly, he decided to take drastic action."

"Okay, Richard, so Putin's unhappy because his efforts to undermine the United States have been exposed in searing stories. It doesn't follow that he'd turn to assassination."

"Well, we believe Putin had a good motive. Owing to the press reports and his incessant lying, Wahl had lost all credibility. Nobody believed the president any longer when he denied Putin's influence on his election campaign and foreign policy. As the president's behavior became more and more erratic, Putin became more and more concerned."

"I agree that Putin might have had a motive, but assassinating the U.S. president is a drastic play, even for the Kremlin. I just can't see it."

"Hear me out. Our team believes Putin came to view Wahl as a serious liability who had to be neutralized."

Bartolo, who could not force herself to take this theory seriously, offered to "play devil's advocate."

"Okay, go for it."

"It's well known that the Russians prefer exotic means to dispose of troublesome actors on the international stage. They wouldn't use something as crude as an assault rifle to bring down a chopper. That's just not in Putin's playbook."

"Joanna, the whole world knows the Russians use poisonous radio-isotopes and deadly nerve agents to take out enemies in the West. If such a weapon had killed Wahl, the crime would have pointed immediately to the Kremlin."

"I agree. And I see where this is going. You maintain that by changing the MO, making it appear like a terrorist attack, the Russians can deflect suspicion away from the Kremlin."

"Precisely. Putin and his cronies had to choose an MO easily associated with radicalized Americans or foreign terrorists. An assault rifle aimed at Marine One suited their purposes perfectly."

"Okay," responded Bartolo, "I grant that you've made a plausible case for motive and explained why the MO departs from the usual Kremlin pattern. But, the question is, do you have any evidence to support your theory?"

Chuckling, Coppersmith replied, "I was afraid you were going to get to that question. The answer is, we don't have anything concrete yet. The CIA is working their human assets and we're both relying on communication intercepts. We have concluded that the Russians have been extraordinarily careful to conceal their involvement. That's another reason to believe Putin himself ordered the hit on Wahl."

"That strikes me as a bizarre argument. There's no evidence, so a lack of evidence strengthens the case against Putin? Richard, I hate to say this, but I think you folks are blowing smoke."

"And I think you're missing the subtleties of our arguments."

"Maybe so."

The agents were comfortable finding flaws in each other's theories, so this disagreement was nothing new or serious. Of all their arguments, however, both knew that this one seemed to have the greatest import.

Bartolo continued, "if your theory is correct, then the implications are dire. Suppose you find a smoking gun, then what? How can the United States retaliate without starting a war?"

"Joanna, that's what covert ops are for."

"What would you do? Shut off the lights in the Kremlin? Sabotage the Moscow subway? Disable Russia's air traffic control system?"

"Naturally, those options would all be on the table—and many that are less obvious but more drastic. Look, our theory so far is an intellectual exercise. Until we have definitive evidence that the Russians did it, talk of retaliation is premature."

"Of course."

"Joanna, what has your team learned?"

"In collaboration with the NTSB, we've figured out how it was done. The shooter stood inside a food truck with an assault rifle and took aim at the chopper through a vent in the roof. He fired off a magazine and got lucky. Several rounds hit the chopper in vulnerable locations. We have DNA from the vent but haven't found a match. The owner of the food truck is an undocumented Guatemalan who's not under suspicion."

"So, you've made some progress. What's the current status of the investigation?"

"It's been hard to identify persons of interest. We can't just bring in every leftist who posted hateful words about Wahl on social media. I've interviewed the number one person of interest, but he's checked out clean. There's a long list of secondary suspects we are now interviewing. Unfortunately, my people have to sit in the same room with some really disagreeable leftists and terrorist sympathizers."

"I don't envy you. Well, I need to go back upstairs. I have a meeting with my team in 10 minutes."

"Thanks for dropping by and sharing. Your theory is intriguing—and frightening."

"Don't I know it!"

CHAPTER 21

BACK IN HER OFFICE, Bartolo compiled a list of the next two dozen persons who had aroused the FBI's interest. She decided to seek warrants wholesale.

Bartolo furnished the FBI attorney with lengthy arguments for a wide-ranging surveillance of all 24: email, social media, telephone, finances—the works. In view of the case's importance, the federal district judge, a Wahl-appointed Republican, issued the warrants. Beginning a week later, Bartolo received daily reports from the analysts assigned to monitor the data streams and dig deeply into the suspects' past activities. On the basis of their recommendations, she would decide who, if anyone, merited an interview.

The investigation had become tiresome. She was merely going through the motions because there wasn't a shred of concrete evidence implicating the assassin. The warrants amounted to no more than a fishing expedition in a vast, murky sea. Wringing her hands, Bartolo said aloud, "I need a glass of grappa."

Bartolo didn't talk about her Italian ancestry in the Hoover Building, for she had detected a lingering suspicion among many WASPs that Italian-Americans still have connections to organized crime. Actually, she was very proud of her heritage. On her father's side, Bartolo was descended from a long line of stone masons, the highly skilled men who did intricate carvings of gargoyles, bible scenes, statues of saints, and other church ornaments. In fact, her uncle Giuseppe had been brought from Italy to help repair earthquake damage the National Cathedral suffered in 2011. "National," she said resentfully, was a misnomer, intended to mislead. The cathedral was, in fact, a cavernous Episcopal church. The only federal involvement was its occasional use for state funerals.

Louis, Bartolo's husband, was also of Italian heritage. Their marriage was happy and stable, marred only by Louis's incessant carping every time she had to spend long periods in the field. Empty-nesters, they enjoyed taking care of their home and getting away for romantic weekends at Rehoboth Beach, nearby in Delaware. The Bartolos especially delighted in taking long walks on the boardwalk, and sampling the offerings of many restaurants within walking distance of their favorite hotel.

CHAPTER 22

IVAN GORSKY WAS AN 18-YEAR CAREER EMPLOYEE of the NTSB who had maneuvered his way onto the Marine One task force. A short man with dark hair and undistinguished features, he was a naturalized U.S. citizen. After earning a Ph.D. in mathematics from Moscow State University in Russia, he returned to his native Chechnya, where he found employment as an actuary with a government-owned insurance company. Gorsky eventually sought asylum in the U.S., claiming to be a freedom fighter in mortal danger because he had resisted Moscow's incursions into his homeland. However, during Gorsky's earlier time in Moscow, the Kremlin had groomed him for an important assignment in the U.S. He was Moscow's mole in the NTSB, keeping tabs on investigations of transportation incidents around world. His current assignment was to inform his handlers, through the Dark Web, about which people or entities the NTSB was fingering for the assassination.

While helping to refine the simulation model, Gorsky attended closely to the buzz about possible assassins that animated coffee break discussions. He had heard about the group responsible proposing for the Putin scenario. Beyond monitoring gossip, he could get no reliable intel, despite his handlers' constant pressure.

One afternoon, the NTSB's Herman Kettering was giving Melanie Ford, head of the CIA's team, a VIP tour of the reconstructed helicopter. After silently viewing the wreckage, they moved into a bleak, windowless conference room adjacent to the hangar where they expected to trade information about their respective investigations. Other members of the NTSB team, including Gorsky, joined them.

A tall, hazel-eyed blonde with angular features, wearing an exquisitely tailored charcoal suit, Ford projected authority. A woman of few words, she made each one count.

Directing her question to Kettering, Ford said, "who was responsible?"

"We don't know that yet."

"Surely you have some theories?"

"Right now, we're thinking it was a lone shooter working with an accomplice."

"Do you believe there was a larger conspiracy?"

"That takes us into very dicey territory. We know that President Wahl made many enemies around the world. Any country could have put this assassination plot together. It was sophisticated in the sense that it worked well, and we haven't identified the perpetrator. But the crime was also unsophisticated because it depended on nothing more than careful planning, two people, a deadly weapon, and an old food truck. And the shooter got lucky. That's why domestic radicals or foreign enemies—anybody—could have planned this crime and pulled it off. We are stumped. If you have any ideas, we'd be happy to have your input."

"I'm afraid I can't divulge much at this point. I can say, with some embarrassment, that we haven't ruled out any foreign actors. The problem is that a dozen or so terrorist groups claimed credit. More puzzling still, anti-American Internet and phone chatter didn't spike in the weeks before the incident. We do know, however, that Putin had become increasingly disenchanted with his puppet in the White House."

Kettering looked puzzled and asked, "are you suggesting that Putin might have ordered the hit?"

"It's just one of many scenarios we're considering."

Gorsky listened to this exchange with great interest. Ford had confirmed the gossip that the CIA believed Putin to be the plot's mastermind. The mole would have to inform his handlers about the CIA's scenario. They would not be pleased at having to pass the disquieting word up the Kremlin's chain of command. Gorsky did not know who had ordered the assassination. He feared that an accusation pointing to Russia might, if given play in the press, trigger an international incident.

CHAPTER 23

A BUSY WEEKEND LOOMED AHEAD for Stella as she prepared for her trip to Hawai'i. Before finishing her packing, she checked the Washington Post online. A front-page article immediately drew her attention with the headline: "Unknown Assassin Still Free." She delved into the article whose byline included four respected journalists who covered the federal beat. The article laid out, in stark terms, the lack of progress in the ongoing investigations. The reporters insisted that many mysteries remained. Perhaps the greatest mystery, beyond the identity of the assassin, was how he had managed to bring down Marine One. The article mentioned neither assault rifle nor food truck.

Post reporters had succeeded in interviewing several FBI agents. The anonymous quotes were devastating: "we've gone the extra mile but there's not one bona fide suspect in sight." Another pinpointed the problem: "we've interviewed hundreds of people around the country, but they're just the tip of the anti-Wahl iceberg." Whoever did this, another source said, "can gloat because the assassination of President Wahl may turn out to be the most infamous unsolved crime in American history."

Stella finished the article, having digested its gist. If the reporters were correct, then the feds were clueless as to the assassin's identity. She couldn't help but feel a rush of excitement in anticipation of meeting the man himself. What would the Joker be like? Was he an Islamist sympathizer? A home-grown radical or terrorist? A hired gun acting at the behest of a foreign government? The article had mapped out these scenarios and others, again quoting unnamed sources, but admitted that no scenario had been ruled out.

Although she had received communications from the Joker, Stella had no idea who he was or what ideology had motivated him—if any. And, despite the considerable risks, she was anxious to meet him. At Malcolm's urging, she promised to be on her guard, to watch for signs she might be heading into a trap. She sighed. It was time, Stella mused, to put these dark thoughts out of her mind and look ahead.

****

Two days later, Stella stepped out of a cab, paid the driver, and walked into the terminal at LAX. Airports were not Stella's favorite places to spend time. In fact, she was convinced that time passed more slowly in airport lounges than anywhere else on Earth. This fact, she was certain, had eluded Albert Einstein and Stephen Hawking. Contributing to the slow passage of time were crying kids, people who hadn't bathed in recent memory, and lonely men trying to make her acquaintance. She was not looking forward to the hour-plus wait before her plane boarded.

Stella passed through the TSA obstacle course with ease and rolled her bag to the nearest place to buy a beer. The line was long but she desperately needed a brew and waited patiently, even as a couple rudely pushed their way ahead of her. She didn't make an issue of it. Beer in hand, she found a seat and began to imbibe.

At long last, seemingly a full day after she arrived at the airport, a gate agent announced the first boarding call. Stella stood up and walked toward the gate, even though there was a long line. When her group was called at last, she handed her boarding pass to the agent who scanned it and waved her in. The jetway was crowded and the line moved slowly. Just one more indignity while she waited to find her cramped seat in economy class.

****

To pass time during the six-hour flight, Stella read one of John Grisham's latest mysteries, *Rooster Bar*, on her laptop. Engrossed in the book, she barely registered the pilot's announcement that the plane had begun its descent into the Daniel K. Inouye International Airport in Honolulu. The landing was smooth and the boisterous crowd, many men already wearing Hawaiian shirts and slightly inebriated, filed out almost speedily. She followed the crowd and rolled her bag to the door whose sign promised taxis outside. Stella waited for a vacant cab and told the driver her destination.

After checking into the Queen Kapiolani Hotel, Stella walked to the elevator and took it to the twelfth floor. She used the key card to open the door and surveyed the room's interior. It was quite nice, she thought. The king-size bed looked comfortable, and there was a desk, recliner, and prints of native Hawaiian birds on the walls. She walked to the window and opened the colorful floral drapes. Far below she could see the swimming pool and children splashing each other. In the distance were Diamond Head and Waikiki Beach.

According to Stella's growling stomach, it was past dinnertime. By local time it was still afternoon. She left the room and explored the hotel. She found the Deck Bar and Grill where people ate and drank in air-conditioned comfort. Stella ordered a mai tai and fish tacos, and sat down to enjoy the repast and to think. She had expected the Joker to make contact by now, but saw no sign of him. After spending a few hours in the Deck and finishing her novel, she went downstairs and approached the receptionist at the front desk.

"Have any messages come for me?"

"What's your name again?"

"Stella Weiss."

He reached below the counter and pulled out a small package. After checking the name, he said, "right. This came for you about an hour ago. I rang your room but there was no answer." He held out a tablet and pointed to a line. "Please sign here." She did, and he handed her the package.

"Thanks."

A courier had delivered the package, which lacked a return address.

She immediately went to her room, carefully unsealed the package and pulled out four items. It contained a note, a round-trip ticket to Samoa departing tomorrow, a Thai passport with a fictitious name and her picture, and a Thai driver's license, likewise with her new identity. Now she would be Sylvia Chung. She looked at her pictures on the passport and driver's license. They were both good likenesses of her but different. She had to admit, this guy is really clever.

The note merely said, "tell no one of new travel plans. Remain registered at Queen Kapiolani. On travel day, walk two blocks west of hotel with luggage; call an Uber to take you to the airport. After that call, turn off phone and shut down computer. Don't turn them on again until you return to Honolulu. Leave credit cards in the room. At Faleolo airport in Samoa, stay overnight at nearby Le Vasa Resort. You'll be met next day a.m."

Whoa, she thought to herself. The Joker was asking her to play a new—and very dangerous—game. She could be arrested if the airline or TSA suspected that her travel documents were fake. She agonized, questioning whether she should really go through with the Joker's plan.

Stella knew that the Joker had devoted considerable effort and expense to bring her to Samoa. This meeting was obviously import-ant to him, but why? Clearly, he wanted to use her. Did he want her to paint a sympathetic portrait of someone who had murdered 10 people? It was a given in her business that everyone who talked to a reporter had an agenda. She was clueless as to the Joker's real agenda. Whatever it was, the story was too important for her to pass up. The words, "scoop of the century," kept echoing in her head. She wanted the story, so she resigned herself to following the Joker's instructions. She would fly to Samoa. In this case, Stella admitted, she was sacrific-ing commonsense in favor of ambition. She texted Malcolm: "Stella may go dark for the next week or so. Do not worry."

To clear her head of lingering doubts, she decided to go outside. First she went to the beach and walked along the shore. Then she took the arduous path to the peak of Diamond Head. On the way up she passed many younger hikers who were huffing and puffing as if suffering from emphysema. She didn't remain long at the peak, as fatigue had set in. After returning from the hike, Stella bought several snacks in the hotel. She ate them in the lobby, enjoying the constant people parade. Finally, she went up to her room.

****

Stella had only vague impressions of Samoa. Google gave her a crash course on the country's geography, history, and culture.

Samoa, Stella learned, is an independent country of 200,000 people in the southwestern Pacific Ocean. It consists of two main volcanic islands, Savai'i and Upolu, and several smaller ones. At 1100 square miles, the land area is slightly smaller than the state of Rhode Island. The country's capital, Apia, and nearby airport are on Upolu.

Samoa had been under the administration of New Zealand until 1962 when it achieved independence. Pago Pago, a popular tourist destination, was on American Samoa—an island to the east that was unaffiliated politically with the nation of Samoa.

Stella was fascinated to learn that Samoa was one of dozens of Pacific island groups originally settled by seafaring Polynesian peoples. Archaeologists discovered that Samoa's first inhabitants arrived around 1,000 B.C., maybe earlier, probably sailing from Tonga on large outrigger canoes. When the first European explorers visited the islands in the eighteenth century, they found an ancient and vibrant agricultural society.

Samoa came to the attention of Americans when anthropologist Margaret Mead published her 1928 landmark study, *Coming of Age in Samoa*. Mead reported on a society whose adolescent girls normally engaged in sexual experimentation. Shocking, indeed, Stella giggled. *Coming of Age* put Samoa into the American consciousness as a tropical paradise replete with free and easy sex, an image the country had been trying to dispel.

But Stella wouldn't be doing cultural anthropology in Samoa, looking for thatched huts and grass skirt survivals of Mead's era. Instead, she hoped her one-on-one with the Joker would furnish all the facts she needed to write about the assassination's greatest mysteries: Who was he? How did he pull it off? What were his motivations? And, on whose behalf had he acted? These were the most important questions, which she hoped the Joker would answer in candid conversations.

CHAPTER 24

THE FOLLOWING DAY PROMISED TO BE WEIRD. Stella would have to spend most of it in Hawai'i because her Fiji Airlines flight didn't leave Honolulu until 6:25 p.m. Stella—a.k.a. Sylvia Chung—decided to devote a good part of the day to exploring. Maybe that would ease her growing tension about flying with fake documents.

She had long known about the Bonzai Pipeline, the place on the north shore where only the bravest surfers challenged the enormous—and treacherous—pipe-shaped waves. Some surfers, she knew, had died in the attempt. She consulted Google and learned about the bus that traveled from Honolulu to the Bonzai Pipeline. It cost only three dollars.

Stella took a cab to the nearest stop for the Pipeline bus. After a few minutes, the bus arrived and she climbed aboard, paid the driver, and found a window seat. The trip took almost two hours, but she enjoyed looking out the window at the spectacular volcanic landscape on the eastern shore, and time passed quickly. The bus let her off just a few minutes walk to the Pipeline beach where she watched surfers challenge the waves. She had only surfed a few times, but in her mind's eye she visualized herself braving the Pipeline. She smiled at the thought, only a pipe dream.

Stella had skipped breakfast and was famished. She recalled that the bus had passed several eateries nearby, so she walked back along the highway for about a mile, checking out menus. Ted's Bakery had an inviting array of lunch offerings. She went in and ordered a mahi mahi sandwich and berry smoothie. The food was well prepared and tasty, and she left feeling satisfied.

After lunch, Stella caught the bus back to Honolulu. Instead of hailing a cab from the bus stop, she trekked back to the hotel on foot.

****

Stella printed out her boarding pass in the business center and then headed to her room. She packed her suitcase, took it downstairs, and withdrew $300 in twenties from a universal teller machine in the lobby. After browsing for a few minutes in the gift shop, she bought a large floppy hat and oversize sunglasses. Then she took a cab to the airport.

Stella believed that the exercise and fresh air had been the right tonic for her anxiety. She knew that passing the security hurdle in the airport required confidence and utmost serenity.

At the TSA checkpoint, the agent asked to see her boarding pass and ID. He looked at her, then at the photo, then back at her. Stella was panicked on the inside, hoping the fear didn't show on her face. The agent returned her documents, and waved her to the conveyor belt.

Letting out a deep breath, Stella joined a line and waited briefly behind a small man who was wrestling with a suitcase. She moved to help him but was too late, as the heavy bag fell to the floor. She helped him lift the bag onto the belt. After putting her own bag on the belt and pushing it forward, Stella placed her purse, shoes, liquids, and laptop into a plastic tub. She passed through the metal detector, grabbed her things, and headed to the departure lounge for Fiji Airlines.

CHAPTER 25

AS STELLA DEPLANED in Faleolo International Airport, she felt a surge of adrenaline that partially overcame her fatigue. The terminal's arrival/departure area was spartan but clean. She found a restroom and freshened up. As a light-skinned Black woman, Stella did not feel conspicuous here, amidst a reassuring rainbow of people. She walked toward the exit, ready for her Samoan adventure but still apprehensive.

The cab ride to Le Vasa Resort took less than five minutes. She had no Samoan currency, but the cabbie was delighted to accept a twenty-dollar bill. The resort had a Polynesian theme throughout, from tiki bar to thatched-roof cabins. She went to the reception area and checked in. Stella was surprised when the clerk told her that Sylvia Chung's cabin and meals had been paid for in advance. Because it was past midnight, she didn't bother to familiarize herself with the resort's many amenities. Instead, she navigated the walkways to her airy cabin. Stella brushed her teeth and set out clothes for the next day. As soon as her head hit the pillow, she fell into a deep sleep.

****

After breakfast, Stella sat in the lounge, not far from the resort's main entrance, impatiently looking around for the Joker. During the next few hours, she waited anxiously, occasionally pacing in the lounge, but he did not appear. For the first time she was frightened, knowing she was vulnerable—an American stranded in a foreign country who had traveled on a counterfeit passport. As it was past lunchtime, and no one had come for her, Stella bought a snack and returned to the lounge.

She was just making herself comfortable when a thirtyish white woman of medium stature approached. The woman had short, strawberry blond hair, blue eyes, and a ski-slope nose. She was wearing a pink blouse with lace trim at the neck and sleeves, a teal skirt, and sandals.

In a friendly voice the stranger asked, "are you Sylvia Chung?"

Stella was about to say no, when she realized that "no" was the wrong answer.

"Yes, I'm Sylvia. Who are you?"

"My name is Tina, but you don't need to know more than that. I've come to bring you to our home where you'll meet my husband, Michael. Together we'll give you the scoop of the century." She held out her hand.

Not in her wildest daydreams had Stella pictured someone like Tina having taken part in the assassination. This was the first of many surprises that awaited the reporter in this Polynesian paradise.

Stella forced a smile and shook Tina's hand. "Nice to meet you, Tina. I've been waiting all morning."

Sensing the irritation in Stella's voice, Tina explained, "Sorry about your wait, but I missed the ferry. Let's get going. We'll take a short ride and be at the dock in plenty of time to catch the four o'clock ferry to Savai'i. My car is out front."

They stepped outside and Stella immediately felt as though she were suffocating in a sauna. The heat and high humidity were oppressive, far more so than in Hawai'i. Accustomed to L.A.'s desert-like air, Stella at once understood the full meaning of "tropical."

Tina led the reporter and her suitcase to the car. Stella had traveled to Europe several times, and was used to seeing tiny cars made everywhere except in America. Tina's car was a Renault Mégane, and it was surprisingly spacious.

As they left for the ferry, Stella looked back at the airport. The main building was topped by a series of arched roofs alluding to the traditional house style of the islands. Nice touch, she thought.

"Tina, what's the plan?"

"After we depart the ferry, we'll take a short drive north along the shore road. Our home is just a few minutes past the village of Salelologa. We'll be home in plenty of time for dinner. That reminds me. Do you have any dietary restrictions?"

"Nope. Put anything on a plate in front of me with a fork and knife and it will disappear."

"Good. I hope you'll enjoy my cooking."

"I'm sure I will."

CHAPTER 26

"HERE WE ARE," SAID TINA, as she turned left into the driveway of what, in the states, would be called a McMansion. Three stories, the house's exterior was entirely Western in appearance; there was not a single Polynesian feature—except for the magnificent sea view.

"How long have you lived here?"

"We leased this place about three years ago."

"It looks expensive. How can you afford it?"

"I don't want to discuss our finances with you. But I can tell you that we managed to squirrel away a large amount of money and invested it wisely. Our stateside careers paid well."

"What were your careers?"

"That's another subject I'm not comfortable discussing, at least not now."

Stella bounced her suitcase up a short flight of lava-block stairs. Tina opened the unlocked door and pointed to the man who had just risen from one of the couches. "Michael, meet Stella."

"Nice to meet you, ma'am," he said as they shook hands.

Barefoot in a flowery shirt and sporty shorts, Michael also seemed to be thirtyish. His auburn hair was neatly trimmed and short; his close-set eyes were steely gray. His face was long with a prominent nose and chin. In no world would Stella have judged him handsome, yet he had a certain masculine *je ne sais quoi*, despite a small paunch on an otherwise buff body.

Stella was dumbfounded. Michael and Tina were what many people would regard as the "all-American" couple. Appearing very WASPy, they did not fit the stereotype of any terrorist or assassin. Not exactly Bonnie and Clyde. No wonder the FBI was spinning its wheels. Maybe she'd been cleverly duped, and they weren't the assassins after all. She was confused—and very jet lagged. Stella couldn't fathom how these two people could have killed the president and nine others.

The reporter looked around at her surroundings. The living room was large, with what appeared to be a dense-pack of dark Danish Modern furniture, a tall ceiling, and a tiki bar of bamboo slats next to a sliding glass door that opened to a large covered patio.

Michael picked up Stella's bag. "Let me show you to your room." They walked up a flight of stairs, passed through the kitchen and dining room, which looked down on the living room, and then took a second staircase to the third floor. Off the center hall were four rooms, only one of which had an open door.

Entering that room, Michael said, "this is your room for the duration of your stay. We hope you'll be comfortable." Pointing to a closed door, he added, "that's the en suite bathroom."

Stella was speechless. Maybe Malcolm had been right, she thought. This seemed more like a vacation than a rendezvous with murderers.

Michael plopped her suitcase down on a small table. The room was lovely, decorated with colorful prints of traditional Polynesian village scenes. The queen bed looked very inviting to Stella after the grueling hours she'd spent on her trip.

"After you freshen up, come downstairs. It's almost cocktail hour."

Cocktail hour? Was she in a dream? These hospitable people, she thought, are really strange mass murderers.

Michael said, "I have to collect your laptop and phone and any other recording devices you brought. And, I hope you'll understand, I have to search your belongings."

He opened her suitcase and gently moved around her clothes, including undies and bras. Stella was embarrassed, for his hands seemed to linger in the lingerie. He probed all around the suitcase's innards but found nothing alarming. Then he emptied her purse on the bed. In addition to two passports, it contained an assortment of apparent necessities, including wallet, sunglasses, coin purse, keys, gum, cough drops, lipstick and lip balm, plus a small digital recorder. He opened the wallet and looked for credit cards, but there were none. Michael seemed satisfied that she hadn't brought along anything threatening.

He picked up the digital recorder and lifted the laptop and phone from the dresser. At least, she thought, he didn't take her wristwatch, which she had reset at the airport to Samoan time.

"Thank you, Stella, I think we're going to get along just fine. Still smarting from the intrusive searches, she managed a nod and strained smile.

Before returning to the living room, Michael entered another room on the third floor and locked up her electronic devices. This room was his office; it contained three large-screen monitors and a host of towers and other gear. In this room Stella would not be allowed to set foot—or even peek in.

CHAPTER 27

AFTER ALMOST AN HOUR IN HER ROOM, Stella was ready to face the couple. She had taken a catnap, awakened by her watch alarm. She held onto the handrail while descending the stairs to the second floor where Tina was working on dinner. Fragrant aromas from the stove diffused throughout the kitchen and dining room.

As if she were visiting a friend, Stella asked, "can I help you with anything?"

"Thanks, but I have it under control. Why don't you join Michael in the living room. He wants to mention a few things to you over drinks."

The bar was large and well provisioned, and Michael asked for her drink order.

"Can you make me something sweet with an umbrella?"

Michael smiled and said, "of course." He mixed a pink rum concoction and filled three goblets. Stella took one from his outstretched hand and slowly sipped the heavenly drink. They left the bar, and he motioned for her to sit in an easy chair. He sat down in a love seat facing her.

"In your visit here, Miss Weiss, there are ground rules."

"Of course."

In an officious voice he said, "I know you have enormous curiosity about what we did and how we did it, so you may ask us any questions that come to mind. However, we are not bound to answer them.

Obviously, we want to protect our identity and our location. So, we won't divulge any information that might enable a third party to track us down. We will always err on the side of caution."

"I understand."

"On the third floor you may enter only your room. All the others are off limits. You may roam freely on the first and second floors, but you will not open drawers or cupboards. Is that clear?"

"Yes," she said and took another sip.

"You may take only hand-written notes. I know these rules will be an inconvenience, but I'm sure you appreciate the great risk we have taken in bringing you to Samoa."

Stella said, "fortunately, I haven't forgotten how to write in cursive. Since you took my phone and laptop, does that mean I won't have access to the Internet?"

"That's correct. We trust you but have to be certain that you won't inadvertently leave an electronic trail that government investigators could follow."

"How do you connect to the Internet?"

"I have a dedicated, wide-band satellite uplink."

"Is there any way I can get a message to Malcolm, my editor? I want to let him know I'm not being held as a sex slave."

Michael laughed and said, with a twinkle in his eye, "how do you know you're not our sex slave?"

Stella laughed, too, surprised that Michael had a sense of humor.

"Miss Weiss, just write out a message and I will send it to Malcolm. Include something in the message so he'll know it's really from you. The message will disappear shortly after he reads it."

"Okay, I can do that. I know he's probably worried sick about me."

"That pretty much takes care of the ground rules, but I may think up more as we go along."

Stella said, "I've had some questions at the back of my mind since you first contacted me."

"Shoot."

"I assume you brought me all this way to tell me your story. So, my first question is, why didn't you just write a manifesto and send it to major newspapers?"

"That's a really good question. I gave the manifesto idea serious consideration but finally decided it was too dangerous."

"Why is that?"

"Did you ever hear of the Unabomber?"

"Yeah, I vaguely remember that name from a journalism class. He mailed bombs and killed several people. Something like that."

"Right. And in 1995 the New York Times and Washington Post published his long and tedious anti-technology manifesto. It was his undoing."

"How so?"

"The Unabomber's sister-in-law, a philosophy professor, read the manifesto and recognized his writing style. She told her husband and he alerted the FBI. They eventually caught him. My writing style is very distinctive. If I published a manifesto, my former co-workers could easily identify me. Once the feds had my name, they could search my travel history and learn about our trips to Samoa. It would just be a matter of time until they came after us."

"I guess that makes sense. Here's another question: why me? There are dozens of well-known investigative reporters in the U.S. You could have chosen someone with a bigger name than mine."

"One reason we picked you is that you work for a reputable paper and are known for journalistic integrity. As you might expect, we also researched you thoroughly; we read many of your articles and all the biographical materials we could find. We learned that you are one of the brightest and most ambitious reporters working today—someone who would go the extra mile to get a story. It seemed like you might be willing to fly halfway around the world with no more than the promise of a big scoop. And besides, you're very pretty, and in my book that still counts. Why should I spend time with some grizzled old goat when I can enjoy your company?"

Stella avoided groaning or rolling her eyeballs. Michael was young but he had some antediluvian ideas. She could live with it; she had to live with it. Playing along, she thanked him for the compliment.

"Michael, despite all your precautions, bringing me down here poses a risk to you and Tina, so you must have a pretty good reason for wanting a reporter to tell your story."

"As you know, ever since the assassination, wackos on the right and left have come out from under rocks to spout their absurd conspiracy theories. We believe it's important to discredit these theories and tell Americans the real reasons why we killed the president. We figured your article would do the trick."

"Why is it so important to refute the assassination theories? What makes your story so compelling?"

"We believe that someday our work will be recognized as a patriotic act because we ended the reign of a tyrant who betrayed America. We may not live to see that day, but at least our story will be in the historical record."

Stella was not entirely convinced by Michael's flimsy rationalization.

Tina leaned over the second-floor railing and said, "dinner is on the table. Come on up!"

****

A large picture window partly covered by lace curtains allowed the late afternoon sun to filter into the dining room. They sat down at a table of light-colored wood Stella couldn't identify. Tina served the first course: an appetizer of large and succulent shrimp. Next came a yellow-fin tuna steak accompanied by slices of sautéed eggplant and sweet potato. Finally, a fruit platter of kiwi and pineapple. Stella didn't say much as she enjoyed the flavorful food.

With obvious pride, Tina said, "Michael caught the tuna."

"And Tina cooked it perfectly," he responded.

Between bites, Stella managed to say, "it's really good, I've never eaten tuna this fresh."

Michael said, "Samoa is a fishing mecca. People come here from all over the world to go fishing. I have a small boat, so maybe we'll go out later this week."

Stella suddenly had a disturbing thought. What if he pushed her off the boat, causing her to disappear forever? Nah, that was a silly idea.

"This has been delicious. Thank you both. I'm overwhelmed by your hospitality."

"We aim to please, unless we aim to kill," quipped Michael.

Tina groaned, but Stella had no reaction. The threesome adjourned to the living room, making small talk about Stella's long trip and the Samoan climate.

Michael abruptly changed the subject. "What have you learned about the government investigations of the assassination?"

A wary Stella stared at him briefly before answering. She wondered, was this the real reason for her trip? Did he simply want to pump her for information? Despite her misgivings, she didn't see any harm in sharing what little she knew. He probably knew as much as she did because he no doubt read newspapers on line.

Stella answered, "as you probably know, the government agencies have kept quiet about their findings. It's generally known that two joint task forces are investigating the incident: one is NTSB-FBI, the other is a supposedly secret FBI-CIA collaboration. So far, neither has issued a report, not even a preliminary one, to refute the more ridiculous theories. Oh, I almost forgot, early on NTSB did publicly rule out pilot error and mechanical failure."

Michael nodded and said, "why do you suppose the agencies have been so tight-lipped about what they've learned?"

"I think the basic problem is that they haven't learned much. You've probably seen the recent Washington Post article that included devastating quotes from FBI insiders. The investigators aren't close to pinning the assassination on anyone."

Michael smiled.

Stella had been troubled by Michael's questions because they implied he had no access to government servers. How could such a skilled hacker be unable to penetrate FBI and NTSB firewalls? Suddenly, she blurted out, "Michael, you had no trouble hacking the L.A. Times servers and my email account. Don't you already know what the government investigators have figured out?"

"Stella, I haven't hacked government servers for two reasons. Number one: they are incredibly well protected. Number two: even if I could hack them, I might set off intruder alerts, which could lead them to me. I'm much more comfortable working my way around commercial servers. I really don't know what the investigations have turned up so far."

His answer made sense to Stella.

"Do you know anything that isn't in the media?" asked Michael.

Stella saw no harm in telling him what he already knew. "The FBI believes the weapon used to shoot down Marine One was most likely a Steyr AUG A3 assault rifle."

Michael nodded and asked, "anything else?"

"There have been hints that a food truck might have been involved, but I don't know any more than that—except for your vague message."

Michael nodded again and said, "after I mentioned the food truck, did you try to verify that information with the FBI?"

"God, no. The food truck connection is obviously very closely held information. I didn't want to risk tipping off the FBI that I knew about it."

"So, that's it?"

"I'm afraid so. Keep in mind that I'm on the city desk at the Times. I only looked into the assassination investigation after you contacted me. I came down here to learn about the incident from you."

"And Tina and I promise we'll enlighten you."

Stella was frustrated. Was she being played? She didn't know. They wanted information from her, but so far had given her nothing in return. This was just her first day on Samoa, and there would be more. She had no choice but to go along at the couple's pace. In the meantime, Stella was deeply fatigued. She excused herself and started to stand up.

"Good night Stella, and sleep well. We rise at eight and breakfast is at nine."

CHAPTER 28

OVER BREAKFAST of scrambled eggs, sausage, toast and jelly, and coffee, Tina pointed to the window and the clouds gathering above the inland volcanic peaks.

"Stella, we're still in Samoa's rainy season. Fortunately, we have an extra raincoat, and we also have plenty of umbrellas."

"How much rain do you usually get?"

Tina replied, "it varies a lot by season and from year to year, but the range is around 100 to 200 inches annually."

"Wow. Did you have any trouble adjusting to all that rain?"

"Nah, we're good with so much rain."

Stella had hoped the question would elicit hints about where the couple was from originally, but it didn't. No need to pry further.

Everyone drifted off after breakfast. Stella sat down in the patio and enjoyed the view of the beach, surprised to see a great variety of birds; she only recognized pigeons, doves, and parrots—the others remained mysteries.

At mid-morning the trio reassembled in the living room. Michael furnished Stella with a spiral-bound notebook, the kind college students once used for taking notes, and a mechanical pencil. The couple moved to the love seat, and Stella slipped into the easy chair.

"Well, Stella, here we go. Tina and I are willing to share some general background information about our lives. It will give you a context for understanding what we did and why we did it."

"Good. That would be very helpful."

Michael looked at Tina, who nodded and began her story. "I grew up in a small town. My father was a minister in a Lutheran church, and my mother taught Sunday school and religious classes there. The church provided housing for our family, which eventually included my sister and two brothers. We were good Christians, as defined by my father's generous interpretations of scripture."

"What do you mean?"

"Well, for one thing, he doesn't believe that homosexuals are sinners. My dad had some scientific background, and he knew that most gay people are born that way. His congregation, part of the Evangelical Lutheran Church of America, is welcoming to all people." She paused as her mind wandered, apparently thinking about a father she would probably never see again.

"Please go on."

"In middle school and high school, I excelled at math. In college I majored in math until my junior year when I discovered geographic information systems. I graduated with a double major in math and GIS."

"That's very impressive," noted Stella.

"Michael and I met in college. We were both attending a meeting of the Young Republicans and caught each other's eyes at the mixer afterwards. Almost immediately we felt a mutual attraction. I was especially impressed with his knowledge of conservative philosophy."

"I thought it was my good looks and buff body."

They both laughed, and he pecked her on the cheek.

"Anyway, we were soon dating and trading lists of books by our favorite conservative authors. In our last semester we returned to my home town, and dad married us in his church."

Stella could barely believe her ears. These people were not radicals or terrorists but, apparently, conservative Republicans.

Tina continued. "After graduation, I didn't want to work for the government or a large company, so I began a consulting career. I must admit, it was amazingly lucrative. I made more money than I ever could have imagined. And I also taught Sunday school at a

Lutheran church."

Michael smiled, obviously proud of Tina's accomplishments. She nodded at him, and he took over the narrative. Stella wondered if their performances had been choreographed in advance.

****

"I also grew up in a small town. My mom and dad owned a hardware store on Main Street. Sadly, the town was in decline, so there was less and less demand for our store's products. Eventually, we left town and moved to a big city where my dad found a job in a large company. He worked his way up quickly to the well-paying position of general manager. I have two brothers, but I'm the oldest."

Stella asked, "are your parents still alive?"

He answered "yes," and quickly resumed the story.

"I was a sophomore in high school when we moved to the city. High school was a total bore, so I spent most of my time reading sci-fi novels, playing video games, and perfecting the fine art of hacking. I didn't become seriously interested in women or conservative thought until I started college."

"Are your parents conservative?"

"No more so than your average Republicans."

"Both of your accents suggest you grew up in the upper Midwest."

Michael answered, "we aren't going to confirm or deny that. And don't even think about mentioning it in your reporting. Also, specific information about our families is also off-limits."

"Okay," said Stella, somewhat reluctantly. "Tina mentioned your interest in conservative literature. Can you elaborate on who might have influenced you?"

"Sure. After I joined the Young Republicans as a freshman, I met a few well-read students who recommended some must-read articles and books. Besides attending meetings and events and working for candidates, I became an avid reader. Soon I developed enormous respect for William F. Buckley, Jr., who founded the influential National Review in 1955. Through that medium and his several books, Buckley became the most articulate spokesman for the new conservatism. Although Buckley was a clear thinker and writer, I wasn't fond of his affected patrician accent."

"I get it," said Stella. She had seen tapes of Buckley on TV and found his speech utterly contrived, though he denied it.

"I was also drawn to Barry Goldwater's rugged individualism, for it seemed more genuine than Ayn Rand's cramped 'self interest' that she championed in novels such as *Atlas Shrugged*."

Stella admitted, "I read *Atlas Shrugged* but didn't care for it."

"Reading more and more American history, I came to understand the significance of Ronald Reagan's election in 1980. As president, he represented the triumph of Buckley-style new conservatism. I became a great admirer of the fortieth president's many accomplishments."

"Tina," asked Stella, "did you also immerse yourself in conservative literature?"

"I read a few things that Michael recommended, but I wasn't much into philosophy. It all seemed so squishy to me; I prefer the certainties of mathematics."

"Michael, what did you major in?"

"This won't come as a surprise, but I double-majored in software engineering and computer information systems."

"You're right. No surprise there. After graduation, did you become a free-lancer like Tina?"

"I interviewed with a dozen companies at my college's job fair. I got several offers and decided to sign on with a large defense contractor whose IT facility was located in a D.C. suburb. I agonized over the decision because the job would put me in a part of the country infested by liberals. Actually, liberals dominate the region. But I took the job anyway. It was time well spent because my knowledge of real-world IT systems grew exponentially, and it paid really well."

"I see," said Stella, who changed the subject. "Am I correct in assuming that you don't have any children?"

The couple turned toward each other with forlorn looks, and Tina answered, "we'd planned to have a family—that's what good Christians do. But after trying to get pregnant for more than a year without success, we finally got tested. The tests proved I have a condition called anovulation, which means I don't ovulate. It's treatable in theory, but in my case the treatment failed."

"I'm sorry," said Stella.

"We talked about the options available to couples in our situation, but never got around to making a decision. We're still young, and maybe we'll finally make a move to adopt. But we have a good life and, I suppose, we've become somewhat selfish. Children require a major commitment of time and resources. That's why people shouldn't have children unless they are ready to completely change their lifestyle."

"Yeah, I get it," said Stella. "Sorry for rubbing salt in that old wound. Michael, I interrupted you. Please go on."

"It's okay. Anyway, I was about to say that I worked for the defense company for several years. But I got bored and restless because I wasn't privy to the big picture. I sat at the same desk in the same cubicle, day after day, month after month, updating subroutines in computer programs others had written years earlier. I longed for the ability to do something meaningful, something politically meaningful. One Sunday I was skimming an expanded employment section of The Washington Post, when I saw an ad for an IT position at a conservative think tank. I filled out the ponderous online application and waited. Finally, an HR official called me in for an interview. I had two callbacks before they finally offered me the job. It was my dream job, and not just because of the $250,000 salary plus benefits. This was during Obama's first term. I regarded him as an ultra-liberal—just this side of socialist. When Obamacare became law, I knew he really was a socialist at heart."

"May I interrupt for a moment?" asked Stella.

"Sure."

"You've given me quite a bit of detail about your careers."

"Yes, I should have told you beforehand, do not mention any specifics about our employment history."

"I was afraid of that. Go on, please."

"When my boss learned that I was very knowledgeable in conservative philosophy and a good writer, he asked me to take on extra duties. I became the go-to guy for writing essays on timely topics. The challenges were immense, but I really enjoyed the work. In fact, I was in hog heaven writing conservative critiques of Obama policies. I like to think my position papers had an impact."

"Is that the last job you held?"

Michael turned to Tina and they conferred briefly in whispers. "Yes, I quit about six months ago."

"Where did you live in the D.C. area?"

Again, the couple exchanged a few words, and Tina answered, "let's just say we had a small condo in a modest suburban community."

"I see you're trying hard to keep me from knowing details of your lives that someone might use to identify you. I wonder, why is that a concern since you live in Samoa now, which has no extradition treaty with the United States?"

"It's very simple," said Michael. "The U.S. government has ways of extracting people from any country. I'm sure you understand that if we were identified and tracked to Samoa, the government would kidnap us and put us on trial in the states."

Stella took a deep breath and said, "yes, I get it." She realized that the U.S. government, President Shilling in particular, would stop at nothing to capture the couple, even risking a diplomatic dust-up with Samoa. If the U.S. could kill Bin Laden in Pakistan, they could easily abduct a married couple in Samoa.

"So," said Michael, "now you understand why we have to keep our families, careers, and location secret."

"I do."

Tina continued. "After Michael got the job in D.C., my consulting work really took off. With Michael's political connections and my GIS background, I helped Republican candidates do micro-targeting of demographic groups."

"You both had interesting and fulfilling careers—careers that paid well—yet you gave them up. How do you make ends meet now?"

"D.C. is a very expensive place, but it's possible to live a frugal Christian life there. Every year we socked away big chunks of money, saving for the proverbial rainy day and the early retirement we had long planned."

Stella nodded her understanding. "I have a somewhat personal question that I hope you'll answer. Both of you have families back in the states. Did you just vanish without telling them? Or do you keep in touch?"

Michael and Tina looked at each other, and he answered, "before leaving for Samoa, we told them we had become Christian missionaries, and we were being sent to the Democratic Republic of the Congo. We claimed it was our calling to civilize the natives in remote villages."

Stella grimaced. Michael noticed the change in her expression, but didn't understand that Jews detest religious proselytizing, and Blacks don't believe Africans need civilizing.

Gazing at Tina, Stella asked, "if they think you're in Africa, do you keep in touch with your families?"

With sadness filling her face, Tina looked at Stella and said, "regrettably, we can't risk it."

"Do they believe you died in Africa?"

"We don't know. Maybe…probably."

"You've made a great sacrifice cutting off all communication with your families."

"Yes," said Tina, now whimpering softly.

Seeing her in distress, Michael hugged her and abruptly changed the subject. "I don't know about you, Stella, but I'm getting hungry. Let's have some lunch."

****

Tina eagerly took the cue and scurried upstairs to fix sandwiches and a salad. Stella didn't say much over lunch, as she had a lot to digest besides food. She was deeply perplexed, wondering why this conservative Christian couple had planned and carried out the assassination of a Republican president.

So far, Stella realized, she was acting more like a stenographer than a reporter. There had been few opportunities to interrupt their stories, but the stories were fascinating. As long as Tina and Michael were willing to talk, she was willing to listen and scribble down notes. Stella hoped their stories would satisfy her curiosity and answer the big questions she had brought to Samoa.

As they ate, Stella could see that the clouds had cleared. Maybe she could take a walk along the beach after lunch. She looked at Michael and asked, "am I allowed to go outside and walk around?"

"Of course! You're not our prisoner. We have plenty of time in the next few days to tell our stories and answer your questions. I should caution you, though: the clouds are gone now but they can return quickly and dump a torrent on us. If the wind picks up from the east, more rain is probably on the way."

"I'll keep a close watch."

"By the way, Stella, there are some tubes of sunscreen on the table in the patio."

CHAPTER 29

STRUNG ALONG THE COAST north of Salelologa were many hotels and resorts frequented mainly by Australians and New Zealanders. Michael and Tina's house was a little beyond the densest group of tourist accommodations. Even so, in taking a long walk along the sinuous shore, Stella had to dodge cabanas, lava outcrops, and lush vegetation. After skirting the obstacles for several minutes, Stella took off her sandals and walked in the lukewarm South Pacific. The white sunbathers must have believed the Black woman splashing through the water was an apparition.

In thinking about Michael and Tina, Stella realized she had been trying to force the couple into an existing category of criminals. They were, of course, mass murderers, though not terrorists; that much was clear. And they were obviously not mentally impaired or under duress. It seemed unlikely they had been hired to do the job. Maybe, she thought, it was better to treat them as a unique case. She would try to understand them on their own terms.

Stella knew that in such a move lurked danger. Would she succumb to the Stockholm syndrome? She wasn't actually a prisoner, though she couldn't leave any time she desired. They set the agenda for her visit. Her hosts were gracious, and it was not easy to dislike them. They seemed so ordinary. She would have to be careful to retain her independence and objectivity when writing her story. She could not afford to fall under their beguiling spell.

Her thoughts were interrupted when, without warning, a strong breeze picked up from behind her. She tried to get her bearings but soon realized she was completely disoriented. With the sun high in the sky, she couldn't tell east from west. Just to be on the safe side, in case the wind augured stormy weather, Stella rapidly retraced her steps, crossed the road, and returned to the house.

She followed the path to the covered patio, where there was an outdoor shower and dry towels. She cleaned and dried her feet and went inside. Michael was not to be seen, in his office she presumed. Tina, in the kitchen thumbing through a cookbook, shouted down to Stella, "did you have a nice walk?"

"Yes, it was good, but I'm used to the long stretches of sandy beach in the L.A. area. This beach is very different and must have taken some getting used to."

"Yeah, it did. We do have long sandy beaches, but not on this part of the island."

"I'm going upstairs to take a little nap. Right now, the jet-lag is giving me a case of foggy brain."

"Come down after your nap, and we can resume our conversation."

"Sounds good."

CHAPTER 30

FBI AGENT JOANNA BARTOLO was having another bad day in the Hoover Building. The pressure she felt from the misogynists in the White House, through the Department of Justice, had become oppressive, bordering on intolerable. Worse still, her health was suffering: she was losing weight and hair, and her guts were in constant turmoil. At home her temper was short, and she experienced bouts of mild depression. Her husband, Louis, had been tolerant and supportive, but even he was becoming impatient, hoping the investigation would end soon in an arrest.

The veteran special agent had often contemplated retirement, for she had been eligible for some years. Yet, she knew—rather, she fervently hoped—her team would solve the great crime someday, the sooner the better. Then she could resume overseeing routine criminal investigations without political meddling. Satisfaction in her job had come when her agents arrested bank robbers, racketeers, embezzlers, and others. During the previous months, there had been only aggravation. She also thought that capturing the killer would be a glorious capstone to her stellar career, perhaps the occasion for retirement. Louis agreed.

When the Wahl-appointed attorney general resigned to take a position in a conservative think tank, Shilling appointed James Moffitt to take his place. In Bartolo's view and that of many career attorneys in the Department of Justice, Moffitt was a mediocrity. Originally from Kansas, he had barely passed the Nevada bar after three tries. Shilling chose Moffitt because they shared a hometown and fervent homophobia. Although loyal to the president, the attorney general ignored Shilling's most inane suggestions. As for ordinary policy matters important to the president, Moffitt was as compliant as a foam pillow. He tried to be a team player, but he also had his own interests to protect. It was a difficult balancing act.

Prodded by Shilling's latest tweet, Moffitt sent a memo to Shirley Abel, Director of the FBI. He insisted that she order the FBI's 56 field offices to immediately begin rounding up and interviewing Islamist-leaning Americans. The FBI and CIA had repeatedly told the president that not a single shred of hard evidence pointed to an Islamist connection. But one of Shilling's foreign policy advisers had reminded the president that many Islamist terrorist groups had claimed credit for the assassination. That reminder sufficed to initiate the tweet-storm about Islamist sympathizers that led to Moffitt's move.

Abel reluctantly complied with Moffitt's onerous order, issuing a directive to the regional offices. Soon FBI headquarters was overrun with requests for warrants to spy on Muslim Americans. Abel asked Bartolo to do a preliminary vetting of the requests. FBI attorneys would then prepare the surveillance warrants and submit them to a sympathetic judge. Bartolo was dismayed as she read about some of the individuals for whom electronic surveillance had been requested. Hardly a civil libertarian, Bartolo regarded some of the requests as batshit crazy. In one case, an elderly man had been targeted because someone reported seeing him buy a book about the history of Islam. She returned this application to the Birmingham, Alabama, field office with a note sharply rebuking the agent in charge.

****

Bartolo's team had no choice but to search for Islamist sympathizers in the D.C. region. Court-approved electronic surveillance of one man, who curiously did not have a Muslim name, raised some red flags. Kevin Bintliff had wired funds to an American-based aid group with suspected ties to the Syrian government. He was apparently unemployed, yet every month a Bermuda-based shell corporation deposited $3,500 in the young bachelor's bank account in the Cayman Islands. And he had large numbers of Facebook friends and Twitter followers in countries that supported terrorism. His posts and tweets were disturbing in their strident anti-Americanism.

Perhaps, Bartolo acknowledged, this man might be a threat to national security, but she was unconvinced he had played a role in the assassination. On social media Bintliff had celebrated the president's death, but Bartolo knew that tens of millions of Americans silently shared a deep antipathy to Wahl, and had shed no tears at his passing. She sighed deeply, deciding it was her duty to interview Kevin Bintliff herself, misgivings aside. To ensure the man's cooperation she obtained an arrest warrant, but she had no intention of employing it without evidence of wrongdoing.

****

Kevin Bintliff lived in an inexpensive, third-floor studio apartment in the Hybla Valley, just south of Alexandria, Virginia. He was awakened when two FBI agents—Paul Yablonsky, a tall Anglo man, and Patricia Murakami, an East Asian woman of medium height—pounded loudly on his door. In unison they said, "FBI, open up."

Still half asleep, the dazed and confused Bintliff hollered "wait a minute," got out of bed, and stumbled to the door. He peered through the peephole and saw two well-dressed people. He shuddered but opened the door, exposing the agents to a messy bachelor pad that reeked of beer and stale pizza. Bintliff had long blonde hair and a scraggly beard. He was wearing only boxers. Murakami averted her eyes.

"Who the hell are you?"

"We're FBI agents Yablonsky and Murakami."

"Show me your IDs."

The agents pulled out their IDs and ordered him to dress quickly. In the Queen's English—he was a naturalized U.S. citizen of

Yorkshire origins—Bintliff protested vehemently.

"You are violating my rights."

Yablonsky said, "you are not under arrest at this time. We are here to bring you to FBI headquarters where Special Agent Bartolo will interview you. However, we do have a warrant, and we will arrest you if you don't cooperate."

With a note of resignation, he said, "okay, okay, I get it," under his breath adding, "bloody fascists."

After sorting through the clothes on his threadbare couch, Bintliff took a green polo shirt and ragged jeans into the bathroom. After he emerged fully dressed, the agents escorted him downstairs and led him to their black SUV for the ride downtown. Forty minutes later at the Hoover Building, they brought Bintliff to the fifth-floor conference room where Bartolo, alerted to their imminent arrival, was waiting with her silent scribe.

CHAPTER 31

IN MID-AFTERNOON STELLA joined Michael and Tina in the living room; they were reading paperbacks. The reporter tore a half-sheet of paper from her notebook and handed it to Michael.

"This is the message I would like you to send to Malcolm Klein at the Times. I assume you already know how to contact him."

Michael read the note. "Dear Malcolm: Having a great time, wish you were here [please insert a smiley face emoji]. I'm learning a lot, but don't expect to hear from me again until I return to L.A. The Joker is treating me well. Stella."

He smiled and looked up, "what's this about the 'Joker'?"

"When you first contacted me, I thought it was a prank, so I referred to you as the Joker. Only Malcolm knows I used that word, so it's my way of proving I'm really Stella Weiss."

"Oh. I guess that makes sense."

"Michael and Tina, is it time to resume our conversation?"

"Yes," replied Tina.

"Good. I'd like to ask a question that's been gnawing at me."

"Go right ahead."

"When did you become disenchanted with President Wahl—and why?"

Michael said, "I suppose those are the questions everyone is asking. It's a long story, but I guess you couldn't write your article unless we told you."

"Right. I've been especially curious since it's obvious you aren't leftwing radicals."

Michael began. "We knew who Wahl was, even before he announced his candidacy. He'd been a media darling for decades, taunting presidents and sounding off on policy issues from A to Z. He was a blowhard, a self-promoter…"

Stella interrupted, "but don't those words describe most politicians?"

"Sure, but Wahl was different because he ripped off honest, hard-working people who owned small companies. The core of his business model was to stiff contractors, especially on his hospital and shopping center projects. After a project went bankrupt, the contractors were left holding the empty bag. He was a crook, a conman, a mobster—plain and simple. But that's not what motivated us."

"Well, then, what did motivate you?"

"He was a Johnny-come-lately to the Republican Party, and he didn't have the faintest idea what real conservatism was all about. Did you watch him when he announced his candidacy?"

"Not really, but I did see excerpts of his speech on TV."

"Let me read from one journalist's take on his grand entrance." He tapped on his laptop for a few seconds and raised the sound level:

"Thousands of people and hundreds of reporters crowded into the Victorian-style ballroom of the midtown Manhattan hotel to witness Frederick "Fred" J. Wahl's long-anticipated announcement. Standing on the mezzanine level at the top of the arc-shaped, gold-carpeted staircase, he waved to the crowd and three times yelled, 'this is magnificent!' With his smartly tailored tux, Wahl was a spectacle. A reporter was heard to quip, 'all he needs is a crown and a cape.'"

"Wahl slowly descended the staircase, still waving, until at the bottom he reached the podium set on a raised platform. Again, he marveled at the huge crowd, as everyone jostled to get a better view of the real estate magnate who had become the star of his own cooking show on the Food Network."

"Wahl's announcement of his candidacy began with a diatribe against America's European and Asian trading partners. These countries were taking advantage of us, he claimed, and called for punitive tariffs..."

"That's enough," said Michael, adding, "I watched Wahl's speech live on my office computer. I was curious about how this reformed Democrat had so quickly morphed into a Republican presidential candidate. I was appalled when I heard him disparage our trading partners. Free trade is as close to holy gospel as any conservative belief, yet this man was trashing it and promoting tariffs."

"Fortunately, I didn't hear the speech," said Tina. "It might have made me ill."

"His speech was more like a rant," resumed Michael. "At first I was puzzled, then I became alarmed. I'm a firm believer that the Republican Party should be a large tent, willing to tolerate a range of conservative views on particular issues. But I just couldn't accept his retreat from free trade. That's outside the tent as far as I'm concerned. I'd only written a few position papers on trade, but I knew enough to recognize that Wahl was faking it, blustering to hide his profound ignorance of how the international system really works."

"I was also surprised when I learned about his anti-trade positions," said Tina.

"He promised to punish manufacturers who off-shored their factories by imposing a 35 percent tariff on products these companies made abroad but sold in the U.S. And he claimed he would immediately renegotiate trade deals. These ideas were straight out of organized labor's playbook. Was Wahl just pandering to traditional Democrat voters? Or was his political philosophy hopelessly muddled? We didn't realize at first that it was both of these."

"Michael, what did you do after listening to Wahl's speech?"

"At home that evening, I gave Tina a synopsis of the speech, editorializing along the way. He was supposedly a Republican, but he was selling discredited Democrat positions on trade, including high tariffs. I just didn't get it. How could he abandon free trade and open markets and still claim to be a conservative? Tina reminded me that Wahl had other liabilities that made him unfit to hold the highest office in our great land..."

"I told Michael that he'd cheated on four wives and didn't attend church. I couldn't see how he could win the Christian vote with that track record of immorality. And worst of all, he hobnobbed with rich New York liberals, and many of them were Jews."

Stella winced but said nothing. Surely, she thought, they knew she was Jewish. Maybe not.

"I agreed with Tina that he'd be a weak presidential candidate, not competitive against any real Republican. I took comfort from the fact that Daniel Harrison, governor of South Carolina, had already raised a ton of money and might sew up the nomination real soon— assuming he didn't blow it. We figured that other qualified candidates would enter the race, and they did, in droves. It was our belief—our hope—that Wahl was just a shiny object that would tarnish quickly."

Tina added, "how wrong we were."

"Wahl's bullying of other candidates and his total lack of civility during the debates stoked our dislike of him. And we weren't the only dismayed conservatives. Two men we respect greatly, George Will and Charles Krauthammer, reluctantly urged Republicans to vote for the deeply flawed Democrat candidate. Wahl, they said, is too mercurial, two unpredictable; a danger to the republic."

"Did you vote for the Democrat?"

"Yeah, but I had to hold my nose."

"Me too," admitted Tina.

****

Michael resumed. "We were stunned when that deplorable human being won the election. Of course we now know that Wahl had help from the Russian government. Putin and his minions mounted a successful social media attack, attempting to sow discord. And after he won the election, Wahl advanced Russian interests. He pulled us out of the Paris Agreement on climate change, the Trans-Pacific Partnership, and hinted that he might withdraw the U.S. from NATO. A stable West under U.S. leadership is another bedrock principle of modern conservatism. And Wahl was undermining it at every opportunity."

Stella was taking notes furiously, hoping she wouldn't get a cramp in her writing hand.

Tina picked up the story. "Many Republicans voted for Wahl expecting him to promote a conservative agenda. Keeping taxes low is of major concern to Republicans, but fiscal restraint and a balanced budget are also high priorities. We were aghast when Wahl proposed a monstrous tax cut. Not that we objected to the fact that most benefits went to corporations and the very rich. No, our objection was that the tax cut was not offset by cuts to entitlement programs, which are ballooning out of control. Even though Republicans controlled both houses of Congress at the time, they rolled over and enacted Wahl's ruinous tax cuts. Now the country is saddled with annual budget deficits of around a trillion dollars."

"And," added Michael, "his embrace of autocrats around the world, especially his 'love' for Kim Jong-un and Vladimir Putin, was treasonous." Shaking his head, he said, "it just kept getting worse."

Stella was anxious for a short break. "I need some water."

Michael said, "why have water when you can drink something better?"

"Okay, surprise me."

He went to the bar and mixed the ingredients for a round of piña coladas.

Stella took a drink and remarked, "were you a bartender in a past life? This is about the best piña colada I've ever tasted."

"I'm glad you like it."

"So," said Stella, "if I'm understanding you both, you believed Wahl was betraying conservative principles and dragging the Republican party to perdition for enabling him."

"Precisely," said Michael. "Something had to be done. He was flouting basic tenets of conservatism and also undermining the rule of law with his quixotic executive orders. And, of course, he filled his campaign staff and cabinet with criminals and grifters."

"When did you decide that you had to take matters into your own hands?"

"When I realized that the Republican Party had sold out completely, that they would do nothing to rein him in. And in the end, he would destroy the party because he would leave it an empty shell, devoid of principles."

"For almost two years Michael and I had long—and sometimes heated—discussions about what we could do. Wahl's Helsinki love-fest with Putin amped up our dislike into pure hatred. We couldn't fathom how our president could take that murderer's word over the judgments of every U.S. security agency. The agencies were unanimous in asserting that Russia had interfered in the election on Wahl's behalf, but he denied it."

Tina raised her voice and added, "it was the most disgraceful performance of any president in U.S. history. He was practically kissing Putin's butt."

Stella asked Tina to repeat her broadside so she could get it down word for word.

"Did the Helsinki summit push you over the edge? Is that when you decided to eliminate Wahl?"

"No, not really," said Michael.

"So, was there something else that did it?"

"Well, let me tell you a little story. It's a bit of a detour, but I'll eventually take you where you want to go."

"Okay, I'm listening."

"My grandfather had two brothers. When the Japs bombed Pearl Harbor, all three of them enlisted in the Army. My granddad had a heart murmur and was turned down. But his brothers Harry and Charles were declared fit. Harry went on to become a B-17 pilot in the Army Air Corps, but his plane was shot down over France early in 1944. None of the crew survived. Charles was in the first wave of soldiers that landed on Omaha Beach during the D-Day invasion. He didn't make it either."

"I'm so sorry."

"An appreciation for the heroism of that generation—the greatest generation—was passed down through my family. We all learned that Harry and Charles were heroes in the fight against fascism. They gave their lives to preserve our freedom and our republican form of government. I grew up fervently believing that fascism is an abomination, as bad as communism, to be resisted if it ever rears its ugly head at home."

"Okay, I'm following so far. You grew up hating fascism. But isn't it true that many Republicans, even Christian conservatives like you, see nothing wrong in having a strong president?"

"Yes, that's true. But a strong president isn't necessarily a fascist. We've had many strong presidents, even a few Democrats, and still managed to preserve the republic."

"Point well taken. So, like most Americans, you hate fascism."

"Yes, I do."

"I'm not getting it yet. Why did you decide to assassinate Wahl?"

"Hang on, Stella, I'm coming to the end of the story."

"Sorry, please go on!"

"Last spring I visited the Holocaust Museum. I'm not sure what drew me there, probably a gut feeling that Nazi-style fascism was on the move in the United States. I walked through the galleries and looked at the exhibits that documented the Holocaust. Some of the images were so graphic they made me cry, especially piles of emaciated bodies and cremation ovens filled with human ash and bones. I'd reached my limit and looked for the exit."

Stella had seen such images before and understood the anguish they could provoke. But how could they have had such an effect on someone who would leave behind 10 burned bodies on Pennsylvania Avenue? Stella gave a big sigh, which Michael misread as fatigue. He picked up the pace.

"I left the museum by way of the gift shop and checked out the offerings. I ran across something excerpted from an article written by Laurence W. Britt. It listed the 14 'early warning signs of fascism.' I read them slowly, one by one, and came to a profoundly disturbing conclusion. Wahl's corrupt and authoritarian regime partly or completely met every single criterion. It was more than sobering; it was the moment of my epiphany. I had to assassinate Wahl before he fully entrenched fascism in America."

Scribbling furiously, Stella said, "okay, now I get it," and then asked, "after you decided to kill Wahl, what was your first move?"

Tina answered. "We had to make a plan for the future—after we did the deed. Fortunately, we could take advantage of our plan for early retirement. Even before Wahl was elected, we went on short vacations to different countries. We wanted to find a nice place for retirement where our money would go far. The first time we visited Samoa, we fell in love with the islands. We had hoped to buy a house, but that's difficult for non-Samoans. Happily, leasing is fairly easy. On our second trip later that summer, we searched for a house to lease long-term. We were lucky to find this one, which had just come on the market. When our plan for the president began to take shape, we realized our vacation home would allow us to escape to Samoa."

Michael, who had been getting restless, said "I don't know about you folks, but I'm getting hungry."

"You're always hungry."

"That's because you're such a good cook."

Looking at Stella, he said, "tonight I thought we'd take you to our favorite restaurant for dinner. It's not the most authentic Samoan cuisine, but the food's decent."

They left the house, climbed into the Renault, and drove a short distance to Dynasty Bar and Grill where they enjoyed a satisfying meal.

CHAPTER 32

AGENT BARTOLO INTRODUCED HERSELF. "Mr. Bintliff, please take a seat and help yourself to coffee and a pastry."

He ignored her friendly gesture and, still standing, bellowed, "I'd like to know why you dragged me out of bed at the crack of dawn and brought me here. How does what you did differ from kidnapping?"

"I beg your pardon. You came voluntarily."

"Bloody hell! Your goons threatened me with arrest. That's hardly voluntary."

"Well, the important thing is that you're here and, I hope, willing to answer my questions."

He finally sat down and asked, "should I call a lawyer?"

"That's up to you, but you're not under arrest. If you have nothing to hide, why wouldn't you answer my questions?"

"Hide about what?"

"We know you are sympathetic to Islamic extremists, and that's concerning to the FBI right now. We're also interested in your source of income. We need you to come clean and tell us what's going on in your life so we can rule you out as a person of interest."

"Rule me out of what?"

Bartolo sensed that Bintliff was genuinely puzzled by the FBI's interest in him. She paused, giving him space to speak.

"It's true that I follow Islamist thought, and I'm sympathetic to the cause. The West has bollixed up the Middle East ever since the breakup of the Ottoman Empire after World War One. The so-called 'extremists' just want a return to a purer form of Islam not contaminated by Western ideas and crass materialism."

"Do you support the use of terrorist tactics in that struggle?"

"Sometimes you have to resort to unpleasant means to achieve desirable ends. The United States supports its vassal state, Israel, even though it was born in terrorism. And the U.S. has used terrorist tactics to overthrow democratically elected leaders in Third World countries. Don't forget about how the CIA kidnapped foreign nationals and tortured them in secret locations. The U.S. claims the high road in the fight against terrorism, but it's bloody hypocrisy."

What Bartolo had heard so far was extremist views whose expression is protected by the First Amendment. She probed more deeply.

"What about terrorism in the United States?"

"What about it?"

"Do you advocate the use of terrorist tactics to achieve political ends?"

"Isn't that the basic definition of terrorism?"

An exasperated Bartolo continued. "Can you think of any domestic terrorist attacks that conformed to your Islamist agenda?"

"In addition to 9/11, Fort Hood, and San Bernardino?"

"Yes."

"Surely you know that the vast majority of terrorist attacks in the United States have been committed by right-wing fanatics: racists, neo-Nazis, and white supremacists."

"What about the downing of President Wahl's helicopter?"

"So, is that what this interview is really about?"

"Was that a terrorist act committed by one of your Islamist comrades?"

"I doubt it was an Islamist group. They would have downed Air Force One, not some wimpy helicopter. Obviously, if you had credible evidence that an Islamist group had killed the president, you would have made arrests by now and wouldn't be harassing me. Do you think I had something to do with the assassination?"

"I don't know. Did you?"

119

"Would I be sitting here answering your questions without a lawyer if I had killed the president?"

Bartolo acknowledged to herself that he had a good point. She decided to change the subject.

"Are you a Muslim, Mr. Bintliff?"

Startled by the question, Bintliff could only sputter, "you have no right to ask that. My religion or nonreligion is none of your bloody business."

"Do you consider yourself a patriot, Mr. Bintliff?"

"I do love my adopted country, but I reserve the right, as guaranteed in the U.S. Constitution, to voice my objections to specific policies. President Wahl was pushing the country in so many wrong directions. Almost anyone could have decided to take him out."

"Even you?"

Looking straight into Bartolo's eyes, he exclaimed, "sure, I hated Wahl, but I didn't kill him."

"Do you own any firearms?"

"No, I do not."

"Have you ever owned any firearms?"

"No, I grew up in a country where citizens have limited rights to own guns, and I'm comfortable with that. More people die in the U.S. annually from guns than from traffic accidents. But the NRA and gun lobby have Congress by the short hairs, and they won't enact sensible laws."

"What were you doing the morning of the assassination?"

"How the hell am I supposed to remember that? It was months ago!"

"So, I guess you don't have an alibi…"

"I don't need one. I didn't kill the president."

"You have a monthly income of $3,500 that comes from a Cayman Islands bank account. Who, or what organization, makes these deposits?"

"So, you've pilfered my financial information. I'm really not surprised. The short answer is, it's none of your bloody business. If you know about my income, then you probably also know I file a tax return every year. I haven't broken any laws."

"But we have to know where that money comes from."

"No, you don't have to know that. You are just invading my privacy because you can. I've had enough. If I'm not under arrest, then call your goons to take me home."

****

Bintliff was escorted home, leaving Bartolo with many questions. The man's qualified cooperation was a point in his favor. He obviously had a favorable opinion of Islamist ideas, but would his beliefs have been a sufficient motivation to assassinate Wahl? Bartolo was surprised that Bintliff wasn't the least bit intimidated by an FBI interview. But that, in itself, was not evidence of guilt. Although still concerned about the source of the man's income, Bartolo wasn't ready to proceed further unless new evidence surfaced. She knew there could be many innocent explanations for the monthly deposits.

As much as Bartolo had wanted the Bintliff interview to provide a break in the case, she couldn't construe the man's words as the utterances of the assassin. Adding to her doubts was the search of Bintliff's apartment. While Bintliff had been downtown, another team of agents had gone through his place. Immediately after the search, they reported finding nothing incriminating beyond a trove of Islamist literature. However, they did remove hair from a comb for DNA and drove it immediately to Quantico for a rush analysis. It did not match the DNA from the TACOMAN truck vent.

Bartolo was not surprised by the DNA results. She had concluded that Bintliff was a leftwing extremist and a jerk, but he probably didn't kill the president. She pored over a new stack of warrant applications, hoping the field offices had turned up someone more promising than Bintliff. After perusing them, she groaned in disappointment and took two antacid tablets. Maybe, she thought, retirement isn't such a bad idea.

CHAPTER 33

STELLA SAT IN THE LIVING ROOM after breakfast, waiting for the couple to arrive. Tina finished up in the kitchen and joined the reporter.

"Where's Michael?"

"He had some business to take care of in his office. He said he'd be down in little while."

"Are you willing to answer a few questions without Michael present?"

"That depends on the questions."

"Well, let me ask them, and you can decide."

"Okay."

"Tina, you mentioned that in the period leading up to the assassination, you and Michael had—I think your words were—'heated discussions.' Could you please elaborate on that for me?"

"Sure. At first I raised moral objections to killing the president. Christians live by the commandment, 'Thou shalt not kill.'"

Stella had to choke back a laugh at what she considered a patently absurd statement. But Tina had taught in a Lutheran school, and maybe she actually believed what she told impressionable children.

"So, you had a deep moral conflict about killing Wahl. Yet, you finally agreed with Michael that it was necessary."

"He made persuasive arguments about how the assassination would serve the greater good of saving our republic from fascism. I was still unconvinced, especially as his plan to shoot down Marine One took shape. We knew there would be other deaths—so-called collateral damage. We didn't know how many people would be aboard or how many people might die on the street. I was terrified at the prospect of becoming a mass murderer."

"Was there some event or argument that finally won you over?"

"I can't put my finger on any one thing. But Michael's harping on and on about the greater good began to break down my reluctance, especially after I saw respected Republican leaders become bald-face liars for Wahl. The country was coming apart, and Republicans in Congress were doing nothing to restrain Wahl. In fact, they were helping him thwart legitimate investigations."

"So, you finally agreed to take part in the plan?"

Almost in a whisper, she replied, "yes. Obviously, it was the most difficult decision of my life. I knew it was a capital crime. If we were caught and convicted, we would probably be executed. Coming to grips with that realization was made easier by the fact that we have no children. I came to accept the possibility of capture and death, even though my parents would be mortified if they ever found out what I had done. Sacrifice for the greater good, as Michael insisted."

"Do you have any regrets?"

"I mourn for the others who died, especially the Secret Service agents and marines." Tina's eyes filmed over as she added, "and we caused untold suffering for the families of the people we killed. I sincerely regret that. But it was for the greater good."

"Any regrets about killing the president?"

"My only regret is that Shilling is now president."

"Shilling is a conservative Republican, a devout Christian. Why would you be unhappy with him?"

"Honestly, he's just a little too pious for my taste. My minister dad warned me about people like Shilling. The ones who so loudly proclaim their faith in public are often hypocrites who in private engage in un-Christian behavior. Without any fanfare or justification, Shilling has continued some of Wahl's worst policies. I can't stand to look at him or hear him speak. But, on balance, I prefer him to Wahl."

Michael, who had just entered the living room, asked, "what's this about Shilling and Wahl?" He seemed concerned that the two women were talking in his absence.

"Stella asked me if I had any regrets about what we did. I told her that I don't care for Shilling, but he's better than Wahl."

Michael raised an eyebrow, wondering what else they had talked about. He didn't ask but planned to quiz Tina later in the privacy of their bedroom.

****

"Stella," said Michael, "I suppose you would like to know something about how we pulled off the crime of the century?"

"Yes, I was expecting you to enlighten me."

"Once we both agreed on the necessity of killing Wahl, we had to make a concrete plan. It was a balancing act. On the one hand, we had to pinpoint when and where he was most exposed, most vulnerable. On the other hand, we had to choose a time and place that allowed for a secure getaway."

"You were unwilling to become martyrs?"

"That's right. I could have easily taken out Wahl when he was giving one of his informal press conferences on the White House grounds. But Secret Service snipers on the roof would have killed me instantly. I didn't want to die that way. I had a lot more fishing to do in Samoa. And, of course, I wanted to live so I could see what happened afterward."

"Michael, how did you come up with the food truck idea?"

"One day I was grabbing lunch at a food truck when I heard Marine One fly by. At that moment, the plan began to take shape. The problem was to find the right food truck that would give me a clear sight to the chopper while providing cover. I cruised the streets of the Washington area for weeks looking for the perfect truck. One day I was checking out food trucks in Alexandria, and came across an old taco truck with the vanity plate TACOMAN. It was perfect because it had an unusual vent on the roof that opened up. I waited until the owner closed up shop and then followed him to his home in

Woodbridge."

"By the way, who held the family at gunpoint?"

"How did you know about that?"

"There was a tiny piece in the Post's Metro section two days after the crash. It didn't mention any names, though."

"I'm surprised we missed that article. Anyway, to answer your question, Tina's brother Harvey was all in on our plan. We wanted to strike on a Friday when Wahl was going to fly to his resort. Early that Friday morning, Harvey drove me to Tacoman's house and waited outside. When Tacoman left the house and went to his truck, we confronted him. Harvey waved his pistol at the man, and I ordered him to drive me downtown and park on E Street. We warned him to cooperate if he wanted his family to stay healthy. Harvey entered the house and held the family at gunpoint."

"Did you wait on E Street for the chopper to fly over?"

"No. The flight path was one block south, on Pennsylvania Avenue. I was waiting for Tina's signal so that I could move into position. She was stationed near the Ellipse with a clear view of the south lawn of the White House. We had heard a rumor that when the president flies on Marine One, his chopper is accompanied by decoy choppers, but we weren't sure. Just to be on the safe side, Tina was on the lookout for them. When Marine One was about to take off, she called me on a burner phone. I stayed on the line until it lifted off and she told me there was no sign of decoys.

I ordered Mr. Tacoman to turn right on 13th Street and then take a left on Pennsylvania Avenue. We parked in the first block, and then I went into action. I stood on a stool and pushed the vent open as far as it would go—and then pushed it even more. I held my weapon up to the vent. My adrenaline was pumping already, but when I saw the chopper approaching, the scene began to play out in slow motion as I fired off the entire magazine."

"Where did you get the gun?"

"Seriously? In the U.S. anyone can buy an assault rifle with no questions asked. I bought mine at a gun show in West Virginia. And I practiced for many months at a shooting range not far from

Centreville and paid cash."

"I've read that Marine One had ballistic armor. How could bullets from an assault rifle penetrate the armor?"

"I did extensive research on Marine One, hacking the websites of the companies that built them—there's a large fleet, you know. I concluded that all the talk about ballistic armor was mainly hype."

"Did you see Marine One go down?"

"Yes, as soon as I knew it was doomed, I quickly put my weapon into a guitar case I had brought along and gathered up the shell casings. I put on my Nationals baseball cap and sunglasses. Before I left the truck, I turned to Tacoman and sternly warned him that if he uttered a word to anyone about what happened, I would kill his family. Then I walked to Metro Center and caught an Orange Line train before they shut down Metro. I got off at the Ballston station and met Tina at a nearby parking garage where she'd left our car. And then we drove home and watched the aftermath unfold on Fox News."

"This incident obviously took lots of careful planning, and it went off just as you expected. But did you have a plan B in case anything went wrong?"

"Not really. We thoroughly scouted out the locations and timing. We worked out every detail. It had to be the perfect crime the first time. Anything less and we would have been arrested or killed."

Stella sat in stunned silence. How, she wondered, could he talk about murdering 10 people so unemotionally?

She posed the same question to him she had asked Tina. "Michael, do you have any regrets about what you did?"

"Sure I do. I feel bad about the collateral damage, but we did what had to be done for the sake of the country and the Republican Party." He said no more.

"Tina, what happened to your brother Harvey?"

"He went his own way after our job was done. We haven't had any contact with him."

"Michael, when did you move here permanently?"

"We moved here in early December, just when it was getting cold in D.C."

"And you're happy here?"

"For the most part it's worked out well. That doesn't mean we're committed to living here forever. We both want to start businesses but there are obstacles for non-Samoans. Who knows? We could move any time."

****

"I guess you've answered all my questions. As you know, my return flight is tomorrow."

"Don't worry, we'll get you back to the airport with plenty of time to spare. As I recall, your flight leaves around dinner time."

"Yes, it does. I must say, this visit wasn't at all what I expected. I almost feel like I've been on a vacation with friends. I guess that's a pretty bizarre reaction, but I never would have taken the two of you for assassins. Yet, you are. For a reporter, it doesn't get any stranger than this!"

Michael said, "there's one ground rule I forgot to mention. Leave Harvey out of your stories."

"That shouldn't be a problem. He'll simply be 'an accomplice.'"

"I guess that's okay. And please don't use our names."

"So, Michael and Tina are your real first names?"

"I'm not going to answer that question."

"Either way, I'll refer to you as Robert and Roberta."

"That works. What will you do after your return to Honolulu?"

"I'm planning to stay at the hotel for a few days. I'll find a nice spot where I can write my story without too many distractions. But I won't send the story to Malcolm until I return to L.A."

"Do you have any idea how you're going to write up what you've learned here?"

"I have a preliminary sketch in my head. I envision a three-part story running on consecutive days. I'm confident it will be on the first page and picked up by wire services and spread around the country and the world."

"I expect you're right. Are you worried?"

"Michael, what should I be worried about?"

"That the FBI or some other government agency will try to force you to give up our identities and location?"

"I've tried to put such thoughts out of my mind. Reporters have constitutional rights that have been affirmed many times by the courts. And the Times' attorneys will be able to assert those rights on my behalf."

"Let's hope so. We're counting on your integrity as a journalist."

****

As promised, Tina and Michael drove Stella to the ferry in mid-afternoon on the following day. Before leaving the house, Michael returned Stella's laptop, phone, and digital recorder, but not before he had scrubbed off his DNA and fingerprints.

Just before boarding the ferry, Stella raised her hand expecting good-bye handshakes. Instead, first Tina and then Michael hugged her. This is just too weird, she thought, as she turned around and stepped briskly aboard.

The hugs, she concluded, were the couple's last gesture to ingratiate themselves with the reporter whose story about them would soon reach a worldwide audience. Michael and Tina wanted the assassination to be told from their point of view. She knew that writing the story would be difficult because, as a journalist, she could not give the impression of sympathizing with their cause or painting them in a romantic or heroic light.

CHAPTER 34

STELLA'S FLIGHT TO HONOLULU was uneventful except for minor turbulence near the equator. A cab ride from the airport brought her to the Queen Kapiolani hotel shortly after one a.m. Exhausted in both body and mind, she changed into nightclothes, brushed her teeth, and fell into bed. Stella's brain wasn't quite ready for sleep, as she mulled over the previous days on Samoa.

Her interviews with Michael and Tina were like conversations among friends. They were stressful conversations because she was sitting with, dining with, the all-American couple who happened to be mass murderers. These people were utterly ordinary, yet had committed a heinous crime. As a reporter, as a human being, she couldn't reconcile the contradiction in their lives. She wondered if this puzzle even had a rational solution. Such thoughts tortured Stella as she tossed and turned before falling asleep, deep into the night.

Following a hearty room-service breakfast of orange juice, Belgian waffles, fruit, and coffee, Stella began to think about what to do with her fake Thai passport and ID. She was tempted to keep them as souvenirs, but then she remembered Michael's ominous question: would the government try to force her to yield information about her sources? If that ever happened, she couldn't let them find the fake documents. By using them to travel abroad, she had committed a federal crime; she had to dispose of them.

In her suitcase was a small pair of fingernail scissors. Stella set to work, methodically cutting the passport and ID into confetti-size pieces. By the time she was done, her right hand had cramped badly. Maybe, she decided, it was time for a swim. Exercise would be restorative.

Stella put on her swimsuit, grabbed a towel, and took the elevator to the lobby where she bought a swim cap in the gift shop. On the way to the pool she deposited the confetti in the abundant trash receptacles that lined the hallways and pool deck. She dove in and swam laps at a leisurely pace for almost half an hour. As the only Black person in the pool, she smirked to herself, thinking about gawkers who might have believed the racist myth that Blacks can't swim because they'd sink like stones.

****

Stella showered and changed into a comfortable blouse and shorts. She opened the lid of her laptop and created a new file, ready to capitalize on the scoop of the century. Before starting to write, Stella realized it was time to give Malcolm a call. He answered his cell on the second ring.

"Oh, Stella, I'm so glad to hear from you. I've been worried sick because I helped put you in a dangerous situation. Are you okay? Are you home? Did you get the story?..."

Stella cut him off before he could pile on more questions.

"Malcolm, it's good to hear your voice. I'm still in Hawai'i and I'm fine. I am about to start transforming the scoop of the century into the story of a lifetime. You won't believe what I've got. But I'm not going to give you details over the phone."

"You can be such a tease!"

"That's part of my job description."

"Bullshit it is!"

"Here's what I will tell you. I envision a three-part story. The first part is general background material on the assassins..."

Interrupting, "there was more than one?"

"Yes, it was a married couple and they had one accomplice. The second part will cover their motivations. And the last part is how they did it. I even have the opening line for the first installment: 'In a place far, far away, I spent time with the people who assassinated President Wahl, learning about their backgrounds, their motivations, and how they pulled off the crime of the century.'"

"Oh my god. This is too good to be true. How did you ever get them to talk?"

"That was never a problem. They wanted their story told because they were tired of all the crackpot conspiracy theories. The couple took a big risk in talking to me, but they felt it was necessary. They were highly motivated to set the record straight, so they gave me the entire story."

"You say that as if there is a surprise punch line."

"Oh yeah! And you won't believe it."

"Well, what is it?"

"You'll find out after I get back to L.A. when I give you the drafts."

Raising his voice in mock consternation, he said, "Stella, please!"

"Sorry, Malcolm. It's better if you get the punch line in context."

A resigned Malcolm changed the subject. "So, when are you coming home? You must be running up a hefty hotel bill."

"I'm going to return on the originally scheduled day because I can do my best work here without all the distractions of life in L.A."

"Well, enjoy your vacation. You've earned it."

"Damn right, I have. Bye, Malcolm."

"Bye, Stella."

During the next several days, Stella sat tethered to her laptop, tapping out the story that, she hoped, would make her world famous. From time to time she paged through her handwritten notes, which were so telegraphic they would be useless to anyone else. She broke up the work with swimming, hiking, and walks along the beach—and delicious seafood meals. Before packing to leave, Stella went outside and walked around the hotel. She found a huge Dumpster and dumped in her spiral notebook and travel-related materials, safely contained in a black trash bag she had taken from a maid's cart.

CHAPTER 35

THE DAY AFTER HER RETURN TO L.A., Stella walked quickly across the newsroom floor, stopping only briefly to answer friendly questions about where she had been. "I was on vacation," she chuckled and said no more.

As soon as Malcolm saw Stella in the newsroom, he stood up and walked out of his office to welcome her. "I could make jokes about your tan not showing, but that wouldn't be PC."

"Truth be told, I didn't spend a lot of time basking in the sun."

"Actually, you look tired."

"Yeah, I'm feeling a little spent. This project has been emotionally draining."

She handed him a thumb drive.

"Is this it, Stella, your bombshell story?"

"Yes, all three parts. I didn't want to risk putting it on our servers until you approved the drafts and the final versions go live. Don't forget: our servers are connected to the Internet and could be hacked."

"You mean hacked by the Joker?"

"Him too, but mostly by the government or right-wingers."

Malcolm was shocked by Stella's statement because she'd never had such worries before. He looked straight into her eyes and said, "what did you do with our Stella?"

"Malcolm. Think about this. I'm the only person in the world who can lead law enforcement agencies to the people who killed Wahl. I fear the feds are going to be on me like a plague of locusts when they read the story, demanding that I surrender my sources."

"Well, you would never do that."

"Of course I wouldn't. But they could arrest me and make my life miserable—or worse. Who knows what Shilling might do? We know he's obsessed with finding Wahl's killer. In his own below-the-radar, ruthless way, he might order drastic action to make me talk. Honestly, I'm becoming a little paranoid. Also, because my stories say the killers are conservatives…"

Malcolm interrupted, "did I hear you right? Conservatives?"

"Yes, the assassins are Christian conservatives, lifelong Republicans."

"You're shitting me, right?"

"It's true. That's who they are. Plug in the thumb drive so you can read all about them. That's why I'm worried that Shilling or the militant right might come after me. They'll just call my story fake news and want to punish me."

Malcolm just stood there, silently shaking his head, uncomprehending. Finally, he said, "I'll put everything else aside and edit your story."

"Thanks, Malcolm. You won't be disappointed."

He smiled and said, "I know."

****

As usual, Malcolm's tweaks to Part 1 were minor. Stella was pleased when he told her it would run virtually as written. Her story, "Crime of the Century, Part 1: The Assassins," appeared first in the online evening edition. She wrote about the small-town origins of the husband and wife couple, Robert and Roberta, who met in college at a meeting of the Young Republicans. There was a persistent vagueness in her descriptions of the couple's post-college activities. She emphasized that the pair were, in all respects, ordinary white Americans, Christians, and politically conservative. Why had they done it? This question was the cliffhanger she promised to answer in the next

133

installment.

Stella left out one crucial detail. She did not mention that the couple made contact first and dictated her travel plans. She allowed the reader to infer that she, herself, had tracked down the mass murderers. No harm, no foul.

PART 2

CHAPTER 36

ON THE WAY TO THE OFFICE, Joanna Bartolo ran into one of the agents on her assassination team.

"Joanna, have you seen this morning's L.A. Times?"

"No, should I?"

"Oh yeah! A reporter wrote that she found and interviewed a married couple who claim to have killed Wahl."

"I don't believe it. If we couldn't find the assassins, no one else could have either."

He grunted his lukewarm agreement, and said, "when I get back to my office I'll forward the story to you. You'll be furious after you read it."

"With my high blood pressure, that's just what I need. Thanks, a lot!"

"By the way, I looked up the reporter. Her name is Stella Weiss, and she has an excellent reputation. We can't just blow off her story. Plus, another installment is promised for tomorrow."

She groaned, took a deep breath, and said, "we need to build dams because the shit's going to start flowing downhill big time."

"Don't I know it!"

In her office, furnished with family pictures and commendations, Bartolo fumed as she read Stella's piece. The reporter's scoop—it was nothing less than a coup—was completely unexpected. How could she have identified the assassins when the FBI had so far failed? More than that, the article made the preposterous claim that conservative Christians—white, no less—had planned and carried out the assassination. Bartolo's entire world had just been turned upside-down.

What could she do? If the story was accurate, then Weiss had information the FBI desperately needed. Bartolo thought about getting the FBI's L.A. field office to pick up Weiss and interrogate her. But a full court press on a reporter, especially one from the L.A. Times, would itself become a story that, Bartolo knew, would come back to bite her on the ass. She had another plan.

****

Bartolo called the Times switchboard. "May I please speak with Ms. Stella Weiss?"

"I'm sorry but she's not taking any outside calls today."

"Well, I'm FBI Senior Special Agent Joanna Bartolo. This is an urgent matter. I need to speak with her now."

"Let me put you on hold, and I'll see if she'll take your call."

"Thanks."

"Ms. Weiss, there's an FBI agent on the line, and she wants to speak to you."

"Holy shit." She hesitated for a few moments before saying, "okay, put her through."

"Will do."

"Ms. Weiss?"

"Yes."

"I'm Special Agent Joanna Bartolo. I work at FBI headquarters in D.C., and I'm heading up the investigation of President Wahl's assassination."

As if Weiss didn't know what Bartolo wanted, she asked, in the most innocent tone possible, "what can I do for you?"

"I just read your provocative story. I was wondering if you could do a good turn for your country. I'm not going to ask you to reveal your sources, but perhaps you could give me some hints as to how you managed to track them down?"

"Oh dear. I'm afraid the article gave you the wrong impression. I didn't track them down. They initiated contact and promised me 'the scoop of the century.'"

"Really? Why would they do that?"

"They were sick and tired of all the crazy conspiracy theories. They wanted to get the truth out so that Americans could appreciate their patriotic motives."

Bartolo was stunned. "Oh. Can you at least tell me the location of the faraway meeting place?"

"I'm afraid I can't do that. But let me clarify one point. I am a patriotic American. Although I didn't personally mourn Wahl's passing, I know that he and nine other people were victims of a horrendous crime. Like you, I believe that Robert and Roberta should be captured and pay for their crimes. But I can't do the FBI's job."

Bartolo was frustrated, but she dared not push harder. Weiss was simply following professional norms by shielding her sources from prying government eyes.

"Ms. Weiss, is there anything you can tell me that would make my job easier?"

"All I can say is that my story accurately reflects the couple's motives and their version of the facts. Obviously, not knowing their real names, I had no way to independently verify their backstories. But they were very convincing, especially in describing how Robert had used a food truck as cover."

Bartolo was shocked by the reporter's mention of the food truck, which hadn't been in the story's first installment. Suddenly, Stella's reporting had gained instant credibility.

"Do I need to wait until the other parts of the story are published? Can you give me a preview?"

"I don't think that would be appropriate."

"I see. Well, I suppose our conversation is over."

****

Bartolo was pleased with herself because she hadn't berated the reporter for withholding critical information. She had reached a dead-end, but it had been worth trying. The conversation was not a complete waste because she had learned some new facts. In the first place—and this was important—the assassins had made first contact with Weiss and, presumably, specified the meeting place. Bartolo would immediately contact TSA to find out if a Stella Weiss had recently flown out of any southern California airport.

In the second place, Weiss claimed ignorance of the couple's real identities. Obviously, they were not Robert and Roberta with no surname.

And third, her reference to the food truck gave Weiss' reporting instant credibility. Bartolo was anxious to see the next installments for they might furnish hints about the couple that would be useful to the FBI.

****

Stella immediately went to Malcolm's office and plopped down in a chair.

"It's started."

"What's started?"

"I just got a call from FBI Special Agent Joanna Bartolo. She's in charge of the assassination investigation."

Malcolm wrote down the name in a small notebook and asked, "what did she want?"

"She wanted to pump me for information. At least she asked nicely."

"What did you tell her?"

"I gave her bupkis."

"Do you think that's going to end the FBI's interest in you?"

"I hope so; I fear not."

CHAPTER 37

PRESIDENT SHILLING WAS IN THE OVAL OFFICE awaiting the arrival of Chief of Staff Alfred Stonehouse. As his name suggested, Stonehouse was a mountain of a man, beefy and six feet, six inches tall. A graduate of Kansas State University, he had been a star linebacker for the Kansas City Chiefs. He was in his mid-forties, with blue eyes, a full head of wavy auburn hair, and neatly trimmed moustache. As always, Stonehouse wore a charcoal suit, powder blue shirt, and paisley tie. Shilling had hired him because he was smart, loyal, and could intimidate unwanted visitors. Stonehouse believed his job was to protect the president from other White House staff members and from himself.

Stonehouse entered the room and wasted no time in delivering the unsettling news.

"President Shilling, there has been some movement in the assassination case, but you're not going to like it."

He handed Wahl a printout of Stella's article.

"Mr. President, I'll wait while you read it because I presume you'll have a response."

Shilling leaned into the article, his face slowly turning red, the veins on his forehead throbbing vigorously. He opened his eyes wide, stood up, and yelled, "this is bullshit, fake news. There is no way in the world Christian conservatives killed Wahl. This was the work of leftwing radicals or terrorists." He shouted, "I won't believe anything else!"

"I regret being the bearer of bad news, but you need to be prepared for the next parts of the story."

Shilling looked at the byline and said, "who is this Stella Weiss?"

"Presuming you'd ask that question, I've already done some preliminary research on her. She's a fairly senior investigative reporter, highly respected for her coverage of L.A. politics and city scandals."

"What else do you know?"

"She's Black and a Jew."

"Oh shit! That's two strikes against her."

"What do mean?"

"Ninety percent of Blacks vote Democrat, and most Jews do too. This is terrible because she'll be biased against Republicans. Maybe she'll make it seem like President Wahl deserved what he got."

"Mr. President, what do you want to do?"

"We need to find out where she got this cockamamie story. Let's put the FBI on this ASAP. I want you to tell Director Abel to have her L.A. agents pick up Weiss and force her to cough up her sources. And they can use enhanced interrogation techniques if they need to."

"With all due respect, sir, giving an order like that to the FBI director is a bad idea. If Abel were willing to carry it out—and there's no guarantee she would—the press would jump on it as blatant intimidation. The story would be big news all across the country, and you would be crucified by the talking heads and every liberal lawyer in Washington. And don't forget about the many organizations devoted to preserving freedom of the press. They'd be filing lawsuits faster than you can blink. I suggest you wait until the rest of the story is published before taking any action."

Shilling sat down to think it over. "Stonehouse, I suppose you're right. Let's wait and see what's in the next installments."

"If you still want to do something, I suggest you begin by requesting a subpoena for Weiss' interview notes. You could go through the Department of Justice."

"An interesting idea, but they're just bureaucrats over there who would tie up my request for months. You know, of course, that DOJ is crawling with leftist lawyers."

Stonehouse sighed and said, "yes, you're right about that."

CHAPTER 38

AS STELLA EXPECTED, her story reverberated through the wire services like a thunderclap, spreading quickly around the country and the world. The reporter's inbox rapidly filled with comments, many of them obscene or worse. Stella shook her head in disgust as she repeatedly pressed delete.

In addition to hate mail, Stella was receiving invitations to appear on cable news programs. She had discussed this possibility with Malcolm, and he urged her to turn them down, at least for now. "Let the expectations build," he advised. "When they reach a fever pitch after the third part, you might want to select one or two quality programs that have maximum impact. It would be good publicity for the Times."

Although Stella craved professional recognition, she had misgivings about becoming a TV celebrity. She followed Malcolm's advice.

CHAPTER 39

When the second installment of Stella's story hit President Shilling's desk, he again raged in the presence of Stonehouse.

"The way I see it," said Shilling after he had calmed down, "these two articles contain no verifiable facts. The first one was on the backgrounds of two unidentified people. Today's is about their supposed motivations for killing the president. All of this could have been easily made up."

"Why would a respected reporter make up a story like that?"

Shilling replied, "to discredit Christian conservatives and Republicans generally. As long as the article contains no verifiable facts, that bitch can get away with it."

"Tomorrow's article promises to have details about how the couple actually committed the crime. We can immediately bring in NTSB and FBI people to do a fact check and blow the reporter out of the water if, as you believe, the article was woven of whole cloth."

"Good. Contact the FBI and NTSB immediately. I want to see Kettering and Bartolo in my office tomorrow at eleven—sharp."

"Of course. I will issue the invitations. That should give them time to read and fact-check the article."

****

The following morning, Herman Kettering and Joanna Bartolo

passed through White House security, and were nervously waiting for Alfred Stonehouse to appear and invite them into the Oval Office. For both of them, this was their first visit to this sacred space, the seat of executive power.

When Stonehouse finally emerged, he gave Kettering and Bartolo a heads-up: "the president is in a foul mood today, worse than usual. I recommend that you tread lightly."

Stonehouse escorted the pair into the Oval Office. The president remained seated behind the ornate Resolute desk, which English artisans had crafted from oak timbers of the British exploration ship, HMS Resolute. Queen Victoria gifted the handsome desk to President Rutherford B. Hayes in 1880.

Awed to be in the very room where so many presidents had made history, Bartolo and Kettering sat down in response to Stonehouse's wave. Casually surveying the furnishings, Bartolo noticed that the Great Seal of The United States, woven into the carpet, was much larger than she had expected. There were two couches, several small cherrywood tables, and two walnut credenzas. Floor-to-ceiling drapes the color of ripe Kansas wheat covered the south-facing windows. Flags of the United States and Kansas bookended the desk. Bronze busts of Shilling's favorite president, Andrew Jackson, sat on the credenzas to the president's right and left. Apart from the symbols of country and power, the ordinariness of the furnishings, except for the Resolute desk, impressed Bartolo. This could be, she thought, the sitting room in any large home.

Interrupting Bartolo's visual survey, Shilling said, "thank you for coming. Stonehouse told you why I called you here. I want Weiss' story totally debunked. It presents supposed facts that your investigations can easily demolish. We have to make short shrift of her fake news reports. I want Weiss blown out of the water, totally discredited."

Kettering and Bartolo looked at each other, their faces contorting with despair. Bartolo's stomach was churning.

Neither agent wanted to speak, but Kettering timidly made the first move. "Umm, Mr. President, umm, what if the facts in the article are correct?"

Shilling pounded the desk with his fist. "That can't be. I won't believe it. Are you telling me she actually interviewed the killers?"

"Umm. I can only tell you that nothing in her story is inconsistent with the facts as we know them."

"What about you, Bartolo?"

"Mr. President, I have to agree with Dr. Kettering. We have turned up no evidence that contradicts Ms. Weiss' account."

Trembling with anger, Shilling said, "when is the NTSB going to release its report on the crash?"

"We don't expect it until the end of the year—at the earliest."

"That's good. In the meantime, I'd like the NTSB to put out a press release saying the L.A. Times story is a complete fabrication. By the time your final report comes out, it will all be old news anyway. No one will care if your original statement was true or not."

Kettering squirmed, looked away, and delayed his response. Finally, in his most measured words, he said, "Mr. President, I'm not authorized to issue press releases. They would have to come through the office of the NTSB's chairman. And the chairman would not authorize the release of any information without having my team's report in hand. My agency would never deliberately mislead the public in the way you suggest."

Shilling pounded the massive desk again. "What about you, Bartolo?"

Without delay she shut down Shilling's request. "We have no basis for a public statement at this time or in the near future."

Exasperated, almost furious with these recalcitrant federal employees, Shilling asked Bartolo, "does the FBI have any leads on this couple?"

"We're working on it, but we have nothing concrete yet."

"Well, get busy!"

"With all due respect, sir, we have been busy."

Shilling fumed quietly, then shouted, "get the hell out of here, both of you."

They stood up and quickly scooted out of the Oval Office. On their way out of the White House, Kettering and Bartolo spoke to each other in hushed tones about their strange meeting with the president.

Kettering said, "he's obsessed with showing that leftwing radicals brought down Marine One. His narrow worldview can't conceive of lifelong Republicans killing one of their own."

"Well, I hope he simmers down and doesn't do anything drastic that we'll all regret."

"You and me both."

CHAPTER 40

SHILLING WAS BESIDE HIMSELF WITH ANGER. He was having a tough time accepting the truth, as Stella Weiss had presented it. In a more rational moment later that day, he acknowledged that his agencies couldn't or wouldn't refute her claims. The next best option was to capture the couple. This was, he finally admitted to himself, the prize. Even if the killers were Republicans, they still had murdered the man he revered. They had to be caught and punished, especially if they now had him in their sights. But who were they? Apparently, he admitted, only Stella Weiss knew that. Despite Stonehouse's advice, Shilling believed it was time to turn up the heat on her.

"Alfred, put in a call to FBI Director Shirley Abel."

Despite his better judgment, he said, "of course, sir."

She answered on the second ring when she saw White House on caller ID. "Hello, Abel here."

"This is President Shilling."

"What an unexpected pleasure, Mr. President. How's your family?"

"I'm not in the mood for small talk, so I'll get right to the point. Are you familiar with the L.A. Times stories about the assassination?"

"Yes sir, I am."

"Well, I'd like you to bring in Stella Weiss and interrogate her until she gives up her sources."

Abel was dumbfounded. Shilling's request was so inappropriate she couldn't even fathom it. Not since Nixon had a president issued illegal orders to the FBI. She mustered up her courage, and said, "Mr. President, I'm afraid I can't do that."

"Why can't you implement my order?" he shouted.

"Mr. President, as far as we know, Ms. Weiss has committed no crime and is not a person of interest in any ongoing investigation. If we interrogate her, we will incur the wrath of every leftist organization and first-amendment defender—especially the ACLU. Lawsuits against the administration will mount so fast we won't be able to keep track of them all. And your allies in the media, especially thoughtful conservatives like George Will, won't be pleased either. It's just wrong in so many ways."

"I suggest you charge her with obstruction of justice because she's withholding information from an ongoing investigation."

"Obstruction laws don't work that way, Mr. President. I admit this is an unusual situation because the assassins were her sources. But that doesn't change the fact that, as a reporter—especially one of her caliber—she has every right to protect their identities. You could try obtaining a subpoena for her notes, but that could take time, and I doubt any judge would approve the request."

"I just don't believe that reporters have any special rights."

"Pardon my French, sir, but if we went after her, as you suggest, we would face a shitstorm of criticism and lawsuits."

"I'm willing to take that chance."

"But I'm not. If you insist that I go through with this interrogation, I will resign immediately and state my reasons publicly."

Shilling was caught off guard by her insubordination and threat. Abel had a well-deserved reputation for integrity and toughness. That's why the last Democratic president had appointed her, even though she was a Republican. She had distinguished herself as the police chief of Fort Worth, Texas, reducing street crime and arresting white-collar criminals by the score.

The president realized he wasn't going to win this fight and backed off. "Obviously, Director Abel, I don't want you to resign. I'll have to find another way." Before she could reply, he slammed down the phone.

Stonehouse had heard only Shilling's side of the conversation, but he easily inferred Abel's negative response. He made soothing noises for Shilling's benefit, but he was appalled by what the president had attempted. God, Stonehouse said to himself, I hope it doesn't get any worse; the president is obsessed with finding Robert and Roberta. Somehow, he mused, I need to temper his autocratic tendencies.

CHAPTER 41

ON THE FIRST DAY STELLA did not appear in the newsroom, Malcolm was only mildly concerned. He knew she was still decompressing from her trip and avoiding the barrage of publicity her story had garnered. Maybe, he thought, she had followed his advice to spend more time working from home. He wondered what her next big story idea would be.

On the second day of Stella's unexplained absence, Malcolm began to worry. She had brought up the possibility that feds or right-wing zealots might come after her. He still believed those possibilities were remote. Malcolm reassured himself that spending time with mass murderers could addle even Stella's fine mind—at least a little.

When the workday was about to end, still without Stella or any communication from her, he moved into mild panic mode. Malcolm dialed her cell, but there was no answer. Then he called down to the Times HR department to obtain Stella's emergency contact information. The receptionist gave him numbers for both parents. He called her father, Daniel, who was just taking off his latex gloves after finishing the last root canal of the day.

A chirpy receptionist answered, "Weiss Endodontics."

"May I please speak to Dr. Weiss?"

"Who should I say is calling?"

"This is Malcolm Klein. I'm his daughter's editor at the L.A. Times. This is important."

"I'll let him know."

"Hello, Dr. Weiss here."

"Hi, this is Malcolm Klein, Stella's editor at the Times."

"Sure, I remember you. We've run into each other at holiday parties. By the way, Stella speaks very highly of your work. What's up?"

"Have you seen or heard from Stella yesterday or today?"

"No, I haven't, but that's not unusual. What's this about? You're starting to scare me."

"Well, I don't want to be an alarmist, but Stella hasn't come to the newsroom or contacted me in the past two days. I'm concerned because she usually keeps me abreast of her activities. I called her cell but there's no answer. I hope she's not sick at home."

"Oh, geez. Let me think." Malcolm could hear the doctor breathing rapidly as he debated what to do.

"Okay, here's my plan. We'll be finishing up here in a few minutes. I'll call Stella's cell and landline. If she doesn't answer, I'll swing by my house and get her apartment key, then go over there to see what's up."

"That's a good plan. Please keep in touch."

"I will."

****

About an hour later, Dr. Weiss called Klein.

"I'm in her apartment now. There's no sign of Stella, but someone else has obviously been here. The place has been trashed. All the drawers were pulled out and emptied onto the floor. The cupboards are open wide. I don't see her laptop or cell, and her purse is on the couch with everything spilled out. This is more than worrisome. I called my wife, Rachel, and she's been working the phone with our relatives and Stella's friends. So far, no one knows anything. Rachel is beside herself with worry. And Stella's car is in the parking lot."

"Oh crap. I recommend that you file a missing person report with the LAPD."

"I'll do it immediately."

"There's something you should know before you fill out the

report."

"What's that?"

"Since the publication of her assassination story, Stella's been afraid that some rightwing nutcase might harm her or the federal government might squeeze her for information. I didn't take her fears very seriously at first, but now I'm not so sure. On the missing person form, be sure to indicate that her apartment was ransacked and that she might be the victim of foul play."

"Oh god. I hope not."

CHAPTER 42

DR. WEISS LOOKED UP THE LAPD NUMBER to report missing adults. He tapped in the number on his phone and was told to go to the Wilshire Community Police Station. He drove over there and filled out the form. The officer on duty told him, "the police will take it from here."

As he was leaving the reception area, Weiss turned around and asked, "do you get many missing person reports?"

"The LAPD receives over 300 missing person reports per month." Weiss was aghast at the news, wishing he hadn't asked. He wondered how much time they would put into finding Stella. He saw no reason to be optimistic and left for home.

Hoping to speed things along, Weiss made several calls, the first one to Stella's city councilman, Henry Carter, who happened to be an acquaintance and one of his patients.

"Henry, this is my daughter. Please lean on the LAPD to take this seriously. Her life could be in danger because of her story in the Times."

"Yeah, Dan, I get it. Believe me, I'll do what I can."

Carter immediately contacted a police captain he knew well who had previously done him favors. An hour later, Daniel received a call from an LAPD officer. He instructed Weiss to meet him later at Stella's apartment.

Ordinarily, the liberal Weisses would rail about wealthy people in L.A. throwing their weight around and getting results from public officials. But, with Stella's life possibly in the balance, they ignored their hypocrisy, thankful they could be the squeaky wheel that got greased.

Daniel and Rachel Weiss drove to Stella's apartment and waited impatiently, fearing the LAPD wouldn't show. After they waited for almost two hours, a pair of officers finally arrived. Seeing the mess and learning that the missing woman was the very same Stella Weiss who had written the bombshell story, the officers sent for a detective and crime scene unit.

After the LAPD had finished their search for evidence, Rachel and Daniel cleaned off the ubiquitous fingerprint dust from exposed surfaces and returned Stella's possessions to drawers and cupboards. They had to make reasonable guesses as to where things belonged.

Throughout the clean-up, Rachel sobbed almost continuously.

"Oh, Daniel, I can't believe this is happening."

He put his arms around her and said, "Rachel, I'm sure Stella will turn up safe. She's strong."

His hollow words of reassurance were not comforting. Rachel had come to believe that Stella's assassination story put her in mortal danger. Before leaving Stella's apartment, her parents' last task was to feed a very hungry Tabitha. Then they took her home.

The next morning the detective called Daniel at work to inform him that Stella Weiss had not turned up in a search of hospitals in L.A. County. Daniel was unsure whether this news was good or bad.

CHAPTER 43

WHEN MALCOLM ARRIVED at the newsroom the next morning, there was still no trace of Stella. He was distressed, feeling guilty that he had approved her story idea. Lacking confidence that the LAPD would do much to investigate her disappearance, he toyed with the idea of getting the FBI involved. He thumbed through his notebook until he found the page on which he had written the name of the agent who had talked to Stella: Joanna Bartolo.

Malcolm wanted to ask the FBI agent to help find Stella. But what if the FBI, unsatisfied with her response to Bartolo's inquiry, had taken her? Well, if they already had her, he reasoned, his call would make no difference. A call to Bartolo would elicit some sort of reaction, which he might be able to interpret. Malcolm had convinced himself that the call was necessary.

He dialed the main number of FBI headquarters in Washington, D.C. When he asked to speak with Agent Joanna Bartolo, the operator wanted to know the purpose of the call.

"Tell her I'm calling about Stella Weiss."

"I'll see if she can take your call."

Less than a minute later, Malcolm heard a click and then a voice.

"Special Agent Joanna Bartolo. Who is this?"

"My name is Malcolm Klein. I'm a managing editor at the L.A. Times. I worked with Stella Weiss on her assassination story."

"Okay. So, what now?"

"Stella has disappeared. She hasn't been seen for more than two days. We fear she's been abducted. Her father told me that her apartment was torn apart. He found her car in the parking lot, but her laptop and phone were missing. I thought you might know something about it."

Bartolo ignored the implied accusation, and said "oh my god, no."

"Look, Mr. Klein, let me assure you that my team and I had nothing to do with her disappearance. Just between you and me, there are people in and out of government who are desperate to bring the assassins to justice. Ms. Weiss is the only known link to them. That's why—and it pains me to admit this—she is in danger. Let me see what I can learn at this end. But I want to emphasize: we didn't do it."

"Who do you mean by 'we'?"

"I only have direct knowledge of my team's activities. And I'm confident the rest of the FBI wasn't involved in her disappearance either."

"Please call me back if you learn anything."

"I'll try, but no promises. If she was kidnapped and we suspect they took her across state lines, then it immediately becomes our case. We may have to take part in the investigation anyway. And if we do get involved, I'll have to go silent."

"I understand. You've got to find Stella. Her parents are frantic, and I'm feeling terrible because I gave her the go-ahead on the story."

****

Bartolo's brief conversation with Malcolm had left her troubled on two levels. First, she could feel Klein's apprehension in his every word. He was obviously fond of his reporter. From Bartolo's brief conversation with Stella, she had come away favorably impressed. True, the reporter was withholding information that could speed up the investigation, but she couldn't fault Weiss for her professionalism.

Second, she reeled off the possibilities of who had abducted Weiss—assuming it was an abduction. She took it for granted that the reporter's story about the killer couple had provoked someone to take drastic action. The timing of her disappearance, coming so close

157

after the publication of Part 3, was just too perfect. Senior special agents don't believe in coincidences. So, Bartolo wondered, who had a motive and what had they done with her? She considered several plausible scenarios. A rightwing person or group, dedicated acolytes of Wahl, might have wanted to punish the reporter. Members of the Christian right could have accepted Sean Hannity's fantastic claim that her stories were fake news designed to stain Christian conservatives. They might have wanted revenge. Plausible scenarios, indeed.

A much more disquieting possibility kept intruding her thoughts. A federal agency might have abducted Weiss in order to force her to reveal more information about her trip and the couple she interviewed. This was also plausible but, in her assessment, unlikely. If such a plot were exposed, it would become the scandal of the century, leading to Congressional hearings, prosecutions, pillorying by the press, and worse. A scandal of this magnitude might eclipse Watergate by an order of magnitude. But she also knew about Shilling's determination to get Weiss to identify Robert and Roberta. Maybe the president had found someone in the government willing to make an unlawful move.

Bartolo decided to nose around the Hoover Building to satisfy herself that what she had told Klein was true: Weiss's disappearance was not an FBI covert operation. The simplest approach was to go right to the top and ask Director Abel. Agent Bartolo easily secured an appointment for later in the day by intimating that she had new information to share about the investigation.

****

Bartolo entered the grand office that J. Edgar Hoover did not live to see, though a painting of him loomed large behind the director's enormous walnut desk. She had been in the office before and didn't bother staring at the grand view from the south-facing window, several floors above hers. For the first time, she did notice half a dozen engraved plaques honoring Abel's contributions to charitable causes.

In her late forties, Shirley Abel was aging gracefully. She had hazel eyes behind thick bifocals, salt-and-pepper hair that cascaded to her shoulders, and finely chiseled features with unblemished alabaster skin. Abel could have been mistaken for a spinster librarian, save for her wedding ring and expertly tailored, cobalt blue suit.

"Have a seat, Agent Bartolo. Can I offer you coffee?"

"Thanks, I'm fine," she said while lowering herself onto a settee across from the desk.

"I've been led to believe you have news about the assassination investigation."

"In a manner of speaking, I do."

"What do you mean by that?"

"There has been a new twist. Stella Weiss, the L.A. Times reporter, has gone missing in Los Angeles."

"Oh no! How long has she been gone?"

"As far as I know, two or three days. I got a call today from her editor, and he's understandably upset. He asked me point blank if her apparent abduction was our work."

Tapping her fingers on the desk, Abel asked, "what did you tell him?"

"I told him that it wasn't my team, and I doubted it was an FBI operation. I hope that last part was true."

"Bartolo, I can assure you it wasn't us. I'd never authorize such a harebrained scheme."

Carefully observing Abel's body language, Bartolo inferred that the director was obviously uncomfortable with the conversation, but she didn't know why.

"I believe you, director."

Finally, Bartolo learned what was causing the director's discomfort.

"I probably shouldn't mention this, but a few days ago I was in a bizarre meeting with the president."

Bartolo's eyes opened wider as she became even more attentive to Abel's every word.

"Please, do tell me more."

"Shilling wanted me to pick up and interrogate Weiss. He's furious that a reporter learned more about the assassination than our agency."

"What did you tell him?"

"I told him such an operation was simply out of the question."

"Good for you."

"I'm worried, though. He might have peddled his illegal scheme from agency to agency until he found a brown-noser willing to go through with it."

"So, you think a fed was responsible for her disappearance?"

"I don't know that, but I can't rule it out, given how adamant Shilling was. Listen, Bartolo, if he found someone to abduct Weiss and the press learned about it, impeachment would be just around the corner."

"Holy shit! The president ordering a kidnapping. Has it really come to that?"

"I hope not, Bartolo. Let's not get ahead of ourselves. Maybe I shouldn't have said anything, but it's been eating at me. I suppose we'll find out soon enough, one way or another. Can you spare some agents to look into possible federal involvement in Weiss's disappearance?"

"Of course. We've got dozens of agents working on the assassination, but I can pull together a small team. I'll turn them loose and see what they can find out."

"Good. By the way, has the investigation made any progress in identifying Robert and Roberta since your last briefing?"

"Well, we still don't know who they are, but we have a lead on where they are. TSA informed me yesterday that Weiss boarded a flight to Honolulu on 25 February and returned to L.A. on 6 March."

"So, she met the assassins in Hawai'i?"

"Apparently. The TSA check did not find a Stella Weiss leaving the islands for a foreign destination during that time period."

"Have you looked into where she might have stayed?"

"She registered at the Queen Kapiolani hotel in Honolulu. The hotel management was very cooperative and allowed our agents to go through their video files. They found something strange."

"What was that?"

"Weiss paid for 10 days at the hotel. But the lobby videos show her leaving through the main entrance with her roller bag, purse, and a tote bag from the hotel gift shop. That was on 26 February; she reappeared on 2 March."

"So, she was taken or sent somewhere else, but where?"

"She didn't take any inter-island flights, so she must have remained on Oahu. We showed Weiss's picture to every cabbie that made pickups at the hotel. One cabbie recognized her. He reported picking her up and taking her to the airport on the day she returned to L.A. In short, we've had no luck tracking Weiss during her absence from the hotel."

"Well, I have a suggestion. Have you examined video surveillance from the airport? Is it possible she boarded an international flight? What about travel on fraudulent documents?"

"I'll immediately ask Honolulu to get answers to those questions."

"If they turn up nothing, where does the investigation go?"

"Honestly, Director Abel, we are stumped. Unless we get some new leads, it goes nowhere."

"Well, we can't let that happen."

Bartolo sighed and nodded in agreement.

Abel said, "while we're on the subject of Weiss, I'm thinking it would be in the FBI's best interest to find her ASAP."

"Why is that?"

"Because as soon as the leftwing media find out about her disappearance, they'll blame us for certain."

"How are you going to find her?"

"I'll put together a team from the L.A. field office. They've got some first-rate agents. I'll assign them to report directly to you, Bartolo."

"Thanks, I can use the extra work," she said, her voice dripping with sarcasm. Her remark managed to elicit a smile from the director.

"Seriously," Bartolo added quickly, "we don't know if she's been taken across state lines. It may not be a federal crime."

"I know that, but we should get ahead of it just in case. Besides, it's a high-profile case, and we should be partnering with the LAPD, at the very least. As you know, their plates are full. They'll probably appreciate our assistance as long as we share the credit for a bust and don't step on their toes."

"Director, are you aware that Stella Weiss is Black and Jewish?"

161

"No, I didn't know that, but I see why it might matter. Maybe a rightwing hate group abducted her. Those groups can't be happy with her race and religion on top of her reporting."

"Precisely."

Abel stood up, and Bartolo responded to the director's cue by heading to the door. As Bartolo was leaving, she turned around and said, "there's an old Chinese curse that seems to fit: 'may you live in interesting times.'"

Abel smiled wanly.

CHAPTER 44

AFTER THE DOOR HAD CLOSED BEHIND BARTOLO, Abel called the L.A. office, identified herself, and asked to speak to the agent in charge. He came on the line almost immediately. After she explained her mission, he recommended agents Benjamin Suarez and Andrew Carrington, and he assured the director that they were an excellent team. She asked for and received their contact information.

In later calls, she informed Suarez and Carrington of their new assignment. They would report directly to Senior Special Agent Joanna Bartolo in Washington. Both L.A. special agents were surprised to be receiving a new assignment from the FBI Director herself, a person neither man had met.

Carrington and Suarez had been a team for six years, and had solved several high-profile crimes in the L.A. region. Perhaps their most famous case was that of the aptly named Jason Kidder. For several years Kidder had run a lucrative Ponzi scheme, enticing wealthy residents of California, Nevada, and Arizona to invest in a private hedge fund. Carrington had posed as a prosperous divorce attorney looking for investment opportunities, while Suarez scoured Kidder's financial records. Their work resulted in an impressive trove of evidence. Kidder's arrest and conviction raised the team's profile in the FBI.

Andrew Carrington was a graduate of Princeton, where he had earned a B.A. in political science. He was married with two teenage children, Tiffany and David, who provided him and his wife, Ellen, with ample challenges. Of English ancestry, Carrington was strait-laced and conservative.

Benjamin Suarez graduated from the University of Colorado with a B.A. in sociology. Single and very eligible, he had yet to meet the love of his life, but not for lack of trying on many dating websites. Suarez was moderately liberal, a fact he did not advertise at work. However, he hadn't voted in the last presidential election because, he believed, neither Wahl nor his opponent was of presidential caliber.

The agents were excited by their new assignment, delighted to put a bank fraud case on a back burner. They knew that a case with national implications, like the Weiss disappearance, seldom landed in their laps. Suarez and Carrington had no idea where the investigation might lead, but they were eager to find out.

CHAPTER 45

TRYING TO CLEAR HER HEAD after awakening from a deep sleep, Stella found herself on a cot in a small windowless room. She forced reluctant eyes to focus on her surroundings: a bare concrete floor and grimy, dark green walls, illuminated by a single fluorescent tube in an ancient fixture hanging from the ceiling. She sat up but felt woozy and grabbed the cot to keep from tumbling over. Stella noticed some fast food wrappers on a table, but doubted she had eaten anything. Through an open door she saw a small room with a toilet and sink.

Her head still foggy, Stella now felt stable enough to stand. There was another door. She walked over slowly and tried the knob. It turned but the door was apparently bolted from the other side. I'm a prisoner, she said to herself, and I have no idea who is holding me or even where I am. Nothing hurt, so she knew she hadn't been beaten or sexually assaulted. Her badly wrinkled blouse and jeans were intact, the same clothes she had been wearing when she opened her apartment door. Was it last night or the night before? She had no idea how much time had elapsed since she'd been kidnapped.

Stella pounded on the outer door and yelled for help. No one came. She pounded and yelled again, this time louder. Same result. Without her phone or laptop, she had no way to communicate with the outside world—wherever it was.

Resigned to waiting until her abductors showed themselves, she used the toilet and then washed her face and hands. She was surprised to find a new bar of soap on the sink and a clean towel on the rack.

****

Sobbing, she muttered to herself, "Stella, oh Stella, what did I get myself into? Is this where the path of unbridled ambition leads? How did I come by such a generous measure of ambition?" The answer seemed obvious: her parents. Rachel and Daniel had invested all of their parenting and love in their only child, and their high expectations were always explicit. She would attend college, maybe graduate school, and then become successful in her chosen profession. They had no preferences as to her career and were pleased when she showed a passion for journalism.

Stella knew it was too easy to attribute her burning ambition exclusively to parental pressure. There was another reason. When she was about ten years old, they told her that she had been adopted. By then she had known it for years; there was simply no other explanation for a Black child being raised by white parents.

An adopted child, Stella had felt the need to excel. Daniel and Rachel claimed to know nothing about her biological parents, but Stella always suspected the worst about her birth mother. Some drugged-out junkie traded sex for a fix and that was it. Stella came into the world nine months later, unloved, until the kindly Weisses adopted her. Sadly, she admitted to herself, she couldn't envision any upbeat scenarios. And she never had an interest in tracking down her birth mother. She had only one mother, Rachel, the one who raised her, the one who loved her, the one who was always there for her.

As Stella grew to adulthood and began her career, her mother sometimes mentioned the importance of marriage and family. Her cousins, mom reminded Stella on many occasions, already had children, and thoroughly enjoyed raising them, despite also having demanding careers. Maybe because Stella was an only child, she did not share the same vision of family as her parents and her aunts and uncles. Stella knew her biological clock was ticking near midnight. It was becoming more certain every day that she'd never gift her parents with grandchildren. Soon the issue of grandchildren would be moot.

Why, she wondered, didn't she just stay in L.A., covering sleaze-balls in city government? But reporting can sometimes be risky; she knew what she was getting into. She made the right decision at the time, allowing the Joker to call the shots. Now she wasn't so sure. Will she be tortured and end up dead? She shuddered and turned to more pleasant thoughts: her days in Hawai'i and writing the story that traveled around the world. Stella was a famous reporter now, a childhood dream realized. Yet, she was a prisoner all the same.

CHAPTER 46

MALCOLM HAD ALLOWED HIMSELF to become very fond of Stella. It was love of a sort, mixed with admiration for her skills and pride in having nurtured her development as a star reporter since college. Now he was beside himself with worry, forced to accept the possibility that he had sanctioned a story that might cause... No, no! He couldn't allow himself to think up worst-case scenarios. He had to do something constructive.

In his prime, Malcolm had been an elite Times reporter. He had covered some of the city's biggest stories, from gruesome homicides to police beatings of unarmed Black men. His uncanny knack for recognizing the potential in a story idea eventually led to his promotion to the editorial staff. Malcolm Klein had power over reporters, something he never craved. He was the liberator of great story ideas and the executioner of poor ones. In this position he felt the resentment of several junior reporters who smarted from what they considered his high-handed dismissal of their ideas.

In the golden age of independent newspapers, when he had started out, reporters had more freedom, and failure was tolerated. They could spend weeks, sometimes even months, on a story idea that didn't pan out without incurring the wrath of managing editors. Wins and losses were all part of the same game. The goal was to have some great wins; the losses didn't count. Now reporters were expected to bring every story to fruition.

Malcolm had closely followed the nationwide decline of print dailies. There was an obvious culprit: the Internet, especially social media. Many people assumed that the Internet had siphoned away billions of advertising dollars from print media. Malcolm knew that the story was more complex because the long-term decline had begun earlier. Seeking to increase profits, greedy owners cut expenses by reducing page size, eliminating sections, and shortening surviving sections. They also cut staff, especially foreign correspondents, and offered early retirement packages to senior staff. Malcolm had refused these offers several times. If reporters were replaced at all, it was by recent college graduates who were cheap but still green. These measures to bolster the bottom line, Malcolm knew, ended up harming the product and driving away subscribers. As the Internet demonstrated its power to attract eyeballs and clicks, advertisers flocked to the new medium. Profits of dailies plummeted. The weakest papers—hundreds of them—disappeared. Survivors, like the L.A. Times, had no choice but to add online editions. Ah, Malcolm sighed, the Internet. No technology better illustrated the law of unintended consequences.

Malcolm looked back on his reporter days with great fondness, though not until today did he have the slightest urge to be in the hunt again. Had his reporter skills atrophied? Was he still capable of chasing down leads, righting wrongs, and maybe affecting people's lives? He didn't know. Because one very special life was at stake, he refused to succumb to self-doubts. Only one question really mattered. Where is Stella Weiss? Malcolm made it his mission to find her.

The best way to generate leads, Malcolm knew, was to publish a story encouraging people to wrack their brains for any recollection that might be relevant. He began sketching out a story idea. He would mince no words: Stella Weiss had been kidnapped; no other scenario fit the facts as well.

Malcolm's story, "Famed Times Reporter Abducted," was published two days later. The story included a flattering picture of Stella with the large-font caption, "Have You Seen Our Reporter?" The plan was to run the picture and caption every day until she was found.

Predictably, his story unleashed a flood of crackpot calls to the newspaper's main phone number, and a torrent of notes to Malcolm's Gmail. The switchboard operators duly forwarded his calls, but few of them needed a personal follow-up.

Malcolm's story also generated speculation in all media about what had happened to Stella Weiss. Predictably, left-leaning talking heads and reporters pointed to the FBI. Right-leaning media insisted that leftists had taken and killed her so that the assassins would never be found.

CHAPTER 47

IN THE FARAWAY TROPICAL ISLAND, Michael was perusing the L.A. Times. He had been following Stella's story, verifying that she hadn't revealed facts that might put the couple in jeopardy. He was pleased with her account of their meeting, for she had told the assassination story accurately while omitting potentially dangerous details.

Comments on the articles, in print and online, were fascinating. Michael was amused by writers who slammed Stella in vacuous broadsides. These people were apparently irate Republicans or Christian Wahl-lovers who ranted about the publication of "fake news" and "obvious tripe." A common refrain was, "what happened to your standards?" He agreed with the latter comment because he saw no earthly reason to publish so many uninformative letters. Oh well, he sighed.

This morning when Michael checked the L.A. Times, he saw the headline of Malcolm Klein's lead article and Stella's picture. He hollered downstairs, "Tina, come up here, I want to show you something."

While he waited for Tina, Michael felt a pang of guilt, knowing that they had initiated the reporter's fateful odyssey. Now she was in trouble and her life might be in danger—assuming she was still alive. He shook his head in disbelief. He was also concerned that whoever kidnapped Stella might force her to reveal their location. That would never do.

Tina read the headline and then the article. She, too, was aghast at the thought Stella might be dead or dying because of them. They looked at each other, both wondering, "what can we do?"

"Tina, we have computer skills and equipment to help us track her down."

"I agree, but we need to have a hunch about who abducted her."

"I have no doubt the feds did it. Think about this: according to her editor, she disappeared without a trace. There's been no ransom note. No body has turned up. This affair smells of a covert op. Some federal agency was tasked with kidnapping her and forcing her to identify us. Nothing else makes sense to me. This was a professional operation."

"If that's right, Michael, then she is most likely being held at a federal facility somewhere."

"I agree. But it would be too risky to squirrel her away in a federal building in the middle of L.A. There would be too many opportunities for someone to recognize her distinctive face. I'm guessing she's at a nearby military base. Let's take a look."

He tapped a few keys, and a map appeared showing military bases in California, Nevada, and Arizona.

"Oh, wow," said Tina, "so many possibilities. You don't suppose she's at that top secret lab in Area 51 where they keep the Roswell space alien?"

"I wouldn't doubt it, but we're going to need some hard evidence to narrow down the list. I'm going to set up a program to monitor two-way Internet and land-line traffic at these bases. We don't need to know the content of the messages, just any anomalous communication patterns."

"That seems sensible to me. That way we're protected."

****

Later that day, Michael again called down to Tina, who was in the kitchen fixing dinner. She put down her spatula and headed upstairs to Michael's office.

"What's up?"

"I think I've got something. Camp Pendleton has been communicating with the White House. I didn't see anything like this at any

172

other base. It's especially odd because military personnel are so compulsive about obeying the chain of command. Why would someone at Camp Pendleton be talking repeatedly to someone at the White House? Surely, under normal circumstances, they'd go through Pentagon brass. This is really odd and probably significant."

"So, what do you want to do?"

"I'll continue the monitoring program to see if anything else suspicious turns up. In the meantime, let's pray they don't torture Stella to force her to give us up."

CHAPTER 48

MALCOLM WAS AT HIS DESK, running through early morning phone messages and reading emails. The phone calls weren't promising, but one email was shocking in its implications. The short message said, "Stella may be at Camp Pendleton." It was signed, "the Joker."

Malcolm wondered who, besides he and Stella, knew her nickname for the president's assassin? He could think of no one else she would have told. Apparently, then, Robert had sent the message. He knew Robert was a computer whiz, so maybe he had discovered something. Ten minutes after Malcolm read the message, it was gone. This was real—a lead he had to take seriously. Why, he wondered, was Robert bothering to help track down Stella? It didn't take Malcolm long to answer his own question: Robert wanted Stella found before she could be forced to yield information about the couple.

Malcolm googled Camp Pendleton, a sprawling base in San Diego County. With 17 miles of coastline and a vast acreage, the base is the largest undeveloped tract between Los Angeles and San Diego. It is the major West Coast installation for training marines and other members of the armed forces. This base, Malcolm noted, could easily conceal Stella. He came up with a plan that would put him on the streets again as an investigative reporter.

It was time to visit Alice McGuire in the suite upstairs where executive editors hang out. With some trepidation, he would present his plan.

"Malcolm, this is a pleasant surprise. Seeing you here in the flesh leads me to believe you want something big, or you have news about Stella."

"You're right on both counts."

"Spit it out, Malcolm."

"I need to spend a few days in Oceanside."

"What's there?"

"A nice fishing pier and lots of bars."

"Come on, Malcolm, tell me what this is really about!"

He gave her a cat-ate-the-canary grin and said, "I received a lead about Stella's possible location."

"Tell me."

"An email just arrived suggesting that Stella is in the vicinity of Oceanside."

"And you believe the lead is credible?"

"Alice, I do."

"And?"

"And nothing."

He was being evasive for fear that if he told her the source of the lead, she might insist on informing the FBI.

Unable to penetrate his veil of secrecy, Alice took a deep breath and let it out slowly. "Okay. What do you want?"

"Motel, per diem, and a car. And, I hate to mention it, but you'll have to ask Juanita Soto to handle my reporters while I'm gone."

"Juanita's not going to be happy about that."

"She'll get over it."

"I guess I understand why you have this sudden urge to be back on the street. Stella means so much to our paper and to you."

"Yeah. She's one of a kind, and if I can do anything to help find her, I will."

"Okay, Malcolm. Your wish is my command. Go to Oceanside and bring Stella home."

"If only…"

CHAPTER 49

ACCORDING TO HER CAPTORS, Stella had been in the dismal room, her prison, for two days. Meals consisted of donuts and coffee for breakfast, burgers for lunch, and Chinese takeout for dinner. She dreaded the thought of stepping on the scale at the gym, so she ate very little. Fretting about gaining weight from the terrible diet was a needed distraction from the undercurrent of terror she felt.

She heard the dull metallic clunk of the bolt lock being pulled open. Two familiar people—she had named them Laurel, the man with the thin face; and Hardy, the woman with the round face—entered the room carrying coffee and donuts. As always, they wore ski masks. Laurel was in a green polo shirt and khakis; Hardy wore a beige blouse and dark gray slacks. And both carried guns. They sat down and told her that another interrogation would begin soon. Laurel and Hardy were feeling the pressure to get results because searches of Stella's computer and phone had come up empty. They had to find another way to extract the information from her.

Laurel spoke first. "Ms. Weiss, you haven't been very helpful. We only need a few facts and then we can take you home."

"You have no warrant for my arrest. And you've added false imprisonment to the crime of kidnapping. You'll do serious jail time for what you've done."

"We're happy to let you to blow off some steam. We know this is stressful for you, but we have a job to do."

"I also had a job to do, and I did it. Your interrogators can keep asking me the same questions, and I'll keep giving them the same answer: no way will I tell them anything about Robert and Roberta. I have the legal right to protect my sources."

Hardy took over. "So, you believe we can't force you to reveal your sources?"

Stella nodded.

"You're wrong."

With no warning, Hardy pulled out her Glock and pressed it against Stella's forehead. Stella winced and pulled back.

"If you kill me, your superiors—whoever they are—will be pissed off because dead reporters don't talk. And you'll eventually be caught and arrested for murder."

Hardy's impulsive bluff had failed, so she reholstered her pistol.

"Okay," she said, "we warned you." Hardy tapped a few times on her phone. About 20 minutes later an older man, also wearing a ski mask, entered the room carrying a small suitcase. When he set it down on the table next to Stella and opened the lid, she immediately recognized it as a polygraph.

"I refuse to be connected to your machine."

Hardy snarled and said, "you don't have the option to refuse anything here."

"Where is here? Can't you at least tell me that?"

"You don't need to know."

"But I would like to know. Better yet," she said, raising her voice, "I'd like to leave, now."

"I'm afraid that's impossible, unless you give us the information we need."

The newcomer tried to attach the sensors to Stella, but she kept pushing his arms away. Suddenly she shoved the machine off the table, and it went crashing to the floor. Stella stood up and, before anyone could stop her, she stomped it, breaking the mechanism that held the moving pens.

The recent arrival muttered, "you broke it, bitch."

"That's right, asshole!"

Laurel, Hardy, and the unnamed man left the room, closed the door, and talked outside. Stella could hear their voices, but couldn't make out the words. But she clearly heard the clunk of the bolt lock as it closed. She was alone again in her prison.

Laurel and Hardy immediately reported the unsatisfactory events to the base's top marine, Commander Otis Griswold, who was just preparing to call in his daily update to the White House.

CHAPTER 50

AN UNHAPPY PRESIDENT SHILLING had just finished listening to Griswold's latest message. He and Stonehouse discussed the brief communication. The agitated president said, "why couldn't they get Weiss to talk? It should have been a walk in the park. Can you believe it? She actually broke the polygraph. What kind of bozos do we have working at Camp Pendleton, anyway?"

"I don't know, Mr. President."

"I want you to arrange a 2:00 p.m. meeting today in the Oval Office with General Leonard Smolinsky. Let's see what the army might have available for a situation like this. I know we have labs all over the country. Maybe one of them has a powerful truth serum."

"Will do, sir. Anything else?"

"Not at the moment."

****

The meeting in the Oval Office took place on schedule. After handshakes, Shilling invited the general to take a seat, and he did.

General Leonard Smolinsky, a member of the joint chiefs, had distinguished himself in the First Gulf War and Iraq. His body was no longer the lean, mean fighting machine of youth. Balding, bespectacled, and slightly stooped with a growing paunch, he looked like an absent-minded professor. He wore a prosthetic device on his lower right leg because his foot had been blown off by an IED in Iraq. But the great strength of his mental muscle, honed at Harvard Law School, was undiminished. Smolinski had been revered by the soldiers under his command, and his voice carried great weight in meetings of the joint chiefs.

"General, I need your advice on an urgent matter. A situation has recently arisen at Camp Pendleton. We are holding a person who has information vital to our national security. Unfortunately, that person has refused to cooperate with our interrogators…"

Smolinski interrupted, "with all due respect, sir, this is the first I've heard of this situation. Can you give me background?"

"For reasons that will become obvious, I want to limit the number of people who know about this operation. But I suppose I need to read you in. We have Stella Weiss, the L.A. Times reporter, in custody, and we're trying to learn the identity of her sources for the assassination story."

"You arrested a reporter?"

"I would prefer to say she's been detained, not actually under arrest."

"I don't give a damn what you call it, Mr. President. If you took Weiss and are holding her against her will, then it's kidnapping and false imprisonment. These are serious crimes. Is that what you did?"

"I'm afraid I had no choice."

"I'm sorry, Mr. president, but I can't be a party to these crimes." The four-star general stood up slowly and limped out of the Oval Office.

"Crap," said Shilling, "I hope we don't have a loose cannon now."

"Don't worry; he'll come around," said Stonehouse. "He likes his job. I'll make certain he knows it's in jeopardy if he doesn't keep his mouth shut."

"I'm afraid it's time for plan B, Stonehouse. Let's see if the CIA has what we need."

"Do you want me to summon Director Smalley now?"

"Yes, get him over here ASAP."

An hour later, Stonehouse led Adam Smalley into the Oval Office.

Smalley was of slight build and medium height. He had blue eyes and dark brown hair, graying at the temples. His thick glasses gave him an erudite appearance, though he could hardly be called a nerd or policy wonk. The late President Wahl had appointed Smalley as CIA director. He had been the head accountant for the tobacco lobby, but came highly recommended for the CIA post by someone at the Heritage Foundation. His tenure at the CIA had been marked by acrimonious relations with senior staff. They regarded him as an ignorant and unprincipled hack, willing to do anything to stay in the president's good graces.

Surprised by the unexpected summons to the Oval Office, Smalley asked, "so, Mr. President, what's this about?"

"Sorry to bring you in here on short notice, but we have a national security emergency and I need your help."

"Read me in, and I'll help in any way I can."

Concerned that Smalley might react like Smolinski when told the nature of the emergency, Shilling took another tack.

"You don't have to know any details right now. I can only say that a domestic terrorist is in custody, and we need to extract vital information from him. I know you have secret labs in several states. Do any of them work on truth serums?"

"Do you mean drugs like sodium pentothal?"

"Sort of like that, but much stronger, more effective."

"As a matter of fact, our Omaha lab has developed a very powerful truth serum. We've been testing it on a few high-value captives in Syria."

"And does it work?"

"Yes and no."

"What do you mean?"

"We've had a fair number of adverse reactions, but fortunately only one fatality. When it works, though, the results have been spectacular."

Shilling heard only "results have been spectacular." Intrigued, he asked, "how soon can we get this drug?"

"I can have it delivered to Washington this evening."

"We need it in Southern California."

"Well, in that case, I can have a batch flown there, if you wish."

The president sat silently, apparently deep in thought. Finally, he asked, "what if I send someone tomorrow to pick it up on his way to California?"

"Of course; I can arrange that."

"Perfect. Stonehouse, page Dr. Graninger for an urgent meeting in the Oval Office."

"Yes sir."

****

While they waited for Dr. Graninger's arrival, the president told Smalley, "I'll dispatch the doc to pick up the drug. He's on my staff and can be trusted. When he arrives at the lab, make sure he gets a full briefing on the drug's protocol."

"Consider it done, Mr. President."

When Dr. Graninger arrived, Shilling told him, "we have a mission for you. Tomorrow you will fly to Omaha and visit a lab to pick up a new truth serum."

Smalley, who had been texting with the Omaha lab, provided Dr. Graninger with the lab's address and a code number. "Give the code number to the receptionist, and he will retrieve the drug while you wait. Then he'll give you instructions on dosage and administration. The president will fill you in on the rest of the mission."

A bewildered but compliant Dr. Graninger said, "I understand."

Smalley asked, "will that be all, Mr. President?"

"Yes, that's all for now. I appreciate your assistance and remind you that this is a top-secret operation."

"I understand."

After Smalley left, Dr. Graninger asked, "what do I do with the truth serum?"

"You will fly on to San Diego, rent a car, and drive to Camp Pendleton. At Pendleton, you'll go to Commander Griswold's office. He'll be expecting you and will give you the rest of your assignment. All the while you will never let the drug out of your sight, and you will not mention this assignment to any living soul—ever."

"You can count on me."

"I know I can."

CHAPTER 51

MALCOLM TOOK HIS OWN CAR to Oceanside so he wouldn't have to waste time arranging for a rental. Traffic was heavy on Interstate 5, as usual. It was one of the many California freeways where rush hour begins at 5 a.m. and ends at 10 p.m.

Malcolm arrived at Oceanside in the late afternoon. He had reserved a room with his credit card at the Best Western just off I-5, so he didn't bother checking in yet. He was hungry and had been looking forward to eating dinner at Ruby's Diner at the end of the fishing pier.

He parked in the nearest lot and walked to the pier. As he strolled toward Ruby's and inhaled the invigorating ocean air, he was on the lookout for lucky anglers. But right now the Pacific was not giving up its piscine treasures.

Seated at a table with a northern view of the coast, he slowly savored his turkey burger with fries. Ruby's was always a good place to find comfort food. Malcolm passed on dessert because they no longer offered his favorite, marionberry pie.

Before leaving his office, Malcolm had googled "bars in Oceanside, CA." The city had an abundance of watering holes. He asked his waitress, who had lived in Oceanside her entire life, if she could recommend any bars favored by marines. She gave him several names, and he jotted them down in his small notebook. Young reporters took notes on their phones and tablets, but Malcolm was satisfied with his dinosaur technology. He thanked the waitress, and added a 25 percent tip to the credit card slip.

Retracing his steps to the parking lot, Malcolm saw a young boy reeling in a small fish. He stopped and watched the kid remove the hook. Neither Malcolm nor the angler could identify it. The scene brought back pleasant memories from his youth. Growing up near the Santa Monica pier, he and his friends often rode their bicycles there with a fishing rod tied to the horizontal bar and a tackle box in the rear basket. They seldom caught a keeper, but had fun gorging on hot dogs and greasy fries, and riding the bumper cars.

Malcolm couldn't imagine today's parents permitting their children to roam freely on the streets of L.A. Regrettably, he ruefully admitted, the media have helped create a culture of fear. Incidents involving children and strangers had not become more prevalent over the decades, but every crime was dutifully reported in print and electronic media, leaving the impression that L.A. was a far more dangerous place for children than it actually was.

Malcolm drove a short distance to the motel, checked into his room, and scrolled through his emails and news feeds. There were no important updates. Next, he looked at the messages on his office landline. He was still receiving calls in response to his story about Stella's disappearance: some were humorous, but a fair number were malicious. He was especially disturbed by the racist and anti-Semitic rants directed at Stella. After checking all the messages—they were unhelpful—he muttered to himself, "L.A. has so many goofballs."

****

Malcolm looked at his watch. It was 7:35 and time to go bar hopping. He wasn't much of a drinker and had never enjoyed the taste of alcohol. The social aspect of drinking he understood, and he could nurse one beer or martini for hours in the company of people he liked. Mixing with strangers in a bar would require social skills that had long lain dormant during his office-bound years as an editor. He hoped that his social skills were poised to revive now.

The first place he visited, Nite Owl, was crowded with noisy patrons, mostly marines, standing room only. This was not his kind of place, dark and somewhat forbidding, but he forced himself to zigzag his way to the bar. A sign on the wall said, "Domestic Beers Only." He eyed the bartender who wore a Harley Davidson jacket and was as bald as a honeydew melon. Malcolm ordered a Bud Lite. The bartender poured it, plunked the glass down, and said, "two bucks." Malcolm paid the tab with three singles. The bartender picked up the money and smirked.

Still standing and feeling out of place, Malcolm asked if the bartender knew of any strange happenings on the base. In return, he received a glare and a grunt. Malcolm tried again, but heard only grunts. Apparently, the bartender didn't want to converse with him. He left his untouched beer on the bar, and squeezed his way through the crowd to the door.

The second bar, Tank You, was a dive smelling of stale smoke even though lighting up inside was prohibited. Among the few patrons were half a dozen marines sitting at wooden, picnic-style tables on heavily worn bench seats. Both tables and benches were covered with carvings of names, initials, and witty sayings, such as "happy Thanksgiving to all my readers." Malcolm chuckled. On the red concrete floor were peanut shells that danced to the ear-splitting country music blasting from huge speakers on both sides of the bar. A sign above one speaker said, "no foreign beers, thank you for not asking."

The bartender was a muscular, fiftyish man with faded tattoos on his arms of shapely women. He shouted over the music, "what'll you have?"

Malcolm shouted in return, "how about a Miller Lite?"

He sipped the brew from the frosty mug, and began asking his questions. Unlike the bartender at the Nite Owl, this one was comfortable using words.

"There's always something strange going on at the base. You know, they store atom bombs there. Not too long ago a bomb floated out to sea, and they never found it. Probably reached Japan by now. Imagine another Hiroshima."

"I'd rather not. Anything else you can think of?"

"What are you, a cop?"

"No, I'm a reporter for the L.A. Times, and I'm trying to verify a rumor."

"Well, I can't help you."

Noting the slight hostility in the man's voice, Malcolm decided not to press further. "Thanks anyway. What do I owe you for the beer?"

"Three bucks."

Malcolm set a five on the bar and returned to his car. He was out of his comfort zone in these bars, no doubt viewed with suspicion. The night was shaping up to be long and unproductive.

CHAPTER 52

Maybe, thought Malcolm, the third bar, Bashful Bandit, would be the charm. He walked in and spotted a few marines in uniform and a dozen or so other drinkers. In this mixed crowd, he didn't feel so conspicuous. The interior furnishings were strictly functional with minimal decoration. Dim lights in glass globes hung from the ceiling. Mottled beige Formica was the material of choice for tabletops and even the bar. A sign advertised the availability of dozens of craft and foreign beers. Malcolm approached the bartender, a man in his thirties with long black hair, olive skin and a full, well-trimmed beard.

"I'll have a Dos Equis." Any Mexican beer, Malcolm believed, had a richer taste than any American beer. The bartender popped the cap off the frosty bottle, gave him a glass, and asked for $3.50. He laid a five on the bar and began nursing his beer.

Watching the bartender drying and stacking glasses, Malcolm finally made his move.

"I'm Malcolm Klein, and I'm a reporter for the L.A. Times."

With a twinkle in his eye, the bartender asked, "are you doing a story about the skinny dippers by the pier, or are you just looking for trouble?"

"Neither, actually. I was hoping you could point me in the right direction."

"If I had a compass maybe I would," he said with a hearty belly laugh.

Malcolm chuckled reflexively.

"Seriously, Malcolm, what do you need?"

"I've heard rumors that something out of the ordinary took place on the base recently. Have you heard about anything like that?"

He looked long and hard at Malcolm, taking his measure, and asked, "is this off the record?"

"If that's what you want. Of course."

"One of my regulars is a chopper pilot, and he's been awfully peevish lately. I figured he was having family problems. Military wives have it hard, you know. And he's got some kids, too. After his second drink two nights ago, he finally loosened up enough to tell me what was going on. Turns out it had nothing do with his family. He began ranting about some weird mission."

"Do you know anything about where he went or what he did?"

"To L.A., I think. But I can't imagine why that would make him so upset."

Malcolm could hardly contain his excitement—and apprehension. Maybe, he hoped, this pilot had ferried Stella to Camp Pendleton.

"Do you think he'll be coming in tonight?"

"Don't know. Hang around, buy another beer. Maybe he'll drop in."

Malcolm ponied up another five for a second Dos Equis even though he'd barely touched the first.

"Thanks, I'll wait and see if he shows. By the way, what's his name?"

"I call him Don. We don't use last names around here."

"What does Don look like?"

"Pretty ordinary. I'll let you know if he comes in."

"Thanks."

****

Waiting for Don, Malcolm spent time on Facebook and kept refreshing several news sites. Not much happening tonight, he concluded. It was close to 11:30, and a tired Malcolm was about ready to pack it in. The reporter turned around and saw a white man entering the bar.

He seemed ordinary enough: a standard-issue buzz cut, clean shaven, undistinguished features, and wearing a camouflage outfit.

"Don," said the bartender, and shot Malcolm a "that's him" look. The reporter sat tight, letting Don order his drink, vodka on the rocks with a twist of lemon. Don sat down two stools away from Malcolm. He pulled his drink closer and dribbled in a few drops of lemon. After his first sip, he sighed and muttered, "just what the doctor ordered."

"Long day?" asked Malcolm.

"Just another day in paradise," was his sarcastic reply, neither hostile nor friendly.

"I was wondering, can I have a few words with you?"

"Go for it. As, you can see, I'm not terribly busy right now."

Malcolm changed stools and moved next to Don, thinking about how to make his approach.

"I'm a reporter from the L.A. Times, investigating a rumor about unusual happenings at Camp Pendleton."

"Is that right?" said Don, neutrally.

"Have you heard anything along those lines?"

He stared at Malcolm for a long time, thinking about the dangers his answer might pose for his career in the Marine Corps.

Finally, he said, "let's find a booth where we won't be overheard."

Malcolm's adrenaline began pumping and his heart pounded so loudly he thought even Don could hear the thump-thumping. They stood up and found an empty booth in the far corner of the bar, away from other patrons.

"I know some things. But if you write a story you can't use my name."

"I don't even know your name."

"It's Don, but I'm the only Don who pilots choppers. So, don't mention Don."

Malcolm took out his notebook and began writing. "Okay, I'll treat you as an anonymous source. So, what kind of things do you know?"

Don scanned the bar, took a long sip of his vodka, and said, "I had a mission a few days ago that made my stomach churn—and it wasn't air turbulence." He paused and gazed down at his drink.

"Please go on."

"I got the order from my squadron leader who said the mission was a matter of national security. Lucky me. My co-pilot and I were ordered to stand by in my Huey to take on two marines in civvies, a man and a woman, and fly them north to the Santa Monica City Airport. After they boarded, neither said a word to me on the brief flight. And I couldn't hear them talking to each other. After we landed, they ordered us to stay put until they returned."

Malcolm's excitement was rising, but he tried hard to stay in control.

"Had you ever seen these marines before?"

"I don't think so. There are thousands of people at Camp Pendleton, and I've never seen most of them."

"Do you have any idea who the two people might have been?"

"It's not rocket science. They were special ops."

"So, you're parked at the airport. Then what happened?"

"We waited a few minutes and a black SUV with dark windows pulled up. I assumed it was an Uber or government-issue. My passengers got out, opened the doors to the SUV, and got in. After they drove off, I cooled my heels in the Huey. It must have been two or three hours later when the same car returned."

"And then?"

"The back door opened and three people got out. The two marines and a woman. She was handcuffed, blindfolded, and gagged. The poor woman was resisting with all her might, so they picked her up and carried her into my Huey. They removed the gag but left the blindfold and handcuffs on. And then I flew them back to Pendleton."

Malcolm's excitement had reached a fever pitch; he feared he might have a heart attack. He began to take slow, measured breaths.

"Can you describe the woman?"

"She was Black, maybe in her thirties or forties. She was wearing jeans and a blue blouse. Kind of pretty for a woman that old."

Malcolm was ecstatic, for this woman had to be Stella. The Joker's tip had paid off. Stella was at Camp Pendleton, unharmed he hoped. He briefly wondered why the Marine Corps—as opposed to any other

191

feds—had staged this operation, and then it came to him. Robert and Roberta had downed a marine helicopter and killed marines. Was this payback or was there a larger conspiracy at work?

Don continued his story. "In the Huey she started flailing around and screaming. She caused such a ruckus that one of the marines shoved a gun in her ribs. That calmed her down for the rest of the trip."

"Then what happened?"

"They told me to return to base."

"And after you arrived?"

"They carried the woman, who was still resisting, to a waiting car. I don't know where they took her."

"You say this was a few days ago?"

"Yeah."

"Do you know if she's still at Pendleton?"

"I have no idea. What I do know is I didn't fly her again. I don't know what they were up to, but it looked like a kidnapping to me. Maybe they had their reasons. I'll tell you this, though, the entire operation made me very uneasy."

"I can see why."

"Do you have any idea who this woman was?"

Malcolm's first thought was to tell Don the truth. On second thought, he decided it was a bad idea because not even Stella's parents knew yet what had happened to her. He would have to keep Don in the dark.

"I can only tell you that this woman is a close friend of mine who disappeared suddenly."

"Then it was a kidnapping and I was part of it? Shit!"

"Don, you have been an amazing help. Don't worry, you're not part of the problem. Before I go, would you be willing to give me your cell number?"

"I suppose so."

"Thank you."

Malcolm laid a Ben Franklin on the table and said, "take your family to dinner."

"Thanks."

"Here's my card in case you find out more about the woman's current whereabouts. I've written my personal cell number on the back."

Malcolm stood up and shook Don's hand. On his way out he stopped and thanked the bartender with a twenty.

****

Running into Don was sheer luck, and Malcolm knew it. He only hoped his luck would last so he could find Stella and bring her home. He left the bar and drove a short distance to the Best Western where he checked in. In room 244 he fleshed out the notes he had taken while talking to Don. His visit to Oceanside had turned out well so far, but he had some thinking to do before making his next move.

He reluctantly admitted to himself that the most appropriate move was to contact Joanna Bartolo. He should tell her what he had learned from Don. Malcolm agonized over the decision, irritated that he—not the FBI—had developed the information. If a hacker and a reporter could figure it out, why couldn't the FBI? After all, they were one of the most respected law-enforcement agencies in the world—and certainly the best funded. The more he thought about it, the less inclined he was to share his information with the FBI. And he didn't.

Maybe, concluded Malcolm, it was time to find out what the base commander knew about the incident. He looked him up: General Otis Griswold, a highly decorated marine.

CHAPTER 53

JOANNA BARTOLO WAS ANXIOUS to receive a briefing from the team investigating other federal agencies for possible involvement in the Weiss disappearance. Today's daily report resembled the earlier ones. Her agents had found no hint that the CIA, NSA, DHS or any of the other alphabet-soup intelligence agencies had mounted the operation. Because kidnapping a civilian would have been a top-secret op, maybe the responsible agency had maintained an effective shroud of silence around it. No way to know, she acknowledged in frustration.

Her team had apparently exhausted all possibilities—except one. President Shilling was Commander in Chief of the Armed Forces. He could order any branch of the military services to undertake special missions, even start a war if he were so inclined. She knew that Shilling shared Wahl's profound distrust of the FBI. That meant her team would have to tread lightly in trying to learn of any White House involvement in the kidnapping.

When Bartolo arrived at her office the next morning, she found a brief report in her inbox. It was from the Honolulu field office. Agents had combed through surveillance videos in Terminal 2 of the airport. They pinpointed a woman who almost certainly was Stella Weiss; she was wearing a large floppy hat and oversize sunglasses. She had entered the departure area for Fiji Airlines. According to the video's time code, she most likely left Honolulu on a Samoa-bound flight. The agents had checked with Fiji Airlines but found no Stella

Weiss on the flight manifest. Apparently, the agents concluded, she must have been traveling on fraudulent documents. There were 57 women aboard that flight, but which one was Weiss? Bartolo knew it would be impossible to single her out with the information in hand.

Bartolo sat back in her chair and shook her head. She was thrilled with the progress, but it wasn't all good news. Samoa was a foreign country. If the woman was Weiss and she had met Robert and Roberta there, the trail would be difficult to follow. Samoa was a proudly independent nation that had no extradition treaty with the United States. The Samoan government might not welcome FBI agents working a case in their country. It was time to consult with Director Abel.

****

Bartolo called upstairs and, after claiming that her call was urgent, she was put through to Director Abel. Bartolo delivered the surprising news she had just received from Honolulu.

"Well, Bartolo, I guess that's a good-news, bad-news situation. We're now in a difficult position. Hang on while I check something."

After a few moments the director reported, "we don't have any agents on the ground in Samoa. If the country is harboring the assassins, this could become a delicate situation. I don't want to precipitate an international incident."

"So, what course of action do you recommend?"

"Well, I could inform the CIA and let them take it from here. They have an infinitely greater capability for international covert ops. But I'd hate to see them close the case when we could do it. And we could use a good score. Smalley is an arrogant prick, and I don't want to give him the lead. I know we're supposed to be collaborating, but... let me think."

While Abel was thinking, Bartolo asked, "among our many thousands of special agents nationwide, do we have any married couples?"

"There's a married couple in Las Vegas, Aisha and Shawan Washington. We all went through Quantico together."

"Why not send them on a South Seas vacation? A married couple won't raise suspicions."

"That's an interesting idea, Bartolo. They could cruise below the radar as tourists and maybe turn up Robert and Roberta. It's a long shot, but I don't see a better option at this point. If we fail, the CIA can pick up where we leave off."

"Yeah, let's give it shot."

"We shouldn't get our hopes up, though. After all, the woman might not be Weiss. And even if Robert and Roberta are in Samoa, our agents might never find them. But it's worth a try. Before I pull the Washingtons from Vegas and give them a new assignment, let's put together an IT task force to see what we can learn from here."

"That's a good idea, director."

"I'll ask them to find surveillance videos from the Samoa airport and vicinity, and also search government records for U.S. visitors, and so on. I'll give them free reign to hack Samoa."

"If they do find Robert and Roberta by hacking Samoan servers, won't our courts throw out the evidence?"

"We had a similar case recently using information hacked from another country. Our attorneys argued that we broke no U.S. laws in obtaining the incriminating evidence of drug trafficking. The federal district judge agreed, and the information was admitted into evidence. The man was convicted. Admittedly, this is a gray area of law, and I suppose we could lose that case on appeal. For now, though, our attorneys believe that foreign cyber-crime laws don't shackle U.S. law-enforcement efforts. In any event, I'll instruct the IT people to report directly to me."

"That's fine, director. I have enough on my plate right now."

CHAPTER 54

STELLA'S PARENTS WERE DISPLEASED with the desultory effort the LAPD was putting into the search for their daughter. The detective assigned to the case was in complete denial, contriving alternate scenarios to account for what he called "her vanishing act." No, Rachel and Daniel insisted, she hadn't run off with a lover or taken an unannounced vacation. The detective seemed willing to consider anything but kidnapping. He even quipped, "it's almost as if she was plucked from Earth by space aliens." The Weisses were not amused. The detective reported that the crime scene team had found no useful evidence in Stella's apartment; and no neighbor on her floor had seen or heard anything unusual. The L.A. police tried pinging her computer and phone, but their GPS systems were unresponsive.

Frustrated with the LAPD's lack of progress, the Weisses were on the verge of hiring a private detective when FBI agents Carrington and Suarez paid them a visit. From now on, the agents said, Stella's disappearance was a federal case. Annoyed by the family's persistent questions, the LAPD had willingly surrendered the lead to the FBI. The Weisses were delighted by this turn of events.

CHAPTER 55

STELLA'S UNHAPPY CAPTORS MADE THEIR NEXT MOVE. They arrived with another masked man who carried in what looked like an old-fashioned doctor's bag.

Laurel and Hardy grabbed Stella and held her down while the newcomer loaded a syringe with a vile-looking liquid. He tapped for a good vein in the vicinity of her left elbow, and emptied the syringe into it.

"Now we'll make rapid progress," remarked a hopeful Laurel.

The man didn't bother to mention that he had injected Stella with an experimental truth serum developed by a secret government lab. Stella was an unwitting guinea pig.

Hardy took charge and began questioning Stella. She closed her eyes and mumbled incoherently. Her head began swaying back and forth, and in a final motion she slumped forward, out cold.

Hardy asked the doctor, "is this supposed to happen?"

"Hell, no. According to the information I received about the drug, we should be having a productive conversation by now. I'm afraid she's having an adverse reaction."

"Can you wake her up?"

"I don't know."

"Try shaking her."

He did but with no effect. "It's no use. I think she's slipped into a coma."

"How long will she stay this way?" asked a worried Hardy.

"God only knows."

Laurel opined, "if she dies on us, we could be peeling potatoes in the mess hall for the rest of our lives—or worse."

Hardy ignored Laurel's black humor and began tapping on her phone.

"Yes, I need to speak to Commander Griswold ASAP. Tell him we have an emergency situation in Building C."

"Griswold here. What's the emergency?"

"The subject apparently went into a coma after the doc administered the drug."

"Oh shit. Do you think she's in danger of dying?"

"I don't know, and the doc doesn't know either. He was taken by surprise but admitted that the drug has caused adverse reactions before."

"Does she have any idea about where she is and who's been questioning her?"

"I don't think she has a clue she's at Pendleton. In fact, she kept asking, 'where am I?'"

"That's good. At this point, let's prepare to abort the president's mission. If she dies here, we'd have a lot of explaining to do. If her condition doesn't improve, we'll have to take her to an off-base hospital. Does the doctor think she's stable, not in immediate danger?"

"Let me ask him."

"Doc, is she stable right now?"

"Her respiration is shallow and her pulse is slow, but she's stable."

"Commander, she seems stable for now."

"Okay. Let's keep her under observation. If she doesn't improve by tonight, you'll have to deliver her to...um...let's say, a UCSD hospital."

"Yes, sir. Will do."

****

The group moved Stella onto the cot, and Laurel and Hardy left her in the doctor's care. They checked on her condition periodically during the day, but the only change was an improvement in her vital signs.

Shortly after 9 p.m., Laurel uttered the pronouncement, "President Shilling's experiment is at an end." Dr. Graninger grimly nodded in agreement.

Commander Griswold had sent an unmarked van for their use. They carried Stella through a dark corridor, down a flight of stairs, and into a loading zone where they placed her on the van's filthy floor.

It was almost 10:30 when the van pulled into the drop-off area near the hospital's emergency entrance. Hardy scouted the waiting room and reported back that it seemed unusually crowded for a week-day evening. That augured well for their distasteful mission. They carried Stella inside, and quickly but gently put her in a chair near the entrance. They departed nonchalantly without looking back. The receptionist at the intake center, seated on the other side of the room, was too busy to notice the latest arrival. Stella was now free but pos-sibly dying.

CHAPTER 56

LATER THAT NIGHT, after the crowd in the waiting room had thinned out, the receptionist, Irma Halperin, first noticed the disheveled Black woman sitting alone, slumped in her chair. Even at a distance, Halperin could see that Stella's hair was a messy tangle, and her blouse was stained with "god knows what." Food, she hoped. She walked over and tried to rouse her, but Stella didn't stir. Halperin saw no purse and concluded the woman was indigent and lacked insurance. Another welfare drop, she surmised, and mused aloud, "I hate these charity cases, but the law says we have to treat them. They're such a drain on hospital resources."

She paged a resident on duty, Dr. James Wessel, who soon joined Halperin at Stella's side. The reporter was still unconscious, leaning precariously to her right, on the verge of tipping over. Dr. Wessel supported her while Halperin called for an orderly to fetch a wheelchair. When it arrived, they gently lifted her into the chair and rolled her to curtain 4 inside the treatment area. Nurses took off her soiled clothes, dressed her in a hospital gown, and placed her clothing and shoes in a clear plastic bag labeled "Jane Doe #3."

Dr. Wessel, young and still at the steep end of the learning curve, sensed that this case was unusual. An apparently healthy woman, with no outward signs of head injury or other trauma, was unconscious, probably in a coma. He searched for evidence of chronic IV drug use, but found none. Dr. Wessel didn't want to miss anything, so he ordered a battery of tests, including a drug screen, comprehensive blood work, and CT and fMRI brain scans. Perhaps the functional MRI could pinpoint areas of diminished brain activity.

The entire suite of test results became available early the next day. An exhausted Dr. Wessel, who had been on duty for 22 hours, couldn't make sense of the results. He decided to call in Dr. Elias Braverman for a neuro consult. A national leader in brain research and an esteemed professor in the UCSD School of Medicine, Dr. Braverman arrived about an hour later. Dr. Wessel gave him a brief introduction to the case and handed him an iPad that displayed the woman's chart.

Dr. Braverman spent a few minutes reviewing the test results. "This is a most interesting case. Thank you for bringing it to my attention."

On a second pass, he read the chart closely and shook his head. Although she had arrived dehydrated with low electrolytes, they were now in the normal range. And there was no sign of brain damage. The fMRI indicated to him that she was just below the threshold of consciousness. He believed she had a good prognosis for a full recovery. Curiously, there were traces of an unidentified substance, perhaps psychotropic, in her blood.

"I'm mystified," said Dr. Braverman, "but I suspect she was given a drug that didn't show up in the drug screen."

Wessel said, "I did notice some redness at an apparent injection site on her left arm. But she had no other signs of IV drug use and her vitals were stable, so I didn't give her Naloxone or Narcan."

"That was a smart move because it avoided potential interactions with the unknown drug."

"What do you suggest?"

"Let's admit her to the ICU for observation. If she remains stable for 24 hours and has no seizures, we'll move her into a hospital room. In the meantime, let's go visit her. As you know, for me a patient is more than a series of tests. And get a swab from that injection site and send it to the lab."

Dr. Braverman stood by Stella's bed and stared at her face. He muttered to himself, "there's something familiar about this woman, but I can't quite place her."

Stella was moved to the ICU and connected to several monitoring devices. The nurse washed her face and combed her hair. Taking a good look at Stella for the first time, she also had an inkling that the face was familiar.

CHAPTER 57

MALCOLM PERUSED THE FOOD offerings at the motel's breakfast bar. Too agitated to eat, he wolfed down a cup of coffee. After the abbreviated breakfast, he returned to his room and prepared to visit Camp Pendleton. The Joker's tip had paid off, and his conversation with Don confirmed that Stella had been abducted and brought to the base. Malcolm was furious but knew he would have to control his emotions. He would gain no advantage by pissing off a marine general.

At the guardhouse Malcolm showed his ID, car registration, and proof of insurance, and he was allowed to enter. He asked for, and received, directions to a parking area near the commander's office. The reporter drove slowly through the sprawling base, following the marine's instructions. After parking, he entered the building and found the reception area in Commander Griswold's office complex.

Malcolm approached the receptionist, Lance Corporal Maria Romero. She was young, probably in her early twenties, with brown hair cropped short. Her striking black eyes were firmly fixed on her phone.

Malcolm asked, "may I please speak to Commander Griswold?"

"What time is your appointment?"

"I don't have an appointment. I'm Malcolm Klein, a reporter for the L.A. Times, and I need to see him about an urgent matter." He handed her a business card.

She responded mechanically, "if you're a reporter, you should be talking to someone in our Media Engagement Office."

He came closer to her and raised his voice. "I'm sorry, Ms. Romero. I guess I didn't make myself sufficiently clear. This may be a matter of life and death."

Romero finally put down her phone, looked up at her insistent visitor, and said, "wait a minute."

Before she could pick up the office phone, Malcolm added, "tell him who I am. And tell him I know he kidnapped my reporter Stella Weiss and is holding her prisoner."

Romero made the call. On the phone with the general, she repeated Malcolm's brazen introduction, almost word for word. She ended the call, and a moment later the commander himself barreled out his office and confronted the reporter. Not intimidated by the six-foot-two general looming over him, Malcolm put out his hand and introduced himself. The general shook it and led him into the cavernous office. Malcolm looked around and saw many mementoes of Marine Corps campaigns, including maps and images from America's many recent wars. Also visible, on his desk, were pictures of the general's wife and two children.

Without inviting the reporter to sit down, the general said, "Klein, what's this nonsense about a kidnapping?"

"It's not nonsense. You brought Stella Weiss here against her will and are holding her prisoner. I have witnesses who can confirm it was a kidnapping. I demand you release her to me immediately."

The general moved slowly to the plush leather chair behind his desk and sat down. Malcolm knew the general had been caught off guard and was thinking up a response. His stalling was a significant tell.

"Klein, I can't release her because we don't have her."

"Sir, that's a flat-out lie. I know she's here."

"Well, I don't know where you're getting your information, Mr. Klein, but you're dead wrong. She is not here."

"I wish I could believe you, but I don't."

"Listen up, Klein. Even if she had been brought here, as you claim, it would have been an entirely legitimate operation."

"Since when is it a 'legitimate operation' to kidnap an innocent civilian, especially a reporter just doing her job?"

General Griswold was losing patience. How could the reporter not understand that the government occasionally did unpleasant things because it had to? Finally, he blurted out, "Klein, sometimes these operations are matters of national security. You don't want to stick your nose in where it doesn't belong."

"I'm afraid, general, you have that ass-backwards. The Marine Corps is interfering in the exercise of the press' First Amendment rights. You cannot legally force a reporter to reveal her sources."

"Klein, let me set you straight. In matters of national security, the president has wide latitude to act in the country's best interest."

Griswold realized he'd said too much and backpedalled. "That was a hypothetical, of course. The president has a variety of special powers. We all know that."

Malcolm didn't want to let the general off the hook. "So, General Griswold, are you saying that orders for this operation came down directly from the White House?"

Griswold averted his eyes from Malcolm, which the reporter took as another tell. "I'm saying nothing of the sort. Don't put words in my mouth."

"With all due respect, your own words implied that the president played the national security card. It's a bogus play. Stella Weiss does not threaten national security."

"As I said, that was a hypothetical. In any event, it's up to the president to determine when national security interests are at stake."

"Let me repeat: release Ms. Weiss immediately into my custody…"

Interrupting, the general boomed, "or what?"

"Or tomorrow's headline in the L.A. Times will blow up this special op. I'll finger you as the villain. Would you be eager to testify to a congressional committee about your role in the kidnapping? I think not. They'll put you on the hot seat, and President Shilling won't pull your chestnuts out of the fire."

Commander Griswold said nothing for a long while. He wanted to arrest Malcolm, but that would only make matters worse. Maybe, he thought, the reporter was bluffing. In fact, he was sure of it. Maybe

Klein had heard some third-hand scuttlebutt, hardly newsworthy. But actual witnesses? Highly unlikely.

"Mr. Klein, our conversation is over. I'm calling your bluff. I don't believe you have anything to report, so I'm not concerned about tomorrow's headline in the Times. Please leave my office now, before I call security to escort you out."

"This has been a most interesting conversation, General Griswold. You'll regret not turning Ms. Weiss over to me."

"Trust me, Klein, she's not here."

"Whatever."

****

Malcolm left the commander's office, and Griswold closed the door behind him. As the reporter walked slowly through the reception area, mulling over what he had just heard, Ms. Romero waved him to her desk. In a whisper she said, "take this." He took the folded piece of paper she offered, immediately stuffed it into a pants pocket, and hurried out the door.

On the way to his car, Malcolm unfolded the paper and saw the ominous words: "UCSD medical." Oh shit, this can't be good, he said to himself.

Before he started the engine, his cell sounded off. Malcolm looked at the caller ID. It was Alice. He hadn't updated her since leaving L.A.

"Good morning, Alice. What's new in your world?"

"I was about to ask you the same question."

"I do have news. Marines abducted Stella and brought her to Camp Pendleton."

"Are you serious? Camp Pendleton?" Alice raised her voice, "now I know why you didn't want to tell me the real reason for your visit to Oceanside."

"Sorry, Alice. I was afraid if you knew, you wouldn't approve the trip and might turn the information over to the feds."

"Malcolm, sometimes you don't give me enough credit. I was a reporter once. And don't you forget it!"

"Alice, I know you were, and a damn good one, too. At any rate, I'm at Camp Pendleton right now. This is a large base with a huge population, but I don't have to search it because she's gone."

"How do you know that?"

"A few minutes ago I got a tip from an insider who directed me to UCSD medical. I assume that's a hospital."

"Damn. I hope Stella's okay."

"I'm really worried. If the tip is correct, she's probably in the hospital because the marines harmed her."

"How did you find out she was at the base? Did you talk to anyone there?"

"Yeah, last night at a bar I ran into the helicopter pilot who flew her to Pendleton. He wasn't happy about the operation because Stella was obviously being abducted. I think he'd be a good witness if this ever reaches a courtroom."

"Terrific."

"This morning I bullied my way into Commander Griswold's office. He fed me some crap but at the same time gave away the whole show."

"How so?"

"From what he told me, I infer that Stella's abduction was ordered by none other than—wait for the drumroll—President Shilling."

"Oh my god, Malcolm. Are you sure it was Shilling?"

"Absolutely. Griswold said the president as commander in chief had the right to undertake this operation in the name of national security. When I pressed him on it, he denied having revealed that his orders had come from the White House, but his tells left no doubt in my mind."

"National security my ass. What a crock. If that were the case, then national security could be used as a cover for any crime. This is truly insidious. Shilling is undermining the rule of law just as Wahl did. Malcolm, get this story. Stay as long as you have to. But—oh god—please be careful. There's no telling how far Shilling will go now that he's already pulled off a kidnapping. Griswold knows you're on the case, so you may be a target now."

"Don't worry, Alice; I love my life. I won't take any unnecessary risks."

"What's next on your agenda—as if I didn't know?"

"Of course. I'm going to the hospital to look for Stella."

"Let me know immediately if you find her."

"I will, right after I call her parents."

"So long Malcolm. And good luck."

CHAPTER 58

COMMANDER GRISWOLD HAD BEEN STEWING in his office after Malcolm left, trying to compose his next update for the president. He also googled Malcolm Klein.

"Romero, put in a call to President Shilling."

"Yes, sir."

A few minutes later she told Commander Griswold that the president was in a meeting and unavailable.

"Thanks."

While he waited for the callback, Griswold continued to agonize over what to tell the president. Klein's visit was not good news; there was no way to sugar-coat it.

An hour later, Romero transferred Shilling's call.

"Mr. President, thank you for getting back to me. We have another problem."

"Another problem? Like what, general?"

"An L.A. Times reporter by the name of Malcolm Klein came sniffing around earlier today. I looked him up. He's a managing editor, probably Weiss' boss. He hasn't published his own investigation in years, but he's on this one like flies on shit. I'm thinking maybe Klein and Weiss are lovers."

"So, general, what's the bottom line here?"

"He claimed to know we had her and threatened to publish a page-one story tomorrow on the abduction."

210

"I hope, general, that you have him under control."

"I'm not sure what you mean by that, sir."

"You know exactly what I mean."

"Mr. President, I respected your right, as commander in chief, to order me to pick up and interrogate Stella Weiss because she posed a threat to national security. But what would be the justification for detaining a second reporter?"

"We have to prevent knowledge of the Weiss operation from becoming public—at all costs."

"I don't get it. The operation has failed, and Weiss may never regain consciousness. I say, let's cut our losses now. Even if she regains consciousness, she's not going to know where she was or who was in the room with her. We were very careful, and I'm confident we're protected. But if we hold Klein, it's a virtual certainty that he'll be reported missing. And then we'll have every investigative reporter in the country working the story. They'll find a weak link somewhere and your goose will be cooked."

"Is that a threat, general?"

"No, no. Of course not, Mr. President. It is a simple calculation based on our slight degree of exposure. Don't order me to detain Klein. No good can come of it."

"What if he knows enough to get the FBI or Congress all riled up?"

"Up to now, I think he's bluffing. I don't see how he could have obtained any hard evidence about the operation. I think we're okay. He's not going to publish a story based on a few rumors."

"I suppose you have a point. Leave Klein alone—for the present. But you might encourage him to stay away from Camp Pendleton. How do you suppose he knew to go to Camp Pendleton in the first place?"

"I wish I could answer that question. I've been half crazy trying to envision who might have leaked at this end. But I'm confident our operation is watertight. My hunch is that the leak came from the White House."

"That's simply impossible."

211

"If you say so, sir."

Shilling ended the call and turned to Stonehouse, who had been listening on speakerphone. "What do you think?"

"He's afraid this situation is going to spiral out of control and leave him holding the bag. If he goes down, he could very well take you with him."

"That's what I'm afraid of. Do you have any suggestions, Stonehouse?"

"I think we have to wait it out. There's nothing we can do at this end. Not now, anyway."

"Hmm. I guess you're right. Unfortunately, my options are limited. What do we do if Klein publishes an article?"

"We issue a blanket denial and accuse him of putting out fake news to sell more papers and harm your reputation."

"Yeah, I can live with that."

"Mr. President, in 10 minutes you have a meeting with the chief lobbyist for the American Pork Council."

"Right. Send in Miss Piggy as soon as she arrives."

A chuckling Stonehouse said, "of course."

CHAPTER 59

FEELING A LITTLE FAINT after his stressful confrontation with General Griswold, Malcolm knew he needed some sustenance. While he looked for a place to eat in Oceanside, he pondered Alice's warning. He hadn't thought about it before, but now realized that he could be in as much danger as Stella. The president, he was confident, had directed a criminal conspiracy. How far would Shilling go to protect his illegal operation? Malcolm wasn't the paranoid type, but from now on he would be much more vigilant. Shilling had many tools at his disposal to deal with someone who might threaten his presidency.

Following the familiar path to the pier and monitoring the rearview mirror for tails, Malcolm ate lunch at Ruby's. While waiting for his meal to arrive, he googled "UCSD medical" on his phone. The results surprised him, as there were a half dozen UCSD medical facilities in the La Jolla and San Diego areas. He assumed that Stella would have been taken to an emergency room. So he googled "UCSD emergency room." There were two: one in La Jolla and the other in a large medical complex in San Diego.

Feeling better after lunch, Malcolm walked back to his car and looked up directions to the La Jolla ER, which was closest to Oceanside. He started his car and drove south on I-5 until he reached his exit, Genesee Avenue. Navigating a couple more streets, Malcolm came to 9434 Medical Center Dr. He parked and strode quickly to the ER entrance. Fortunately, it wasn't crowded, so he stepped up to the receptionist and asked, "have you treated a Stella Weiss recently, say in the past few days?"

She said brusquely, "I'm prohibited from giving out patient information."

"I'm only interested in knowing if she was brought to this facility."

"I can give you that much. What was that name again?"

"Stella Weiss. W-E-I-S-S."

"Let me check." She keyboarded briefly, then turned back to Malcolm and said, "I'm sorry; we haven't treated a Weiss."

Malcolm was stumped. He wondered if her captors had tortured her, maybe just left her in the ER, totally incapacitated.

"What if someone were dropped off here without identification and couldn't talk? Would you treat that person?"

"The law says we have to provide treatment in those cases. I'll check to see if any Jane Does came in recently."

She turned back to the screen, tapped a few keys, and said, "nope. No Jane Doe since two weeks ago Sunday."

****

A downcast Malcolm said thanks and returned to his car. One more chance, he glumly thought, as he returned to I-5, then switched to I-8 eastbound and followed Google's directions to the UCSD Medical Center-Hillcrest on West Arbor Drive. At the medical center's parking structure, he took a ticket from the machine and drove in. He found an open space, parked, and chirped the doors locked. The ER entrance was on Front Street, so he walked east on Arbor, and turned left on Front. Another block and he was finally at the ER.

The ER's waiting area was much busier than the one in La Jolla. He padded his way to the receptionist, a young woman of East Asian ancestry with a ready smile. He decided to play the journalist card.

"Hi. I'm Malcolm Klein, a senior reporter and managing editor at the L.A. Times. Maybe you saw my story about Stella Weiss, the reporter who went missing?"

"No, I'm afraid not."

"Well, I have reason to believe she was brought to this hospital within the past few days. She might have been dropped off here with no ID and unable to speak."

The receptionist had been listening intently and said, "I can check to see if we treated a patient by that name. If that doesn't get a hit, I'll try our Jane Does. How do you spell Weiss?"

"W-E-I-S-S."

"Sorry, no Stella Weiss. Let me see here. Well, we've had run of welfare drops lately."

Malcolm raised his eyebrows and said, "she's a Black woman in her late thirties."

She scrolled through a screen and triumphantly exclaimed, "we have a Jane Doe #3 who fits that description."

Malcolm could barely contain his excitement. He felt strongly that he was getting closer to liberating Stella.

"Where is she now?"

"She's been admitted to the hospital. I need to call my supervisor to let him know the good news that we likely have an ID on JD3. By the way, does she have insurance?"

Malcolm did a double take at the tacky question but held his tongue, merely saying, "of course."

"That's good. Do you have her insurance information?"

He glared at the woman in disbelief. "No, I don't have that information, but I can probably have someone at the Times send it down. Can I see her now?"

"Yes, but please wait here for my boss to escort you to her room. She was in the ICU for a day, but the consulting neurologist said it was okay to move her into a hospital room."

CHAPTER 60

TEN MINUTES LATER, as Malcolm stood by the receptionist, a handsome, middle-aged Black man wearing a dark blue suit walked up to him and said, I presume you're here to make the ID on JD3?"

Malcolm was nonplussed by how quickly this man got down to business, even before introductions. Instead of answering the question, Malcolm said, "I'm Malcolm Klein from the L.A. Times. I'm here to find my missing colleague, not to solve your billing problem."

The other man recognized his faux pas and said, "I'm sorry. Let me begin again. I'm John Morrill, Assistant Director of Emergency Services. I'm going to escort you to JD3's room and, hopefully, witness a positive ID."

"Nice to meet you, Mr. Morrill. Let's go."

As they walked, Morrill asked, "I take it you two are very close?"

"We've worked together at the L.A. Times for almost two decades. I mentored her while she was still in college, and I've watched her develop into one of the country's most respected investigative reporters."

They continued to make small talk while working their way through the maze of gray hallways. Malcolm decided the less Morrill knew about how she ended up in the hospital, the better. Finally, they took an elevator to the sixth floor, and Morrill led the way to room 634.

"She's in the far bed."

Malcolm walked past the other patient in 634 until he reached JD3.

Once he saw her face, Malcolm's eyes began glistening and he exclaimed, "oh, thank god. It's Stella."

A voice from the next bed said, "don't bother trying to wake her up, she's in a coma and can't talk."

Malcolm turned to Morrill. "Is that true?"

"Yes, she's in a coma, but I don't know anything more about her condition, and if I did, I couldn't tell you."

"I understand. The HIPAA gag at work."

"Yes. So, you're sure she's…what was her name again?"

"Stella Weiss."

"Right. I'll come back with some paperwork for you to sign. In the meantime, it's still visiting hours so you can sit down by her bed if you like."

"Thanks, I'll do that. I'm going to call her parents and let them know. They've been worried sick. I expect they'll want to come down here as soon as possible."

"Where do they live?"

"In the L.A. area."

****

Morrill left, and Malcolm moved one of the green plastic chairs next to Stella's bed and sat down. He studied her face closely but saw no trace of an injury. And no casts or bandages were visible. She was peacefully dreaming, her eyes moving rapidly under their lids.

During this calm interlude, Malcolm took stock of his surroundings and Stella's medical accessories. She was hooked up to an IV and several monitors, one that provided a continuous display of her blood pressure and pulse. He knew that a BP of 102 over 68 was good. Her pulse was 61, about right for someone who worked out regularly. He had no clue how to interpret the other numbers. Malcolm also spied the bag containing Stella's filthy clothes, wondering what they signified.

Stella's bed was next to the window. Malcolm got up and walked around the bed to check the view. He raised the shade and saw only a cinder-block wall.

Back in the chair, he pulled out his phone, found Dr. Daniel Weiss on the contact list, and made the call.

"Weiss Endodontics."

"Hello, this is Malcolm Klein, the L.A. Times reporter. I need to speak with the doctor ASAP. I found Stella."

"Oh my god. Hang on, he's in the middle of a procedure, but I'll drag him away."

She ran to the treatment room and gave Dr. Weiss the good news.

"Is Malcolm still on the line?"

"Yes."

Daniel was in such a hurry to talk to Malcolm that he dropped his drill on the patient's lap. He picked it up, saw that it wasn't damaged, and said, "Mrs. DeVore, I'll be right back. Don't go away."

Flustered, Mrs. DeVore gurgled incoherently and nodded. Daniel ran to the front desk where he grabbed the receiver and said, "Malcolm, is it true you found Stella?"

"Yes, I'm sitting next to her. She's in a hospital in San Diego."

"Oh no. What's wrong with her?"

"She's in a coma. And they won't give me any information because I'm not family."

Shifting the phone from one gloved hand to the other, he said "I have to finish a root canal. She's my last patient for the day. It should only be another 15 minutes or so."

"Are you going to come down?"

"Of course. I'll come down with Rachel. I believe she only had to take one deposition this morning, so she should be home already. I'll swing by the house and pick her up. We'll grab overnight bags and come down directly."

"You should probably go to Stella's apartment; she needs some clean clothes."

"Right.

"Are you going to drive or fly? I can pick you up at the airport."

"Time-wise, it's going to be about three or four hours either way. But I think we'll drive; then we won't have the hassles with TSA and renting a car."

"Dr. Weiss, I hate to bring this up, but there's no family resemblance between you folks and Stella. They're sticklers for HIPAA here, so I recommend you bring some documentation of your relationship. Otherwise, they might not answer your questions."

"Yeah, we've faced this issue before, most recently when Stella had a kidney stone."

"Give me your cell number so I can text you the name and address of the hospital and her room number. I'll be waiting for you in her room or in the seating area by the nurses' station."

"I can't wait to hear how you found her."

"It's a very strange story."

"Anyway, hold Stella's hand and talk to her."

"I will, as soon as I inform my boss and the FBI."

"Right."

He tapped his cell a few times and reached the switchboard at the Hoover Building. He asked for Special Agent Joanna Bartolo.

"I believe she has already left for the day."

"This is an emergency. Can you give me her cell number?"

"I can't do that, but I can call her and pass along your message and number."

"That works. Tell her I found Stella Weiss."

Five minutes later, his phone buzzed. It was Bartolo.

"Agent Bartolo, I have some news. I'm sitting in a hospital room in San Diego next to Stella Weiss. She's in a coma, and I'm waiting for her parents to arrive so they can quiz the doctors about her condition."

From the next bed, behind the yellow curtain, Stella's neighbor called out, "speak up, I can't hear you."

"Agent Bartolo, I need to move. Please wait while I find a more private place to talk."

****

Malcolm relocated to the end of the hall by a window where phone reception was strong, and there were no nosy neighbors.

"I'm back."

"So, how did you find her?"

"It's a long story. An informant led me to Camp Pendleton where I interviewed the helicopter pilot who helped abduct her."

"Damn, damn, damn. The feds did it after all."

"Yeah, I'm afraid so. I went to Camp Pendleton and talked to Commander Otis Griswold; he's the Marine Corps general in charge. He wasn't directly helpful but he let it slip that the operation was on the order of the president himself."

"Shit."

"Yeah. Someone at Pendleton suggested I go to UCSD medical. I finally tracked down Stella in San Diego. She was dumped in the ER and treated as an indigent Jane Doe. The ER administrator was thrilled I was able to identify her."

"I'll bet he was."

"So, Agent Bartolo, what's your next move?"

"First I'll notify our office in L.A. handling the case that Ms. Weiss has been found. Usually, the military services conduct their own investigations of wrongdoing by their personnel. NCIS may want to handle this without FBI involvement. In my experience, this kidnapping is unprecedented. We have to proceed very carefully."

"I understand your situation, though I'd be much happier if the FBI took the lead in the investigation."

"I can assure you, we'll be watching very closely for any White House interference."

"Agent Bartolo, I have to warn you, I'm going to write up this story and name names."

"I figured you would."

"But I'll wait a few days, maybe longer, because I'd like Stella to regain consciousness first. I hope she can fill the gaps in the story." Malcolm paused, his eyes glistening again, and said, "geez, I hope she's going to be okay."

"Me too. In the meantime, you do the reporting and we'll do the law enforcement. It's kind of ironic, though, the FBI and the press are on the same side in this case."

"Yeah, go figure. But we're both trying to get at the truth."

"And we'll get there."

"I hope so."

Bartolo ended the call and took a deep breath. She needed some time to think. Although Klein was certain that marines from Camp Pendleton had abducted Weiss, Bartolo decided to keep that knowledge to herself for the present. Klein would eventually blow up the mission, but not until he had more information.

CHAPTER 61

THE NEXT MORNING, when FBI Director Abel checked her email, she found a preliminary report from the IT task force seeking Robert and Roberta in Samoa. They had accessed back files of airport video surveillance. It didn't take them long to confirm that the woman who departed Honolulu in the floppy hat and large sunglasses was in fact Stella Weiss. Arriving at Faleolo International Airport during the night, she had shed her tourist camouflage. Her entire face was visible as she walked through the baggage area. Outside cameras showed Weiss entering a taxi. Unfortunately, the IT team was unable to access the cab company's files.

The report ended with a preview of the team's next move. Because she had taken a cab, they assumed Weiss was heading to a hotel for the night. They planned to hunt for her by tapping into the computer systems of nearby hotels and resorts.

Abel was pleased with the team's progress and thanked them. She decided it was time to send the Las Vegas agents to Samoa, even though they had no firm fix on Robert and Roberta's location. But the fugitives were almost certainly somewhere in the small country. She would put the Washingtons in place and ask them to await instructions for the extraction of the president's assassins.

In the meantime, Abel forwarded the IT report to Bartolo and told her about the Washingtons' imminent departure for their "South Seas vacation."

CHAPTER 62

MALCOLM RETURNED TO STELLA'S ROOM and sat down. He bent over and kissed her on the forehead, grasped her right hand, and whispered in her ear, "Stella, please wake up. We're all so worried about you. Your parents are on their way down. You may not be aware of what's happening, but you're in a hospital in San Diego. They did something to you at Camp Pendleton, and we're going to get to the bottom of it."

Suddenly Malcolm felt Stella's hand gently squeeze his. There was no other movement, but he was thrilled by the feeble sign, hoping she was on the verge of regaining consciousness.

A nurse arrived to check Stella's vitals, and she also put on a fresh IV bag.

"She squeezed my hand," he said to the nurse.

"That's a good sign for sure. Keep holding her hand and talk to her. It's the best medicine in this kind of case. With any luck, she'll bounce back as good as new."

"I hope so."

The perky nurse left, and Malcolm returned to his perch at the end of the hall. He called Alice at the Times and delivered the good news. She was thrilled that he had found Stella, but appalled that the federal government had treated an innocent civilian this way—especially an L.A. Times reporter.

****

It was already past dinnertime, and Malcolm was getting hungry, but he didn't want to leave Stella until her parents arrived. Finally, a few minutes after eight they stormed into the room and went straight to Stella's bedside.

Rachel said, "she looks so peaceful. I only hope she's having pleasant dreams." Realizing that she had ignored Malcolm, she made amends. "Oh, Malcolm, I'm so sorry. I can't thank you enough for finding her." She hugged him tightly.

Daniel joined the hugfest and asked, "have you learned anything more about her condition?"

"Not from the medical people. But when I was talking to her and holding her hand, she squeezed mine."

"That's a terrific sign," said Daniel. "I'll go to the nurses' station and request that her doctor pay us a visit. We need to know what's going on."

Daniel returned and said that a doctor was on his way. About 20 minutes later Dr. Braverman entered Stella's room. After a round of introductions, the doctor asked to see some proof of their relationship to Stella. He glanced cursorily at the papers Daniel had removed from a manila envelope.

"That's fine." Pointing at Malcolm, Dr. Braverman asked Daniel, "you don't mind if he hears our conversation?"

"Not at all. He's practically family."

Malcolm quickly cut in to mention Stella's hand movement. Dr. Braverman nodded knowingly and said, "that bodes well. I can't really tell you much except that she has no brain damage. The blood work and the red spot on her left arm indicate that someone injected her with an unidentified drug. We believe it will slowly work its way out of her system, maybe sooner rather than later."

"So, do you expect a complete recovery?" asked Rachel.

"I do. Just stay with her and keep talking. I've instructed the nurses' station to ignore the regular visiting hours. She needs verbal and tactile stimulation—24/7, if possible."

"We'll do our part."

****

The trio tagged-teamed talking to Stella and visiting the cafeteria.

As dawn approached, Stella began tossing and turning, her motions accompanied by the occasional groan. And intermittently her eyes flickered open. Daniel, who was at Stella's side, stroking her hand, heard her mumble, "dad, I'm hungry. Where the hell am I?"

His eyes began to tear up. He bent down and kissed her. "Thank god you woke up. We've been worried sick about you."

Stella raised her head off the pillow and saw Malcolm and her mother. Haltingly, she managed to say, "I remember... some quack injected me...when was that?"

"Malcolm thinks it happened a couple of days ago," said Daniel, gently sobbing. "By the way, you can thank him for finding you."

Hearing the conversation, the others woke up. When Rachel realized that Stella was conscious, she burst into tears.

A nurse who arrived to check Stella's vitals choked up when she heard Stella's voice. She spread the good news, and an hour later Dr. Braverman dropped by to see for himself. He was pleased with her rapid progress.

"Hello, Stella, I'm Dr. Braverman. I'm glad to see you're with us this morning. I don't know what you were injected with, but it was bad stuff. Do you have any idea?"

"They said it was a powerful truth serum."

"Who did?"

"The people who abducted me."

It finally dawned on the doctor why her face had seemed familiar. "Stella. Stella Weiss? Aren't you the reporter who wrote the article about the president's killers, and then you went missing?"

"Yes, that's me."

"That was an impressive piece of reporting."

"Thank you, but my captors weren't so pleased with it. They tried everything to force me to reveal my sources' names and location. I hope I didn't tell them anything."

"You don't know?"

"I was out like a light after they injected me."

"I'm sorry Stella. It sounds like a terrifying experience."

"It was, but I don't want to talk about it right now."

"When can she come home?" asked Rachel.

"I'll sign the release papers this afternoon."

"Thanks, doctor."

CHAPTER 63

STELLA RODE BACK TO L.A. with her parents. They stopped at her apartment where she picked up clothes for the next few days. At her parents' urging, she had agreed to stay with them for the time being. Stella didn't need to be convinced it was a safer option. When they arrived at her apartment, Rachel pulled the key out of her purse and opened the door.

Stella gasped in disbelief as she surveyed her apartment. "I've been dreading this moment. My kidnappers made a big mess, but now it's all cleaned up."

Looking at her mom, Stella said, "I think I know what happened."

"Yeah, your dad and I came over and did some straightening up."

"Thank you! And what about Tabby?"

"She's fine. We have her at home. She'll be so happy to see you."

Stella suddenly remembered that her abductors had taken her phone and laptop. "Oh shit," she said, and told them what was missing.

"It makes sense they'd want to search them to find your sources," said Daniel.

"Well, they would have been disappointed because neither device contained that information."

"Stella," said Rachel, "let's go home."

"I'm ready—and really, really tired."

CHAPTER 64

AFTER TAGGING ALONG with the Weisses until they left for L.A., Malcolm returned to his motel room in Oceanside. He was eager to gather more information about the bizarre happenings at Camp Pendleton. Stella called him the following morning and briefed him on her memories of the time she had spent in the dreadful little green room.

She remembered encountering six people during her imprisonment: her captors, Laurel and Hardy; two male interrogators she called Tweedledum and Tweedledee; the polygraph man; and Dr. Death, the "quack" who injected her. Malcolm listened, his anger growing, horrified by the details of her ordeal. But he did chuckle when she described the fate of the polygraph machine at her hands—and feet. Thank god, he thought to himself, she survived. Stella was fine physically but her emotions were somewhat flat. He suspected that she would eventually need counseling for PTSD. As they ended the call, Stella managed to say, "we have to get those bastards."

"We will," he said, not entirely convinced it would be possible. The government, he knew, had ways to cover up its crimes.

****

Next on Malcolm's agenda was another visit to Camp Pendleton. He wanted to snoop around to see if he could find out more about the six mystery people who had made Stella's life so miserable. He drove to the gate, but this time he was not waved through.

"Sir, you have to make a U-turn up ahead and leave the base."

"Why? I was just here the yesterday."

"I'm sorry, sir, but you're on the entry-denied list."

"Who made up that list?"

"I really don't know. The list just appears every morning on my monitor. Please pull ahead and turn around, cars are piling up behind you."

Malcolm was furious. He had no doubt that this was Commander Griswold's doing, but he couldn't fight it—not here, not now. He complied with the order. After leaving the base, Malcolm pulled into a restaurant parking lot to calm down and assess his options. He was still registered at the motel, expecting to return for the night after buttonholing people on the base all day. That was now impossible. It was still early enough to check out and return to L.A., yet he felt there was still more to learn, if not on the base, then maybe in Oceanside.

Malcolm was so incensed by his treatment at Pendleton that he couldn't create a coherent plan. What's more, he was feeling the after-effects of the emotional roller coaster he had been riding since the day Stella disappeared. It was a gnawing fatigue spiced with anger. He returned to the motel, checked out, and drove to L.A., looking forward to being back at his desk.

****

Immediately after Alice heard Malcolm's good news about Stella's recovery, she posted a note on the staff listserv: "Malcolm found Stella. She's okay."

In the early afternoon, when Malcolm returned to the newsroom, reporters and editors greeted him with congratulations and high fives. One of the young bucks said, "looks like the old dog can still hunt." Malcolm was touched by the warm reception and waved off the praise. He set to work on a brief note merely announcing that Stella had been found unconscious in a San Diego hospital. He kept details to a minimum, not mentioning her abduction and involuntary stay at Camp

Pendleton. He wanted to follow through on his threat to Griswold, but believed it would be better to delay until he could piece together the complete story.

CHAPTER 65

THE NEXT DAY STELLA BOUGHT a new computer and phone. Fortunately, the company easily transferred her old number to the new phone. One of the first calls she received was from the L.A. office of the FBI, which still had an open missing-person case, ostensibly in collaboration with the LAPD. After Stella had been found, the case morphed into a full-blown FBI kidnapping investigation.

Agent Suarez arranged to interview Stella at the Weiss' home that evening. Before the agents arrived, she and Rachel set up a video camera to record the interview. Malcolm said that she had been abducted and imprisoned by the Marine Corps at the direction of President Shilling. She didn't know if the FBI or any other federal agency could be trusted. Would they conduct a thorough investigation of this incident or were they just going through the motions? Would the FBI agents badger her about the identities and whereabouts of Robert and Roberta? If they did, she would have a record of their inappropriate questioning. And she would also have the transcript for later use when writing stories for the Times.

****

The two L.A. agents arrived promptly at 7:00 p.m. and introduced themselves. Almost six feet tall, Benjamin Suarez had wavy black hair and olive skin with dark brown eyes. Like his partner Andrew

Carrington, he wore a charcoal suit. Carrington was Suarez' opposite in every way: short with blonde hair, fair skin, and steely blue eyes. Neither agent seemed prone to smile.

Rachel welcomed the men into the sitting room with its charming antique sofas and chairs. She left them sitting across from Stella. Suarez looked around at the furnishings, thinking to himself that the original oils and watercolors on the walls seemed appropriate for a Beverly Hills McMansion. The furniture included a solid oak breakfront and coffee table, though it held no coffee. The plush purple sofa was as comfortable as it looked. On the opposite wall was a bookcase; he spotted the video camera nestled between two books but said nothing.

Suarez began the interview with a brief preamble.

"Ms. Weiss, we are pleased that you have turned up safe. But our investigation continues because we need to know everything about what transpired during this incident. We are counting on your memory to furnish details we can use to track down the perpetrators."

Apparently, Bartolo hadn't told the L.A. office that she knew, in general terms, who was responsible for Stella's abduction. This had been a deliberate move on her part because she didn't fully trust the director of the L.A. office. If he were to find out that Camp Pendleton's base commander and the president had conspired to commit this crime, he might insist that his agents back off or tread lightly. Bartolo wanted the investigation to continue full bore. To ensure that it was moving ahead, she asked the agents to furnish her with daily progress reports, including copies of all written, audio, and video materials.

"I'll be asking the questions today," declared Carrington.

Stella looked at him and said, "that's fine."

"Ms. Weiss, how are you doing?"

"It's been a difficult time, but I'm doing reasonably well, considering the circumstances."

"I'm glad to hear it." She thought he sounded sincere.

"Ms. Weiss, tell us what happened on the night you were taken."

"I appreciate the opportunity to collect my thoughts and tell you my story." Looking from one agent to the other, she paused briefly before unwinding her tale.

"I arrived home shortly after six p.m., parked in the lot, and went directly to my building."

"Did you see any strangers in the parking lot?"

"No. And I didn't notice anything else unusual." She paused, sorting her recollections.

"Please go on."

"I took the elevator to my floor, walked down the hall, and unlocked my apartment door. I went in and put my purse down. I had just changed into casual clothes and was getting ready to make dinner when the doorbell rang. I live in a safe neighborhood and didn't think twice about opening the door. Big mistake. A man and woman wearing ski masks pushed their way into my apartment. One of them was holding a gun."

"Do you know what kind of gun it was?"

"It was a pistol but not a revolver. That's all I know about it."

"Can you describe the intruders?"

"As I said, they wore ski masks so their faces were almost completely hidden. Oh, they were also wearing tight-fitting latex gloves. But the tiny areas of visible skin told me they were both white. The man was about six feet tall and had a thin face. The woman's face was round and she was a few inches shorter. I named them Laurel and Hardy."

Suarez lost control for a moment as a slight smile crossed his face.

"Did you see any tattoos or other distinguishing features on either person?"

"I couldn't see enough of their skin."

"Did either of them have accents?"

"I think Hardy was from the south, maybe Virginia or North Carolina. She had a soft, molasses-sweet Southern drawl."

"Do you remember anything distinctive about Laurel's speech?"

"He spoke very standard English. He could be from anywhere in the urban West or even Midwest."

"Then what happened?"

"Laurel held the gun on me and ordered me to sit on the couch while Hardy tore apart my apartment. She didn't find anything except my laptop and phone, which she put into one of my grocery tote bags. Laurel ordered me to stand up. He put handcuffs on me, followed by a blindfold and gag. Then I heard the door open. Hardy, who must have looked down the hall, said 'it's safe now.' Laurel shoved his gun in my back, and told me to 'get moving and you won't be hurt.'"

Stella paused and looked down, as if reliving the horror of those moments. Carrington said, "please go on when you're ready."

"One of them grabbed my arm and pulled me a short distance down the hall to the stairwell. We took the stairs to the first floor. I almost fell a couple of times because I couldn't see or hang on to the railing, but Hardy—I think it was Hardy—steadied me. She seemed to be unusually strong. When we reached the first floor and stepped outside, Laurel made a call, saying something like, 'we're ready to go.' A car pulled up, and Laurel and Hardy dragged me inside."

"Did you notice anything about the car?"

"I sat between Laurel and Hardy, so I know it had a spacious bench seat. Once we got rolling, I was pretty sure it had a V-8 engine."

"How did you know that?"

"I've lived in L.A. all my life, and I'm a reporter. I notice sights and sounds. The car had a V-8's low rumble. I could also tell it had an automatic transmission with five or six forward gears."

The agents looked at each other and nodded. They were thinking big SUV—maybe government-issue or an Uber.

"Do you know the destination and what route they traveled?"

"It seemed like we were on the road for about an hour, though obviously I can't be sure about how long the ride took. There were lots of red lights on the way and constant traffic noise. We were on surface streets and never took a freeway."

"Can you remember anything else about the trip?"

She paused for a long moment and replied, "not really."

"And where did the trip end?"

"We stopped somewhere, and then they pulled me out of the car. I heard the sounds of a nearby helicopter. I put up a fight as they tried to get me to walk to the helicopter. They finally picked me up and carried me over to it and lifted me inside."

"Do you have any idea where you were?"

"The place might have been an airport, but I'm not sure. The helicopter was obviously at ground level, so I knew it wasn't on a helipad at the top of a building. There was no loud jet noise, so it couldn't have been LAX or Burbank. Anywhere near those airports and you can hear the constant whine of jet engines."

"Did you notice anything about the helicopter?"

"Not really. I don't know much about aircraft. And, of course, I couldn't see it."

****

Suarez held up his hand to indicate a pause in the interview. He said to Carrington, "after we're done here, let's have the FAA search for chopper landings and takeoffs at small airports on the evening of the incident. Let's specify airports within a 50-mile radius of Ms. Weiss's apartment."

"Got it," said Carrington, and resumed the interview. "Then what happened?"

"We flew for—I don't know, maybe half an hour or forty-five minutes—and landed in a fairly quiet place. A car picked us up and we drove for a few minutes."

"Can you tell us anything about the car?"

"Not really. Honestly, I was so terrified I didn't give the car any thought."

"Okay, please resume."

"After the car stopped, they pulled me out. Then they steered me into a building and led me up one flight of stairs, then down a hallway. We turned once to the right, and then entered a small room. Laurel and Hardy immediately left and bolted the door from the outside. Every time they locked me in I heard that horrible metallic clunk. I can still hear it, banging in my brain."

"How did you know it was a small room?"

"I didn't know it at the time, but later when they removed my

235

blindfold, I could see where they'd taken me."

"After they removed the blindfold, did you see their faces?"

"No. They always wore ski masks."

"What else did you notice about the room?"

"It had grimy green walls and one crummy light. I felt totally disoriented. By the way, I'm still having flashbacks to that wretched room. Hour after hour I stared at the walls and saw faces—grotesque and threatening faces. I was afraid I was going to die there." Stella began to sob quietly.

After pausing briefly while Stella regained her composure, Carrington asked, "did you learn anything more about your captors while you were in that room?"

"I think they were about my age, maybe a little younger, probably mid-thirties."

"How did you determine that?"

"From their voices. As people age their voices change."

"Anything else?"

"Yeah, I'm pretty sure they're military. They both called me ma'am and occasionally Laurel referred to Hardy as 'sir.' Don't forget, Hardy was the woman. And they were wearing boots, too."

"Were they wearing any distinctive clothing?"

"Not really. Casual, long-sleeve clothing, not uniforms."

"That's very interesting."

The agents looked at each other, and Carrington said to Stella, "I think we've done enough for one night. We'd like to come back tomorrow morning so you can finish the story."

"That would be fine."

"Would ten o'clock be convenient?"

"No problem."

"We'll see ourselves out. Sleep well, Ms. Weiss."

"I'll try."

After the agents left, Daniel and Rachel checked the video recorder, confirming it had done the job with perfection.

"What's your impression of the agents?" asked Daniel.

"They seemed sincerely interested in my story. I didn't sense any skepticism. They asked good questions, though I couldn't answer all of them. By the way, they'll be back tomorrow morning at ten to finish the interview. I still wonder whether they'll eventually begin asking me about Robert and Roberta."

****

Daniel went to another room, but Rachel stayed with Stella and asked, "do you ever think about giving the government the information they want?"

"Is that a gentle way of asking, why do I continue to protect mass murderers?"

"No, not at all. I'm just thinking out loud. It seems like you have an inherent conflict between being a patriotic American and being a responsible journalist. And I just wonder how you've resolved that conflict."

Stella shook her head and said, "I don't see that as a conflict at all. By being a good journalist and protecting my sources, I am also being a patriotic American. There is nothing more sacred to our democracy than the free press."

"Of course, I agree," said Rachel, "but…"

"Mom, at a deeper level it bothers me that I could, with one phone call, help the government find President Wahl's assassins. But I won't do it. I can't do it! And I don't have any guilt about it. Let the government do their own investigations and bring Robert and Roberta to justice. I would applaud that, but I can't help them get there."

Putting her arms around Stella, Rachel said, "I'm proud of you for resisting all the pressures and standing by your principles."

"Thanks, mom."

CHAPTER 66

WHEN DR. CHARLES GRANINGER, the physician on the White House medical staff, returned from California, he braced himself for an uncomfortable grilling from President Shilling. "Shilling's grilling," he laughed bitterly to himself. He should have feigned illness and refused to go to California. The mission was a disaster, and now he owned a big part of it. No doctor should be put in the position of having to administer an experimental drug without the patient's consent. On top of that, he had no license to practice medicine in California. He knew it was malpractice, but he also knew that refusing Shilling's order might have ended his sweet life in the White House.

The meeting was scheduled to begin an hour after Graninger's plane landed at Reagan National. He took an Uber directly to the White House, arriving five minutes before the appointment. Stonehouse ushered him into the Oval Office and urged him to take a seat.

The president began the meeting by demanding to know what went wrong at Camp Pendleton. With a dramatic flair, Shilling immediately put Graninger on the defensive. "Doctor, I'm inclined to fire you for botching the Camp Pendleton operation."

Graninger sat there in disbelief at the president's harsh words. He looked down but didn't speak.

"I won't make a final decision on your employment status until after I complete the debriefing."

"Yes, Mr. President," he said softly.

"Dr. Graninger, did you give Weiss the recommended dose?"

"Of course."

"When the drug was in your possession did it ever exceed the maximum temperature?"

"No sir, never. It was in my bag the entire way. I did not let it out of my sight."

Shilling took a deep breath of frustration and let it out quickly.

"So, what happened after you injected her?"

"She quickly passed out, and we couldn't revive her. She had fallen into a coma."

"Were you surprised?"

"Of course I was, Mr. President."

"What do you think went wrong?"

"The drug must have been defective, or else she suffered a rare side effect. We knew that an overdose could be fatal, but I was extremely careful to follow the protocol."

Shilling just shook his head and said, "we're done here. You won't get the axe today. But I warn you, not a word to anyone about this incident."

Graninger nodded, stood up, and swiftly left the office before Shilling had time to change his mind. Stonehouse closed the door behind the departing doctor.

"Stonehouse, let's get Smalley in here ASAP and see what he has to say."

"Yes, Mr. President. I'll summon him immediately."

****

Later that day, Stonehouse brought CIA Director Adam Smalley into the Oval Office.

Shilling said, "thank you for coming. We need to get to the bottom of the screw-up at Camp Pendleton. Dr. Graninger claims he did everything according to the drug's protocol. He believes the drug might have been defective. What's your assessment?"

"Mr. President, our scientists in the Omaha lab packaged up several doses of the drug in readiness for Dr. Graninger's visit. Since I learned about Weiss's adverse reaction, I ordered an investigation to see if anything went wrong at the lab. The lab director got back to me very quickly and said everything had been normal. The doses they sent with Dr. Graninger were from the same batch that had yielded good results in Syria. The number of adverse reactions among Isis fighters was below 15 percent, which they regard as acceptable in the earliest trial of an experimental drug."

"So, you're saying that there was no problem at your end?"

"That's correct, Mr. President."

"Thank you, Smalley. You may go now."

"Thank you, Mr. President." Smalley couldn't leave the Oval Office fast enough.

When the door closed behind him, Stonehouse wryly remarked, "the mission was a disaster but no one was responsible."

CHAPTER 67

SUAREZ AND CARRINGTON ARRIVED at the Weiss home a few minutes early but rang the bell anyway. Stella, the only person at home, immediately turned on the video camera and walked warily to the door. Ever since her abduction, she had become far more cautious, reflecting an understandable paranoia. She worried constantly that the marines might make another attempt to capture and interrogate her. She was terrified at the thought.

Stella asked, "who's there?"

A familiar voice said, "agents Suarez and Carrington." She let out a sigh of relief, opened the door, and greeted them with handshakes. Then she led them to the sitting room and invited them to take seats. This time the coffee table held coffee in a large pot, ornate porcelain teacups and saucers, and a selection of fresh muffins.

"Gentlemen, you can thank my mother for the coffee and munchies."

"Thanks," said Carrington, as he poured a cup, added cream from a matching pitcher, and picked up a walnut-pumpkin muffin. He immediately began nibbling on the muffin, taking care not to get crumbs on the Persian rug.

Suarez said, "I'm good for now, thanks." His eyes were fixed on a watercolor scene on the opposite wall, to the left of the bookcase. He recognized it as the Isabel II Bridge over the Guadalquivir River in Seville, Spain. This was a place his paternal grandparents knew intimately. Their families had fled that beautiful city and the country of their ancestors during the Spanish Civil War before the fascists took over under Franco.

Carrington said, "now that I'm comfortable and caffeinated, shall we begin? Suarez will ask the questions today."

Stella took a deep breath, let it out slowly, and said, "I'm ready."

Suarez gave her a sympathetic look and asked, "Ms. Weiss, how are you doing today?"

"I feel like I've escaped from the set of a horror movie and had to adjust to the outside world again. It's taking time."

"I understand."

****

"When we ended yesterday, your captors—Laurel and Hardy, as you call them—had taken you to a small room. What can you remember about the room?"

"It was like a jail cell without bars. It was maybe 12 by 12 feet, and there were no windows. My bed was a cot, the kind with canvas on a wooden framework. There was a beat-up wooden table and several metal folding chairs. Opposite the door was a tiny room with a toilet and sink."

"When did you first take note of your surroundings?"

"I woke up—I think it was the next morning—but I'm not sure how long I'd been asleep. I felt like I'd been drugged. That's when I began looking around. There were fast-food wrappers and a Pepsi cup on the table. I guess they'd fed me, but I didn't remember eating anything. And I wondered what they'd put in the drink that knocked me out."

"When Laurel and Hardy returned that morning, what happened?"

"They brought me coffee and donuts, and then left me alone."

"How long before they returned?"

"A couple of hours, probably. The next time the bolt was retracted and the door opened, Laurel and Hardy brought me lunch and two new people. Both of them were men wearing ski masks."

"What did you notice about them?"

"They were white, maybe in their forties or fifties, not very tall. I didn't detect any particular accents. I named them Tweedledum and Tweedledee. They wore casual clothes and boots like Laurel and Hardy. For the rest of my captivity the two teams traded off duties. Laurel and Hardy brought me meals and took people in and out of the room."

Suarez and Carrington shot knowing glances at each other and nodded.

Observing the nonverbal communication, Stella asked, "what does that mean?"

Surprised by the question, Suarez said, "nothing."

"Really? Come on now!"

"We're thinking that the two men were interrogators."

"Well, you got that right. Tweedledum and Tweedledee were in my face, repeating the same questions, over and over again."

"What did they want to know?"

"It was quite predictable. They made no threats, and they were friendly, trying to con me. They even said they were on my side, hoping I would be released soon. Then they asked about my education, my family, my pets, how I liked being a reporter. I just went along and answered. What choice did I have?"

"At some point, I assume they started playing hardball?"

"Yes. They said that if I were a patriotic American, I would help them. Then they came to the point: they wanted me to reveal the true identities of Robert and Roberta and their whereabouts."

"What did you tell them?"

"I said, 'I don't know their real identities and I won't tell you where they are. I'm a patriotic American whose occupation is recognized and valued in the First Amendment to the U.S. Constitution.' They knew exactly what I meant: there was no way I was going to furnish information about my sources, even though Robert and Roberta were mass murderers. And I had to keep repeating the refrain: 'the courts have spoken; I have the right to protect my sources.' We went around and around for several hours. Finally, Tweedledee said, 'do yourself a favor

243

and tell us what we need to know.' I again made my position clear. I told them, 'you can stay here and question me until we all grow old together, but I'm not telling you anything about Robert and Roberta that's not already in my Times story.' Then I insisted they release me because they were breaking the law. They said nothing. Eventually, Laurel and Hardy appeared carrying a carton of cold chicken chow mein and a soda. And then everyone left me alone."

"What happened then?"

"I picked at the pathetic dinner and just waited, my anxiety spiking. I pounded on the door a few times and yelled for help, but no one came."

"Did anyone return later on?"

"No one came back."

"What happened the next day?"

"Tweedledee and Tweedledum returned in the morning, right after Laurel and Hardy brought me coffee and donuts. As for the questioning, we pretty much went through a rerun of the previous day. I was exhausted. I just wanted to lie down on the cot and sleep for a week."

"So they left without learning anything new about the assassins?"

"That's correct."

"What happened during the rest of the day?"

"Laurel and Hardy returned in the late afternoon with another man carrying a polygraph machine."

Stella went on to tell the agents about how she broke the machine, and Suarez laughed out loud. Carrington glowered at him and urged her to continue.

"Before they left for the day, Hardy promised me I would be sorry."

"Except for deliveries of food and drink, I was left alone until the next afternoon. By this time I was going batty. I was angry and mentally spent. I expected to die in that crummy little room."

She paused, reflecting on her experience.

"Ms. Weiss, please continue when you're ready."

"The next time I heard the bolt move, I got up from the cot and stood by the door. Laurel and Hardy were making their food delivery. I decided to release some anger, so I kicked Laurel in the nuts. He bent over and lost his balance. He dropped the food and fell to the floor gripping his groin. I made a run for it through the open door with Hardy chasing after me. She caught me and forced me back into the green room. As soon as Laurel was able to stand up, they left. On the way out he gave me a menacing warning in a strained voice, 'you'll pay for this.'"

"Did they return that day?"

"No, and they didn't bring me any more food. I guess that was payback for Laurel's aching nuts."

Suarez reined in a smile.

"What happened the next day?"

"Laurel and Hardy brought in another man wearing a ski mask and a shabby suit. He was carrying an old-fashioned, black doctor's bag. The kind you see on reruns of 1950s TV shows. I had this deep sense of foreboding when I saw him, so I named him Dr. Death."

"What did you observe about the newcomer?"

"He was short and stout, and he spoke with a slight foreign accent I couldn't identify."

"Then what happened?"

"I was sitting on the cot when I saw Dr. Death take a syringe and tiny vial out of his bag. As he filled the syringe with a gray liquid, I felt a wave of fear wash over me. Actually, it was more like tsunami of terror. I jumped up and began flailing around, trying to get past him as he approached me with the needle. Laurel and Hardy grabbed me and held me down. Dr. Death gave me a painful shot in the arm. And that spot's still red."

"What happened after that?"

"I have no idea. My next memory is waking up in a hospital bed with my parents and my editor, Malcolm Klein, nearby. They were all sobbing."

Stella was trying to keep from crying, which did not escape the agents' notice.

"You've had a terrible experience, Ms. Weiss. We hope it leaves no lasting effects."

"I do have recurrent visions of a cartoonish, wild-eyed Dr. Death hovering over me with a horse-size hypodermic needle, then plunging it into my gut."

Suarez winced noticeably as Stella began sobbing loudly.

Carrington said, "you may need to seek counseling, Ms. Weiss. In the meantime, we're finished for now. At some point we may return and ask more questions."

"I understand. I'll answer them to the best of my ability." But, she wondered, would there be a third interview when they broached the subject of the assassins? She wanted to trust them, but she was stingy with her trust after what had happened.

"Let me assure you, we are committed to following this investigation—wherever it leads."

"I hope so. But what if it leads to a government agency?"

They did not answer.

"I was afraid of that. They could kill your investigation if it gets too close to the people responsible."

"Let's not speculate," said Suarez.

****

"Now," said Stella, who had recovered her composure, "may I ask you a few questions?" She aimed to get their answers on tape, for possible use in a story.

"Feel free to ask, but we may not be permitted to answer."

"I understand. First of all, you're FBI agents on this case, even though I wasn't transported across state lines. So, what's up?"

Carrington answered. "Yes, as far as we know, you've remained in California. This case began as an LAPD missing person. But when our superiors in Washington realized who was missing, the FBI offered to help the LAPD. Eventually, they assigned us to the case. We're both from the L.A. regional office, but we report to Washington headquarters. In theory, we're helping out the LAPD, but in practice it's our show now."

"Do you know who my captors were or where I was?"

"As of now, we don't."

Stella was surprised at Carrington's answer because, according to Malcolm, she had been a prisoner at Camp Pendleton. Maybe Carrington didn't know. Maybe he didn't want to implicate the Marine Corps. She let it slide.

"Well then, do you at least have any hunches about who kidnapped me?"

"We prefer not to speculate on that subject. Let's wait until we have some hard evidence."

"If the people are caught, what will they be charged with?"

"That determination is above my pay grade, but they'll face a laundry list of charges, beginning with kidnapping."

"Who will you interview next?"

"Sorry, that's also above my pay grade." A convenient untruth. Carrington didn't want Stella to give Malcolm a head's up that he'd be interviewed next.

Disappointed with their empty answers, she said, "thanks, gentlemen, I'll see you to the door."

As they walked out, Suarez paused, turned around, and smiled at Stella. Surprised, she forced a smile in return, wondering what his kind gesture was all about. He was handsome and seemed nice. Was he flirting? Stella was intrigued.

On the way to their car, Carrington asked, "what do you think?"

Apparently without thinking, Suarez answered, "I could be falling in love with Stella."

"I'll pretend I didn't hear that. Seriously, do you have any idea who abducted her?"

Suarez responded coyly, "I do. But let's begin by adding up the number of people involved in these crimes. Let's see: one or two chopper pilots, Laurel and Hardy, Tweedledum and Tweedledee, the polygraph guy, and Dr. Death. That's seven or eight right there. And those are only the people we know about. They did all the dirty work. Someone else gave them the orders."

Carrington chewed over the numbers for a few seconds, then blurted out the obvious conclusion. "This was no amateur operation! I'm thinking this was a federal op. Ms. Weiss said Laurel and Hardy were wearing boots, and he addressed her as 'sir.' That's got to be military."

"You got that right. We're sleepwalking into a hornet's nest. So, Carrington, what do we do now?"

"Malcolm Klein is the only other person we know of who has any direct knowledge of this op. Let's get to him ASAP before all hell breaks loose."

"My thoughts, exactly."

"Hang on, I just got a message from the FAA. They have a record of a chopper at the Santa Monica City Airport in our timeframe. Here's the kicker: it was a marine Huey."

"Oh shit!"

CHAPTER 68

BARTOLO CALLED A MEETING of the entire assassination team. Before the meeting began, she could sense the tension rising in the room. The agents were chagrinned that a reporter had beaten an elite FBI team to the perpetrators. Weiss knew who the assassins were, but the FBI did not. It was galling, even demoralizing. Bartolo felt these sentiments even more acutely because she led the team whose mission had so far failed. True, Robert had initiated contact with Stella, but...

Bartolo presented her agents with a challenge: "let's treat Weiss's story as a resource for us. What does her report tell us about the assassins?"

Team members offered many suggestions, and Bartolo took careful notes on the ideas she believed had merit. Later, in her office, she drafted a brief memo to Director Abel summarizing her notes. She also presented a plan:

We know that Robert was IT savvy, almost certainly a professional IT guy. Let us assume that a company employed him for his computer skills. Given the level of planning involved in taking down Marine One and making a clean getaway, we may assume that Robert and Roberta were intimately familiar with the D.C. area and probably lived and worked here. Roberta is a total enigma. At some point, probably well before the incident, the couple must have quit working. This gives us a possible way to identify Robert. My plan is to send agents to companies in the D.C. region, beginning with the largest. Our agents will contact the director of HR in each company and request a list of all IT employees who left the company in a three-month window both preceding and following the incident. That will take much legwork, of course. They will seek basic information: phone number(s), email address, home address, and emergency contacts. We know there's much lateral movement among IT specialists. Therefore, the goal of our analysis will be to identify the ghosts: the men who left a company but who don't show up in another company. Admittedly, it's a needle-in-a-haystack problem, but we have little else to go on. Unless you advise otherwise, I will put this plan in motion tomorrow.

A few hours later, Abel called Bartolo. "Interesting plan. We'll have to depend on the patriotism and good will of HR managers, because we have no basis for requesting warrants until ghosts show up. By the way, how's the other investigation going?"

Bartolo had hoped the matter of Weiss's abduction wouldn't come up during their conversation. She gulped hard and said, "we're making progress building a timeline for the abduction and imprisonment."

"Anything else?"

"Umm. Not at this time."

"Bartolo, that sounds like an evasion to me."

"I guess it is. You're not going to like our preliminary findings, so I thought I'd save them until they were no longer preliminary."

"This is about Shilling, isn't it?"

"Let's wait and see."

"I suppose."

"Director, has our IT task force made any progress figuring out where Weiss went after she landed in Samoa?"

"They're still working their way through surveillance videos. The hacking of resorts and hotels hasn't been as easy as they expected, and there are dozens and dozens of places to check. I'll let you know if they make a breakthrough."

CHAPTER 69

SUAREZ AND CARRINGTON ARRANGED TO MEET Malcolm Klein at his Times office. Malcolm wasn't happy that two FBI agents would be traipsing through the newsroom. He hoped the agents would be mistaken for businessmen. A visit here, he knew, was preferable to inviting them into his home, an alternative they had suggested. He feared that his wife, Miriam, and teenage sons, Jason and Mark, would conclude he was under federal investigation because of his close working relationship with Stella Weiss.

After introductions, Malcolm offered the agents chairs, and they sat down. Suddenly the office seemed much smaller.

Carrington began, "I'll be asking the questions today, Mr. Klein. Thank you for agreeing to this interview."

"Did I really have a choice?"

There was no answer.

"We are interested in the entire sequence of events from the time you learned about Ms. Weiss' disappearance…"

Interrupting, Malcolm said, "you mean her abduction."

Carrington backpedalled, "of course. So, we'd like to hear your account of events from the time she was abducted to the time you found her in the San Diego hospital. We will be recording this interview."

"So will I," responded Malcolm, pointing to the digital recorder on his desk and turning it on. He looked back at Carrington and said,

"I will answer your questions up to a point."

"What do you mean?"

"Don't bother asking me about the identity of my sources or about Ms. Weiss's sources. And, by the way, she has not disclosed them to me."

"Let me assure you, Mr. Klein, our work is entirely independent of the FBI's assassination investigations. We will not be inquiring about the identities of Robert and Roberta or about Weiss's trip to Hawai'i."

Malcolm wasn't surprised they knew about Stella's trip, but he wondered why Carrington had mentioned it. He had a hunch. Maybe Carrington was letting him know that the FBI has many ways to obtain information not available to the public. In effect, it was a warning not to lie or mislead the agents, for they could check his account against other facts and other witness statements. The more Malcolm thought about it, the more anxious he became. He was beginning to feel like a suspect.

Malcolm began his story. "After I received a tip that Ms. Weiss was at Camp Pendleton, I drove down to Oceanside, the nearest city to the base."

Klein's mention of Camp Pendleton supported the agents' inference that marines had carried out the kidnapping. Carrington asked, "can you tell us where you got this tip?"

"I'm afraid not."

"Fine. Continue your story."

"I ate dinner on the pier and decided to do some bar-hopping. The waitress gave me the names of a few bars where marines hang out. I'd hoped to run into someone who knew about Ms. Weiss."

"Did you have any luck?"

"Not at the first two bars. In the third one the bartender told me he'd heard rumors about some unusual happenings at the base."

"Did he reveal the content of those rumors?"

"Not really, just something about a strange helicopter mission. When a marine pilot entered the bar, he suggested I go talk to him."

"And did you?"

"He was reluctant to talk to a reporter near other people in the bar. We picked up our drinks and moved to a booth that gave us some privacy. He told me about a recent mission that had upset him."

"Did he tell you what took place during that mission?"

"Yes, he did. He flew his Huey to Santa Monica City Airport. His passengers were two marines, a man and a woman, wearing civilian clothing. After landing, the pair got into a waiting car and returned a few hours later with a Black woman. She had been handcuffed, blindfolded, and gagged."

Suarez and Carrington looked at each other and nodded. No longer was there a scintilla of doubt: marines from Camp Pendleton had kidnapped Stella Weiss. Carrington looked glum and shook his head in dismay. Klein had confirmed their conviction that the Weiss kidnapping had been a federal op. Malcolm noticed the change in Carrington's demeanor. The veteran agent seemed shaken.

Carrington said, "please continue, Mr. Klein."

"Of course. The next morning, I went to speak with General Otis Griswold, Camp Pendleton's Commander. At first his receptionist refused my request. Finally, I said, 'tell him I know what he did to Stella Weiss.' The receptionist called the general, and a moment later the general himself came out of his office and led me into it. He denied any role in Ms. Weiss's kidnapping. Eventually, perhaps because I got under his skin, he made noises about national security. The president, he implied, could order such an operation. He didn't go so far as to admit that Shilling had actually issued the orders, but I had no doubt the White House was behind the kidnapping."

Suarez and Carrington again glanced at each other, this time with looks of dismay. Neither could fathom why the president had made such a foolhardy move.

"What happened next?"

"I told the general that he would end up taking the fall when the truth came out. Then he sent me away. Before leaving the base, however, I came into possession of a note that simply stated, 'UCSD-medical.'"

"What did the note mean to you?"

"I assumed the worst—that Ms. Weiss had been injured and taken to the hospital."

"What did you do next?"

"I learned that UCSD-medical has two emergency rooms, one in La Jolla and the other in San Diego. I was closer to the La Jolla ER, and so I went there first. She wasn't there. Then I drove to the San Diego hospital. It took me a while in the ER, but I finally found out she had been admitted as an indigent—and unresponsive—Jane Doe."

Suarez shook his head and said, "Jane Doe, really?"

"Yeah, she'd been dumped, unconscious, in the ER with no ID."

Carrington stepped out of his stiff investigator persona momentarily and said, "this is a sad day in America. We don't treat people that way. We shouldn't treat people that way." But he quickly regrouped and resumed the questioning. "How were you able to find her in the hospital?"

"The receptionist in the ER told me that an unknown Black woman had been transferred from the ER and admitted to the hospital. When I said that the woman could be the person I was looking for, the receptionist called her boss. He was eager to have the unknown woman identified and led me to her room. It was Stella, and she was unconscious."

"Then what?"

"I called her parents and they came down a few hours later. We sat around Stella's bed. Thank god, she finally came out of the coma." At this recollection, Malcolm began to tear up. Suarez and Carrington looked on sympathetically, but said nothing. They turned off their recorder.

Suarez said, "thank you, Mr. Klein, you have been an enormous help. If we have more questions, we'll set up another appointment."

Malcolm responded, "I want the bastards who did this to Stella to pay for their crimes, no matter how high up this goes in the government."

The FBI agents, in a cynical moment, knew that the full justice Klein sought was an unlikely outcome. There were too many powerful players on the other side.

****

"It's lunchtime," said Suarez.

"I'm not very hungry. I lost my appetite when Klein implicated President Shilling in ordering the operation."

"We know Shilling is obsessed with finding the assassins, but the puzzle to me is how he managed to convince Commander Griswold to kidnap Weiss and falsely imprison her."

"That's a good question," said Carrington.

"I hope we can learn the answer."

"Suarez, do we dare go down to Pendleton and interview the general?"

"It would be an extraordinary move on our part. To my knowledge, the FBI has never before investigated a commanding officer suspected of kidnapping a civilian. We should clear it first with Bartolo."

"Yeah, she'll probably want to give NCIS a heads-up before we meet with Griswold."

"I'll make the call right now."

"Bartolo here."

"This is Agent Suarez."

"Nice to hear from you. I've been impressed with the daily reports you and Carrington have been sending me on the Weiss case."

"That's why I called. We now have good reason to suspect that the commander of Camp Pendleton, General Otis Griswold, was involved in the kidnapping."

"I must confess, I'm not surprised to hear that. We've speculated all along that this could be a military op. I suppose you want my go-ahead to interview him?"

"Yes, we were hoping to drive down today."

"By all means, proceed. While you're on the road, I'll set up a joint operation with NCIS."

"Do you really trust them?"

"What do you mean by that?"

"They botched dozens of investigations that preceded the 'Fat Leonard' scandal. Don't we run the risk of them derailing or even sabotaging our investigation? They would have many reasons to protect a Marine Corps general, especially the commander of one of their most important bases."

"I see what you mean. I'll bring Director Abel into the loop. I assume she'll make it clear to NCIS that we won't tolerate any obstruction. And, of course, we'll retain the lead in the investigation."

"Okay, Agent Bartolo, you have your work cut out for you. So, in the meantime, we go ahead with the Griswold interview?"

"Yes, ASAP. Record it and read him his rights."

"Should we arrest him?"

"No, just rattle his cage. He's not going anywhere, so hold off on the arrest until we identify others who can furnish evidence against him. At some point this may end up in Congress. But let's proceed as if the case is ours to see through to the end."

"Got it."

CHAPTER 70

WHEN COMMANDER GRISWOLD read the brief L.A. Times article on Klein's discovery of Weiss, he let out a sigh of relief. His earlier surmise had been correct: Klein was bluffing about having evidence. The reporter had no direct knowledge linking Camp Pendleton to Weiss' disappearance. He expected Klein's tantrum in his office to be the last of the affair.

Arriving unannounced, Suarez and Carrington presented their IDs to Commander Griswold's receptionist. Romero called the general and told him who was in the outer office. He clenched his fists and gritted his teeth, fearing the worst. The general composed himself and told her to show them in. He stood up and moved out from behind his desk just as Romero was leading the agents through the door.

Offering an outstretched hand, the general said, "good afternoon, gentlemen. I'm Commander Otis Griswold."

Suarez and Carrington introduced themselves and shook his hand.

"To what do I owe the honor of a visit from the FBI?"

Carrington answered, "we'd like to speak with you about a recent incident involving some of your personnel."

"Is that so? Well, why don't you take a seat. I'll have Miss Romero bring us some coffee."

"That won't be necessary," said Suarez.

"Suit yourself, but this time of day I need a caffeine infusion."

He moved back to his desk, sat down, and ordered his coffee.

"Commander Griswold," said Suarez, "I hope you don't mind, but we will be recording this interview."

Without waiting for a reaction, Suarez turned on the digital recorder he'd removed from his pocket.

"Oh, and just to cover all bases—so to speak—please read this card and tell us if you understand your Miranda rights to remain silent."

"Gentlemen, this is deeply offensive. I'm a Marine Corps general, Commander of Camp Pendleton. I know my rights. What I don't know is, why do I have to affirm my understanding of these rights to you?"

"We have reason to believe that you would protect the personnel under your command. Informing you of your rights is our way of letting you know that lying to the FBI is a federal offense, punishable by prison time."

"Gentlemen, I don't believe you have the authority to interrogate a member of the U.S. Marine Corps. That's the exclusive job of NCIS."

Carrington replied, "with all due respect, general, you are mistaken. Military personnel are also subject to state, local, and federal laws. If we obtain evidence that you committed a federal crime, we can arrest you on the spot."

Suarez added, "and we recently received word from Washington that the FBI and NCIS have formed a joint task force to investigate the Weiss affair, with the FBI taking the lead."

Shaking his head, Griswold was stunned by the news. He swiveled in his chair, looking around his office and then at the ceiling, as if redemption lay there. He was in a tough spot. The FBI must know more than he suspected. They've probably already interviewed Weiss and Klein. Tiny beads of sweat began to sparkle on his upper lip.

Griswold knew that exercising his right to remain silent at this point would be tantamount to an admission of wrongdoing. He pondered the possibilities, and finally said, "what do you want to know?"

Suarez asked, "are you familiar with the incident concerning the abduction and recovery of Ms. Stella Weiss, an L.A. Times reporter?"

"I don't live in a cave. Everyone's read about it."

"We have evidence, strong evidence, that her abduction was carried out by Camp Pendleton personnel involving a Huey and special ops team. Further, we have evidence that Weiss was falsely imprisoned here, subjected to brutal interrogations, and administered a dangerous drug that caused her to become comatose. Base personnel then transported her to a San Diego hospital and dumped her in the emergency room with no ID."

Griswold sat with his mouth open, seemingly unable to speak. He couldn't imagine how they had learned so many details about the marines' role in the operation. Apparently, he thought, Klein's story hadn't shown all his cards.

Carrington then asked the crucial question: "do you, Commander Otis Griswold, have personal knowledge of these events?"

Griswold was fighting off nausea. He got a momentary reprieve when Romero carried in a silver-plate tray holding a pot of coffee and three mugs. She poured the coffee, and Griswold, stalling for time, took a mug and very slowly added cream and sugar. All the while he was struggling with his dilemma. Klein's words echoed in his head: President Shilling would not come to his rescue. If he lied to the FBI, he might be arrested. If he went silent, he might still have some options later on, perhaps a plea deal in which he gave up the president in exchange for probation. Silence might be golden.

Finally, Griswold made his decision. "Gentlemen, I believe this meeting is at an end. I have nothing more to say."

"You won't answer the question as to your knowledge of this incident?"

"That is correct."

"It is your right to do so," said Suarez sullenly.

Carrington added, "I guess we are done here. I can assure you, General Griswold, you'll be hearing from the FBI again."

****

As soon as the FBI agents left, Griswold had a mild panic attack. He leaned back in his chair and slowly inhaled and exhaled. When he was back in control, his first inclination was to call President Shilling to break the news that the FBI was homing in on the ill-fated operation.

The commander agonized for hours until, finally, he decided that maybe the president could call off the FBI, especially since Attorney General Moffitt was a Shilling loyalist. That gave the president some leverage over the Department of Justice and the FBI. It was already late evening in D.C., so he put off until the following morning what promised to be a difficult call.

CHAPTER 71

THE NEXT MORNING, when the White House switchboard put Griswold through to the president, the general minced no words.

"Mr. President, two FBI agents interviewed me yesterday about the Weiss affair. It's bad. They know details of the operation that apparently were leaked by someone inside Pendleton. They implicate me directly."

"Have they got me in their sights, too? Did you say anything about me?"

"No, Mr. President. The conversation never reached the point of discussing your role. I shut it down, invoking my right to remain silent. They left but threatened to return. I fear they'll come back with a warrant for my arrest."

"Griswold, that would be unfortunate."

Shilling knew that he could hardly depend on Griswold to take the fall for him. He had approached Griswold with his plan, knowing that the downing of Marine One was a festering sore in the Marine Corps. Every marine wanted to see the assassins caught and sentenced to death. Shilling had assumed that the marines' desire for revenge was a near certainty. That's why he had turned to the marines first, expecting them to extract the assassins' identities from Weiss. Shilling believed that Griswold undertook the operation, not out of loyalty to him, but out of loyalty to the Marine Corps. That was now a cause for worry: if Griswold were arrested and serious charges piled on, he might be persuaded to flip. The president was distraught at the thought.

"So, Mr. President, what should we do about our common problem?"

"Don't you worry about it, Griswold. We'll take care of it."

The president ended the call, turned to Stonehouse, and said, "Attorney General James Moffitt is loyal to me. Why don't you contact Moffitt and tell him what's at stake. Maybe he can find a way to quietly end the FBI investigation."

CHAPTER 72

"STELLA, WHERE DID YOU COME UP with such nonsense?"

Stella and Rachel were finishing breakfast in the sunroom off the kitchen in the Weiss home in Beverly Hills. The early morning light filtered in, warming up the maple paneling, a vestige of the previous homeowner's quirky decorating tastes. They sat on white wicker chairs at a round wicker table with a glass top, sipping coffee from handmade ceramic mugs.

"Mom, I know my ordeal was as painful for you and dad as it was for me."

"Hardly, dear."

"My stories have sometimes taken unexpected twists and turns, but the trilogy on Robert and Roberta led to an unreal odyssey. There have been times when I wish I'd never responded to Robert's tease about the scoop of the century."

"But you produced a fabulous piece of journalism."

"Maybe the cost has been too great: my flashbacks, my guilt over the unimaginable worry you and dad felt not knowing whether I was dead or alive."

"When we encouraged you to follow your dreams and become a journalist, we knew the job was sometimes dangerous. You were prepared to accept the risks, and so we went along, knowing it was your decision. You've made a great career at the Times, and we have no regrets about supporting your life in journalism."

"Thanks, mom. I guess I needed some reassurance that you don't resent me for having caused you and dad so much worry."

"Stella, how could you think that? We respect your work, and we're proud of you for doing it."

Stella stood up, walked behind Rachel, and gave her a big hug.

"Mom, you and dad have been hinting that you'd like to know more about how I took advantage of the scoop of the century."

"Well, I must confess, we have been curious."

"I'd love to give you details that aren't in my story, but I can't. Not even Malcolm knows everything. It's better that way. No one else is put in danger, and my sources are protected."

"I'm fine with that. You have to stick to your journalistic ethics."

"Thanks for understanding."

"I know you're probably anxious to move back to your apartment, but you can stay with us for as long as you like."

"Thanks, mom. Honestly, I've been reluctant to move home. The memory of Laurel and Hardy barging in and trashing all my things is still too fresh—and painful."

Rachel chuckled at the mention of Stella's nicknames for the abductors.

"I feel so violated, the way they scattered all my belongings on the floor. So, I'd like to stay here until I've recovered a little longer. Maybe I'll move home after I return to the newsroom."

"That's fine with us. Stay as long as you want."

"Thanks, mom."

"By the way, Stella, how are the counseling sessions going?"

"I think they're helping."

"I'm glad to hear that. What's your therapist like?"

"She's a very pleasant Asian-American woman, maybe in her late forties. She asks me how I'm feeling and offers suggestions for reducing the flashbacks, including special eye exercises. It's getting better. The terrifying image of Dr. Death hovering over me with his monstrous syringe is becoming less sharp, less vivid, and I don't see it as often now."

"I guess Malcolm recommended a good therapist."

"Another reason to thank god for Malcolm. Who knows what would have happened if he hadn't found me in the hospital."

"Stella, not everyone is lucky enough to have a Malcolm in their life. Dad said that when Malcolm called from the hospital to say he found you, he broke down. If I didn't know better, I'd think he was in love with you."

****

"Mom, while we're on the subject of men, I have to tell you something interesting."

"I'm all ears."

"Remember the taller FBI agent who interviewed me here?"

"Sure. He seemed nice, and he's good looking, too."

"Well, his name is Benjamin Suarez. When he was leaving after the second interview, he turned around and gave me a very flirty smile."

"Ooh! Tell me more!"

"Yesterday he followed up the smile with a phone call. He asked if I wanted to go to coffee with him."

"Do you think he's too shy to ask you out on a real date?"

"An FBI agent shy? I don't think so. He's probably just afraid he might cross an ethical line if he dates the victim in an ongoing investigation."

"That does make more sense. So, what did you tell him?"

"We're going to meet tomorrow afternoon at a Starbucks on Wilshire near Rodeo Drive."

"Hmm. That is very interesting."

CHAPTER 73

BARTOLO WAITED PATIENTLY outside Abel's office for her eleven o'clock appointment. The FBI director had requested—no, ordered—her to report on the progress of her two major investigations.

The special agent was finally invited into the office after the FBI's assistant director departed, looking somewhat dejected. Bartolo hoped it was not a bad omen for her meeting.

"Bartolo, thanks for coming. Take a seat. We haven't talked in a few days, and I'm sure you're anxious to update me. When you've done, I have some news to share."

"Yes, I'm eager to fill you in."

"Has the needle-in-the-haystack strategy found the golden needle?"

"We obtained information on 268 IT employee departures for 138 of the largest companies in the region. Only 23 companies refused to provide us with data. We identified nine possible ghosts. Unfortunately, we were able to track down every one of them."

"So, no Robert in the haystack?"

"I'm afraid not."

"How do you account for the failure of your strategy?"

"There are several possibilities. First, Robert is a skilled hacker but might not be an IT professional. For all we know, he could be a carpenter with a computer hobby. Second, maybe he worked in IT but at a small company or nonprofit that fell outside our net. Third,

Weiss exaggerated Robert's computer capabilities."

"What is your assessment? Which, if any, possibility is most likely?"

"I'm afraid, Director Abel, I haven't a clue. The strategy seemed promising, but it didn't yield Robert."

"Does that mean you won't be ferreting out employee departures in smaller companies and other organizations?"

Bartolo hesitated and looked around the room before replying. "I don't think it's worth continuing this long-shot strategy. It wouldn't be a good use of our agents' time."

"I think that's the right decision. Do you have any other plans for identifying Robert?"

"I'm planning to put more effort into our IT task force that's hacking Samoa. They just reported this morning that Weiss had checked into the Le Vasa Resort using the name Sylvia Chung. Obviously she traveled on fake documents."

"Are you planning to arrest her?"

"God no! She's suffered enough already."

"I agree, Bartolo. If we arrested her, there would be a huge public backlash against the FBI."

"Yeah, we don't need that."

"Do we know where she went after her stay at the resort?"

"I'm afraid not, but our team is still working on it. I'm optimistic that we'll soon give the word to the Washingtons to collect Robert and Roberta. In the meantime, director, I'll convene my assassination team again. We'll have another brainstorming session to see what we can come up with."

"Maybe your team can devise a successful plan this time."

Abel was rubbing it in, but Bartolo took no offense. Instead, she asked, "Director Abel, are you still getting pressure from the president?"

"Curiously, it has been all quiet on that front lately."

"He may be worried about the progress of our investigation, perhaps unwilling to pressure you."

"Tell me what you have learned so far."

"Our L.A. team has put together a fairly complete timeline of

Weiss' abduction and imprisonment."

"I assume you'll copy me on that report soon?"

"Of course, you should have it in a few days. In the meantime, let me give you an executive summary."

Abel listened intently as Bartolo ran through the brief version of the timeline. The director nodded knowingly at the mention of Camp Pendleton's role. Bartolo concluded the summary by stressing, "Commander Otis Griswold almost certainly set the operation in motion, most likely at the insistence of President Shilling."

Abel nodded again. "What evidence supports the basic events of the timeline?"

"Agents Suarez and Carrington interviewed Stella Weiss twice in her parents' home. They said she was lucid and forthcoming, despite the lingering psychological effects of her ordeal."

"Has she been diagnosed with PTSD?"

"I'm not sure, but I do know she's undergoing counseling now."

"What else?"

"Our team also interviewed Malcolm Klein. Remember, he's Weiss' editor at the Times and the person who found her in San Diego. It's worth noting that he had previously interviewed the chopper pilot who took part in the abduction."

"I've got some news about that. I'll share it with you in a moment."

Bartolo looked surprised but continued. "Finally, their interview with Commander Otis Griswold did not go well."

"How so?"

"After they informed Griswold that they had pieced together some details of the illegal operation, he invoked his right to remain silent and ended the interview. In fact, he refused to answer even the simplest question: 'did you have knowledge of these events?'"

Abel raised her eyebrows and said, "he's digging a deep hole for himself."

"At the rate he's going he'll pull Shilling into it, too."

"How strong a case can you build against Griswold now?"

"Honestly, I think we have the right guy, but the case is still weak. We need to interview people who took part in the operation, but we have no names…"

Abel interrupted, "I can remedy that in a moment, but please continue."

"Klein hasn't given us the chopper pilot's name. And I doubt he'll give up his source. We need to establish that Griswold himself gave the order to plan and implement the operation. Simply arguing that he—as base commander—must have been the one to issue the order carries little weight without supporting evidence. After all, officers of lower rank could have done it."

****

"I believe the dearth of viable leads has been remedied," said Abel.

"How so?"

"An hour before you arrived, I received a call from my counterpart at NCIS. When I first contacted him, he was a little skeptical about our investigation, but he quickly got on board after seeing the chopper logs from Pendleton. It seems that a Huey in Viper Squadron left Pendleton at 16:19 and returned at 21:47 on the day Weiss disappeared."

"Oh my, isn't that interesting!"

"And can you guess the destination?"

"L.A., I assume."

"Better than that: Santa Monica City Airport."

"That fits our timeline perfectly. And corroborates the FAA info that a Huey had landed and taken off from Santa Monica."

"The Viper Squadron is led by Major Thomas McPherson."

"Did NCIS also get the name of the chopper pilot?"

Glancing at her notes, Abel said, "yes, he's Donald Emerson. If I were you, I'd hold him in reserve for a later interview. He was obviously following McPherson's orders. The question is, who ordered McPherson to send the Huey?"

"I'll pass McPherson's name along to our L.A. team. They can set up an interview. By the way, did NCIS find out who was on the Huey?"

"That information is missing from the record. Not surprising for special ops. Are you ready for the cherry on top of the sundae?"

"Sure."

"NCIS also obtained Griswold's phone records."

Bartolo could barely contain her excitement. "What did they show?"

"There were many calls to and from the White House. We can't be sure he was talking directly to the president, but it's a good working hypothesis."

"Holy shit!"

"Yeah, that's what I've feared all along since Shilling asked me to detain Weiss and I refused. I assumed he would peddle the idea around the government until he found a taker. For some reason, Griswold bought in. Evidently the president bypassed the Pentagon brass and made direct contact with a base commander. That was a highly unorthodox move. It strongly hints at something nefarious."

"It certainly does. There would be no legitimate reason for the president to short-circuit the chain of command."

Abel stood up, signaling to Bartolo that the meeting was over. The special agent returned to her office and called Carrington, bringing him into the loop on the NCIS findings. He was eager to arrange an interview with Major Thomas McPherson.

CHAPTER 74

STELLA'S MENTAL STATE HAD BEEN steadily improving. Therapy was helping but perhaps not as much as her mother's cooking. Stella had lost three pounds during her captivity at Camp Pendleton. Rachel's meals were helping her to regain the weight. Beyond having wholesome food, Stella was benefiting from the long talks she and her mom were having in the sunroom and lounging by the pool.

Malcolm called her nearly every day, asking how she was feeling and encouraging her not to return to the newsroom until she was fully up to it. This day, Stella did not give her usual perfunctory, "don't worry, Malcolm." Instead she said, "I'm ready. We have some stories to write. I'll be in your office at nine tomorrow."

"That's music to my ears."

"Hasta mañana."

CHAPTER 75

COMMANDER GRISWOLD HAD THOUGHT about placing Suarez and Carrington on his "entry denied" list but decided against it. The general knew that jacking around the FBI was not a smart play, especially under the fraught circumstances in which he found himself.

Driving down to Oceanside for the second time in less than a week, the agents amused themselves by spinning out scenarios of arresting Griswold and his gang. Would the arrests come in the commander's office? Would they resist being cuffed? Would Griswold become indignant and belligerent? But the most interesting question was: which of the many front-line participants in the incident would become witnesses for the prosecution in exchange for immunity? Griswold was the local big fish and they had to hook him. Maybe through McPherson.

"You know, Suarez, it would have been so much easier all around if Weiss had just surrendered the information on Robert and Roberta. I just don't see why reporters get special protection and don't have to reveal their sources."

"Really? I'm surprised to hear you say that. I'll try to make the argument."

"Okay, give it your best shot."

"First of all, do you support special protection for attorney-client and doctor-patient relationships?"

"Yeah, in principle. But sometimes I've been tempted to strangle a lawyer. Remember the time when the lawyer invoked his privilege even though lives were in danger from his client's gang?"

"I think that case was before my time in the L.A. office."

"Well, I'll tell you about it. The lawyer knew that his client was a member of a multi-state gang hell-bent on revenge against a rival gang. In meetings with his client, the lawyer had gotten hints of an upcoming confrontation. But he refused to violate his so-called 'sacred trust.'"

"I did hear about it. Fortunately, no one was killed in the shoot-out."

"But that was sheer luck."

"Well, then, maybe a few more exceptions could be carved out for rare cases like that one," said Suarez.

"So far, you haven't defended the reporter's privilege."

"I'm getting to it. As you know, the First Amendment to the U.S. Constitution guarantees freedom of the press."

"Of course."

"How can the press be truly free to do its job if reporters can't protect the identity of their sources? Robert and Roberta would never have been willing to meet Weiss and tell their story if she could have turned around and given them up to the government."

"I get all that, but in some cases wouldn't the government's right to know outweigh a reporter's rights? In the Weiss case, I would argue, the government has a compelling interest in finding and prosecuting the couple, especially if they might be planning more assassinations."

"But those concerns wouldn't qualify as an exemption under California's Media Shield Law. The exemptions are few and far between, mainly to protect the right of a person on trial to challenge witnesses. Also, in the event of an emergency or imminent disaster, a judge may force journalists to reveal their sources. If the government's interest in this case was so compelling, the FBI should have arrested Weiss, allowing the courts sort it all out."

"I suppose I agree with that. Kidnapping Weiss in the hope of learning about Robert and Roberta was as stupid as stupid gets."

****

273

Suarez turned into the base and presented his ID and driver's license to the guard at the gate. Carrington showed his ID, and the guard waved them through. They found McPherson's office in a small building a mere stone's throw from an aircraft maintenance hangar.

McPherson was expecting them, and his door was open. He warily introduced himself to the agents. They reciprocated and shook hands.

"Come in and sit down."

They looked around at the military-grade office furniture and aircraft images on the walls. On his desk were a vintage PC and family pictures. One image showed the married couple and five girls, perhaps taken at a recent family gathering.

McPherson, probably in his late thirties, had short black hair sprinkled with silver strands. He had close-set brown eyes, an aquiline nose, and an early five o'clock shadow.

"Major McPherson," began Carrington, "I'll be taking the lead in today's interview. Oh, and we'll be recording this meeting."

Suarez handed him a card with Miranda rights printed in large font. McPherson knew his rights but was willing to talk to the agents. Carrington turned on the recorder.

"Do you have any idea why we're here?"

"I'm afraid I do. When the NCIS agents showed up and demanded the Huey logs, I sensed that our secret op was no longer secret."

"What was your role in this operation?"

"I chose the pilots and coordinated with special ops to take their people to Santa Monica and return."

"Did you know that the special ops team was planning to abduct Ms. Stella Weiss, an L.A. Times reporter?"

"I didn't know that at the time the operation was being planned. In fact, I didn't know it was an abduction until the next morning when I debriefed Emerson and learned the terrible truth."

"So," interjected Suarez, "your claim is that you knew nothing about the specific purpose of the operation in advance?"

"That is correct. I only knew that Emerson and his co-pilot would be transporting a special ops team to Santa Monica and return."

Carrington resumed the questioning. "Major McPherson, I'm

going to ask you a different question, so please take time to think about it before answering. Keep in mind that lying to the FBI is a felony offense."

McPherson held his armchair in a death grip, his knuckles turning white. Then he began to fidget. He looked around the room and then settled his gaze on Carrington.

"I'm ready."

"Who ordered you to undertake this operation?"

"Earlier that day, the special ops team came to my office with their superior officer. He gave me the assignment."

"Did he have line authority over you?"

"Actually, no. However, in some cases, an important operation takes precedence over protocol. When special ops needs a ride, we are more than happy to provide it."

"Fair enough. But did anyone in special ops tell you who had delivered their marching orders?"

"I asked and was told, 'it came from the top.'"

"Did you take that answer to refer to a particular individual?"

"Of course. Decoding the answer wasn't rocket science. I assumed it was Commander Griswold."

"Please provide us with the name of the special ops officer who requested the chopper transportation."

"I can do that. His name is Luke Petersen. Do you want his contact information?"

"That would be helpful."

McPherson jotted down Petersen's phone number and email address and handed the paper to Carrington. The agents stood up, thanked Major McPherson for his cooperation, and left the office, taking along their recorder.

CHAPTER 76

"SUCH A TANGLED WEB THEY'VE WOVEN," remarked Suarez as they returned to their car.

"Hang on. We've got plenty of day left, so let's see if we can snag an interview with Petersen in the next couple of hours."

Petersen, who also held the rank of major, answered Carrington's call.

"I've been waiting for your call. Major McPherson gave me a heads up."

"We would like to speak with you this afternoon. We have a few questions regarding a recent special op."

"I don't want you anywhere near my office, so let's meet at a restaurant in Oceanside."

"That works for us. It's past lunchtime anyway, and we haven't eaten."

They agreed on a time and place. Forty-five minutes later they were sitting at a red Naugahyde booth in La Fuente, an old Mexican-style cafe. The setting was replete with plastic cacti in colorful ceramic planters, pictures of churches and fiestas on the walls, and a small tray of hot sauces and other condiments on every table along with menus. A waitress brought a bowl of tortilla chips and took their lunch order. They all chose the day's special, a chile relleno and cheese enchilada with sides of beans and rice. Sin cervezas.

Suarez took the lead after placing his recorder on the table and ensuring that Petersen understood his Miranda rights.

"Two of your people boarded a Huey and traveled to Santa Monica City Airport. After landing, they were driven to Stella Weiss' apartment. They abducted her at gunpoint and returned to Camp Pendleton. Is that correct?"

"Well, you guys don't waste any time, do you? But I would be careful tossing around a strong word like 'abducted.'"

"Let's not get distracted by semantics. Was that an accurate rendering of the operation?"

"I suppose so."

"Okay, then. Now we need to know, Major Petersen, did they carry out this operation on your orders?"

Petersen looked around to be certain that no one could overhear their conversation.

"Gentlemen, I received what I believed was a lawful order, and we followed it. I admit, it was out of the ordinary, even for special ops."

"Did you have any reservations about the operation at the time?"

"Many unusual ops move forward under the cover of national security. This was one of them. I had to assume that people above my pay grade knew what they were doing. I had no reason to doubt that we were acting in the national interest."

"I hope you will answer the next question without equivocation."

"Of course."

"Who gave you the order for this operation?"

"As I made clear to Major McPherson, the orders came from the top."

"By top you mean…"

"Commander Griswold, of course."

"How did he communicate the orders to you?"

"He personally came to my office and spelled out the requirements in considerable detail."

"Did he tell you where he got his orders?"

"He did not. He said only that it was top secret and a matter of national security. That was all I needed to know."

"Did he tell you who you would be abducting?"

"That word again."

"Please answer the question."

"He merely said it was a woman who had committed a serious crime."

"And where did your team take Ms. Weiss after returning to Camp Pendleton?"

"They loaded her into a waiting car, drove her to Building C, and put her into an interrogation cell."

"Isn't it a bit strange that they wore ski masks?"

"Not really. We do that sometimes. We have to protect the identity of our personnel. Don't forget: most of our operations are secret."

"When Commander Griswold was in your office, did you raise any questions about the operation's legality?"

"Why would you expect me to challenge the orders of the base commander?"

"So, you had no reservations about abducting and falsely imprisoning a civilian woman?"

He winced and said, "for all I knew when I got my orders, she could have been a serial axe-murderer. I had no reservations at that time. My job was to ensure that my people carried out the operation efficiently."

"How do you feel about the operation today, knowing the woman was Stella Weiss, a respected reporter?"

"I believe Commander Griswold ordered an operation that, in his judgment, served national security interests. If you're trying to get me to admit regrets about the special op, you're wasting your time. I'd do it again tomorrow if given the same orders."

"Major Petersen, we would now like to turn to the personnel who took part in the operation."

"I may not be very helpful in that regard."

"Why not?"

"As I told you earlier, we jealously guard the identities of our special ops personnel."

"Well, let's see."

"Were the man and woman who abducted Ms. Weiss members of

your team?"

"I can give you that much. Yes, they were. But don't bother asking for their names."

"Were the interrogators also part of your team?"

"Yes, they were also my people. And, again, I must withhold their identities."

"What about the man with the polygraph machine?"

"Yes, him too."

"And the supposed doctor who administered the drug to Ms. Weiss?"

"No, he arrived at Pendleton a day or two after Weiss broke the polygraph machine."

"Do you know his name?"

"I didn't know it while he was here. He just said to call him 'doc.' He was a strange one, for sure."

"Who sent him?"

"I assumed it was Commander Griswold because I had informed him about the polygraph incident. He said he'd find another way to get Weiss to talk."

"So, you don't know the doc's identity?"

****

Petersen was weighing the pros and cons of telling all he knew about doc. When he considered the penalties for lying to the FBI versus covering his own ass, the scale tilted toward candor. After all, doc wasn't under his command, so he wouldn't be betraying one of his own.

"Honestly, Agent Suarez, I was very curious about the supposed doctor who came out of nowhere, especially after he botched the interrogation, and we had to take Weiss to the hospital."

"Are you telling us that you now know who he is?"

"Yes, I do. He stayed at the base in our guest quarters. After he left the base, we searched his room and found some useful materials in the wastebasket."

Carrington and Suarez were dumbfounded at this revelation.

"What did you find?"

"Besides orange peels, candy bar wrappers, and dirty tissues, we came up with two used boarding passes. The man's name is Dr. Charles Graninger. He departed from Reagan National Airport and flew to Omaha. And from Omaha he took a flight to San Diego."

"Do you know anything more about this doctor, apart from his name and the fact that his trip originated in D.C.?"

Petersen hesitated again, poking his fork at the last piece of enchilada, and remained silent for many minutes.

"Major Petersen, I'm not a dentist. Don't make me feel like I'm pulling teeth trying to pry answers out of you."

Petersen groaned and then dropped a bombshell. "I looked him up. He's on the White House medical staff."

"Oh my god," said Suarez under his breath, while Carrington just looked down and shook his head.

Without missing a beat, Suarez resumed the questioning.

"When you learned his identity and place of employment, did you draw any conclusions?"

"I think the conclusion is fairly obvious."

"Can you please spell it out for the benefit of the record?"

Seemingly unsettled by this line of questioning and his admissions so far, Petersen reluctantly said, "it appears that Dr. Graninger was sent by someone in the White House."

Suarez and Carrington looked at each other, and nodded; a faint smile appeared on Suarez's face.

Carrington said, "I think we have what we need right now, Major Petersen. Thank you for your time."

****

On the walk to the car, Suarez said, "it's been a good day."

"Better than we had any right to expect after Commander Griswold stonewalled us."

"Maybe McPherson and Petersen cooperated because NCIS is working with us."

"I wouldn't be surprised. NCIS can destroy their careers. All we can do is annoy the hell out of them—at least for right now."

"But surely we have enough on McPherson and Petersen to arrest them?"

"If they were civilians, probably. But arresting two Marine Corps officers would be highly unusual. The armed forces are supposed to take care of their own law-breakers. We should let NCIS do it. But if NCIS doesn't act, we have the authority to make the arrests. Anyway, Director Abel will make that call after we submit our final report to Bartolo."

"Right you are."

The agents reached their car and entered with Carrington taking the wheel. On the return trip to L.A. they continued talking.

"You know, Carrington, one thing surprised me in the interviews today."

"Yeah, what's that?"

"Neither officer asked about Stella's condition."

"No surprise, really. She's just a name to them."

"If they had met her they might feel differently."

"Suarez, I hesitate to ask, but I will anyway. How did your date go with Ms. Weiss?"

"It didn't."

"What do you mean?"

"You gave me some good advice, which I took to heart. If I dated the victim in an ongoing investigation—even doing something as innocuous as meeting her for coffee—a defense lawyer could use it to undermine my credibility. So, I broke the date."

"A wise decision."

"But I told Stella, 'as soon as we submit our final report, I'll get back to you for a real date.'"

"You two would make a nice couple. I hope it works out."

"Thanks for saying that."

PART 3

CHAPTER 77

BARTOLO'S EYES ALMOST BUGGED OUT of their sockets when she read the transcripts of the McPherson and Petersen interviews. These marines not only admitted their roles in Weiss affair, but they also implicated the base commander and, indirectly, the White House. "This is golden," she said out loud, as she forwarded the latest L.A. report to Director Abel. In an accompanying note, Bartolo wrote, "request NCIS obtain names of Petersen's special ops team members and an account of their whereabouts on the days in question."

Abel wrote back an hour later. "These are fabulous interviews. I've already sent the report to NCIS so they'll know who is in our sights."

NCIS did more than furnish names and places. A week after Abel's request, they supplied transcripts of their agents' interviews with the persons of interest. Having access to base personnel records, NCIS agents were able to identify and interview Laurel and Hardy, Tweedledum and Tweedledee, and the polygraph man. They even tracked down Don Emerson, the helicopter pilot. And the NCIS did their own interviews of McPherson and Petersen. Apparently, they had not interviewed Commander Griswold—or he had refused to cooperate.

Abel had mixed feelings after receiving the cornucopia of NCIS evidence. On the one hand, she was delighted with their cooperation and the high quality of the interviews. They had asked pertinent questions and elicited apparently truthful answers. With these materials

285

the FBI case was nearly complete.

On the other hand, the expeditious and thorough way NCIS had handled the interviews raised a disquieting possibility: NCIS might mete out military justice, in the form of courts martial, to the marines involved. Such an NCIS move might preclude any FBI enforcement actions—or at least make them bureaucratically problematic. Unsure of NCIS's motives, Abel had no choice but to wait for Bartolo to wrap up the FBI's investigation.

CHAPTER 78

ACTING ON THE PRESIDENT'S BEHALF, Stonehouse had communicated with Attorney General Moffitt about both FBI investigations. In his first call, Stonehouse merely requested the AG to assign a low priority to the Weiss investigation. Top priority would remain the discovery and apprehension of Robert and Roberta. But the tone of Stonehouse's advice to the attorney general changed drastically after Griswold informed the president, "all hell is breaking loose at Camp Pendleton with NCIS and FBI agents snooping around." In his latest message to Moffitt, Stonehouse passed along the president's "suggestion" to shut down the Weiss investigation and transfer all pertinent files to the White House.

Moffitt, who had been periodically briefed on the investigation's progress by Abel, was a strong supporter of Shilling. He had publicly praised his policies, and often took actions that furthered the president's agenda. However, shutting down an important FBI investigation was unthinkable, out of the question. Eventually, Moffitt surmised, knowledge of the president's misdeeds would leak to the press. In the aftermath of the media frenzy, Moffitt feared that he would be called to testify before congressional committees. He had no choice but to push back hard against the White House, even if it meant falling out of favor with the president. If Shilling fired him, he would land on his feet as a lobbyist with a seven-figure salary. America truly is the land of opportunity, he smirked to himself.

****

President Shilling was already in a cranky mood before Stonehouse told him that Moffitt wouldn't play ball.

"That son of a bitch. I thought he was on our team. What brand of loyalty is this? I make a simple request to my attorney general and he refuses. I don't get it. I may have to take drastic action. In fact, I see no alternative. Stonehouse, why don't you invite FBI Director Abel to come by my office this afternoon for a little chat."

"What are you going to do?"

"You'll find out when the time comes."

"Mr. President, with all due respect, need I remind you that a cover-up can have more dire consequences that the original crime…"

"Stonehouse, let me tell you for the umpteenth time: I've committed no crime. As the commander and chief of the armed forces it was within my powers to order the marines to detain and interrogate Weiss."

"I doubt the FBI sees it that way."

"Well, it doesn't matter. As president I'm protected from the FBI."

"That's true because long-standing DOJ custom says a sitting president cannot be indicted. But you are only protected as long as you remain in office."

"Does that mean the FBI could come after me when I'm no longer president?"

"It's a possibility, sir."

"Well, that's another good reason to kill the investigation now. I'm not going to put up with this shit any longer. Fuck 'em."

"I strongly advise you not to take any action that could come back and bite you on the ass."

"Stonehouse, you worry way too much."

"Yes, sir. Even so, Mr. President, you may want to refresh your memory on presidential history. Look up Richard Nixon."

"Sure. I'll do it right away," was Shilling's sarcastic reply.

****

Abel deliberately arrived 10 minutes late for her 2:30 appointment with President Shilling. She gave no excuse to Stonehouse who, while pacing, had almost worn a thin spot in the carpet outside the Oval Office. Sensing that Shilling had put her near the top of his disloyalty list, Abel's tardiness was sending a message. She wanted to assert her continuing independence and her unwillingness to dance to the president's tune.

Stonehouse hurriedly opened the door and led Abel into the sacred space. Shilling was watching himself on Fox News delivering a speech to the Clean Coal Coalition. Stonehouse looked up at the monitor and said, "that was a truly brilliant performance, Mr. President."

Abel glanced at the monitor but said nothing as the president reluctantly pressed the mute button.

Shilling looked up at Abel with a strained smile.

"I'm glad you could drop by; I've been looking forward to our little pow-wow."

She winced at his last word and merely nodded.

"Why do you suppose I've asked you here today?"

"To present me with the Presidential Medal of Freedom?"

There was no laughter.

"No, Abel, that wouldn't be it. No, indeed. I want an update on the two FBI investigations looking into the assassination and its aftermath."

In a neutral voice, she said, "I'm happy to oblige, sir."

Before she could provide the update, Shilling said—in a loud and accusatory tone, "why have you failed to arrest the killers? Why haven't you identified Robert and Roberta? Why don't you know where they are?"

"Mr. President, since you already seem to know the status of that investigation, I really have nothing to add."

She did not want to mention that her IT task force had verified Weiss' trip to Samoa for fear the White House would pass the information along to CIA Director Smalley. "I want to emphasize that our agents are working their tails off. The investigation is moving forward in a deliberate manner. Unfortunately, our results to date have been limited."

"That is simply unacceptable."

"It is what it is, Mr. President. We are competent investigators, not magicians."

"I've learned from other sources, Abel, that the investigation of the Weiss incident is nearing completion."

Abel feared that if Shilling believed the investigation were about to wrap up, he would move quickly to suppress its findings. She had to stall for time.

"Your sources, I regret to say, are misinformed. In collaboration with NCIS we have conducted interviews with several personnel at Camp Pendleton. We have yet to draw major conclusions from the growing body of evidence."

"I'd lay money on the entire affair being a rogue operation. Maybe some marines want credit for cracking the case."

Dumbstruck by Shilling's preposterous idea, Abel held her tongue. Maybe agreeing with him would be a smart tactic.

"Well, Mr. President, I have to admit it's a good possibility. In fact, right now it's one of the most likely scenarios we're exploring." He nodded approvingly.

The shadow boxing continued for several more minutes until Shilling delivered a demand. "Let's assume it was a rogue operation, confined to low-ranking personnel. In that case the operation reflects poorly on base leadership and, by extension, on the commander in chief. The entire matter is moot anyway because Weiss was found safe and unharmed. Nothing would be gained by continuing the investigation. Its only effect would be to embarrass good people in positions of authority. That outcome is unacceptable. That's why you will terminate the Weiss investigation immediately."

Abel showed no outward reaction. Inside, a volcano of anger was ready to erupt. She struggled to keep it bottled up.

Shilling added, "and you'll turn over to my office all original source materials and copies, both paper and electronic. That includes records searches, transcripts and audios of interviews, draft reports, and so on. No exceptions."

Regardless of the president's orders, Abel had no intention of shutting down the investigation. But she needed to protest, just a little.

"Mr. President. I don't agree with your decision. My people have worked very hard and will be terribly disappointed if all their work was for naught."

"It simply can't be helped. I've made my decision and I expect you to implement it."

She nodded her head in feigned acquiescence. "As you know, sir, pulling together all those materials is going to be a big job. How soon do you want them?"

The president turned to Stonehouse who said, "I believe 72 hours will give you ample time to comply with the president's order. Bring the materials to me when you're done."

"Yes, I believe we can do it in that timeframe."

Shilling glared at her and said, "you know, Abel, failure to follow my orders will have dire consequences for your career."

"I understand."

"I'm glad we're on the same page."

Turning to Stonehouse, Shilling said, "show her out."

After Abel had been escorted out of the Oval Office, and the door closed behind her, Shilling asked, "well, Stonehouse, what do you think?"

"You handled that delicate situation very well, sir. She seems to be falling in line. She likes her job and wants to keep it."

"Yes, my sword hangs over her head but will fall at the slightest sign of betrayal."

****

Not more than five minutes after she had returned to the Hoover Building, Abel had already formulated a plan. She immediately went to Bartolo's office. The door was open, the special agent seated at her desk.

"Bartolo, we have a problem."

"Let me guess, you just returned from your meeting with the

president."

"Right. Shilling has ordered me to shut down the Weiss investigation."

"Oh crap!"

"Worst of all, he wants to remove all traces of our work. He has demanded every document—original source materials and all copies. Fortunately, Stonehouse gave us 72 hours to comply."

"Shilling wants to remove all evidence that the investigation ever took place?"

"Precisely, Bartolo."

"What a dumbfuck. He's completely naive when it comes to IT capabilities. Our investigation will live on, accessible to any third-rate government IT specialist."

"And, let's not forget, Weiss and Klein will publish their accounts of the plot in the L.A. Times. He can't bury that story. I have a feeling they may eventually publish a very full account of the affair." Wink, wink.

"I suspect you're right, Director Abel. They're damn good journalists."

"How soon can your team complete the final report?"

"I believe they're very close to finishing it. Maybe a day or two."

"Let them know about Shilling's edict. Request the final report ASAP—with copies to you and me. And tell them to assemble all source materials, just as the president directed. However, they are to hold the documents until they hear from me."

"Good. We can't let Shilling bury his crimes."

CHAPTER 79

WITH STELLA FINALLY BACK AT THE TIMES, she and Malcolm worked on their stories, which were published without delay. The online demand to read their account of the kidnapping was so great that the Times' servers crashed. The emergency IT team got them up and running again within an hour.

Most readers, had they been questioned, would have admitted that Weiss's account of the events brought them to tears. She had told the story in great detail, and it was highly believable. The tale ended with Laurel and Hardy restraining her while Dr. Death delivered the painful injection. Because the story included only what she knew first-hand at the time, it made no reference to Camp Pendleton or to Commander Griswold—much less to President Shilling.

Malcolm's story began in the first frantic days of Stella's disappearance. He included quotes from her parents and from Times co-workers who praised her journalistic chops. He described the ransacking of her apartment, and mentioned the L.A. Police Department's cursory investigation and the FBI's subsequent takeover of the case. Malcolm alluded to an anonymous tip that sent him to Camp Pendleton in search of his reporter. An interview with someone on the base confirmed that the marines had abducted and imprisoned Weiss. The tense interview with Commander Otis Griswold had yielded little except a hint that the operation was justified on the basis of national security. Malcolm was vague in describing the tip that led him to visit

UCSD emergency rooms in search of Ms. Weiss.

To embellish the story's human-interest angle, he told how the marines had dumped Ms. Weiss, an unconscious Black woman with no ID, at the ER. There she had been classified as an indigent Jane Doe. Jane Doe #3, to be precise.

Malcolm's story ended on a high note as he recounted the heart-warming scene when, with her parents and the editor at her bedside, Stella regained consciousness and managed a wan smile.

The twin stories went viral on the Internet. In online comments, the majority of readers expressed outrage at how the Marine Corps could have so mistreated an innocent civilian, a respected journalist. Some comments, however, were rightwing rants about Weiss as a traitor who refused to help the government identify President Wahl's assassins. A handful of comments were obscene or racist.

President Shilling fumed as he read the stories. He hoped the uproar would subside quickly without provoking Democrats in Congress to call for an investigation of Stellagate—the name given to the incident by a talking head at CNN.

CHAPTER 80

CARRINGTON AND SUAREZ, informed by Bartolo of the existential threat to their investigation, worked almost around the clock, surviving on pizzas, Thai takeout, and coffee.

For maybe the tenth time during the second morning following Shilling's edict, Carrington exclaimed, "I can't believe the president would shut down an FBI investigation and want to confiscate our entire work product."

Suarez replied with the same message but different words each time. "I understand your shock at this turn of events, but we have to make the best of a bad situation."

"And how do we do that?"

"Our report has to set forth and highlight every shred of evidence that directly or indirectly implicates Shilling for issuing the orders that resulted in Stella's ordeal."

"The strongest evidence we have is Petersen's identification of Dr. Charles Graninger as Dr. Death. How could a doctor on the White House staff end up on this op without the president's authorization?"

"But here's the rub: all we have is Petersen's statement. It's suggestive evidence but not definitive."

"I agree, Suarez. Maybe we need to interview Dr. Death."

"Better yet, let's ask Bartolo to do it because we can't spare the time for a round trip to D.C."

"Brilliant idea. She'll understand the importance of this. I'll call her right now."

"Bartolo here."

"This is Carrington. We are working feverishly on our final report, but it has one hole you can fill."

"Tell me."

"We would like you to interview Dr. Death—I mean Dr. Charles Graninger—because he's in your neighborhood. Perhaps you can get him to name the person who sent him to Camp Pendleton with the drug."

"You're right. He is a crucial link. And it makes sense for me to do the interview. As soon as I'm finished talking to him, I'll send you an audio file and transcript so you can incorporate the new material into your report."

"We'll be waiting."

****

After Bartolo ended the call, she wondered, how am I going to pull off this interview without Graninger immediately alerting the president? She had an idea. In fact, several ideas. With the help of her IT team, Bartolo searched dozens of data bases to gather information about Dr. Charles Graninger's life. Behind the White House firewall, her team turned up his work schedule. He was due to end his shift in about an hour. The bachelor, she learned, usually summoned an Uber to take him to his Logan Circle townhouse.

Bartolo rode the elevator to the garage under the Hoover Building. A few minutes later, she pulled out of the garage in a black Chevy Suburban with an Uber sticker on the window and a D.C. license plate that said "vehicle for hire." An agent in another FBI vehicle immediately followed her.

She drove the counterfeit Uber to Graninger's most likely pick-up spot, and awaited his arrival. The agent in the second car intercepted and waved off the genuine Uber. When the doctor appeared, Bartolo unlocked the passenger doors for him. He climbed into the back seat, and she locked him in. Preoccupied with his phone, scrolling through

Facebook, Graninger didn't realize he was now in FBI custody.

Looking up from his phone, Graninger suddenly shouted, "hey, you're going in the wrong direction."

"There's been a change of plans, Dr. Graninger. I'm FBI Special Agent Bartolo. You are subject to arrest on suspicion of conspiracy, attempted murder, and practicing medicine in California without a license."

Graninger was too startled to argue with Bartolo's transparent bluff. She pulled to the curb and turned around, pointing her 9mm Sig Sauer at his head.

"I'll take your phone now."

His hand was shaking as he passed her the phone. Her mention of California signaled to him that she was aware of his role in the Weiss affair. He knew he was in deep trouble.

Feigning ignorance, he asked, "what's this all about?"

"You'll find out after we're settled in the Hoover Building."

"I think you have me confused with someone else. This must be a mistake."

"Is your name Dr. Charles Graninger?"

"Yes."

"Then there's no mistake."

****

Bartolo returned with her protesting cargo to the FBI garage. They rode the elevator to the fifth floor, and she led him down the hallway to the conference room. Her inscrutable scribe was already seated, the audio-visual equipment turned on.

"Dr. Graninger, have a seat and help yourself to coffee and pastries. I apologize because they're a little stale this time of day."

He sat down reluctantly, quaking with fear, his face as white as porcelain. She handed him the Miranda statement, and he acknowledged his understanding.

"I see that your medical degree is from the Jagiellonian University Medical College in Krakow, Poland. Is that correct?"

"Yes."

"What is your specialty?"

"General surgery."

"Why does the White House need someone with your qualifications?"

"We must be prepared for any medical situation. I can remove an appendix or a bullet, close a knife wound, even amputate a limb."

"Have your services ever been required?"

"Sure. Many times for simple things, like cleaning and bandaging a visiting child's scraped knee. But once I did an emergency appendectomy on the White House pastry chef. I didn't believe there was enough time to transport her to Georgetown University Hospital. And she could have waited in the ER for hours before a doctor saw her. So, I made the decision to operate and probably saved her life."

"Very impressive. Now I'd like to turn to the matter at hand. Are you familiar with the name Stella Weiss?"

He began to look away, but at the sight of the scribe, who seemed to be scowling, the doctor turned back to Bartolo and said, "yes, I've followed that little morality play."

"You didn't just follow it, you were a lead actor. Is that not so? Before you answer, I want you to understand that lying to the FBI can jeopardize your freedom."

"Am I under arrest?"

"It depends."

"What do you mean?"

"It depends on whether you cooperate."

He nodded his understanding.

"Good, let's get started. We know you flew out of Reagan National Airport to Omaha, Nebraska. Then, later that day, you flew on to San Diego."

"Is that itinerary correct?"

"Where did you get this information?"

"That's not important. What's important is that you answer my questions truthfully. Now, I'll ask again: was that itinerary correct?"

"What happens if I don't answer your questions?"

"In that case, I will deem you uncooperative, arrest you, and charge you with several felonies."

"And if I tell you what you want to know?"

"Then I might not arrest you."

"That doesn't seem like much of a choice. If I incriminate myself I might not get arrested. Can you give me a better incentive to cooperate?"

Bartolo was losing patience with the doctor, and her voice became more strident.

"You need to cooperate. Answer my questions about your travel, now. You have 10 seconds."

"Yes, I took those flights."

"See, that wasn't so hard. Now, what did you do for part of the day in Omaha?"

"I stopped by a laboratory to pick up a drug."

"Which laboratory?"

"I don't really know anything about the laboratory. It was located in a small commercial building with no exterior signs. I had been instructed to go to a specific room and give the receptionist a code number."

"Who told you where to pick up the drug?"

"I was in the Oval Office. The president told me about a new drug the government had developed to use on foreign captives who had double-crossed the U.S. It would make them speak the truth. I was to deliver it to Camp Pendleton and inject it into a person who had betrayed our country."

"So, if I understand you correctly, President Shilling asked you to obtain the drug in Omaha and administer it to someone at Camp Pendleton?"

"Actually, there was another man in the Oval Office besides the president and Stonehouse, but I wasn't introduced to him. He was the one who told me where to go in Omaha."

"Did you ask why this clandestine operation was necessary?"

"Yes. The president said it was a matter of national security."

"When you received your assignment, did you have any knowledge of that person's identity?"

"No. When I got my orders, I didn't know who she was. I learned her identity at Camp Pendleton."

"Did you ask about the drug's status in the FDA approval process?"

"No. The question never occurred to me. Don't forget, Agent Bartolo, I was in the Oval Office with the President of the United States. Did you expect me to give him the third degree? I'm a patriotic American. I assumed he knew what he was doing."

"So, Dr. Graninger, you were prepared to administer a drug about which you knew virtually nothing to a person who was not your patient?"

He took a deep breath and glanced at the plate of pastries as he stalled before answering.

"Yes, I suppose so. Again, I want to emphasize that I was not in a position to question my orders."

"It was an order and not a gentlemen's request?"

"I did not believe I had a choice in the matter. He gave me an assignment, and I did what I was asked to do."

"Asked you to do, or told you to do?"

"Surely you understand that these words have the same meaning in the Oval Office."

"As a physician, Dr. Graninger, do you believe that you acted in the best interests of Ms. Stella Weiss?"

"Is that a trick question? She wasn't my patient, and I wasn't even introduced to her. From the time I entered the room to the time she passed out was a span of about five minutes."

"Do you have any regrets about what you did?"

"Of course I do, but only with the benefit of 20-20 hindsight."

"So, you were just following orders?"

"That is correct."

"What happened after Ms. Weiss passed out?"

"We waited during the rest of the day, hoping she would regain consciousness so the interrogators could get back to work."

"And what happened when she didn't revive?"

"Well, that's when I heard them mention her name for the first time. I was shocked."

"Who is the 'them?'"

"A man and a woman who weren't in uniform, but I assumed they were marines. And, of course, the two interrogators; both of them were men. They were all wearing ski masks, as was I."

"Then what happened?"

"They said my services were no longer needed. I went to my quarters and made travel arrangements to return to D.C. the following day."

"Do you know what happened to Ms. Weiss after you left?"

"I didn't learn about her trip to the hospital until I read about it in the Post."

"What happened upon your return to the White House?"

"I had no choice but to tell my side of the story to the president. He threatened to fire me but eventually seemed to understand that I carried out the mission as he had directed. It was the drug that failed."

"These are all the questions I have for the present time."

"Are you going to arrest me?"

"I'm still deciding. In the meantime, you'll be my guest in the Hoover Building during the next day or so. Tomorrow morning, under my watchful eye, you will call the White House and tell them you contracted a sudden illness, and won't be reporting to work for the next couple of days."

"You have no right to hold me here."

"Actually, I have every right to hold you for 48 hours before charging you with a crime."

"This is outrageous."

"It is what it is."

CHAPTER 81

AFTER HAVING DR. GRANINGER'S INTERVIEW transcribed, Bartolo sent the text and audio file to Carrington. Sitting in his cubicle, Carrington read the transcript and immediately forwarded it to Suarez with the subject line: "Bartolo nailed it."

Suarez finished reading the transcript then said to Carrington, who had just joined him, "this is incontrovertible evidence that the president ordered Dr. Graninger to Camp Pendleton to inject Stella. More than that, it provides strong evidence that Shilling was aware of, and sanctioned, the entire operation."

"But I'd sure like to get Griswold to come clean."

"Maybe we should interview him again."

"It would be a long shot for sure. NCIS couldn't make any headway with him either. But it might be worth a try. Can we spare the time for the trip?"

"I think we have to. Look, our draft report is complete except for a summary of the Graninger interview. It won't take me long to add it. We have to go the last mile for Griswold."

"Then," said Carrington, "we better get going."

"Let's just show up at his office, and not give him time to prepare or disappear."

"I agree."

****

On the drive to Camp Pendleton, Carrington took the wheel while Suarez drafted the new section of the report on his laptop, frequently pausing to get feedback from his partner. When they were satisfied with the wording, Suarez asked, "what do think will happen?"

"You mean when we submit our final report?"

"No, I mean after. Is this the beginning of the end of the Shilling presidency?"

"I doubt it. That guy is a survivor. He wants to bury the report and sequester all our files. Even if the report is leaked, Shilling has enough Republican allies in Congress to excuse his bad behavior. They'll invoke national security and all the rest. They'll paint Weiss as the villain, a traitor to our nation."

"I hope you're wrong. Shilling needs to pay the price for what he did to Stella."

"Well, I wouldn't put any money on it."

****

After being waived into Camp Pendleton and parking, the agents headed straight to Commander Griswold's office. Several men in uniform were standing in the reception area, talking in hushed tones, apparently waiting for a meeting with the general. Carrington and Suarez stepped passed the group and approached Romero at her desk.

"We're FBI Agents Suarez and Carrington, and we're here to speak with Commander Griswold."

"Yes, I remember you from the last visit. Let me inform him that you are here again without an appointment."

The general opened the door, entered the reception area, and approached the agents. In a low voice he said, "I'm getting sick and tired of federal agents coming around here and pestering me. What do you want this time?"

Suarez replied, "we still need an answer to the question we asked you last time. Did you know what had transpired with respect to the abduction and false imprisonment of Ms. Stella Weiss?"

"Well, gentlemen, I'll give you the same answer as before. I have nothing to say. And you may leave now. As you can see, several officers are waiting to meet with me."

In a threatening tone, Carrington said, "we have ironclad evidence that you ordered the Weiss operation. If I were you, I'd cooperate."

"Well, you're not me, and my position is unchanged; I have nothing to say."

The agents looked at each other, and Carrington said, "well, I guess we're done here."

As they turned to go, Suarez shouted, "will you answer that question when a congressional committee asks you?"

Griswold cringed but said nothing, and then he invited the uniformed men into his office.

Suarez and Carrington returned to L.A. They spent the next 14 hours putting their report into final form and preparing the supporting documents for transmittal to Bartolo and Abel.

CHAPTER 82

Oh my god, Abel uttered over and over as she read the final report and selectively skimmed the appended documents. When she had finished going through the materials, she called Bartolo.

"Bartolo here."

"Your L.A. team did outstanding work on the Weiss case."

"But will it lead to justice for the wrongdoers?"

"I don't know. Maybe for some of them."

After ending the call, Abel made a small but significant addition to the report's cover sheet. She printed out several copies of the final report and put one copy along with the appendices on a thumb drive. She could have driven to the White House, but it was a crisp and clear spring day, and she decided to walk instead. A leisurely stroll to the White House would give her time to further contemplate making a risky move. And she could also enjoy the tulips blooming in concrete containers scattered along Pennsylvania Avenue amidst throngs of texting tourists. As she passed by the site where Marine One had crashed, she stopped for a moment of silence.

Earlier in the day, Abel learned that her IT team working Samoa had made more progress. Video surveillance at the ferry terminal had captured a Renault with two women inside. There was a clear view of the woman in the passenger seat, and it was Stella Weiss. The video had also recorded the car's license number. A search of Samoan auto registration files identified the car's owner: one Michael Armstrong.

All signs pointed to him being Robert. Further sleuthing had iden-tified his wife as Tina Armstrong, a.k.a. Roberta. The couple lived in a leased house on Savai'i. Upon receiving the good news, Bartolo requested arrest warrants for the Armstrongs. She also told the Washingtons to stand by for further instructions.

Finally arriving at the White House, Abel passed through security and delivered the thumb drive to Stonehouse. "This thumb drive con-tains everything the president asked for."

He said "thanks" as he took the package, adding, "President Shilling will be pleased." Neither he nor the president would bother to read the report.

****

The next morning, Malcolm checked his email and found a message from an unfamiliar sender. Unlike many Americans, he didn't imme-diately consign the email to the trash, though he was wary of its large attachment.

He opened the note and read, "Dear Mr. Klein: I have attached a report about matters of mutual concern. You are free to make use of the information contained therein." The note was signed, "a friend of truth and transparency in government."

With some trepidation Malcolm opened the attachment, hoping it wouldn't unleash a virus that could ravage his computer's hard drive. He smiled when he saw a federal document with long appendices. It was the final report of the FBI task force on the disappearance of Stella Weiss, written by Special Agents Andrew Carrington and Benjamin Suarez. He took special note of the unexpected phrase on the cover page, "Available for Public Dissemination." Malcolm's eyes were fixed on his computer screen as he carefully read the lengthy and seemingly comprehensive report. He was pleased to find that the quotes attributed to him were accurate.

When he was done reading, Malcolm felt like running through the newsroom shouting "stop the presses!"—a trope he had seen in many old movies. But he resisted the urge and merely walked rapidly to Stella's desk where he found her immersed in the report he had already forwarded to her.

"Malcolm, can you believe this?"

"Stella, wait 'til you get to the end. They nailed Dr. Death. Excuse me, Dr. Charles Graninger."

"So, he's a real doctor?"

"Yes, he is."

"I guess he won't be practicing medicine much longer."

"Let's hope not. But here's the real punch line, Stella: he's on the White House medical staff."

"Oh, my god!"

"I shouldn't tell you anything more and spoil the other surprises." He said, "read on," and padded back to his office, grinning from ear to ear, still tempted to shout, "stop the presses!"

After Stella had read the report and paged through the appendices containing the interview transcripts, she went quickly to Malcolm's office and said, "how did you get the report?"

"It was in my inbox with a phony sender address and a note saying we could use it."

"It's strange that a report with such dire implications for the White House would be cleared for dissemination."

"Right. Someone in the FBI is doing a thorough ass-covering. If the leaker were exposed, he or she couldn't be prosecuted. After all, the report is unclassified."

"Fabulous. And don't forget, it protects us, too."

"And now, Stella, it's time to plan our next story. Best of all, we can name names."

"I love it."

****

In the give and take between Stella and Malcolm during the writing of the story, only one argument had arisen. Stella wanted Malcolm to be the first name on the byline; Malcolm wanted Stella to be the lead author. After going around and around, they finally decided the order by the flip of a coin.

Before publication, the Weiss-Klein story was carefully vetted by Alice McGuire and by Times attorneys. Three days later it appeared on page 1. The headline read: "Shilling Ordered Weiss Abduction."

Americans became transfixed by Stellagate. Stella cringed every time she saw or heard the word "Stellagate," hoping it would quickly disappear. But the name stuck.

The cable news networks insistently begged for interviews with the Times' star reporters. Both Stella and Malcolm refused all requests, claiming that their story spoke for itself. They hoped that people would turn off their TVs and phones—and read newspapers instead.

CHAPTER 83

DEMOCRATS IN BOTH HOUSES of Congress clamored for impeachment as did the op-ed pages of newspapers around the country. Republicans asked, "where is the smoking gun?" In cable TV interviews, Republican legislators maintained that Dr. Graninger was lying. The entire affair was, they insisted, a rogue operation conceived and conducted by junior officers at Camp Pendleton. And, they added, even if President Shilling had ordered the operation, he had the legal right to do so in the service of national security.

The chair of the House Judiciary Committee, representative Todd Russell (D-Illinois), announced that his committee would hold hearings and call witnesses to testify in open session. When pressed by journalists, he refused to use the word impeachment. He stated repeatedly that the hearings had only one purpose: "to bring to light the facts surrounding this disturbing incident." From Director Abel, Russell had secured a pdf of the FBI's final report and passed it along to all committee members.

Russell proceeded methodically, scouring the report for the names of people likely to furnish informative testimony. The first tier of witnesses would, according to Russell's plan, speak to the facts of the crimes, verifying that they had occurred. Each committee member would be allotted five minutes for asking questions. He would forgo the usual wordy introductions, allowing the witnesses themselves to carry the evidentiary load.

****

Summoned by the Judiciary Committee, Stella and Malcolm arrived the day before the hearings, and took rooms at the Harrington Hotel. The hotel was old, but the rooms were clean and—for downtown D.C.—a bargain. Best of all, the Harrington's location was convenient. On the hotel's ground floor was Ollie's Trolley, the restaurant where they ate dinner. Ollie's Trolley served comfort food that diners could enjoy surrounded by kitschy antiques.

The two journalists ordered platters: he had a hamburger, and she had a crab cake. Both meals featured fries made with "26 herbs and spices."

"So, Stella, are you ready to tell your story?"

"Honestly, I can't wait."

"You're not nervous about having to testify before members of Congress?"

"Well, of course I'm apprehensive. Who wouldn't be? But I'm also eager to let them know what happened."

"I hope members of the Judiciary Committee ask you the right questions."

"Representative Russell called me yesterday with a heads-up on what to expect. He's going to throw me some softball questions, but he also said the Republicans will be out for blood and accuse me of being a traitor."

"A traitor? Seriously?"

"That's what he said. But I'm ready. If the Republicans throw me hardballs, I'll blast them into the bleachers."

"That's our Stella!"

CHAPTER 84

HEARINGS OF THE HOUSE JUDICIARY COMMITTEE took place in room 2141 of the Rayburn House Office Building. With its tall ceiling, the austere room seemed much larger than it was, though it could still hold more than a hundred people plus dozens of photojournalists. By the time Russell gaveled the hearings to order, the room was packed.

Russell was in his late sixties. He had a full head of short, salt-and-pepper curls, black eyes, and fleshy features on his dark brown face. When standing in his sleek black suit, Russell's six-foot, eight-inch frame was a reminder that he had been a star forward on the Chicago Bulls. His basketball career had been cut short by a motorcycle accident, which left him with a broken ankle that healed poorly despite two surgeries. After his playing days ended, Russell earned a law degree at Fordham University, graduating near the top of his class. He was serving his seventeenth term in the House and thoroughly enjoyed exercising power as chair of the Judiciary Committee.

Stella Weiss was witness number one. After she had been sworn in, Russell invited the committee's ranking member, Lawrence Maxwell (R-Oklahoma), to begin the questioning. Stella was puzzled. Why had Russell given a far-right Republican first crack at her? She assumed he must have his reasons.

In his fifties, Maxwell was stout and of medium height. He had thinning gray hair and a pasty complexion, brown eyes, and sharply defined features. He wore a dark brown suit with no tie and left his jacket unbuttoned.

Before asking the first question, Maxwell looked around at the gaggle of photojournalists seated on the floor and smiled at the familiar faces. He had already agreed to provide Fox News with an exclusive interview immediately following the hearing. At last he turned to Stella.

"Miss Weiss, thank you for appearing before us this morning. I'd like you to explain to us why you refused to divulge the names of the mass murderers you interviewed and are now protecting."

Surprised by Maxwell's aggressive opening, she answered, "as I've said in my L.A. Times stories, I do not know the real names of Robert and Roberta. And if I did, I would not disclose them. It is true that they are mass murderers, but they were also my sources. If we couldn't promise anonymity to our sources, people would not agree to be interviewed. Then it would be impossible for us to do our job of keeping Americans fully informed on significant issues. And, Representative Maxwell, the First Amendment to the U.S. Constitution explicitly recognizes the role of the free press in our democracy. Let me remind you, court decisions have supported the right of journalists to keep their sources confidential."

"We don't need a civics lesson, Miss Weiss. What I wish you would provide instead are the real names of Robert and Roberta. I can't believe you don't know their identities and…"

"Are you calling me a liar? How dare you! I've sworn an oath to speak the truth and that's what I'm doing." She raised her voice and repeated, "I do not know their real names."

"So," he said with sarcasm dripping from every syllable, "do your journalistic ethics require you to protect mass murderers?"

"I believe I've already answered that question."

"Let us assume for the sake of argument that you are telling the truth, that you don't know the murderers' true identities. But do you know where they are?"

Stella was not surprised by the question. "I only know where they were when I met them."

"Would you be kind enough to identify that location for the benefit of the committee?"

"I'm afraid I can't do that. Someone could use their whereabouts to track them down. I cannot provide information that directly or indirectly compromises my sources."

"Your attitude is treasonous. You are a traitor to this nation. You should be ashamed of yourself."

A dull rumble pervaded the packed room, as many legislators, reporters, and spectators reacted to Maxwell's aggressive line of questioning.

Stella hesitated before responding to his latest provocation. "Representative Maxwell, I am not ashamed. Rather, I am proud of my work. Let me remind you: my work is not the issue here. The real issue is the kidnapping and imprisonment of a journalist."

A small group of spectators began to applaud. Russell asked that order be restored and informed Mr. Maxwell that his time was up. Maxwell grumbled, "I need more time."

"I'm sorry, but you'll have to adhere to the five-minute limit."

Stella finally figured out why Russell allowed Maxwell to ask the first questions. He wanted everyone to have a preview of the Republican strategy to impugn her integrity and patriotism.

****

Russell next recognized Sheila Dominguez (D-Minnesota). Dominguez was a petite woman with short auburn hair, radiant hazel eyes, and thin lips. The former attorney general of Minnesota, she was a newcomer to the House and, many believed, was destined for a leadership role. She dressed the part in a black, Georgio Armani pantsuit, which complimented her alabaster skin.

"Thank you, Mr. Chairman."

Turning to the witness, she said, "Ms. Weiss, I'm pleased to see that you have recovered from your horrific experience. Perhaps you could tell us what happened, beginning with the day you were abducted from your Los Angeles apartment."

"I had just come home from work and was getting settled in my apartment. There was a knock at the door and I foolishly opened it. A man and a woman wearing ski masks barged in."

Stella went on to describe how she had been kidnapped at gunpoint, driven to an airport, and taken by helicopter to an unknown destination where two masked men interrogated her at length.

"I assume you told them nothing about your sources?"

"That is correct."

"What happened after the initial interrogations?"

Stella described the episode with the polygraph, which elicited laughter and scattered applause. Russell again called for order and threatened to have the boisterous spectators removed. Stella then recounted Dr. Death's role in affair.

Dominguez asked, "were you physically abused?"

"Only to the extent that I had to eat god-awful fast food during my imprisonment. And, of course, I was forcibly held down while the doctor injected me with the drug that put me into a coma."

"Is there anything else about this incident you would like to share with us?"

"I do have something important I want to say."

"Please proceed."

"As most of you know, President Wahl was a tyrant who abused the power of the presidency, appointed a cabinet of thieves and incompetents, promoted his own economic interests, lied incessantly, and engaged in other unpresidential behaviors that, in the opinion of many respected Americans, should have resulted in impeachment long before his assassination. Unfortunately, Republicans—especially those in Congress—were Wahl's enablers." Pointing to Maxwell, she added, "you excused his every transgression and repeated his lies because he supported your legislative agenda. If you and other Republicans had done your jobs and removed Wahl from office, he would not have been assassinated." She paused for dramatic effect, stood up, and concluded with a shout, "Republicans, President Wahl's blood is on your hands."

Republicans on the committee and in the audience were stunned by her accusation. Many voices shouted epithets at Weiss, but she had no intention of responding. She had made her point and was confident her accusation would be the sound bite on evening news programs. And it was.

****

The commotion settled down, and Russell continued alternating between Democratic and Republican committee members. Democrats asked Stella to elaborate on several points, such as what happened after she received the drug. Republicans to a man harped on her for "betraying your country by protecting murderers."

One reporter tweeted that "even a casual observer of the proceedings would notice that Republicans were all asking the same questions, apparently reading from the same script, intent on portraying Ms. Weiss as a traitor."

Russell thanked Stella and adjourned the hearing for a 15-minute break. Several septuagenarian legislators nearly crashed into each other rushing toward the restrooms.

CHAPTER 85

WHEN THE HEARING RESUMED, Russell called on Malcolm Klein. His testimony was brief, as he was simply asked to describe Ms. Weiss' condition when he found her in the San Diego hospital. Members of the audience who had not read the FBI report gasped and expressed outrage when Malcolm reported how Stella had been dumped in the ER, treated as an indigent Jane Doe.

The next witness was Major Thomas McPherson. After he was sworn in, Russell began the questioning.

"Major McPherson, thank you for agreeing to give testimony before this committee. Are you the leader of Viper Squadron at Camp Pendleton?"

"Yes sir, I am."

"Would you please describe the unusual mission your team conducted on the day in question?"

McPherson admitted to giving the order for a Huey pilot to ferry two special ops personnel to the Santa Monica City Airport. With prodding from Russell, he conceded that the Huey returned with Stella Weiss.

"And who ordered this operation?"

"Major Petersen, head of special ops, arranged for the transportation."

"Did he tell you where his orders came from?"

"He implied that he was acting under orders from General Otis Griswold."

"And who is General Otis Griswold?"

"He is the base commander."

"Was Major Peterson's request out of the ordinary?"

"No, sir. We often transport special ops teams."

"Thank you, Major McPherson."

The major breathed a sigh of relief, but the relief was premature.

Representative Donald Perkins (R-Alabama) was recognized. A bald and grizzled nonagenarian whose attention had wandered, he was holding up his head with great difficulty. Russell prompted him to respond. At last Perkins pulled it together, and began reading his questions from Maxwell's script.

"Major McPherson, isn't it true that you have no written evidence that General Griswold issued the orders for this operation?"

"That is correct."

"Do you consider yourself a patriot?"

"Yes sir, I do. I've devoted my life to the Marine Corps and the values it stands for."

"Were you disturbed by Miss Weiss' articles and her failure to identify Robert and Roberta?"

"Of course, sir. She should have immediately furnished their names to the authorities. And if she didn't know their real names, she should have told the FBI where to find these deplorable people."

"Did you feel so strongly about this, Major McPherson, that you and Major Petersen decided to take matters into your own hands?"

"What are you implying?"

Before McPherson could respond, Perkins's attention wandered, and he repeated the question twice. Puzzled, McPherson asked for clarification again, louder this time, which helped Perkins to focus.

"Did you in fact conspire, without authorization from your base commander, to abduct and detain Miss Weiss in order to obtain the information about Robert and Roberta?"

"No sir, we did not."

"But you have no evidence, only Major Petersen's word, that you were complying with General Griswold's order. Is that correct?"

McPherson was stunned by Perkins' accusation.

"With all due respect, sir, this was not a rogue operation. I had every reason to trust Major Petersen's word."

During the remainder of McPherson's questioning, Democrats did their fair share of grandstanding, and took special delight in ridiculing the rogue operation story. Republicans took a different tack. They pounded McPherson relentlessly for the alleged "unauthorized mission." The rogue operation narrative was gaining traction among those who wanted to protect the president.

****

After lunch, the hearing resumed with the swearing in of Major Luke Petersen. Russell gave Republican Maxwell the first crack at the new witness.

"Major Petersen, are you the head of special operations at Camp Pendleton?"

"Yes, sir."

"On the day in question, did you request helicopter transportation from Major McPherson?"

"Yes sir, I did."

"Who authorized the operation to pick up and detain Miss Weiss?"

"Commander Otis Griswold gave me the orders."

"And have you preserved a copy of those orders?"

"They were verbal orders, sir. So, no, there is no email or paper trail."

Maxwell went on to accuse Petersen of conspiring with McPherson to conduct an unauthorized operation. Petersen vehemently denied that they had done so. Democrats were frankly puzzled by the Republican strategy, concluding that they hadn't read the FBI report very carefully. Surely even they had to realize that Dr. Graninger would implicate the president—and thus, Commander Griswold. Democrats believed the testimony of the White House physician would be bulletproof. Republicans, however, held no such belief.

****

As his next witness, Russell called Thomas Parke (a.k.a. Laurel). Russell and the Democrats managed to elicit Parke's role in the kidnapping. Parke also admitted that he and Amanda Foshay (a.k.a. Hardy) were both special ops who brought Ms. Weiss to Camp Pendleton, oversaw the interrogations, and delivered her meals. Republicans passed on the opportunity to question Parke.

Russell had anticipated calling Amanda Foshay and Donald Emerson, the helicopter pilot. But in the final analysis, he and the other Democrats didn't believe their testimony was needed. The witnesses had established the occurrence of criminal acts, and those facts were now in the public record. It was time, Russell concluded, to move on to the second tier of witnesses to establish, insofar as possible, who ordered the operation. Because it was already 3:40, Russell adjourned the hearing for the day.

CHAPTER 86

STELLA AND MALCOLM WALKED CALMLY through the gauntlet of reporters who poked microphones in their faces, shouting questions. Both kept repeating, "no comment."

Once outside the building, Stella said, "Malcolm, it's still a nice day. Let's walk back to the hotel."

"Terrific idea."

It was too early in the season to feel the stifling humidity of a Washington summer. The temperature was in the mid-70s with puffy white clouds floating lazily across the sky, crisscrossed by fuzzy contrails. The pair walked west on Pennsylvania Avenue, and then turned north on 12th Street. They carefully dodged the many tourists seemingly oblivious to their surroundings, reading maps on their phones.

"Stella, that was quite a speech you gave."

"I have to confess it wasn't spontaneous. I've been thinking about the basic idea since my time with Robert and Roberta."

"I'm glad you had the opportunity to vent, but I'm sure the Republicans just blew off your criticism."

"I know. This country is so screwed. Republicans still hold the presidency and the Senate, so they'll continue to roll back consumer and environmental protections, and pack the courts with rightwing zealots. Oh, and don't forget about the war against women. It just keeps getting worse."

"Did you have any misgivings about revealing your political leanings? Won't the Republicans say it compromises your credibility?"

"Frankly, Malcolm, I don't give a shit about what Republicans say. They are the ones who lack credibility."

"Don't hold back, Stella, speak your mind."

They both laughed.

"Seriously, Stella, do you think the public admission of your liberal views could affect your reputation as an impartial journalist?"

"Malcolm, what are you implying?"

"I'm just saying that some people in our business might frown on what you did."

"If those journalists don't hold Republicans responsible for rationalizing and enabling Wahl's horrific acts, then they can't be taken seriously. But you have me worried. Do you think this is going to affect my position at the Times?"

"Not a chance. But I would recommend you choose stories without overt political content—at least in the near term."

"I can manage that, but it's irksome."

"Just take the advice of your old mentor."

"Yes, Malcolm. I know you have my best interests at heart."

"Stella, I really do."

CHAPTER 87

WHEN THE HEARINGS RESUMED the following morning, Russell called Dr. Charles Graninger, who was duly sworn in. Before Russell turned over the proceedings to Maxwell, he announced that three Republican committee members had ceded their five-minute slots to the ranking member. Democrats groaned, as they feared a Maxwell marathon was in the offing.

"Dr. Graninger, please state the position you hold in the White House."

"I'm a surgeon on the White House medical staff."

"When did you assume this position?"

"I was appointed by the late President Wahl in March of his first year in office."

"And before that, what position did you hold?"

"I was in private practice in Philadelphia."

"Is it true that you were President Wahl's personal physician in Philadelphia before he took office?"

"That is correct, Mr. Maxwell."

"Did you perform President Wahl's annual physical examination last year?"

"Yes, I did."

"Did you state, at a press conference, that President Wahl was the healthiest person ever to occupy the Oval Office?"

"I said something to that effect. But I don't understand why you are asking me these questions. They have nothing to do with the matter at hand."

"Be patient, Dr. Graninger, because they have everything to do with it. You pronounced President Wahl to be in excellent physical health despite his lack of exercise, his poor diet, and his obvious obesity."

"It was my professional opinion that he was the picture of good health."

"Did President Wahl insist that you render that opinion instead of relying on the test results showing he had cardio-vascular issues?"

Dr. Graninger paused and turned toward Chairman Russell, as if begging him to intervene.

Russell said sharply, "answer the question."

"Representative Maxwell, I believe you are aware of President Wahl's unusually strong personality. He had a unique ability to bend people to his will. Yes, he asked me to put the most favorable spin on his health assessment."

"In other words, you lied to the American people about the president's health."

"I wouldn't exactly call it lying."

"Well, it was so far from the truth that I don't see how it could be construed as anything else. Dr. Graninger, we have now established the fact that you are a liar."

Graninger protested vehemently, but no one came to his defense. Maxwell kept badgering the doctor, demanding repeatedly to know what other falsehoods he had told in the course of his White House duties. Several Democrats at last voiced loud objections, interrupting the flow of Maxwell's performance.

"My Democrat colleagues have displayed a singular lack of politeness. Please allow me to resume without interruption. I have proved that Dr. Graninger is a liar, which bears directly on the matter at hand, as my next questions will demonstrate."

"Proceed," said Russell reluctantly.

"Dr. Graninger, we have heard testimony that you administered a drug to Miss Weiss at Camp Pendleton. Was that testimony correct?"

"Yes, it was."

"How is it that you went to Camp Pendleton?"

"I don't understand your question."

"Let me see if I can make it any clearer: who sent you to Camp Pendleton?"

"I was sent by President Shilling."

There was a loud murmur in the room, but it subsided before Russell reached for his gavel.

"We can't take your answer literally because you and the truth are easily parted. Do you have any evidence to support your claim?"

"Unfortunately, I don't have any documents. But there was a reputable witness."

"I assume you mean that Chief of Staff Stonehouse was present?"

"Yes, he was in the Oval Office, but there was someone else, too."

Blindsided by the doctor's answer, Maxwell was reluctant to ask for the witness' identity because it might undermine his strategy to discredit Graninger. A hush fell over the hearing room, as Chairman Russell interrupted with his own question, "who was this witness, Dr. Graninger?"

Before he could answer, Maxwell stood up and yelled, "how dare you interrupt me, Russell!"

Russell calmly retorted, "Dr. Graninger, you will please answer my question. Who was the witness?"

Graninger at last replied. "When President Shilling gave me the orders, Director Adam Smalley of the CIA was in the Oval Office. Both he and Mr. Stonehouse can confirm my account. Also, Mr. Smalley was the one who told me how to pick up the truth serum in Omaha."

This was an unexpected revelation. Russell was puzzled and said plaintively, "but, according to the FBI report, when Special Agent Bartolo interviewed you, you made no mention of the CIA director's presence."

"I said there was another man in the room. He looked familiar but at that moment I didn't remember who he was. More recently I saw Director Smalley interviewed on Fox News. He was the other person in the Oval Office."

Graninger's explanation of the delayed identification of Smalley caused the room to erupt in loud side conversations and recriminations. Russell called for order and allowed the questioning to resume, but neither Republicans nor Democrats elicited new facts.

Republicans were nonplussed, worried that if the CIA director were called to give testimony, he might support Graninger's account. If that happened, the finger of blame for the Weiss incident would come to point squarely at President Shilling.

After the questions to Dr. Graninger had been exhausted, Russell adjourned the hearings. They would resume, he said, at ten the next morning.

Russell returned to his office and immediately contacted Smalley at the CIA to arrange for his appearance. Smalley at first refused the invitation, but Russell persuaded him that his appearance was in the national interest. Though a Shilling acolyte, Smalley was also a loyal patriot. In giving testimony, he would have to find a way to navigate between his conflicted loyalties.

CHAPTER 88

GENERAL OTIS GRISWOLD was also scheduled to testify before the Judiciary Committee during the next day. Because the Cherry Blossom Festival was in full swing, Griswold had brought along his wife, Marianne, and their two young children. The entire family was staying in the Marine Barracks, a small D.C. base built in 1801 during the first year of Thomas Jefferson's presidency.

Marianne was a stay-at-home mom who busied herself with cooking and scrapbooking when the kids were at school. She was slim, of medium height with curly red hair, large blue eyes, and a forest of freckles.

After the children went to bed, the Griswolds watched a recap of the Congressional hearing on Fox News. They were tired from the trip but not yet sleepy. Marianne noticed that her husband was fretting over something, obviously upset.

"Otis, what's wrong?"

"I had no idea the CIA director could confirm Dr. Graninger's claim that President Shilling ordered him to go to Pendleton."

"Why does that matter?"

"Because I stonewalled the FBI and NCIS when they questioned me. I didn't tell them that my orders came directly from the president. But at least I didn't lie. I don't want to lie tomorrow, either."

"What are you going to do?"

"I don't know. I'm torn between my loyalty to President Shilling and my duty to tell the truth. Maybe my best option is to invoke the Fifth Amendment. Just stay silent."

"May I offer an observation, as a parent?"

"Sure, go ahead."

"I believe that no matter what you say tomorrow, President Shilling is headed for impeachment. When our children are old enough to be studying American history in high school and college, they will read about Shilling's misdeeds and his subsequent fate—whatever it is. Do you really want them to find out that their father took the fifth in a congressional hearing? Can you imagine how they'd feel?"

As the general's face contorted in pain, he put his arm around Marianne's shoulders and began to sob.

CHAPTER 89

THE NEXT DAY THE HEARINGS resumed on time. Smalley, the first witness called, was sworn in. Russell began the questioning.

"Mr. Smalley, what is your position in the federal government?"

"I am Director of the Central Intelligence Agency."

"Does this agency have a laboratory in Omaha, Nebraska?"

"Yes sir, we do."

"And what is the purpose of that laboratory?"

"It makes a variety of drugs useful in our work of protecting America from foreign adversaries and terrorists."

"Does that include making drugs that promote truth-telling?"

"Yes, it does."

"Dr. Graninger testified before this committee that, while he was in the Oval Office with President Shilling, you instructed him on how to acquire the truth serum from the Omaha lab. Was his testimony accurate?"

Smalley slowly looked around the room as if seeking guidance from the army of spectators and journalists. He raised a glass of water and took several sips.

"Director Smalley, please answer my question."

"I prefer to assert my right under the Fifth Amendment of the Constitution to remain silent."

"If you didn't give Dr. Graninger instructions, how did he know where to obtain the drug?"

"Again, I assert my right to remain silent."

"Director Smalley, you are not being very helpful this morning. Let me turn over the questioning to Representative Maxwell. Perhaps he can persuade you to be more responsive."

"Director Smalley, many of us on this committee believe that Dr. Graninger is a notorious liar who, for whatever reasons, is helping to cover up a rogue operation perpetrated by officers at Camp Pendleton. Do you agree with our assessment?"

Choosing his words carefully to avoid telling an outright lie, Smalley responded, "in my opinion, your assessment may be correct."

"Thank you, I have no further questions."

In the remainder of Smalley's testimony, he stonewalled the Democrats and, without perjuring himself, gave lukewarm support to the Republican narrative. Chairman Russell was so frustrated that he kept gently and silently pounding the table with his fist and glowering at the witness. At long last, Russell dismissed Director Smalley and adjourned the meeting until two o'clock.

****

The first witness of the afternoon session, General Otis Griswold, was sworn in. Chairman Russell again led off the questioning.

"General Griswold, what is your current position in the Marine Corps?"

"I am Commander of Camp Pendleton."

"And where is Camp Pendleton?"

"It is located in Southern California between Los Angeles and San Diego, on the coast adjacent to the city of Oceanside."

Russell now pivoted to the crucial questions, fully expecting General Griswold to remain silent to avoid self-incrimination.

"Did you know in advance that a special operations team planned to abduct Ms. Stella Weiss and transport her to Camp Pendleton?"

With his hand shaking, a stressed-out Griswold grasped a water glass. He raised it to his lips, and carefully took several sips. Sweating profusely, the general was stalling, taking time to make the final decision about whether to testify or invoke the fifth. He finally put the glass down, and with his gaze fixed firmly on Russell, Griswold replied, "yes, sir. I knew about the plan."

Loud murmurs echoed throughout the room, and Russell called for order.

"And were you aware, in advance, that Ms. Weiss was to be imprisoned at Camp Pendleton."

"Yes, sir, but I prefer to use the word 'detained.'"

Russell's eyes opened wide, as the glimmer of a smile crossed his face.

"Major Petersen testified that you, General Griswold, authorized this mission. Is that correct?"

In a low voice, he said "yes, sir."

"Please speak up."

"Yes, I gave the orders to Major Petersen."

The room was again abuzz, but the disturbance quickly subsided.

"Were you acting under orders from a higher authority?"

"Yes, sir."

"Please divulge the identity of the person who gave you the orders."

Griswold slowly elaborated. "Two days before the abduction, my receptionist notified me that I had a call from Washington. When I answered the phone, I was astonished to find President Shilling on the line. He said he wanted me to carry out a top-secret mission."

"And what was that mission?"

"He said I was to pick up, detain, and interrogate Miss Stella Weiss. This woman, he insisted, had committed treason against the United States and possessed information of vital importance to national security. He tasked me with obtaining that information."

"And what, precisely, was that information?"

"I was to learn the identities and whereabouts of Robert and Roberta."

"At the time you received the president's orders, did you know who Stella Weiss was?"

"Yes, I read the L.A. Times."

"Did you have any reservations about abducting and imprisoning a civilian journalist?"

"I didn't have time to think through all the implications of following the president's orders. When the commander in chief gives you a mission and insists it is critical for national security, you don't question him. I told the president that I would see to it that the mission was carried out. And I did."

"Thank you, General Griswold. I now turn the questioning over to Representative Maxwell."

"General Griswold, have you, in any form, actual documentation of the president's orders you allegedly received?"

"No, sir, I do not. We carried out all communications about this mission by telephone."

"So, we have nothing but your word that you were following the president's orders?"

"Yes, sir."

"In fact, isn't it true that you undertook a rogue operation because you wanted the glory for capturing Robert and Roberta?"

"With all due respect, Representative Maxwell, your insinuation is outrageous. I did what the president ordered me to do. You are coming perilously close to accusing me of lying to this committee, and I cannot abide that. Let me point out, as emphatically as possible, that Dr. Graninger's testimony is consistent with mine. And CIA Director Smalley's refusal to answer the committee's questions also supports my account by implication. I am confident that impartial observers will conclude that we at Camp Pendleton did our jobs in service to the nation as President Shilling required."

"Notwithstanding your desperate attempt to put the blame on President Shilling, you have provided no hard evidence—no memos, no emails, absolutely nothing—that accords with your account."

"Your time is up, Representative Maxwell," asserted Russell.

Surprisingly, there was little further questioning of General Griswold. Democrats were apparently satisfied that the general's testimony was truthful. Republicans knew that they would have to find a different strategy to protect the president in light of Griswold's credible testimony.

CHAPTER 90

WATCHING HER HUSBAND ON TV, Marianne Griswold teared up as he acknowledged his role in the Weiss affair. She was both proud and concerned. What would happen to him and the other fine marines at Camp Pendleton now that the mission had completely unraveled? When she had gently urged him to be truthful, she'd given little thought to the possibility he might be court martialed. Reflecting on his testimony, she realized Otis could end up in prison. It was more than just a possibility. After all, he did order Weiss's kidnapping and imprisonment.

If he was imprisoned, she wondered, what would happen to her and the children? Marianne's apprehension had turned to worry and anguish. Maybe, she thought, it would have been better if she hadn't broached the subject with him. Yet, she believed fervently he had done the right thing—and would have done the right thing, even without her prompting.

When Otis returned to the Marine Barracks after his testimony, Marianne and the children were waiting for him in the lobby. As soon as he came through the door, she rushed forward and gave him a huge hug and kiss. The children followed and hugged their dad.

"Oh, Otis, I love you so much, and I'm so proud of you."

"Thanks, Marianne, for setting me straight. I don't know where my testimony will lead—I might be headed to prison—but I remained faithful to Marine Corps values."

"You did the right thing, and that's all that matters. We'll worry about the fallout later."

He hugged her again and kissed her tenderly. They both began sobbing.

CHAPTER 91

ALFRED STONEHOUSE WAS the day's final witness. After he was sworn in, Maxwell asked the first questions.

"Mr. Stonehouse, please inform the committee, what is your position in the White House?"

"I am the president's chief of staff."

"I see. Do you have frequent conversations with the president?"

"Yes, we talk often." Getting ahead of the questions, Stonehouse added, "in fact, I can't reveal to this committee or any person the contents of my conversations with President Shilling, inside or outside the Oval Office."

"And why is that, Mr. Stonehouse?"

"Because all such conversations are subject to executive privilege, which I am claiming on President Shilling's behalf."

"So, if I understand your position, you are unable to confirm or deny any of the allegations against the president put forward by Dr. Graninger and General Griswold?"

"That is correct."

"Thank you, Mr. Stonehouse, I have no further questions."

A furious Russell immediately asked, "Mr. Stonehouse, has Mr. Maxwell or any other Republican on this committee discussed today's testimony with you beforehand?"

Stonehouse stalled and looked plaintively at Maxwell, who turned his eyes downward.

In a voice of utter frustration, Russell shouted, "would you please answer my question!"

"Yes," he whispered.

"Speak up, I can't hear you."

"Yes, Mr. Chairman. I had a brief conversation with Mr. Maxwell yesterday evening."

"And what was the subject of that conversation?"

"He advised me to invoke executive privilege if the questions became uncomfortable."

"Mr. Stonehouse, do you find candor to be uncomfortable?"

"No, sir. But I cannot imagine a president doing his job well if the wise counsel of his most trusted advisers can be made public at the whim of a congressional committee."

"For the record, Mr. Stonehouse, our hearing is not based on a whim. It is based on the certainty that serious crimes took place. This committee is in the business of learning who was responsible for committing those crimes. By protecting the president, Mr. Stonehouse, you have failed the American people."

Russell adjourned the meeting until the next morning at ten.

CHAPTER 92

RUSSELL BEGAN THE QUESTIONING of Special Agent Joanna Bartolo after her swearing in.

"Ms. Bartolo, what is your position in the federal government?"

"I am a senior special agent in the FBI."

"Were you assigned to investigate the disappearance of Ms. Stella Weiss?"

"Yes, sir. Director Abel herself gave me the assignment. The LAPD had initially opened the case, but they were overwhelmed with missing person reports. That's why they were willing to give the FBI the lead in the investigation, especially after they realized that Ms. Weiss was a well-known Los Angeles Times reporter."

"What did you know about the case when you took it over?"

"We knew very little. We did know that Ms. Weiss had disappeared. Our job was to find out if her disappearance resulted from foul play. And, if so, we would aim to identify and arrest the perpetrators."

"How did you carry out this investigation?"

"Director Abel had arranged for two highly respected agents in our L.A. field office, Mr. Benjamin Suarez and Mr. Andrew Carrington, to conduct the investigation. They reported to me."

"And what did they learn?"

Maxwell rose and said, "anything she says about the investigation's findings is merely hearsay or speculation. I strenuously object to this unfair tactic."

Russell responded, "Mr. Maxwell, if you had read the entire FBI report that I sent to all committee members, you would understand that Special Agent Bartolo's testimony is based entirely on facts, as presented in the supporting documents. In the meantime, you may sit down. You will get a turn to ask questions. Please wait until I call on you."

Maxwell's face turned red. He was furious that Russell had upbraided him as if he were in elementary school. But he did sit down.

"May I continue?" asked Bartolo.

Russell said, "by all means, please proceed."

Glaring at Maxwell, she said, "agents Suarez and Carrington wrote in their report that personnel at Camp Pendleton had abducted and detained Ms. Stella Weiss."

"Did you come to any conclusions as to who had ordered this operation?"

"Yes. We were confident in our conclusion that Commander Griswold received his orders directly from President Shilling."

"And, apart from the information supplied by the witnesses that your agents interviewed, did you find evidence indicating suspicious contact between the president and Commander Griswold?"

"As a matter of fact, we did. Once our investigation was underway, we requested and received the collaboration of NCIS. They identified several key personnel involved in the operation. And, relevant to your question, they also obtained Commander Griswold's telephone records and passed them along to us."

"And what did you learn from those records?"

"We found a series of calls between Commander Griswold and the White House."

"When did these calls take place?"

"The calls occurred during a period that began a few days before the incident in question, and they continued for about a week afterward."

Hushed conversations filled the room but tailed off quickly.

"Was there anything unusual about these calls?"

"Their very existence was unusual."

"Why is that?"

"Base commanders do not report directly to the president. They respect the chain of command. Unless the president was planning a dog-and-pony show at Camp Pendleton, any contact between the White House and the base commander would be suspicious."

"Who made the first call?"

"It came from the White House."

"Did you obtain intercepts revealing the content of the conversations between the White House and Commander Griswold?"

"Unfortunately, there were no intercepts."

"Thank you, Agent Bartolo."

****

Russell turned the questioning over to Amos Reidhead (R-Utah). Another veteran House member, Reidhead was in his fourteenth term. He was short and gangly with white hair. His face was heavily wrinkled, and his eyelids drooped. He was wearing a much worn, charcoal gray suit. It was rumored that he had bought the suit during his first term in Congress.

"Ms. Bartolo, my esteemed colleague from across the aisle asserted that the president himself communicated by phone with General Griswold. But this is nothing but conjecture, intended to cast aspersions on President Shilling. Do you have any knowledge as to who in the White House was the other party in these conversations?"

"I believe that the preponderance of evidence makes it highly likely the other party was the president."

"But you don't know that for certain, do you Agent Bartolo?"

"I believe it is a near certainty. Nothing else makes sense in light of the total pattern of evidence and the testimony of previous witnesses."

"So, in fact we don't know the identity of the party in the White House who communicated with General Griswold, and we don't know what the conversations were about. Isn't that correct, Ms. Bartolo?"

"With all due respect, Representative Reidhead, I've already answered those questions."

The questioning of Bartolo continued for some time. Democrats elicited more specific information about the findings of the FBI's investigation. Republicans continued to emphasize uncertainties about the identity of the "other party" in the White House. However, they were unable to elicit from Bartolo a plausible alternative to President Shilling.

Russell adjourned the hearing.

CHAPTER 93

WHEN THEY HAD ARRIVED IN SAMOA, FBI Special Agents Aisha and Shawan Washington rented a car and took up residence in a resort on the coast of Savai'i between the ferry terminal and the Armstrong home. Abel had assigned them to keep a discreet watch on the Armstrongs' comings and goings, to get a general fix on the couple's activity patterns.

Although Abel was unwilling to bring the CIA into the operation, she did need help to pull off a successful extraction of the criminal couple. Her agency couldn't go it alone, risking a diplomatic dust-up from an operation that might violate Samoan sovereignty. She grudgingly admitted the necessity of getting assistance from State Department officials.

Abel arranged to meet with Aaron Snow, the Assistant Secretary for the Bureau of East Asian and Pacific Affairs. He had an interesting history, she learned. His parents had been Mormon missionaries in Japan, where he was born in 1962. The family returned to the United States when Aaron was in his late teens. He graduated from Georgetown University with a B.A. in justice and peace studies and an M.A. in political science. After graduate school he entered the diplomatic corps. When he had obtained a secure position in the State Department, he returned to Japan and married his childhood sweetheart, Akiko Senzaki, who had converted to Mormonism.

Abel met Snow in his office at the Harry S Truman Building in

340

Foggy Bottom. She passed through security, and an aide led her into his office. The large room was decorated with Micronesian story boards, antique Japanese prints, Chinese and Korean porcelain vases, and other art objects from East Asia and the Pacific. Looming in one corner on a manikin was a full suit of Samurai armor, a gift of Japan's ambassador to the United States during the Johnson administration. Abel marveled at the beautiful and colorful creations.

Although they had not met previously, Abel and Snow exchanged warm greetings. Wearing a dark suit and bifocals, Snow had short blond hair, hazel eyes, and a wide, smiling mouth.

After they sat down, Snow wasted no time in asking, "what can I do for you?"

"We have placed two agents in Samoa and are prepared to launch an operation. We need your assistance."

Taken aback by her blunt revelation, he said, "this is highly irregular. At this time there is no provision for an FBI presence in Samoa. Who authorized this operation?"

"As FBI director, I did. And this morning I also informed Secretary Moffitt, who okayed it contingent upon the State Department's cooperation. As you no doubt know, the FBI can operate in other countries."

Frowning and raising his voice, he said, "there are no authorized FBI attachés in Samoa. In our experience, the Samoans prefer to be asked before allowing any foreign intervention."

"That's why we want you to smooth the way."

"Well, you had better tell me what this is all about."

"I will tell you, and I trust your discretion to keep this information confidential."

"Of course."

"We have tracked down President Wahl's assassins to Samoa. They live on Savai'i."

"Holy cow! But how good is your intel?"

"It's bulletproof. We had good stateside intel on their whereabouts, so we sent agents Aisha and Shawan Washington to Savai'i to confirm. The assassins are there."

"Robert and Roberta in Samoa. That's truly disturbing."

"Yes, they live in a leased house by the beach."

"Okay. So, the FBI is already in Samoa. This could be a real problem."

"They haven't made any moves against the couple. In fact, the Washingtons are posing as tourists, standing by, awaiting my instructions. Naturally, I didn't want to make any moves that would jeopardize the friendly relations we enjoy with Samoa."

"That was a smart decision, Director Abel. But I'm quite unhappy that you jumped the gun."

"Now you see why we need your help."

He frowned again and paused. "I assume you want us to devise a feasible extraction plan that won't ruffle Samoan feathers?"

"Precisely."

"Okay, but this might be tricky."

"I'm truly sorry for putting you in this awkward position. But we had to have visual confirmation and couldn't risk losing track of Robert and Roberta. For the record, their real names are Tina and Michael Armstrong."

"I guess I understand, but this is going to take some delicate diplomacy. By the way, Emory Goodyear III, our ambassador to Samoa, actually lives in New Zealand."

"Why is that?"

"It's a holdover from the time when Samoa was under New Zealand administration. At any rate, our plan will have to rely on his diplomatic skills. I can tell you right now, the Samoans will be displeased to learn that FBI agents are already in their country."

"I should think they would be more concerned about the world finding out that Wahl's assassins took refuge there."

"In any event, it may take Goodyear some time to convince the Samoans that we've acted out of necessity, and that we still respect their sovereignty. He'll have to eat some crow on behalf of the United States."

"I'm truly sorry, but it couldn't be helped. Do you think the Samoan government will eventually approve the extraction, even though we have no extradition treaty with them?"

"It's hard to say. But if they agree to the extraction, I can almost guarantee they will insist on making the arrests themselves."

"I don't care who makes the arrests as long as the Armstrongs are eventually put in the custody of the Washingtons and returned to the U.S."

"Assuming we can smooth things over with the Samoan government, we can arrange for a military plane to provide air transport back to the states."

"Perfect. I'll send you copies of the warrants and relevant intel."

"After I've reviewed the intel, I'll give Goodyear his marching orders and let you know if, and when, the arrests can take place."

"Then we can arrange for the handoff to our agents and put them on the flight home."

They stood up and shook hands. Abel returned to her office and updated the Washingtons.

CHAPTER 94

DEMOCRATS ON THE JUDICIARY COMMITTEE had heard enough testimony to believe President Shilling had, at the very least, abused the power of his office. But, with considerable reluctance, they agreed that ordering the kidnapping of a reporter, heinous act though it was, did not unequivocally meet the Constitution's criteria for impeachment: "high crimes and misdemeanors." What's more, they reasoned, no Republican in the House of Representatives would support an impeachment resolution. And further, no Republican would vote to convict the president in a Senate trial. Because Republicans still held a majority in the Senate, committee members agreed that initiating impeachment at this stage would be an exercise in futility. Democrats reasoned that if they could build a much stronger case against Shilling, perhaps some Senate Republicans would eventually support his removal from office.

****

Behind closed doors on the following day, Russell and fellow Democrats on the committee planned their next move.

Russell began, "in the hearings just concluded, we have held in abeyance any reference to President Shilling's efforts to obstruct justice. Let us now lay the foundation for a second set of hearings. Representative Dominguez, would you please remind us of the intelligence you gathered from your contacts at the Department of Justice."

"Initially, I just heard some rumblings," said Dominguez, "that Shilling tried to end the Weiss investigation."

"How did he go about doing that?"

"I dug deeper and found out that Shilling instructed Stonehouse to ask Attorney General Moffitt to back off. However, Moffitt ignored the president's suggestion."

"So, maybe Moffitt would be willing to testify?"

"I can't speak to that issue, but we could always issue a subpoena if he refused to testify voluntarily."

"I'd like to avoid a subpoena, if possible. In any event, Moffitt is one potentially promising witness."

Russell next turned to Representative Sharon Holmbeck (D-Connecticut). "Please refresh our memories as to what you learned from your friend at the FBI."

"I have rock-solid information that Shilling tried to bury all traces of the Weiss investigation."

Russell asked, "did your friend furnish any details?"

"She said that Shilling ordered Director Abel to assemble all copies of the report and supporting documents for transmittal to the White House."

With a straight face Russell remarked, "I guess Abel didn't comply." His comment elicited much laughter. "I doubt it's worth our time to call Stonehouse to testify, though watching him assert executive privilege again might be as good as an admission. We'll see. In the meantime, I'll set up the new hearings for next week and invite Attorney General Moffitt and FBI Director Abel to testify. If we could nail Shilling for abuse of power and obstruction of justice, impeachment would become a necessity, our constitutional duty. And maybe the Senate would go along."

CHAPTER 95

THE DAY AFTER THE FIRST HEARING ENDED, Stella and Malcolm had returned to L.A. He wanted to resume editing his reporters' draft articles; she wanted to decompress.

Stella had moved back to her apartment, but she was still apprehensive when she heard the doorbell ring or even a gentle knock. Through the closed door she would question the visitor to make sure it was safe to open up. At some level, Stella knew she was overreacting, perhaps behaving irrationally. Nonetheless, the precaution gave her peace of mind.

Two days after returning to L.A., Stella was relaxing comfortably at home in the evening, reading Alice Hatcher's debut novel. This was a gloriously creative work whose narrators were cockroaches in a taxicab. Cockroaches, she chuckled to herself—a perfect metaphor for half the politicians in Washington.

Her phone's ringtone startled Stella momentarily until she saw the name on the caller ID: Benjamin Suarez. She smiled and answered, "hello Benjamin."

"Hi Stella. And please call me Ben. How have you been?"

"I'm still a little tired from my D.C. trip. You know, jet lag. Plus, testifying before the Judiciary Committee was more emotionally taxing than I had expected."

"I can imagine. But you really nailed it."

"You watched the hearing?"

"It was early morning here, but I wouldn't have missed your testimony for the world. You were very brave to blame the Republicans for Wahl's assassination. Your claim jump-started lots of conversations in our office."

"Really?"

"Yeah, and they were pretty heated at times. Even Carrington and I got into it after he saw excerpts of your testimony on Fox News."

"I hope you and Carrington are still friends."

"We're still partners, and we work together well, but we've never been close friends."

"Oh, I didn't know that. Anyway, I'm just glad it's all finally over."

"Now you can get back to your normal routine."

"Whatever that is. In the meantime, I've been fending off dozens of personal injury lawyers who want me to sue the government and the Marine Corps from Griswold on down."

"What do you tell them?"

"I just ignore their overtures. If they are very persistent, I simply say I'm not interested. I've come to believe that the only person who should be punished is Shilling. Maybe Congress will take care of him."

"Considering all you've been through, you are remarkably forgiving."

"Actually, my motives are selfish. There's no need to drag out my ordeal in the courts. I'd have to testify again, and I really don't want to. It's time for me to move on."

"I understand."

"How have you been, Ben?"

"I'm fine, but lonely. I've been longing for a woman's company, and the only woman I can think about is you."

"Does that mean we're on again for coffee?"

"Sure. I think we should get together, ASAP. In fact, it's still early. Would you like to go for coffee now? I can pick you up."

"Talk about short notice for a date! Why not? I'll be ready in 10 minutes."

"And I'll be there in 11."

Ben lived in an apartment in West Hollywood, a short drive to

Park La Brea Towers.

Stella refreshed her eye shadow and lipstick, and changed into a frilly white blouse and a black skirt short enough to reveal more than a hint of her shapely thighs.

Ben knocked gently, and she opened the door after verifying his identity. He entered, and they stood close, smiling, and in silence both leaned forward and embraced.

"Thanks, Ben, I really needed a good hug."

"I bet you did, after all you've been through. How about another one?"

They hugged again.

Ben scanned her apartment, taking note of Tabby and Stella's preference for modern furnishings, so different from the antiques in her parents' home. He also noticed the Picasso prints.

"I see you like Picasso."

"Yes, he was so immensely creative; I just love his work."

"My great-grandfather bought one of his early cubist paintings before he became a world-famous artist."

"No kidding? Did you inherit it?"

"I wish. It was trashed in the Spanish Civil War."

"Oh, that's awful."

"Fortunately, my great-grandfather survived."

She asked, "where would you like to go for coffee?"

"How about the Coffee Bean and Tea Leaf? It's nearby on Third Street."

"I know the place. It's pretty decent for a chain cafe."

In her parking lot, Ben led Stella to a 2008 Mustang painted black cherry. He had bought it used, preferring the earlier styles because they retained more of the charm of the 1960s classic Mustangs.

****

Sipping their coffees and picking pieces off a nutty fudge brownie, Stella remarked, "you know a lot about me, Ben, but everything I know about you would fit in a thimble."

"So, what would you like to know?"

Smiling mischievously, she said, "I think I'll begin my interrogation with an easy question. Are you married?"

He laughed loudly, attracting stares from nearby customers. "No, of course not. I was married once when I was young, but it didn't work out. Our lifestyles and careers drove us in different directions."

"Let me guess. Was she a criminal defense attorney?"

He laughed and said, "no, not that. She was a bank manager who earned a big promotion to the company's head office in New York City. I didn't want to leave the West because this is where I grew up and where my family lives. And I enjoy working in the L.A. office. So, with great reluctance, I told her she should take her dream job in New York. And we went our separate ways. It was a friendly divorce. That's all there was to it. But I don't want to spend more time talking about my ex."

"Okay. Now that I know you're single, I can move on to the next question on my list."

She smiled and he chuckled.

"You said you grew up in the West. Where in the West?"

"I'm from Denver. My dad—may he rest in peace—was a senior chemical engineer at the U.S. Mint. He made a good living, and we had a nice house in the Cherry Creek area, a Denver suburb."

"So, you were named for the $100 bill?"

"Hmm. Never heard that one before!"

"What was your childhood like?"

"My mom didn't work outside the home. So, she had plenty of time to raise me and my younger siblings, William and Andrea. Mom encouraged us to read and pursue our interests." He sighed, "she's not doing well these days, and we might have to move her into assisted living fairly soon."

"Oh, I'm sorry. It's tough watching parents get old. I'm fortunate that my folks are still relatively healthy."

"Yeah," he said, as he took another piece of brownie and sipped his coffee.

"My mom's career allowed her to spend most of her days working at home. She was always there for me, and we're still very close."

"We're both lucky to have been raised by nurturing parents."

"And what were your interests, Ben?"

"I love music and took piano lessons all through school. I even started college as a music major, but music theory didn't resonate with me."

She laughed at his lame pun and asked, "what kind of music do you like these days?"

"I still like classical music, but I also listen to jazz."

"I also enjoy jazz."

"I have a feeling, Stella, that one day soon we'll have a date at a jazz club."

Stella nodded and asked, "where did you go to college?"

"University of Colorado. It's not the most prestigious school, but I received a good education."

"What did you finally major in?"

"After I gave up on music, I floundered around for the first two years. I eventually ended up in sociology and graduated magna cum laude."

Stella looked surprised and asked, "and the FBI hired a sociology major?"

"Strange but true!"

"What drew you to the FBI?"

"I was turned on by driving big black SUVs." He waited for her to laugh, and she obliged. "Seriously, it was the mystique of solving crimes. I'd read a lot of crime novels when I was young, and was drawn to the intellectual challenges. My sociology background has been useful because it helps me understand the complex intersections of race, ethnicity, social class, and so on that affect behavior."

Stella said, "as a journalism major at USC, I took several sociology classes. Maybe sometime we could compare notes on our favorite social theorists."

"You're kidding, right?"

She smiled and admitted, "of course!"

"To prepare for our interviews with you, I read many of your articles in the Times and was impressed by your ability to tell a compelling story in sparkling prose. Stella, you do terrific and important work. And, I must confess, when I saw your beautiful face in a photograph, I let my imagination run wild."

Stella smiled demurely. "Where did it run to?"

"To the conclusion that I might easily fall in love with you."

"That's so sweet, Ben."

"One thing I couldn't find on the Internet was anything about your love life."

"I've never been married, but I've had a few brief romances. Unfortunately, first dates are too often last dates. I'm not sure why, but a lot of men just don't call back."

"You probably intimidate them."

She laughed. "What do you mean?"

"Well, you're attractive and smart—and accomplished in your career. A woman like you makes some men very uneasy."

"Ben, are you uneasy with me?"

"Not in the least."

"That's good!"

"Oh god, Stella, I hope I'm not making you uncomfortable. I'm prone to saying the wrong things to women."

"Ben, complimenting me is not the wrong thing." She reached over and patted his hand but couldn't stifle a yawn.

"I see you're tired, Stella. After all, you've had a busy week. I suppose it's time to take you home."

"Yes, I'm tired, but I'm also happy. This has been a delightful first date, and I hope you'll call me again."

"Count on it. In fact, how about dinner on Sunday?"

"That works for me."

"I'll pick you up at seven."

"Great."

They stood up and walked slowly to the door. Outside, Ben grasped her hands and gently pulled her close. Their lips met in a tender but fleeting kiss.

CHAPTER 96

THE HOUSE JUDICIARY COMMITTEE began its second hearings with the same cast of characters. The audience was prepared for another duel between Democrat Russell and Republican Maxwell.

James Moffitt was sworn in.

"Mr. Moffitt," asked Russell, "what is your position in the federal government?"

"I am the Attorney General."

"Would you say, then, that you are the top law-enforcement officer in the United States?"

"That is correct."

"Do you have jurisdiction over the FBI?"

"Yes, the FBI is an agency within the Justice Department."

"Were you read in on Special Agent Joanna Bartolo's investigation of Ms. Stella Weiss's disappearance?"

"Of course."

"Did you approve that investigation?"

"It's my practice not to second-guess the FBI's decisions. Personally, I believed the investigation was warranted."

"Do you know how the White House regarded this investigation?"

"As a matter of fact, I do."

"Please elaborate."

"Mr. Stonehouse, the president's Chief of Staff, at first asked me to assign a low priority to the Weiss investigation. Then, as the investigation continued anyway, he told me to terminate it."

"Did you ask him where his marching orders came from?"

"Of course. Stonehouse said he was acting on the president's behalf."

"And what did you do?"

"I told Mr. Stonehouse that I was a strong supporter of President Shilling, but I couldn't interfere in a lawful FBI investigation."

"And how did he react?"

"He told me the president would be very unhappy to learn of my refusal to cooperate. And he reminded me that I serve at the pleasure of the president."

"Did you understand that to be a threat to your position?"

"How else could I take it?"

Russell turned over the questioning to Maxwell.

"Mr. Moffitt, in what manner did Stonehouse communicate to you what he said were the president's wishes?"

"All of our communications took place by phone."

"Does that mean there are no memos, no emails, nor other hard evidence to verify your claim?"

"I'm afraid there is no documentary record, as such. However, I do have a phone log that lists several conversations with Mr. Stonehouse."

"So, we have to take your word that President Shilling, acting through Mr. Stonehouse, asked you to end the investigation?"

"That is correct. But I assure you that it happened that way. Keep in mind that I am under oath and I am telling the truth."

"Can you recall the exact words that Stonehouse used when making the request?"

"I only remember the substance of the conversation. Frankly, I was appalled."

Maxwell said, "I have no further questions for this witness, but I want to make it clear: Attorney General Moffitt provided no evidence to support his allegation that the president ordered him to shut down the Weiss investigation."

Moffitt stared daggers at Maxwell.

The questioning continued. A few committee members wanted

more details about interactions between Moffitt's office and that of FBI Director Abel, but there were no revelations. According to Democrats on the committee, the case for obstruction of justice was building nicely.

****

FBI Director Shirley Abel was sworn in and took her seat. Russell thanked her for agreeing to testify. He then made a surprise move, handing off the witness to Maxwell.

Maxwell looked puzzled but asked, "Ms. Abel, what is your current position in the federal government?"

"I am Director of the FBI."

"And how long have you held that position?"

"For seven years."

"So, I guess you have a lot of investigations under your belt?"

"Yes, we have a very fine record of identifying and putting away bad actors."

"There's one big blemish on your record, though. You haven't arrested Robert and Roberta. In fact, you don't even know their real names. Isn't that correct?"

The last thing Abel wanted to say in a public hearing was that the arrest of the assassins in Samoa was imminent. She couldn't endanger that operation by being forthcoming about the status of the investigation. Abel hoped that it would not be necessary to lie.

"It is unfortunate that we have not yet made arrests in that case."

"And why is that?"

"As any experienced investigator will tell you, it's a very challenging case. We've pulled out all the stops trying to solve it, and we've explored many investigative avenues. I am confident that we'll eventually have a break in the case."

"Have you made this investigation your highest priority?"

"Yes, it's one of two recent high-priority investigations. Fortunately, we did close the case on the Weiss incident. The assassination case remains priority número uno."

Democrats on the committee expected Maxwell to lay a foundation for defending the president against the inevitable obstruction charges. But Maxwell wasn't going there. Instead, he drilled deeper on the FBI's failure to arrest Robert and Roberta, questioning the agency's competence and Abel's leadership. According to most observers, it was an ineffective move, but Maxwell apparently thought that Republicans would gain an advantage by undermining the FBI director.

****

Democrats took their turn at the witness, with Dominguez asking the first questions. Russell and Dominguez had conspired beforehand to co-opt several obvious Republican lines of questioning. In fact, she planned to ask questions whose answers she already knew.

"Director Abel, in your professional opinion, was finding Robert and Roberta a matter of national security?"

"In my professional opinion, identifying and arresting the assassins was obviously important, that's why we assigned it a top priority. But it had nothing to do with national security."

"And why is that?"

"Ms. Weiss's interviews with Robert and Roberta clearly showed that the assassination was a one-off crime. Thus, we had no reason to believe that there was an ongoing threat to this nation, much less a conspiracy to undermine our government. And, let me add, there was no justification for President Shilling ordering the abduction and detention of Ms. Weiss."

Dominguez then pivoted to the crucial question, "Director Abel, did the president ever try to interfere in the Weiss investigation?"

"Yes, he did."

Members of the audience murmured and stirred, surprised at her revelation.

"Please tell us how that came about."

"He summoned me to the Oval Office and directed me to terminate the investigation. What's more, he asked me to assemble all copies of the final report and supporting documents. He gave me 72 hours to gather the materials and deliver them to Mr. Stonehouse."

Many in attendance audibly gasped.

Anticipating a Republican question, Dominguez asked, "so, is it reasonable to assume there is no actual written documentation of his order?"

"To my knowledge there is not."

"And what was your response to his demand?"

"I told him, reluctantly, that I would comply."

"And did you comply?"

"Not exactly."

"Would you please be more specific."

"Following the president's demand, I did deliver a thumb drive to Mr. Stonehouse with the requested materials. But I also retained copies."

"Why did you defy the president's orders?"

"Because I believed the findings of the Weiss investigation had to be made public. I had no desire to participate in a cover-up of President Shilling's crimes."

"Did you leak that report to Mr. Klein of the L.A. Times?"

"The report was unclassified, available to the public. So, no, I didn't leak it; I merely emailed it to Mr. Klein."

The audience was buzzing upon learning of Abel's stratagem. Democrats smiled and nodded; Republicans scowled and groaned.

"Isn't it highly unusual for a report of this kind, which implicates some fine marines by name, to be unclassified?"

"It was somewhat unusual, but making that determination was entirely within the scope of my powers as FBI director."

"I have no further questions."

****

Russell turned over the questioning to Republican Amos Reidhead.

"Ms. Abel, I find your behavior reprehensible. You disobeyed the president's order."

"As far as I was concerned, Mr. Reidhead, the president had himself committed a crime by ordering me to terminate and bury the

Weiss investigation. Obstruction of justice is a serious offense."

Reidhead's face was turning red, the veins on his forehead throbbing. He raised his voice, "I condemn your act of insubordination."

"Mr. Reidhead, I understand your frustration, but I acted to protect the integrity of the FBI's investigation."

"What if the president had insisted that his order was a matter of national security?"

"As I said in my answer to Representative Dominguez, the Weiss investigation was not a matter of national security, so I would have done exactly the same thing. Regardless of how President Shilling justified his order, the bottom line was simple: he was trying to prevent his wrongdoing from becoming public. And in making that move, he was obstructing justice."

"That's a serious charge, Ms. Abel. But doesn't it boil down to your word against the president's?"

"What do you mean?"

"You have admitted that his order lacks written documentation. Without supporting evidence, we are not compelled to believe your story. And isn't it true that Democrats on this committee are simply using you as a tool to undermine the president?"

For once Abel raised her voice. "I will not dignify that slander by answering you."

"Then I have no more questions."

Director Abel answered a handful of repetitious questions from Republicans and Democrats, but her testimony did not waver from two strong claims. First, she insisted that President Shilling personally ordered her to end the Weiss investigation and turn over its findings to the White House. Second, she did not believe that national security was at stake.

Russell adjourned the hearing, leaving ample time for the committee to meet behind closed doors to discuss the day's testimony. Russell brought several hours of heated discussion to an end by tasking a subcommittee of Democrats to draw up articles of impeachment. Republicans stormed out of the room. "Good riddance," shouted one Democrat.

CHAPTER 97

AMBASSADOR GOODYEAR HAD BEEN appalled when Snow briefed him on the FBI's misstep. His initial thought was to keep the Samoan government in the dark about the presence of the Washingtons in their country. He could simply ask permission for the FBI to send their agents. He realized, however, that he would have to provide the names of the agents to whom the Samoans would transfer the Armstrongs. It would be a simple matter for Samoan officials to determine when the Washingtons had arrived in their country. Goodyear could not risk being caught in a lie while seeking permission for a fait accompli.

Goodyear arranged a meeting with three high-level Samoan officials. He informed them of the plan to arrest the Armstrongs, admitting that two FBI agents were already on Savai'i. The meeting did not go well. The Samoans took offense at what they regarded as a breach of protocol, stood up, and walked out.

After giving the Samoans a cooling-off period of several days, Goodyear was able to arrange a second meeting. In that meeting Goodyear offered a formal apology on the behalf of the United States government. Even after receiving the apology, the Samoans did not immediately approve the operation, taking it under advisement.

Two weeks later Samoan officials at last informed Goodyear of their willingness to proceed. They placed only one condition on the agreement: the Samoa Police Service would make the arrest. This condition posed no problem.

CHAPTER 98

WHEN THE DOORBELL RANG at 7:00 a.m., the Armstrongs awoke, startled. Michael rolled out of bed and walked to the window facing the street. He pulled the curtain aside and peered outside. When he saw a police car parked in the driveway, his heart almost stopped.

"Tina. It's the police!"

"Oh my god. What do you think it's about?"

As Michael struggled to get dressed, he said, "I have no idea what's going on. I'll head downstairs and find out. In the meantime, you better get dressed. I have a feeling they're not here to sell us Lotto tickets."

The police officers rang the bell again, more insistently this time, and then pounded on the door just as Michael was about to open it. When he pulled the door inward, he saw two huge Polynesian policemen.

"Are you Michael Armstrong?"

Terrified, he answered, "yes, I am."

"Does Tina Armstrong also reside here?"

"Yes, she'll be down momentarily. She's getting dressed. You woke us up. What's going on?"

One of the officers, apparently the spokesman, said, "I am Officer Malala, and he is Officer Tofilau. We have come to arrest you and your wife for the murder of Frederick John Wahl, President of the United States. Let us all step inside."

Michael came close to fainting but quickly turned around, walked to the couch, and sat down. A frightened Tina, her cheeks already streaked by tears, joined him a few minutes later.

"You can't arrest us for allegedly committing a crime in the United States."

"We are conducting a special operation in collaboration with the U.S. government." He showed them the search and arrest warrants and said, "we'll be delivering you to FBI agents who will escort you back to the United States to stand trial."

Michael and Tina looked at each other in disbelief. They held hands briefly before Malala handcuffed them. He said, "if you know what's good for you, you won't move while officer Tofilau searches the premises."

Tofilau took a good look around the main floor. He found the tablet and laptop computers and placed them on the table near the front door. Then, in the kitchen and dining room, he opened the cupboards and pulled out the drawers, but found nothing of interest. Finally, Tofilau climbed the stairs to the third floor. He entered Michael's office and whistled in disbelief, staring at the cornucopia of IT equipment. It took him four trips to bring everything downstairs, including a small stack of documents. He also collected the couple's phones from their nightstands.

Tofilau said, "that should do it for now."

After allowing the Armstrongs to pack one suitcase each, Officers Malala and Tofilau loaded the couple, their luggage, and the confiscated items into the police car. Tofilau drove to the ferry terminal, where they awaited the next departure.

****

Almost two hours later, Tofilau pulled into a distant part of the Faleolo airport. Near the U.S. Air Force C-130J transport plane were parked several official vehicles of the Samoan government.

The foursome exited the police car and approached the group standing near the plane. After introductions and handshakes, Malala and Tofilau handed off the Armstrongs to FBI agents Aisha and Shawan

Washington. American and Samoan videographers documented the unusual event. Neither Tina nor Michael smiled for the cameras.

Uniformed men loaded everything into the C-130J, and the Washingtons and Armstrongs climbed aboard. The big plane taxied to the runway, made a turn, and took off. The four turboprop engines effortlessly carried the plane northward across the Pacific.

The Armstrongs had been silent and slept during most of the grueling flights. At one point, while they were on the ground, refueling in Los Angeles, Michael asked the FBI agents, "how did you know where we were?"

Shawan responded, "the FBI has IT capabilities you can only dream about."

"In her testimony to Congress Stella Weiss said she didn't give us up to the government. Was she telling the truth?"

"Yes. She never stopped insisting that she couldn't reveal her sources. And she didn't reveal them, despite unrelenting pressure from the Shilling administration. For your information, our IT people in D.C. pieced together your location."

"How did they do it?"

"Using video surveillance, our team followed Ms. Weiss to Samoa and monitored her travels there. The crucial image was Ms. Weiss sitting in your car at the ferry terminal. The car's license number led to your name and address. Your big mistake was leasing the car and house in your own name."

Michael shook his head, recalling that he had leased the car and house even before Shilling had been elected. Underestimating the FBI's IT capabilities had been a serious—perhaps fatal—miscalculation.

After refueling stops and crew changes in Hawai'i and Los Angeles, the big plane with its precious cargo landed at Joint Base Andrews. Aisha texted Abel to announce their arrival.

The next morning Abel called the White House. She was put on hold and had to wait almost 15 minutes. At last Shilling came on the line.

"I'm surprised to hear from you, Abel. You know, I wanted to fire you for making the FBI report public, but Stonehouse talked me out

of it. You should consider yourself very lucky to still be the FBI director. I'm very busy, so what do you want?"

"I called to inform you that Robert and Roberta are in custody.
Their real names are Michael and Tina Armstrong, and they arrived
early this morning on a flight from Samoa."

Shilling replied coldly, "it's about time" and ended the call.

CHAPTER 99

STELLA HAD CLOSELY FOLLOWED press reports of Michael and Tina's arrests in Samoa and their arrival in D.C. A story in the Washington Post quoted an unnamed FBI source as saying that video surveillance at the ferry terminal purportedly showed Stella Weiss in the Armstrong's car. At the disturbing news, Stella tensed, terrified she might be called to testify. What would she do? Although she had found the couple personable and hospitable, they were mass murderers who deserved to be arrested and punished. Stella was deeply conflicted because she opposed the death penalty.

Several days after the arrest, Stella was having dinner at her parents' home. She was assembling the salad while Rachel prepared the main course, chicken marsala. Daniel was in the dining room, setting the table and opening a bottle of merlot.

"So, Stella, it seems the saga of Robert and Roberta is finally coming to an end."

Cutting slices of tomato, Stella replied, "actually, mom, it's just the beginning of a new chapter."

"I assume you mean the trial?"

"Yes, of course. It's going to be a media circus because journalists from around the world will be covering it. And the inevitable demonstrations outside the courthouse will themselves become news."

"Who would want to demonstrate?"

"I'm guessing that fringe groups on the right and left will both use the trial as an opportunity to advance their causes. They can count on extensive media coverage to get their messages out to a large audience."

"Are you interested in going to D.C. to cover the trial?"

"No way. My beat is still L.A. city government. In a few weeks I hope to be working on new stories that affect Angelinos," remarked Stella as she drained the liquid from a can of Mandarin oranges and added them to the salad.

"I almost hesitate to ask you, dear, but what happens if the prosecution subpoenas you to testify against the Armstrongs?"

"That would put me in an impossible position. The FBI has an image of me sitting in their car. The prosecution would no doubt ask me to verify the location and identify myself and the driver."

"What would your options be in that case?"

"I've already posed the question to a Times attorney. He said my first option is to refuse to answer the questions."

"But would you?"

"If I refuse to answer, the judge would most likely declare me in contempt of court. I could end up in jail."

"Is there another option?"

"The attorney said I could invoke the Fifth Amendment and refuse to testify because I might incriminate myself. He said that if a judge questioned me about my reasons for taking the fifth, I could claim to be worried about being arrested as an accessory after the fact."

"What does that mean in this case?"

"It means I knowingly protected the president's assassins."

"Would you actually invoke the Fifth Amendment?"

"It's tricky because people who take the fifth are assumed to be guilty of something. I wouldn't want that stain on my reputation."

"If I'm hearing you correctly, you have two choices: bad and awful."

"True, but that assumes the case goes to trial. I'm praying the entire affair will end soon in a plea bargain."

"And if it doesn't?"

"Then I'll take the "bad" choice even though it involves the risk of going to jail."

"Stella, you know that people might say you refused to testify in order to protect two murderers."

"The people I care about will know I did it to protect freedom of the press."

"Stella, your dad and I are very proud of you—worried, but proud."

"Thanks, mom."

"The chicken is done, so let's eat!"

CHAPTER 100

DEMOCRATIC MEMBERS OF THE Judiciary Committee had taken several weeks to debate the merits of impeaching the president. All agreed that Shilling's conduct met the constitutional criteria. But several representatives were dead-set against proceeding to an impeachment vote.

Myron Goldberg (D-California) offered the first, and most obvious, argument. "How can we vote for impeachment without assurances that the Senate will remove him from office?"

In countering Goldberg, Dominguez insisted, "any objective observer, even Senate Republicans, would have to agree that Shilling had abused the power of the presidency and attempted to obstruct justice."

In addition, she pointed out, "Shilling and Griswold were engaged in a criminal conspiracy. If Shilling were any other citizen, he would have been arrested by now. We cannot shirk our constitutional duty. We must hold the president accountable."

No one disagreed with her on the merits, but several worried that the Democratic Party might lose credibility—and future elections—if the Senate failed to convict the president.

The second argument concerned public opinion. The most articulate spokesperson for this position was Tanya Holtzman (D-Oregon).

"My esteemed colleagues, I call your attention to a recent poll. Sixty-three percent of voting-age Americans oppose impeachment. We have to move the needle on public opinion before taking this

366

drastic action. Posterity will be very unkind to us if we go against public opinion and Democrats lose the next presidential election."

Russell, who had been silent during most of the discussions, finally opined, "Representative Holtzman, the problem with that argument, I would wager, is that 63 percent of Americans conflate impeachment with "removal from office." We can sway public opinion simply by educating the public on the civics lessons they ignored in high school. We have to stress, at every opportunity and in every medium, that impeachment merely means that the president has been indicted, his reputation permanently besmirched. Only the Senate has the power to render a verdict and remove a president from office. If we do a full court press on the media regarding this constitutional point, I predict polls will swing our way before the Senate trial."

After several more hours of committee discussions, the Democrats passed a resolution declaring their intent to impeach Shilling. Chairman Russell agreed to work on the two articles of impeachment. Several days later, he sent the draft articles to the remainder of the committee, welcoming their suggestions.

The committee met again with no Republicans in attendance and voted unanimously to forward the revised articles of impeachment to the Honorable Elaine Naismith, Speaker of the House.

Democrats held press conferences and appeared on talk shows to emphasize the meaning of impeachment. In the last poll taken before the Senate trial began, the needle had moved. Fifty-one percent of likely voters now supported impeachment.

CHAPTER 101

STELLA PREPARED FOR HER third dinner date with Ben. The previous date had been at the Catalina Bar & Grill on Sunset Boulevard, well known for topflight jazz performances. They had both enjoyed themselves thoroughly. With every date Stella was becoming increasingly smitten with Ben, who was already madly in love with her.

She chose a pastel orange blouse, teal skirt, and medium heels. Ben arrived promptly at 7:00, and she welcomed him into her apartment. He was wearing a lively orange shirt and khakis.

"Oh my god, we're both wearing orange," said Stella.

"I'm horrified," he replied, and they both broke out laughing. And then they hugged.

"Ah, Stella, when I'm in your arms, I feel like we are the only two people in the world."

She smiled, and said, "there's something very special about hugs."

"Where would you like to go for dinner?"

"Ben, have you ever been to Canter's on Fairfax?"

"I've been to the bakery part, but I've never eaten in the restaurant."

"Do you want to give traditional Jewish favorites a try?"

"Why not? I'm an omnivore."

"There's nothing really scary on the menu—unless you count calories and salt and cholesterol."

"I'm an eater, not a counter."

Stella giggled.

They took the elevator to the ground floor, and walked to his car in the parking lot. The pair got into the Mustang, and he drove the short distance to Fairfax Avenue.

"Ben, there's a parking lot at the beginning of the block on the left side. We can park there if it's not full, and Canter's validates."

He eased the Mustang into the last empty space and took a ticket from the attendant. They walked a half block north on Fairfax and entered the restaurant. A hostess led them to a table where they sat down and studied the menus.

"Stella, you'll have to give me some tips on these items. What's good?"

"My favorite is pastrami on rye with sides of coleslaw and potato salad. You also get a slice of dill pickle. The food's delicious."

"Well, I'll take your word for it. Let's make it two of them."

After the waitress took their order, Ben asked in a low voice, "Stella, how are you doing?"

"I'm feeling better every day. Malcolm is keeping me busy at the paper, and so I don't have time to dwell on the past."

"That's wonderful news. But, what about the future? Are you concerned about the upcoming trial of the Armstrongs?"

"Of course. I'm worried sick that I might be called as a prosecution witness. To tell you the truth, Ben, I'd rather not talk about it. Let's not spoil our time together."

"I understand; sorry for bringing it up. Let me change the subject. Are you working on any interesting stories?"

"Right now, I'm just doing grunt work for Malcolm, going through public records and doing other research to shore up the stories of our cub reporters. It's low stress work that suits me just fine right now. Honestly, I haven't been looking for a new story to pursue on my own. My investigative groove isn't back yet. I don't know what's the matter. Maybe in a week or two I'll find something to get excited about."

"It's understandable you haven't jumped into a new story. Your last jump was almost a fatal plunge."

"I can live without all the drama."

Their plates arrived, and Ben marveled at the size of the pastrami sandwiches. He opened wide and took his first bite. With a full mouth he managed to say, "wow, this is delicious, and big enough for two people. I could get used to Jewish food."

"In my family, Canter's is a place for special occasions."

Ben looked deeply into Stella's amber eyes and asked, "is this a special occasion?"

"Being with a man who respects me is special."

He reached across the table and grasped her hand, gently stroking her dainty fingers. She looked up and smiled.

"You know, Ben, after dinner we could take a nice long walk in the Grove and then go back to my apartment for a nightcap and maybe more exercise."

"Sounds like good plan."

"So, Ben, what are you working on these days?"

"Just a run-of-the-mill armed robbery at a bank on Western Avenue. Fortunately, nobody got hurt."

"That's good. And how's the investigation going?"

"We're just wrapping it up. The dumbass robber left his car within sight of a surveillance camera. We ran the license plate and arrested him. After we finish the paperwork, the case will go to an assistant D.A."

****

They finished dinner, left the restaurant, and forgot about the walk. After returning to Stella's apartment, they made themselves comfortable on the couch. Tabby jumped on Ben's lap and began purring. Stella took that as a good sign.

"Ben, would you like some sherry?"

"I'd love some, thanks."

They snuggled on the couch and slowly sipped sherry. One touch led to another, one kiss to another. Stella and Ben soon adjourned to the bedroom where they pleasured each other.

"Stella, this could be habit-forming."

"Do you have a problem with that?"

370

"Nope."

"Neither do I."

CHAPTER 102

THE UNITED STATES ATTORNEY'S OFFICE for the District of Columbia indicted Michael and Tina Armstrong on charges of conspiracy, multiple counts of murder in the first degree, destruction of government property, and several lesser charges. During the most perfunctory hearing on record, the judge denied the Armstrongs bail.

With impeachment looming, President Shilling was eager for the trial to distract the public, though there would be some downsides. A trial would become the occasion for every leftist group to remind the country of President Wahl's moral and political failings. That could exacerbate the electorate's growing disenchantment with Shilling's presidency and the Republican Party. Despite his misgivings, the president urged Attorney General Moffitt to bring the Armstrongs to trial ASAP.

Moffitt, Abel, Bartolo, and several assistant attorneys from the Department of Justice held a lengthy and contentious conference about the advisability of going to trial. When Bartolo laid out the case against the Armstrongs, admitting that nothing incriminating was found on their computers or in the documents taken from their home, the attorneys groaned. The only hard evidence linking the Armstrongs to the crime itself was Stella Weiss' stories. The stories had achieved credibility because the image of Weiss in the Renault placed her in Samoa where the Armstrongs lived.

The lead federal attorney was blunt: "our best shot at getting convictions is to have Weiss take the stand as the chief witness for the prosecution." The other attorneys nodded in agreement. Without Weiss's testimony, they feared that a battery of top-notch defense attorneys would turn their case into mincemeat.

In the back of everyone's mind was one salient fact. Bartolo expressed it aloud: "to protect her sources' identities, Stella Weiss would almost certainly refuse to answer questions, risking a contempt citation." Abel opined, "and if we put Weiss on the stand, we could end up with a public relations disaster. Journalists would pile on, reminding everyone about what the government had already done to her. It would look like government prosecutors were prolonging her suffering."

Abel and Bartolo gave other reasons for avoiding a trial. One of the most compelling was the revelation that the DNA recovered from the food truck's vent did not belong to Michael Armstrong. Everyone knew that the defense would seize on that fact and claim it was exculpatory, even though it was not. Michael no doubt wore gloves, and a maintenance person could have touched the vent and left DNA at any time.

Initially offering strong pushback, the federal attorneys reluctantly agreed that a plea agreement was the best option. They would not have their trial of the century.

****

Washington Post op-eds had been predicting for weeks that the assassination saga would end with a plea deal. Meeting the Post's expectations, attorneys for the government and for Michael and Tina Armstrong held a conference in the chambers of federal district Judge Thomas Rakita to discuss terms of the agreement.

Government attorneys indicated a willingness to avoid trial despite having a "slam dunk case" with Ms. Stella Weiss as the star witness. In exchange for a nolo contendere plea, which is equivalent to an admission of guilt, the government would take the death penalty off the table. In its place the government would accept a sentence of life in prison without the possibility of parole. The Armstrongs' attorneys pointed to holes in the government's case, but presented the deal to the couple, expecting them to turn it down.

Deliberating the terms of the deal in phone calls, the Armstrongs reasoned that a jury would likely find them guilty in order to achieve closure on the president's assassination. In the event of convictions, they would have to live on death row for decades while appeals worked their way through the courts. And that would be intolerable. The couple decided to accept the deal, opting for the certainty of life in prison over the possibility of conviction and an interminable wait on death row. In prison, they would at least have the opportunity to spread conservative ideas among other inmates.

After Judge Rakita approved the plea agreement, federal marshals delivered the Armstrongs to separate high-security prisons. The notorious couple quickly faded from public view. Behind the scenes, however, they received death threats from other inmates and occasionally were put in solitary confinement or transferred to other prisons for their own protection. This was not the early retirement they had envisioned.

CHAPTER 103

NAISMITH CIRCULATED THE ARTICLES of impeachment to all House members and set a date and time for debates to begin. From this larger venue Republicans did not flee. Rather, they used every weapon in the legislator's arsenal to hinder the proceedings against the president. Their strongest argument was not entirely frivolous.

Speaker of the House Elaine Naismith had, according to Republicans, a serious conflict of interest. If Shilling were impeached in the House and convicted in the Senate, she would become president according to the law of succession. Shilling could have appointed someone to fill the vacant vice president position, but he knew that House Democrats would block that move, so he hadn't bothered. Naismith asserted repeatedly that she had but one vote; the decision to impeach rested with the remaining 434 representatives.

In view of the controversies and the decision's importance, Naismith allowed the discussion to lumber along, day after day. Finally, tired of the acrimony, repetitious arguments, and frivolous Republican objections, she brought the articles of impeachment to the floor for a vote.

Naismith had some concerns because many Democrats in swing districts had argued against impeachment. These members worried that they could lose their seats in the next election, diminishing the Democratic majority in the House. She urged them to vote their conscience.

The articles of impeachment passed 230-202. The vote was much closer than expected because 21 Democrats voted "no" and three voted "present." Naismith thanked the members of the House for discharging their constitutional duty. It was, she said, "a bold and historic move. Posterity will remember that we held President Shilling accountable for his criminal behavior."

****

In the Oval Office Shilling and Stonehouse watched the vote on C-SPAN. The president was livid. He earnestly believed he had done nothing improper, much less illegal. He couldn't fathom why he was being persecuted. Stonehouse tried to console the president, insisting, "the Senate is filled with our friends. They will never remove you from office."

"I agree. Republicans will remain loyal to me. But just being impeached and tried in the Senate is a black mark on my presidency."

"You have many accomplishments to your credit." In a spasm of wishful thinking, Stonehouse added, "history books will showcase your accomplishments, not your impeachment."

"I hope you're right."

"Don't worry, Mr. President. We'll get through this."

CHAPTER 104

BARTOLO, TOO, HAD BEEN WATCHING the House vote on C-SPAN. Since receiving the final report from Suarez and Carrington, she had been pondering the fate of the people at Pendleton who had perpetrated the Weiss incident. She counted them up: seven marines, all with excellent service records and no criminal histories. They had merely done what good soldiers do: they followed Commander Griswold's orders, believing them to be legal. For that reason, NCIS had taken no action against any of the marines ranked below Griswold. After much fretting and soul-searching, Bartolo reluctantly seconded the NCIS decision and filed no charges.

General Griswold, Dr. Graninger, and CIA Director Smalley were special cases requiring special consideration. They, too, were following orders—President Shilling's. Bartolo concluded that Smalley's role in the affair was sufficiently minor to give him a pass. She could not think of a charge that would compel a jury to convict him.

A friend confided to Bartolo that lengthy and contentious discussions had taken place at NCIS about how to deal with General Griswold. NCIS attorneys had agonized over the man who had played a central role in the affair, having conspired with the president. Could he also be given a pass because he had obeyed Shilling's orders? Strictly speaking, Griswold did not report directly to the president. His superior officers were in the office of the Marine Corps Commandant. The president had bypassed the chain of command by issuing orders directly to Griswold. Thus, several attorneys reasoned, the prosecution might argue that Griswold could not legitimately invoke the superior orders defense to justify his actions. The commander should have insisted that the president go through channels. But Griswold didn't do that. Instead, he bought into and implemented the president's plan. And he authorized the dumping of the unconscious Stella Weiss in an emergency room. In his favor, though, Griswold admitted to having had conversations with the president and passing along his orders to Major Petersen.

In the end, according to Bartolo's friend, NCIS attorneys agreed that a court martial would result in an acquittal because, regardless of the chain of command, Griswold was following what he believed were a superior's lawful orders. Bartolo was unhappy with the NCIS decision but accepted it.

Dr. Graninger was punished for his role in the Weiss affair. He lost his license to practice medicine in Washington, D.C. Shilling, if he remained in office, would have to find another White House physician.

CHAPTER 105

STELLA AND HER MOM WERE SITTING in the sun room, enjoying coffee and blueberry muffins on the day after NCIS had publicly given Griswold a get-out-of-jail-free card.

"He should be in prison for what he did to you," said Rachel.

"I suppose so. But Griswold was just a good soldier, obeying his orders. And besides, he has a wife and two young children, so maybe it's okay that he's been let off the hook."

Taking another bite of muffin, Rachel said, "it's very generous of you to say that. But what about Shilling? How do you think the Senate will vote?"

"He'll get away with his crimes. The vote will no doubt be along party lines. The Republicans will defend Shilling regardless of his reprehensible acts. They tipped their hand in the hearings. Mark my words: Republicans will put party over country every time."

"Well, Stella, you're in a cynical mood today."

"Not entirely. In fact, I have some upbeat news."

"Tell me."

"Mom, I think I've finally found my soul mate."

"That came out of the blue! Is this about your FBI friend, Ben?"

"Yes. You know we've been dating, and we really enjoy each other's company. He's obviously good-looking, but there's so much more to him than that. We just talk and talk and talk. He's very worldly and a great listener. And Ben really opens up when he's talking about himself and his family. He's so different from the stereotype of FBI agents as humorless automatons. Ben is warm and affectionate, and he has a terrific sense of humor. He makes me laugh."

"And do you make him laugh?"

"I try—and sometimes succeed."

"It sounds like you might be falling in love with Ben."

"I've met a lot of men over the decades, but Ben is special. If I'm not in love with him now, I will be soon."

"You've never seemed interested in a permanent relationship."

"That's true, mom. And I know my attitude has bothered you because you've dropped gentle hints about how nice it would be for you and dad to have grandchildren."

"I've never pushed you about having kids because you've always insisted that marriage and children would interfere with your career."

"Mom, I know I've said that, but I've done lots of thinking lately. I've had a life-changing experience. Maybe I need a better balance in my life. I love being a journalist, but it's been an all-consuming career. I think about you and dad, your strong marriage despite two demanding careers. You are a very special couple."

"Yes, as we've aged, our appreciation for each other has grown. We are a team held together by love and mutual respect."

Rachel began to tear up, and Stella's eye's glistened.

"Honestly, mom, I don't know if Ben and I could achieve anything like the relationship you and dad enjoy, but it might be worth trying."

"How does Ben feel about a more permanent relationship...about marriage?"

"We've never talked about marriage, but he's dropped hints about wanting to spend the rest of our lives together. It's not quite an endorsement of marriage, but it's damn close."

"I have to admit, Stella, you've caught me by surprise. I never thought you'd become so serious with a man."

"It caught me by surprise, too. Ben and I are just so simpático. We want to spend more and more time together. He even wants me to meet his family in Colorado."

"Hmm. Is it time for me to hire a wedding planner? And when do we go shopping for your gown?"

Stella and Rachel couldn't stop laughing.

CHAPTER 106

ACCORDING TO THE CONSTITUTION, the Chief Justice of the United States presides over impeachment trials in the Senate. Appointed by Wahl, Chief Justice Max Panovsky was in his late fifties. He looked much younger with a wrinkle-free face and a long, wavy mane of bottle-black hair. Behind his bifocals were expressive brown eyes. Although he was a constitutional originalist, even Democrats respected his meticulously crafted opinions. But no court case had ever induced the level of anxiety Panovsky felt when he entered the Senate chamber for the first time as presiding judge in the trial of a sitting president.

Testimony for and against the charges spelled out in the articles of impeachment—abuse of power and obstruction of justice—endured for weeks. After the witnesses were heard, every senator, it seemed, wanted to express an opinion for the record, and Judge Panovsky was willing to give all of them time to do it. In his view, the grave matter at hand required a thorough airing. There was no need to rush to a vote, even though other important Senate business was at a standstill.

In open session Republicans admitted that detaining a reporter was a drastic move. But they insisted it was necessary because Shilling was acting on behalf of national security. He could not be faulted for his patriotic motives, much less removed from office. They also claimed that the witnesses in the House hearings and in the Senate trial had lied about Shilling's alleged attempts to obstruct justice.

In the privacy of their offices, talking with staff and with each other, Senate Republicans told a different story about why they would vote to acquit the president. A vote for conviction, they lamented, was a vote to elevate Speaker Elaine Naismith to the presidency. That outcome, they agreed, was anathema.

Journalists were not fooled by the Republicans' patriotic rhetoric. Op-ed pieces in the major dailies repeatedly called out Senate Republicans for their transparent party-first, country-second stance. Would scolding by the press sway any Republican votes? Some Democrats were guardedly optimistic that reason and good judgment would prevail, but they were in the minority.

During the third and final week of the trial, several Republicans finally broke ranks with the party. Senator Gavin Shackley, the outspoken senator from Vermont, gave an impassioned speech, which included several poignant remarks.

He began, "the impeachment clause in the Constitution gives Congress the only remedy for dealing with a lawless president. In the present case, President Shilling's wrongdoings have risen to a level never before seen in the glorious history of our republic. If we do not convict President Shilling for these crimes and remove him from office, history will judge us harshly. Worse still, future presidents will believe that they are free to pursue illegal agendas without fear of consequences. It is time to end Shilling's presidency and move on. We are all frightened by the prospect of a radical liberal becoming president, but with the election looming soon, we can field a strong candidate and defeat her at the polls. For now, do not fear a Naismith presidency because we have the power to hold her worst impulses in check. But now we must carry out our solemn duty and pass righteous judgment on a president who has repeatedly, and flagrantly, broken the laws of our land. I urge my fellow Republicans to pay close attention to your moral compass. I, for one, will vote to convict."

A hush fell over the Senate chamber as members ruminated over Shackley's surprising remarks. Other Republicans were stunned and dismayed by his brief, heartfelt speech; Democrats saw a faint glimmer of hope that he might have convinced a few Republicans to break with the party. But a handful of Republican votes would be inconsequential because a two-thirds majority was required for ending the Shilling presidency.

Two days later Justice Panovsky gaveled an end to the Senate's deliberations. Despite the seriousness of Shilling's misdeeds, only three Republicans voted for conviction. The articles of impeachment were defeated 55-45. The Senate majority leader, Henry Tortuga (R-Nebraska), immediately stripped the three defectors of their committee chairmanships.

Fox News had been carrying the Senate vote, and Shilling had watched the coverage in the Oval Office. He was pleased with the outcome though it was expected.

After the vote, crestfallen Democrats filed out of the Senate chamber. They had miscalculated. It had been utter naiveté, or wishful thinking, to believe Republicans would vote against their president. The articles of impeachment and supporting testimony demonstrated convincingly that Shilling was unfit to hold the highest office in the land. Democrats could do nothing to prevent Shilling from remaining in office until the end of his term. They groused that he would not be held accountable for his deplorable deeds.

****

Stella and Malcolm had watched the final tally of the Senate vote in his office. They were disappointed but not surprised.

"Malcolm, the hearings and trial have all been a waste of time. Shilling is still in office, and he's getting away with his crimes."

"Maybe not for long. The most recent national polls are showing reduced support for him. If the Democrats nominate a strong candidate in the upcoming election, Shilling might very well lose."

"We'll see," she said as she left his office, shaking her head.

CHAPTER 107

STELLA HAD CONTINUED ATTENDING counseling sessions throughout the early summer. Her therapist marveled at the reporter's resilience and rapid progress. Disturbing flashbacks to the green room and Dr. Death had ceased, and the entire ordeal was fast become nothing more than a fuzzy memory. Stella was bitterly disappointed by the Senate's exoneration of Shilling, but his trial was also in the past, and the verdict would not change. Stella had a bright future to think about, perhaps a full life to spend with Ben.

On an early Saturday afternoon in mid-July, Stella picked up Ben at his apartment. He greeted her with a huge hug and long kiss. They left his apartment and walked two blocks to the only parking space she had been able to snag. In her three-year-old Volvo, she drove to one of L.A.'s many fine independent theaters. This week the theater was featuring movies based on D.C. Comics superheroes. Today's showing was Wonder Woman.

At the snack counter Ben bought a tub of popcorn, M&Ms, and two drinks.

"Ben, how am I supposed to stay in shape if you keep spoiling me with treats?"

He just laughed and said, "this is a one-time indulgence."

"You mean, once a week or whenever we get together!"

"Well," he said through a grin, "you could stop seeing me."

"Oh, Ben, please don't even joke about that. You know how much

I care for you. I'll gladly suffer with the treats."

They both laughed.

The couple was still in the lobby when a young man approached Stella and said, in a menacing tone, "you are a traitor. The marines should have beat the crap out of you."

Ben took a quick step toward him and said, "stand back and go on your way." Looking up at Ben, who towered over him, the young man turned around and scurried away.

This was not the first time self-proclaimed patriots had recognized and accosted Stella in a public place. She had become a minor celebrity, her face familiar to most Angelinos because her picture had been in newspapers almost continuously since she had gone missing. Some strangers tried to make eye contact and nodded or smiled; others offered nasty comments. She regarded these unwelcome encounters as a minor annoyance.

"Thanks, Ben, but he was just expressing his opinion. Jerks like that don't really bother me any more. I'm used to their rudeness."

"I just don't like it. You never know when one of them might take a step beyond rude and become violent."

"Let's go inside and find seats. I think the previews are about to begin."

Actually, the couple had to sit through ten minutes of advertising before the previews started.

Stella said, "they should pay us to watch the commercials."

"That's going to happen. Not!"

After the show, which they enjoyed, Ben and Stella drove to Chinatown for dinner. Both used chopsticks skillfully, eating an assortment of dishes favored by non-Asians including chicken chow mein, shrimp eggrolls, and egg foo yung.

"Stella, I've planned a special treat for next weekend. You'll need to bring along a bathing suit and lots of sunscreen. We'll be going on a little cruise. You don't get seasick, do you?"

She laughed heartily. "No, happily I don't. What's this all about?"

As he took another bite of eggroll, Ben replied, "you'll find out next Saturday. Just block out the entire day for spending quality time with me."

"Yes, sir!"

CHAPTER 108

FOR STELLA, THE NEXT WEEKEND couldn't come soon enough. Ben arrived at 10 a.m. on Saturday. After taking the elevator to the ground floor, the couple walked across the parking lot to his Mustang. She was wearing a white blouse, jeans, and a stylish blue sun hat. He was also dressed casually in khakis, powder blue shirt, and Dodgers cap. They drove to Marina del Rey where, after a long hunt, he finally found a parking spot not too far from the boat slips. He opened the Mustang's trunk and pulled out a picnic basket filled with takeout food from Canter's. Stella could smell the savory food, even though the basket was covered with a large linen napkin.

"Oh, Ben, this is awesome!"

"Wait until you see the boat."

The couple walked several short blocks, and he led her down the row of slips until they came to a small yacht named Lover's Lane. At the sight of the boat, Stella smiled and gave Ben a hug. They climbed the ramp and clambered aboard. Then they took the stairs to the lower deck where they changed into bathing suits and sprayed on sunscreen.

"Ben, are you going to be the captain?"

"No," he chuckled, "I have more important things to do...with you. Our captain will be arriving at noon. We'll have lunch, and then he'll take us past the breakwater into open ocean."

"I can't wait."

In the meantime, they sat on the upper deck and watched seagulls.

She commented that their graceful, almost effortless soaring was mesmerizing.

The captain arrived unobtrusively and fired up the diesel engine, and so began their journey.

Sitting at a table on deck, the pair split a pastrami sandwich and dug into the paper cartons of coleslaw and potato salad.

Stella remarked, "Jewish comfort food. Hmm. Is there some reason I need to be comforted today?"

"Possibly," he said with a sly grin.

Stella chuckled. She wasn't worried, just curious and a bit anxious. After lunch and more applications of sunscreen, the couple settled into lounges.

In the cloudless sky, the July sun had warmed the air, but a slight sea breeze kept them at a pleasant temperature. It was a perfect day for sailing up the coast. Soon they passed Venice Beach, a stretch of sandy coast not yet turned into high-end hotels and high-rise condos. Venice still had funky stores and street people selling trinkets and art on the boardwalk.

Farther north was Santa Monica. There were upscale developments, city parking lots, and volleyball courts where, decades earlier, passersby watched Wilt Chamberlin at play. The pier, which had had bit parts in hundreds of movies and TV shows, offered fishing, restaurants, and an amusement park. As they sailed past the end of the pier, Ben gazed at the patient anglers who were hoping to catch a keeper.

The cacophony of seagull squawks slowly gave way to a humming, buzzing sound. Stella looked up and saw, coming from the south, an old biplane streaming a banner from behind. As the plane passed by, Stella was able to read its wavy message: STELLA, MARRY ME, BEN.

She was floored. "Ben, you are such a romantic."

They stood up, embraced, and shared a long and passionate kiss.

"Well, Stella, what's your answer?"

With a grin, she asked, "what was the question?"

"My darling Stella, will you be my wife? Will you be the woman I wake up to every morning? The woman I see every night? The woman

I will love and cherish for the rest of my life?"

She looked deeply into his eyes, gripped his hands tightly, and said, "yes, Ben, I love you too, and I want to be your wife."

They both began to tear up. From under a lounge cushion he pulled out a placard with large lettering, and aimed it at the shore: SHE SAID YES. Over the sounds of surf and seagulls, the newly engaged couple heard applause and cheers coming from the crowded beach.

The lounge yielded one more surprise. Ben pulled out a small velvet-covered box, and handed it to her. When Stella opened it, her eyes almost bugged out of her head. It was an engagement ring. The diamond, of at least one carat, was framed by a grouping of smaller diamonds, all set in gold. After removing the ring from the box, Ben slid it easily onto Stella's slender finger.

"It's lovely and fits perfectly. Ben, how in the world did you figure out my ring size?"

"I asked your mother."

"Oh." And then she laughed. "So mom knew about this?"

"Yeah, I had a pleasant chat with her early last week. She assured me that she and your dad would welcome our marriage. Their only concern was your happiness."

"And I am very happy!"

Stella had not been entirely surprised that Ben popped the question. Their romance had been heading in that direction. In long conversations, they had tossed around the idea of living together. They decided that the best time to make that move would be early next year, after they found an apartment large enough for both of them—and Tabby.

After more hugs and kisses, the engaged couple returned to lounging as the boat made its way north to Malibu. On the way they changed back into street clothes. They ate an early dinner at the Moonshadows Malibu restaurant with its stunning sea view and tiki decor. Stella was still so excited by the events of the afternoon that she could hardly keep her mind on the menu. Finally, after the server had come by several times, they ordered a seafood medley and mai tais. They enjoyed a leisurely meal and talked about their future life together as they sipped Champagne.

"Ben, what do you think about a spring wedding?"

"Stella, that could work, though it's a long way off. Whatever tickles your fancy is fine with me."

"Maybe later you'll tickle my fancy…"

They laughed.

Back on the boat, Ben told the captain to set sail for Marina del Rey, and they arrived just as the sun was setting over the Pacific. Admiring the orange glow of haze on the horizon, they kissed and hugged again.

The couple left the boat, navigated back to Ben's car and drove to Stella's apartment. They spent the night there and made love for the first time as an engaged couple.

CHAPTER 109

THE SEASON OF NOMINATING conventions for the Democratic and Republican parties was near. Still smarting from their defeat in the Senate, Democrats hoped that Naismith would be their presidential nominee. The Democratic National Committee had made some minor rule changes to increase her odds. In this election cycle, 15 percent of the votes would be cast by superdelegates: governors, Democratic members of Congress, and party officials. Intense lobbying of superdelegates had been going on since the fateful Senate vote.

The Democratic convention took place in the Kohl Center in Madison, Wisconsin. It was a boisterous affair, marked by thousands of signs, journalists buttonholing celebrities and politicians, and nominating speeches that stirred progressive hearts.

The state-by-state reporting of delegate counts went on interminably. After more than three hours of bloviating by delegation spokespeople, the final vote took place. As the press had predicted, Governor Joseph Samuda of Pennsylvania outpaced Naismith—but by only a handful of delegates. However, when the tally of superdelegates was added to the state totals, Naismith became the decisive winner. The arena erupted in demonstrations that continued for hours.

The next day Samuda gave a gracious speech endorsing Naismith's candidacy. In turn, she chose the young and charismatic governor to be her running mate.

Delegates and journalists alike wondered whether the Naismith-

Samuda ticket could prevail over the Shilling-Maxwell ticket. Many believed that wealthy, conservative PACs would have an outsize influence on the election, enough to secure an Electoral College victory for Shilling. The advantages of incumbency and fund-raising aside, some Republicans fretted that their worst nightmare—a liberal president—might still come to pass.

Elaine Naismith was 62 years old. She had been elected speaker after serving nine terms in the House of Representatives. Before that, she had been Minnesota's attorney general. Her husband, Ronald Gustafson, was Professor of Anthropology at Macalaster College in Saint Paul. They had raised two daughters and both had become, like their mother, attorneys.

Naismith comfortably accepted the label of "liberal," though she tended to be somewhat more fiscally conservative than fellow progressives. She was a strong campaigner, noted for the unusual trait of answering, succinctly, the questions reporters and constituents actually asked. Unlike many past elections, this one did not feature candidate debates. Shilling and Maxwell had refused to participate.

The election was vigorously contested, with polls showing the election to be a dead heat. Excerpts from the articles of impeachment figured prominently in Democratic TV ads. Republican ads played on patriotic themes, including Shilling's tough decisions to keep America safe. Republicans also touted the economy, still humming along at an annual growth rate of 2.3 percent with low unemployment. Combined spending on the presidential campaigns totaled a record $4.7 billion. The media rejoiced.

In normal times a strong economy favored the incumbent. But these times were not normal. A well-qualified woman was running for president against an incumbent man of diminished stature.

****

On election night, Stella and Ben were at her parents' home, watching the returns on MSNBC. The most recent polls had called the election a toss-up. Once again, predicted the pundits, the fate of the

393

presidency would depend on two states, Ohio and Florida. Both party bases had been energized by the hard-fought election, and turnout was expected to set records. And it did, as weather was unusually mild across the country.

Talking heads did not call the first states until 7 p.m., Eastern time, and there were no surprises. Results from the rest of the country trickled in over the next several hours. In the running count of the Electoral College, Naismith and Shilling were never more than a few dozen votes apart; in the popular vote Naismith was ahead by millions. At 10:39 p.m. NBC called Ohio for Shilling, which gave him a seven-vote lead in the Electoral College. Stella and Ben and her parents were distraught. How could another election come down to Florida?

Florida's county-by-county updates were posted, and the trend favored Shilling. When the large urban counties began reporting, however, there was a surge of support for Naismith. But would it be enough?

NBC did not call Florida until 1:48 a.m., California time. The United States, for the first time in its history, had elected a woman as president. Despite the early morning hour, crowds gathered in streets and parks and city squares throughout the country to celebrate the Democratic victory. The highest and most rigid glass ceiling had at last been shattered.

Ben and Stella had fallen asleep on the couch and didn't know that Naismith had won. Daniel gently prodded them awake and delivered the scintillating news.

"Thank goodness our country will be rid of Shilling in January," said a groggy Ben. Stella hugged him and said, "sometimes justice is delayed."

EPILOGUE

THE INAUGURATION OF ELAINE NAISMITH took place on the Capitol steps during a very chilly January morning. The new president delivered a stirring speech that, according to media reports, hit all the right notes. By the best available estimates, more than three million people attended in person. They stood cheek to jowl from the Capitol to the Lincoln Memorial, watching the ceremony on jumbotrons and shivering. Live coverage of the inauguration gave rise to rallies around the world, especially in Western Europe.

An important inauguration-day ritual usually takes place immediately after the new president is sworn in. The outgoing president boards Marine One, which then flies over the National Mall on its way to Joint Base Andrews. Shilling refused to climb aboard the helicopter, his fear of being shot down still palpable. However, Secret Service agents told him he had no choice; the flyover tradition allowed no exceptions. Shilling reluctantly acquiesced and, along with his wife, haltingly climbed aboard.

Marine One swooped low over the Mall, but not low enough for Shilling to hear the crowd singing "nah, nah, nah, nah, hey, hey, hey, good-bye." Americans bade farewell to the defeated and dishonored president with middle-finger salutes.

Marine One set down on the tarmac at Joint Base Andrews. Shilling stepped out of the helicopter and prepared to walk several hundred feet to Air Force One, which would take him and his wife home to Kansas. Before he had gone 10 steps, a black SUV pulled up, and FBI Director Abel stepped out. A surprised Shilling thanked her for coming to say good-bye.

"Mr. Shilling," said Abel, "you are under arrest for criminal conspiracy, kidnapping, and other felonies." The ex-president was shocked and looked around for someone to protect him from the FBI. No one, not even members of his Secret Service detail, stepped forward to intervene. He was, for once, speechless. A second FBI vehicle pulled up and two burly agents got out; they grabbed the ex-president, handcuffed him, and pushed him into the car. Four more SUVs followed, escorting Shilling and his wife to the Hoover Building.

Two blocks from the fortress the motorcade suddenly veered off course and headed west on Constitution Avenue. Shilling, it seems, had been complaining of chest pains. With lights flashing and siren blaring, Shilling's car pulled into the ambulance bay at George Washington University Hospital. Attendants loaded him onto a gurney and rolled him inside the crowded ER.

A few hours later the hospital issued a terse news release: "Earlier this afternoon, Former President Shilling suffered a massive heart attack. At 4:38 p.m. Dr. Leonard Libby, Head of Emergency Medicine, pronounced him dead."

****

The wedding of Stella and Ben took place on the last Sunday in June. It was held in the spacious backyard of the Weiss home in Beverly Hills. Almost 200 family members, friends, neighbors, and co-workers attended, including Joanna Bartolo who, with her husband Louis, had recently retired to San Diego.

Stella wore a white satin wedding gown, and Ben donned a tuxedo with a blue dinner jacket. The couple preferred a simple ceremony without bridesmaids or groomsmen.

For months preceding the wedding, Stella and Ben had discussed the "religion problem." Ben's mother, Liliana, had preferred a Catholic wedding, and the Weisses predictably favored a Jewish ceremony. Either option would have required Ben or Stella to convert to the other's religion, but both gently but firmly refused.

After heartfelt discussions, the couple chose a largely religion-free wedding. Neither a priest nor a rabbi would officiate. Instead, Malcolm Klein bought an officiant's certificate online and presided over the ceremony.

At Daniel and Rachel's urging, the couple took their vows under a traditional Jewish canopy called a chuppah, decorated with pink orchids and surrounded by all three parents. And Ben stepped on a wine glass, another nod to Jewish tradition. As a token of respect to the Suarez family, Malcolm invited Ben's brother William to recite three of his mother's favorite psalms, and she in turn presented Stella with a Catholic Book of Prayers. The bride graciously accepted the gift from her mother-in-law.

Ben and Stella had written their own vows, which they read with glistening eyes. Malcolm nodded to Ben—the cue for the kiss. During the long kiss, the guests began applauding and cheering the newlyweds.

The Weiss home was also the venue for the sumptuous reception. Buffet-style food stations offered selections to satisfy every taste— Jewish, Spanish, and Mexican dishes—and Champagne flowed non-stop. Multi-colored lights and streamers decorated the seating area.

The cake had three layers: the top and bottom were chocolate, the middle was white. Stella and Ben mugged for the cameras as they fed each other, leaving behind chocolate mustaches.

After the wedding, a limousine drove the newlyweds to LAX where they boarded a plane for their honeymoon.

On their second full day in Paris, Stella received a message from the L.A. Times: She and Malcolm had jointly won a Pulitzer Prize. Ben and Stella celebrated her award by taking a Champagne cruise on the Seine.

ACKNOWLEDGMENTS

Writing this story, during the period December 2018 to August 2019, gave me much satisfaction. The comments and suggestions of beta readers have helped me to shape and improve *Scoop of the Century*. I am grateful to Annette Schiffer, Jay Carsman, James M. Skibo, and especially Adam J. Schiffer and Stephanie M. Whittlesey for their critical insights.

Lightning Source UK Ltd.
Milton Keynes UK
UKHW021611230720
367047UK00009B/477